"The ghastly puzzle comes together in a breathtaking, suspenseful finale."

—*Publishers Weekly*

"Compelling, grittily gruesome in a Jeffrey Deaver kind of way."

—*Booklist*

"This exhilarating but dark and vividly violent (don't eat just before reading this novel) police procedural sequel hooks the audience with the first coded formula and never slows down. . . . The story line flows with blood as the killer keeps rolling sevens while Granger and Pulaski shoot snake-eyes at each other. The climax will prove to be one of the year's best as advanced mathematical concepts have rarely been more fun to follow."

—Harriet Klausner

"What makes this story unique is the unanticipated twists and turns experienced not only by Pulaski, but also the sharp edges tagged to those that work with Pulaski and those that wish her ill will, or worse yet, her own gruesome ending. Not for the faint of heart or stomach, *Strip Search* provides a thrill ride; at times, at a relentless pace. . . . Bernhardt has captured the seediness of Las Vegas in a way that will stay with you until the end!"

—armchairinterviews.com

Praise for

DARK EYE

"*Dark Eye* . . . may well be the beginning of a new series, and his best work to date. . . . Bernhardt, who already has a winning protagonist going with [Ben] Kincaid, has hit the bull's-eye once again. Highly recommended."

—Bookreporter.com

"Bernhardt and Las Vegas go together like fire and gasoline."

—Stephen Coonts, author of *Liars and Thieves*

"A thriller that will chill you while its two unique and endearing protagonists steal your heart."

—Lisa Scottoline, author of *Devil's Corner*

"Bernhardt keeps his foot flat on the accelerator, producing action at every turn of the page."

—*Orlando Sentinel*

"Who knew we had an author with such a dark and twisted imagination living among us? [*Dark Eye*] is an unflinching tale of abject terror. . . . Let me formally thank Mr. Bernhardt for scaring the wits out of me."

—*Oklahoma Gazette*

"*Dark Eye* combines elements of *Friday the Thirteenth, The Silence of the Lambs,* and *CSI: Las Vegas* to form a macabre detective story set in Las Vegas. . . . If a diverse cast of characters and a story line with detective work and cliff-hanging suspense is your cup of tea, then *Dark Eye* is worth your time."

—*The Roanoke Times*

"A suspenseful thriller."

—Wichita Falls *Times Record News*

"*Dark Eye* begins a new series offering readers a thriller with a pair of protagonists full of shock and awe. . . . The antagonist, the man the police and FBI call Edgar and who calls himself 'The Raven,' is a work of art."

—*Tulsa World*

ALSO BY WILLIAM BERNHARDT

The Code of Buddyhood
Double Jeopardy
Legal Briefs
The Midnight Before Christmas
Natural Suspect
Final Round
Dark Eye

Featuring Ben Kincaid

Primary Justice
Blind Justice
Deadly Justice
Perfect Justice
Cruel Justice
Naked Justice
Extreme Justice
Dark Justice
Silent Justice
Murder One
Criminal Intent
Death Row
Hate Crime
Capitol Murder
Capitol Threat
Capitol Conspiracy

Strip Search

A Novel of Suspense

William Bernhardt

BALLANTINE BOOKS • NEW YORK

2008 Ballantine Books Mass Market Edition

Published in the United States by Ballantine Books, an imprint of The Random House Publishing Group, a division of Random House, Inc., New York.

This book contains an excerpt from the forthcoming hardcover edition of *Nemesis* by William Bernhardt. This excerpt has been set for this edition only and may not reflect the final content of the forthcoming edition.

Originally published in hardcover in the United States by Ballantine Books, an imprint of The Random House Publishing Group, a division of Random House, Inc., in 2007.

ISBN 978-0-345-47020-1

Cover design: Carl D. Galian
Cover photographs: Jupiterimages

Printed in the United States of America

www.ballantinebooks.com

9 8 7 6 5 4 3 2 1

For Valerie, my sister,
always smiling

BOOK ONE

ALGEBRA AND ALCHEMY

"I want to know God's thoughts."

—Albert Einstein

1

JULY 11

I DON'T CARE what you've seen on television. This is the truth: Most days, being a cop is one of the most boring jobs on earth. Except when it isn't. Or to clarify, it's huge patches of tediousness punctuated by brief moments of stark terror. That's why so many cops turn in their badges before retirement. That's why eight times more cops die from suicide than homicide. The badge ain't for sissies.

I love it. All of it—the tediousness and the terror—even now, six months since my badge was officially yanked. I was a cop for almost ten years; now I'm a consultant, which means I work twice as many hours for half as much money. At least I'm in the game. Tediousness and terror. But still in the game.

The officially designated casino escort met Darcy and me at the front door. He was dark and muscular and obviously worked out and I disliked him almost immediately. "You the chick Chief O'Bannon sent over?"

Just to prove that I'm not high-strung, hot-tempered, rabidly feminist, or any of those other female cop clichés, I let that one slip. "I'm Susan Pulaski."

"You're the shrink?"

"I'm a psychologist. I work as a behaviorist for the LVPD."

"Whatever." Sure, it sounded rude, but I suspect he was compensating for the fact that he didn't know what a behaviorist is, so I let that one slide, too. "The boss says I'm supposed to take you upstairs to see the floor boss captain."

"Then let's do it."

"Sure. And afterward . . ." His eyes narrowed and he got that smirky expression that you only get from men who think everyone finds them as sexy as they find themselves. ". . . I could give you a personal tour of the casino."

"Thanks, but I've been here before."

"You have gorgeous eyes, you know it? I bet you get that a lot. Unusual. One looks darker than the other."

"Cat scratch. I was five. Now if you don't mind—"

I tried to push past him, but he grabbed my arm. "I could show you parts of this place you've never seen. Including some very private rooms. Huge suites. Mirrored ceilings." And then, I swear to God, he actually winked as he added, "Vibrating beds."

Grotesque. Repellent. Wildly inappropriate. But I am a trained professional, cool and detached, and I was sent here to do a job. So I let it pass. "Maybe it would be best if you just took us to the captain."

"Us?" He glanced behind me for the first time. "Who's the punk?" He was pointing at Darcy, the tall, lanky twenty-six-year-old hovering uncertainly behind me. "The boss didn't say anything about some kid coming along." Darcy flushed, stared at the floor, talked some barely audible gibberish, then began flapping his hands. "Why is he here?"

"I'm babysitting," I said. "You know how lousy cop pay is. I have to moonlight."

"I don't want to get into any trouble with the boss. The kid looks . . . weird. What is he, some kind of retard or—"

I flattened him. One punch, on the nose, down and out.

Yeah, I know, I shouldn't have done it. Someone will report me to IA, and they'll throw it in my face the next time I make my periodic pathetic application for reinstatement.

But honestly. A girl can only put up with so much.

IT WAS YOUR TYPICAL Vegas casino, if there is such a thing, an exquisite blend of tony, trendy, and tacky. No windows, no clocks, nothing to remind gamblers of the outside world, everything designed to encourage them to settle in and play, play, play. So noisy that Darcy covered his ears and I was tempted to follow suit: the cacophony of slot machines, the clinking of glasses, the jingling of chips, the whirring of security cameras, the incessant chatter about what place dealt the smallest number of decks and who had the cheapest buffet and whether to split tens. And the smoke—my God, what a stink! Darcy was practically gagging, and who could blame him? I suppose they still have to cater to the old-timers, the high rollers who can't put down the big money without a weed dangling from their mouths. Give it another ten years or so and those dinosaurs will die out and casinos will go no-smoking like the rest of the civilized universe.

In an attempt to stifle the stench, I focused my attention on the décor—the fake gold wall paneling, the gaudy, dark (to disguise spills), and durable (because a million dirty shoes trod upon it daily) carpet. The gorgeous smoked glass ceiling, which would be even more gorgeous if I didn't know there was a platoon of security officers beyond it watching everything happening on the floor.

There was even something different about the air. The rumor is that casinos pump oxygen through the air vents to keep everyone awake (and thus playing longer) and to deliver a mild O_2 buzz, thus ensuring that even those not partaking of the free drinks enjoy themselves. I don't know if it's true or not. But as I surveyed the room—the tourists, the suckers, the sharks, the shills, the obvious hookers, the less obvious and thus much more expensive hookers, the dealers, even the pit bosses—I did notice one thing they all had in common. They were having a good time. They were losing money, blowing hours of their lives playing some of the stupidest games ever invented—but they were having fun.

Eventually Steve, the replacement flunky, got us through the casino. Steve was blond and looked more like a tennis pro than a casino employee, but maybe I'm just working off stereotypes formed by watching *The Godfather* films way too many times. He seemed a little nervous, uneasy, but I suppose being called in to replace a guy I'd just decked might induce a certain wariness in anyone.

Frank Olivestra, the owner of the casino, the man with sufficient pull to get me sent here *unofficially,* was waiting with his floor boss captain, Dominic Castle, in the latter's office.

"Hey, Frank," I said, waving a hand.

"Hiya, Susan. How's it hangin'?" I'd worked with Frank before—strange as it might seem that a casino would have any links to the world of crime. Or aberrant personalities. We'd always gotten along well. I assume he asked for me personally or in all likelihood, I wouldn't be here.

While we small-talked, I strolled unobtrusively and soaked in as much of the office as I could without being too obvious. Nothing overtly unusual—standard desk and chair arrangement—but it told me a lot about Olivestra's floor boss captain, Mr. Castle. He was a detail man, which I suppose is exactly the quality you'd want in the employee supervising the transfer of large sums of money. He was a neat freak, extremely fastidious. The stapler on his desk was perfectly symmetrical to the telephone and the pen cup, and I spotted the corner of a Dopp kit in his bottom desk drawer. Judging from the absence of photos, he was single and childless. The bookshelves behind his desk told me even more. He was smart, patient, and he liked to fish. He was a Republican, a member of the NRA, and he preferred nonfiction to fiction.

And I could tell one other thing from his office, too. He did it. He took the money. Don't ask me to explain how I knew. I get people. I can absorb them, their environments, key into their thoughts. But trying to explain the process makes it sound more calculated than it actually is. I'm not Sherlock Holmes and I didn't go through a long series of logical deductions. I just knew.

Now all I had to do was prove what I knew.

"Thank you for coming over, Susan." Olivestra was short, rotund, and had a harsh quality to his voice. He couldn't have looked more like a casino boss if he'd been chomping a half-gone stogie between his teeth. "Haven't seen you since . . . well, that business with the clown from Dubuque and his magnetic slots gizmo. Thank God you were able to figger that one out."

"Just wish I'd done it about five grand sooner."

"Heard you had an altercation with one of my men out in the lobby."

"Well, yeah."

"Tell me he wasn't pushin'. I know you hate pushers."

"No, no. It was just a . . . personality conflict."

"What was the problem?"

"The problem was . . ." I sighed. "I'm trying to think of a nice way to put this. He was annoying as hell and made me want to rip off his testicles."

"Well, then," Olivestra deadpanned, "I'd say he got off easy." He took me by the arm and lowered his voice.

"The money disappeared a little over an hour ago. We're still hoping we can handle this internally. Don't like the negative publicity. People visiting the Florence need to know they're safe."

"Understood. Can you show us where you think the theft occurred?"

He and Castle led the way to a much smaller room with a few chairs, curtained windows behind a high riser all along the far wall, and an elevator with only a down button.

"You're certain this is where it happened?" I asked Castle. He was short, especially standing beside me, but he had that Napoleonic swagger you sometimes find in guys his size. He was overcompensating with muscle, manner, and manicure. Immaculately groomed. Even wore French cuffs.

"It's the only place it could have occurred. We've reviewed the tapes. No one intercepted the money on the floor. If someone had stashed the dough in the elevator downstairs or intercepted it on its way to the vault, we'd have tape. And once it's in the vault, Superman couldn't get it out."

"Why don't you have a camera in here?"

Olivestra answered. "We did. The line was cut. The security officer in the video control room noticed immediately, but by the time he determined it wasn't a power or monitor blip—which was only about five minutes—it was all over. The thief thunked poor Dominic over the head, took the cash, and climbed out that window—we found it gaping open. It leads to a parking lot. From there, he could be halfway down the Strip in sixty seconds."

"And you're sure it wasn't taken from the vault?"

Castle looked at me as if I were stupider than stupid, but I got the general impression he thought anyone with breasts was stupider than stupid. "Let me guess—you've seen *Ocean's Eleven*? Let me assure you that in the real world, getting into a casino vault isn't that easy. You'd have better luck trying to steal plutonium from Los Alamos."

Which I believed, because I knew perfectly well he'd taken the money. But I didn't want him to know that I knew. "How much was swiped?"

Castle gave his boss a look, got the nod, then replied. "Two hundred sixty-eight thousand, four hundred twelve bucks."

I whistled. "Day's take?"

He gave me another withering look. "One hour."

"And none of your videos show any unauthorized personnel coming in here?"

"Unfortunately, none of the cameras are trained on the outer door to this particular room."

"That is unfortunate." Or perfect, if you're the thief. Or a person picking a place to pretend there was a thief. "Darcy, what do you think?"

Darcy was standing on a chair, his face flattened against the windowpane, sniffing the curtains.

"Darcy?" I repeated, wiggling my fingers. "Yoo-hoo?"

He looked up, startled. His foot slipped off the chair and he tumbled to the carpet, barely avoiding a head injury. He pulled himself up, tugged down his T-shirt, and grinned his goofy, angelic grin. "Did you ever know that humans spray two-point-five drops of saliva into the air for every word they speak?"

I was mildly puzzled. The expressions on the faces of Castle and Olivestra suggested that they were, well, more extremely puzzled. "No, I must confess I didn't."

"That comes to, on average, three hundred drops per minute. When someone is talking."

Castle appeared irritated and annoyed. "Is this some kind of joke? Is he making this up?"

"Darcy never makes anything up," I replied. "He doesn't know how."

Olivestra gave Darcy a quick once-over—the long shaggy brown hair, skinny frame, worn sneakers. Darcy was twenty-six, but he looked younger. "May I ask what exactly is this young man's function? He doesn't appear to be a member of the police department."

"He works with me. As a consultant," I bluffed.

"But I was told you were—"

"And he's the consultant's consultant, okay? Don't sweat it; he won't cost you any extra."

Olivestra folded his arms, frowned, but let it go.

"Notice anything else, Darcy?" I asked.

"Did you see me try to get the window open? I tried really hard to get that window open. I couldn't make it budge."

"Perhaps you should reconsider that gym membership."

"I think that maybe even for a strong man opening this window would be tough."

"But the window *was* open," Olivestra insisted. "The shark was obviously strong if he clubbed Dominic unconscious, yanked open the window, and survived that jump."

Darcy ran his fingers through his hair, as if washing it with invisible shampoo. "No one jumped out of that window."

That caught us all by surprise. "How do you know?"

"That would be twenty-two and three quarters feet straight down to the concrete."

I glanced out the window. "Looks about right."

"That is exactly right. I think that if I had stolen that money—I mean, I would never steal any money, but if I did, I would be in a hurry. And I would be carrying a heavy sack or briefcase or something. I see no sign that there was a rope or ladder. The officer outside told us that they looked really really hard but they found no blood or torn clothing on the concrete. And look at the mud." He pointed down below the window. "That is from last night's rain. I do not see any footprints. Do you see any footprints?" He grinned sheepishly. "Or butt prints, depending on how well he fell. I do not think that anyone could possibly have jumped out that window with all that money." He continued staring at the transparent pane of evidence.

"I already had my boys go over that window with a fine-tooth comb," Olivestra said. "There's no prints on it."

"Which proves Darcy's point," I said. "If this was some outside crook or hopped-up crackhead making a desperate run for it, why stop to wipe his prints? No, the thief had to wipe the window clean after he got it open, because he knew you'd be able to ID his prints." I slowed, giving Olivestra a minute to catch up. "Because you print all your employees before you hire them, don't you, Frank?"

I didn't wait for him to respond. I already knew the answer. "The open window was just a decoy. A clever bit of misdirection. What else have you got on the thief, Darcy? Who was he?"

"Even though it was hard to get the window open," he replied, "he got the window open, so I think that he was a strong person. Do you think that he was a strong person? I do not understand why he would go to all the trouble of opening the window if he was not going to go through it, though. Do you think that maybe it was really hot in here? Because it does not seem that hot now."

In this perfectly climate-controlled casino? I don't think so. "Darcy, if you can't tell us anything use—"

"And he was five foot five."

"Excuse me?"

"Or less. Five foot five or less."

"But how—"

Darcy raced to the other side of the room, then

pressed himself up against the wall, giggling excitedly. "See how all the chairs are lined up against the wall? Evenly spaced. Except one. I hate that. They should all be in an evenly spaced straight line. Don't you think they should be evenly spaced? And then I thought—maybe they're not evenly spaced—"

"Because he needed to move one to get up on the window riser."

"If he'd have been five foot six or more, he could've stepped up there himself. But five foot five—"

"He needed a chair." I glanced across at Mr. Castle, who was looking distinctly uncomfortable. I'm not nearly as good at estimating height or distance as Darcy—well, in his case, it isn't estimating, it's just plain knowing—but I'm almost six feet tall, and Castle appeared to be eye level with my clavicle. Which suggested to me . . .

"I think that maybe he took off his shoes and walked around in his socks when he was in here, because he did not leave tracks," Darcy continued. "As soon as he left the room, he put his shoes back on."

Which would be easy to do without attracting notice, if you worked right next door. But we still didn't have any proof.

"I think that even though he was a strong man he had to work really hard to open the window," Darcy continued.

"I know, Darcy, you've already—"

"He probably maybe even said a swearword, like my dad does when he can't get the attic door unstuck."

"Your point being . . . ?"

"If he said something . . . he left behind saliva."

My eyebrows rose. "Two-point-five droplets a swear word?"

Darcy nodded. "Plus sweat. I smell sweat."

"Both saliva and sweat could be tested for DNA, if we can find enough of it."

"And Skin Bracer Cooling Blue aftershave lotion."

I did a double take. "You can smell his aftershave?"

"In the curtains." Darcy shrugged, then stared at the floor, fidgeting with his fingers.

"This is absurd," Castle protested. "This isn't real detective work. It's like . . . a stand-up comedy routine."

"Funny you should think that, Mr. Castle," I said, deciding to make my move. "Because it's clear to me we're looking for someone on the inside, someone your height, your strength, someone with intimate knowledge of the casino security system and how money is transported from the casino floor to the vault. Someone with an office nearby where the cash could be quickly stashed during the five-minute camera blackout. Someone who is smart, patient . . . and extremely fastidious."

"What the hell are you implying?"

"Well, I don't have Darcy's sense of smell, but that spray or pomade or whatever it is you have on your hair is practically gagging me."

"Also the foot powder," Darcy murmured quietly. "Pee-*yew.*"

"You know what I think, Mr. Castle? I think you knocked yourself on the head, pried open the window with a crowbar or something, then stashed the cash in your office."

"Now look here, Susan," Olivestra said, throwing back his shoulders and poking out his paunch. "I invited you here to solve a crime, not to latch on to the first suspect you met. I've known Dominic Castle for over fifteen years. He's one of my main men and there's no way I'm going to believe that he—he—" His face reddened and I was pretty sure he was exceeding the average saliva droplet expulsion rate. "—that he *stole* from me."

"Well, I could call Forensics, but you said you wanted to keep this quiet. I know you take DNA samples from your employees at the same time you fingerprint them, so I'll leave it up to you. Test the curtain for saliva and sweat, compare them with a sample from your main man, and see what you come up with, okay? You lay out enough money, you can have the tests done downtown in forty-eight hours. In the meantime, I noticed Mr. Castle has a grooming kit in his bottom desk drawer. Why don't you go open it and see if it has any Skin Bracer Cooling Blue aftershave? 'Cause if it does . . ." I wagged my finger under Castle's nose and put on my best faux-Cuban accent. "Lucy, I think you've got some 'splainin' to do."

Olivestra remained silent, but I could see his indignation concretizing into a cold realization of truth.

Castle began to sputter. "This—this is an outrage. Utterly reprehensible. I'm calling my lawyer and filing charges for slander and gross police misconduct. You haven't heard the last of me, Ms. Pulaski."

I stared deeply into Olivestra's simmering eyes. "Somehow, Mr. Castle, I kinda think maybe I have. Like, maybe, everybody has." I grabbed Darcy by the shoulder. He flinched but didn't pull away. "C'mon, Darcy. You've earned yourself a custard. My treat."

2

"WHY?" AMIR PLEADED, his hands pinned behind his back and his body pressed against the stainless steel plating of the fast-food grill. "Why are you doing this to me? I do not even know you!"

"I know you. I know who you are. More important, I know *what* you are."

"Please do not hurt me, sir. Please!" Amir cried, but it was no use. Thunderbolts of pain radiated up his arms and through his shoulder blades. "Is it my skin color? I am not from Iraq, if that is what you are thinking. Or Iran, or Saudi Arabia. I am from New Delhi."

"I don't care about that," Tucker said, pulling the man's arms even tighter.

"Then please stop. Please. I have a wife. I have three daughters. A newborn son."

"Uh-huh. And when was the last time you saw any of them?"

"I saw them—I saw them—why do you ask me this question?"

"Just wonderin'." Tucker was a big man, not tall, but thick, and rippling with muscles, muscles born of hard work, physical labor, not pushing weights around in some fancy-ass gym. He shoved Amir forward, pressing his bare chest against the edge of the cooking stove. Amir screamed, trying to push himself away. "Be careful! Please! I have not yet turned off the equipment."

"I noticed. I'm cookin' a little somethin' up for you."

"But why? I am nothing. I do not even run this place! I am just the assistant manager." His face was stricken, desperate. "Please—my wallet is in my back pocket. I do not have much, but whatever I have, it is yours."

Tucker tightened his grip on both of the man's arms, bending them almost to the breaking point. After all those years living off the streets, moving from one hard-scrabble job to the next, Tucker knew what he was and what he wasn't. He might have many failings. But he was not a thief. The very suggestion made his blood boil. He wrapped a rubber cord around Amir's wrists, then secured him to the grill. "You got pictures of your little girls in that wallet?"

Amir hesitated. "Well . . . no. There is not so much room."

"Pretty much written them off, haven't you?"

"That is not true. I love my little darlings. I—"

"You got a new piece of ass, some slutty teenager who's workin' as your fry cook and will spread her legs for the cost of a quarter pounder."

"That is not true!" Amir squirmed, trying to keep his stomach off the super-heated stainless steel.

"Is. She's makin' it with Wilfred, too. The janitor. You know. The one with more acne than face."

"I—I do not believe it."

"And for that you gave up your family. Your wife. Your three girls."

"Listen to me, my man. There are things you do not know. Financial matters. My wife is better off—"

"And what about Anna, Khouri, and Indira? Are they better off?"

"Please. I do not know why you are asking me all

these questions. I do not know . . . what business it is of yours. But I take care of my girls. I visit whenever I can—and I give them whatever—"

"When was the last time you made your child support payments?"

"My—" Amir stopped short. "Is that what this is about? Are you from the DHS? I know I am a little behind—"

"More than a little."

"But it is so hard, trying to make a living in this country, working sixty hours a week at a Burger Bliss. I barely clear twenty thousand American. I have told them that. I filed a report. Talk to your bosses."

Tucker gave the knot a twist, sending another searing bolt of pain coursing through the man's body. "Do I act like I'm from DHS?"

"Then—why are you here? Why did you knock me out? Why did you rip off my shirt? Why me?"

"Why here? Because I had to catch you at your place of work, alone, after everyone else left the joint." Tucker's expression flattened, and then he added. "And why you? Because you are Keter."

"Keter? I do not know this word Keter."

"Doesn't matter. I do."

They both heard the abrupt ring of the oven timer. "Ah," Tucker said. "The appetizer's ready."

He put on a pair of oven mitts, opened the door, and withdrew what at first appeared to be a long fireplace poker with a protective handle at one end. It was so hot smoke emanated from the end piece.

Amir took a closer look and realized that it was not a poker. It was a branding iron. At the far end of the metallic prong, glowing at him like a fiery monogram, was the letter *K*.

Amir stepped away from the pulsating heat, cowering,

begging for mercy. "Please," he said. "Do not do this to me. Please!"

"Friend, this is just the beginnin'." Tucker brought the iron nearer; though it was still inches away, Amir could feel it cooking his skin. "No! Please, *no*!"

Tucker pressed the brand into the man's solar plexus.

Amir screamed. With a howl that might've been heard for miles—if anyone was awake within miles—he cried out as the searing metal burned into his flesh. His knees buckled, he lost all control of his body, he wet himself. The skin on his chest began to blister and water rushed from the surrounding tissues in an ineffectual effort to cool the piercing wound. He went into shock, looked as if he might have a stroke . . . which would make the rest of the plan far more complicated.

He untied Amir's bonds—there was no risk that he was going anywhere on his own—and walked him over to the deep fat fryer, still burning at full boil, still bubbling with the super-heated oil that had flash-fried thousands of frozen potatoes that day. Tonight, the recipe would be somewhat different.

"No," Amir said, crying, barely able to muster a whisper. "Please. No."

"You are part of the Sefirot," Tucker intoned. "The time for the termination of your predestined number has arrived."

"Number," Amir whispered, the aching in his chest still making it difficult to think, much less resist. "I tell you—I have done nothing wrong. This is . . . this is madness!"

"It ain't madness that's doomed you," Tucker said, as he lowered the man's face toward the bubbling cauldron. "It's math."

With a decisive thrust, careful to keep his gloved hands out of it, Tucker pushed Amir's face into the churning pool of boiling oil.

Had he been able, the man would surely have screamed. But the intense three-hundred-fifty-degree heat melted his mouth, his lips, the skin on his face, even his tongue, long before any such response was possible.

3

JULY 12

I ACTUALLY STUCK my hand out of the shower and said, "Would you hand me a towel, sugar bear? I can't—" Before I stopped myself.

Even after all this time, my brain still blipped, and I expected David to be standing on the other side of the fogged-up shower door. "Idiot," I said, slapping myself on the forehead for good measure. As if that minor blow might get my brain working right.

Mind you, I had made progress. I didn't have conversations with him anymore. I didn't see him at night during that twilight time just before you fall asleep. And I had fully and formally forgiven him for . . . well, whatever I thought he needed to be forgiven for. But some part of my brain, especially when I was deep in thought about something else, still instinctively expected David to be there. We had spent so much time together, so many happy times.

I've read that people who lose limbs in adulthood experience something called phantom pain—the arm or leg they no longer possess still seems to hurt. I guess I have a phantom husband.

And it still hurts.

BACK WHEN I WAS IN DETOX, I hated Dr. Coutant. Of course, I was forced to see him three times a day. If I had refused I would've never been discharged, not after what I'd done. So I went to his little closet at the clinic, always refusing the couch, and rambled on about whatever pleased him, blowing off questions whenever possible, deflecting them when I knew he was getting too close ("Okay, like now could we talk about my other parent for a while?") and never never never letting him start in about David. If he wanted to call me a drunk, let him. If he wanted to harp on my dismissal from the detective squad, losing my house, losing custody of my niece, he had that right. But my husband was my business. It was insulting, really. After all, I'm a trained psychologist. Was I supposed to believe he could lord it over me just because he went to school a few more years and could prescribe drugs? I was an experienced, educated career woman. And yet, for the entire six days he had me in his clutches, he treated me like I was some barely potty-trained street junkie.

Actually, I *still* hated Coutant. But these days, it wasn't because I didn't think he knew what he was talking about. It was because I knew he did.

"How long has it been?" This was always his first question. I made a point of calculating my answer before I arrived.

"Five months, two days, and about fourteen minutes."

He seemed genuinely pleased. "That's very impressive."

"Hardly a lifetime."

"For an alcoholic? It's several lifetimes. I know people who've been under considerably less stress than you who haven't made it half as long. Still . . ." His pencil slowed, and he made sure I was looking at him. "If you think the struggle is over . . . it isn't."

"I know that."

Coutant was a short, round man with a full beard and round-rimmed glasses, but now that I was seeing him in his private office, he didn't wear the white coat. His office was tastefully decorated in soothing colors, mostly beige. Like he borrowed his interior decorator from Banana Republic. "Can you still remember what that last drink tasted like?"

"Well, that last drink was laced with a hypnogogic drug that led to me getting kidnapped."

He batted his eraser on his legal pad. "Okay, the last drink you enjoyed."

I thought for a moment. A long moment. "Actually, no."

"That's a good sign. It tells me you were well past the point of drinking for pleasure. You were drinking to relieve stress, to deal with your demons. Neither of which booze accomplishes. If you can remind yourself of that, if you can remember that it isn't actually fun for you and never will be again, it'll be a little easier to keep off the sauce."

I saluted him. "Message received and understood."

"The problem is—the demons may still be there. Have you been depressed lately?"

I hesitated. "I am a little . . . lonely. I miss having Rachel at home. And I miss . . ." I didn't have to finish the sentence.

"Unfortunately, depression and anxiety are not uncommon in your profession, Susan. Much less to someone who's been through everything you've been through."

"Don't you have some kind of magic pill you can prescribe? Prozac, or whatever's trendy these days."

"I could, but I'm not going to."

"You prefer to let me suffer."

"I think we both know that you have an addictive personality, Susan. I can't in good conscience recommend anything to you that might create a dependency. Hell, if I could, I'd restrict you from drinking coffee."

"You are a cruel bastard."

"Yeah, I get that a lot." He smiled. "I'd still be happier if you were in an AA group."

"I'm not the talky-feely type."

"Nonetheless, AA has the highest recovery rate of any program—"

"You're assuming I need a program."

He rubbed the rim of his glasses. "Susan, when will you get it through your head that you do not have to do everything on your own? There's nothing shameful about getting help. You have many friends who love you. Amelia, Rachel, Darcy, Chief O'Bannon." He paused. "Me. Let us help. Talk to people who've been through what you're going through. Even if you don't join an AA group, I could find you a sponsor—"

"Please don't."

"I'm sorry, Susan, but I can't help but think this . . . insistence on doing everything yourself is another indication of your self-destructive behavior. The same instinct culminated in you beating some poor frat boy to a pulp in—"

"That's not fair!" I shot back. "I was out of my head. I thought he was a drug kingpin." I took a deep breath. "Besides, he had the sorriest pickup lines you've ever heard in your life."

In an apparent act of resignation, Coutant changed the subject. "How's Darcy?"

"Doing great. He's made enormous progress these past months. I've done a lot of reading on autism and worked with him and given him useful things to do, and I think it's making a real difference. He was invaluable to me on an investigation yesterday."

"How long have you two been seeing each other now?"

I stared at him through furrowed eyebrows. "I assume that was an unintentionally suggestive phraseology. I took care of him for five weeks. While his father was recovering from a gunshot wound."

"And even thereafter dropped by to visit almost every day."

"His father was weak and barely ambulatory. And besides, we like each other. What are you getting at?"

"Nothing. Why are you so defensive?"

"I don't like what you seem to be implying. Darcy is a kid."

"He's nine years younger than you."

"He looks more."

Coutant held up his hands. "Look, I'm not trying to suggest that you initiate a physical relationship, especially given his neurological difficulties. But I am wondering if you're using him as . . . well, as a sort of shield."

I pursed my lips. "You know, Doc, I guess that M.D. did make you smarter than me, because I have no idea what the hell you're talking about."

"Then let me be blunt. Your husband died over a year ago. Right or wrong, many people blamed you for his death. You used alcohol to defend yourself. The first time you attempted another relationship with a man, that FBI agent—well, we both know how that turned out. But now that's ancient history, too. You should be seeing someone. It would be healthy for you. And if it isn't going to be Darcy—"

"It can't be Darcy."

"Then you need to stop spending all your time with him and find someone else."

"You think it's that easy?"

"Las Vegas is a big city."

"Which makes it harder, not easier. Where am I going

to find someone decent to go out with? And I warn you, if you say, 'An AA meeting,' I'll slug you."

Coutant smiled. "In my personal opinion, it's all a matter of attitude. If you're scared of trying again, then you'll hide behind your work or your friends or whatever else is available. But if you really want to find someone—you will."

"Where'd you get that pearl of wisdom? Dr. Phil?"

"What does it matter? Whether you care to admit it or not, pushing everyone away is just another example of self-destructive behavior." He leaned forward. "Susan, you're a smart, healthy adult female. You need a smart, healthy adult male."

"And get trapped in a relationship? With the mess I am right now? Sounds pretty risky to me."

"It is a risk. Of course it's a risk. So what?" Coutant checked his watch, then laid down his pen and paper. Apparently the fifty-minute hour had come to an end. "Susan, how is it you've managed to live in Vegas your entire life but you've never learned how to gamble?"

DESPITE HIS YEARS of experience and training, despite the steady succession of suicides and homicides that had inevitably hardened his stomach, if not his heart, despite his almost obsessive concern with self-image and making a good impression on his superiors and inferiors, the moment Lt. Barry Granger stepped behind the counter at the fast-food restaurant to which he had been summoned and took a look at what lay beyond, he fell to his knees and began uncontrolled retching.

It didn't make him forget what he had seen. A deep fat fryer with blood splattered all around it. Severed flesh simmering in the oil.

"Still think we don't need to bring her in on this one?"

Chief Robert O'Bannon asked, hovering over his convulsing chief homicide detective. He was using a cane to keep himself on his feet.

Granger took long slow controlled breaths. "What . . . happened?"

O'Bannon paused reflectively before answering. "I'm not sure there's a word for what happened here." He glanced over his shoulder and shouted at one of the crime scene techs working the site. "Hey, Crenshaw! Is there a word for dissolving someone's face in an industrial-strength deep fat fryer?"

The tech looked up, grimaced, then returned to his work.

"There's just no precedent for . . . death by melting. Unless you count *The Wizard of Oz.*" Steadying himself with the cane, O'Bannon reached down and slowly pulled his detective to his feet.

"I'm—I'm sorry, sir," Granger said feebly, wiping his mouth. He had sandy hair and, normally, a sun-baked ruddy complexion. At the moment, his face was ashen white. "I don't know what came over me."

"Don't feel bad, Barry. I've been a cop for over thirty years, and I've never seen anything like this. You should've seen the poor chump teenager who came in this morning to open—and found this mess of blood and melted flesh where the french fries are supposed to be."

"Where's . . . the rest of the body?"

"We don't know. Apparently, melting off the guy's face wasn't good enough for this killer. He wanted to take the body home with him as a souvenir."

"That's bizarre."

"Agreed. Which is why we need to bring in Susan."

Despite the aching in his stomach, Granger managed to mount a protest. "We don't need her. Give me and my boys a few days—"

"Granger, we have a bona fide psychopath on our hands."

"Brutality alone doesn't prove craziness, Chief, not in this day and age. It's still possible there was some rational explanation."

"You're in denial, Granger. It's a psycho. We need a profile. We need Susan."

"You know I have issues about working with her."

"I thought you'd grown out of them."

Granger pressed his lips together. At the same time he was talking to the chief, he was also watching the CSIs crisscrossing the wax paper laid on the floor, the med techs from the coroner's office, the uniforms posted at all the entrances, wondering how many of them had seen him break down and spew like a newbie. He knew he wasn't popular. A lot of people thought he didn't deserve his promotion, that he had taken advantage of Susan's breakdown to seize something he hadn't earned. Didn't matter how many perps he'd caught in the last few months. Didn't matter that he hit the gym four times a week, keeping himself in prime physical condition. Once the gossip mill started, nothing could stop it, and this humiliating display wasn't going to help.

"It's not that easy, Chief. I was David's partner."

"Yeah, and she was David's wife. You think that gives you one up on her?"

Granger wiped his hand across his brow, trying to make this make sense, even though deep down he knew he wasn't really thinking rationally. He just knew what the chatter would be, back in the locker room. Granger couldn't solve a murder if he'd committed it himself. Granger can't wipe his ass without Pulaski's help.

"I think you should give your homicide squad a crack at the case before bringing in outside consultants."

O'Bannon frowned. "I'll admit, I hate to dump something like this on her. I've kept her busy since the Edgar mess, but far away from anything that might be too . . . traumatic. Tried to give the girl a chance to heal, for God's sake. Get off the booze, pull her life back together. She always gets so wrapped up in these psychos, trying to think like they think, trying to make some sense out of the craziness. If I pull her into something as ugly as this—"

"She'll be back in the drunk tank in twenty-four hours. You and I both know it."

O'Bannon's nostrils flared, making the purple veins on the tip of his nose darken. "She's kept herself clean for months."

"And we want it to stay that way, right? So, I say—keep her out of it."

"Unfortunately, it isn't your decision to make."

"Hey, Chief! Have you seen this?"

It was Tony Crenshaw, one of O'Bannon's best forensic experts, waving at him from the other side of the kitchen.

Granger followed O'Bannon over, with considerable relief. Any excuse to get away from that damn deep fat fryer. At least until the techs had finished taking samples and someone from the scrub squad had swept away the remains. They rounded the central cooking console and came out facing a large flat grill that looked as if it had been designed to fry a hundred burgers at once.

"Check it out," Crenshaw said, pointing.

The grill was coated with a thick layer of grease, but in the grease, someone had left a message. Like a kid writing WASH ME on a dirty car, except this wasn't written in the English language. Or any other language. It was all numbers and symbols and things Granger remembered from school only hazily if at all.

It wasn't a message. It was an equation.

O'Bannon glanced at Granger out of the corner of his eye. "Still think there's some rational explanation?"

Granger didn't bother answering. The chief was already on his cell phone.

4

TUCKER WAS EXHAUSTED. He was a strong man—built like a bull, his mother had said, since he was a toddler. Ten hours of construction work six days a week would build strength in anyone. But he was used to that. Hauling a corpse around—that was something new.

He didn't mind the bloody stuff. A change of pace from the repetition of his day job, the cutting and sawing and measuring. He was never much good at anything but grunt labor; they only kept him around to do the heavy lifting no one else wanted—or was able—to do. But he knew how to use his fists. He'd learned that early on. He knew how to take someone down and take them out, quickly and painlessly, or slowly and painfully, whichever worked best.

Tucker grunted, then shifted his burden from one shoulder to the other. Hard work, lugging this through the darkened streets of one of Vegas's seedier downtown districts in the dead of the night. Maybe he had made a mistake, coming on foot. But the distances had to be exactly right, to the number, so he needed the pedometer. His van's odometer might get him close, but close wasn't good enough.

It had all started at that damned grade school, he supposed, in a small town near the Utah border. He didn't know why he couldn't make friends. Maybe it was his father and . . . everything that was going on at home. Maybe it was the way he looked. Who knew? He wanted friends, he wanted people to like him. But they never did. No matter what he did or tried, they never did. Tucker was an unusual first name back then, and kids being what they were it wasn't long before "Tucker the Fucker" became the chant he heard every time the teachers were out of sight, till finally he couldn't stand it anymore. He popped an older kid three times his size and a huge fight ensued. Tucker ended up with a broken nose, so mangled it was still crooked, and he permanently lost his sense of smell. Which might be a blessing, given his current activities.

The worst of it was, even though the older kid started the fight, Tucker was the one who got in trouble. The teachers didn't like him any more than the other children did. He scared them, so they paddled him till he was raw and there was nothing he could do about it. Nothing he could do to them, anyway. A stray calico cat made the mistake of crossing his path on the way home from school. So he killed it. Twisted its neck with his bare hands, so hard the head nearly came off.

Not that different from last night's work, now that he thought about it.

He shifted his load back to his left shoulder. How much farther? He checked the pedometer. Only about a tenth of a mile. Hell, he could do that standing on his head. Wasn't any harder than . . . well, ripping the head off a kitten. Which as it turned out, he really enjoyed. He did it again and again, every time he saw one running loose, each time envisioning the face of someone from school, some kid. A teacher. His father.

How many times had dear old dad popped him in the face, huh? And he'd never hit him back, never once. He was afraid to. How could they expect him to learn anything at school? Didn't matter. He already knew more than those teachers, at least about the things that were really important, about the way the world really worked. He just ignored them. All of them. Taking his little pleasures where he could find them. The cats.

Except one day, when he was out in the woods behind the McKinley place doing a black and white Maine coon, that damned meddling Suzie Connery saw him. She threatened to tell everyone.

So he did to her what he did to the cats. Or tried, anyway. She managed to get a few screams out, and one of Old Man McKinley's wives came running, screaming her head off, and he had to run. Not long after that, the police found the trash dump where he'd been leaving the cats, more than fifty of them. The police grabbed him and told him he was a "nasty boy" and had "violent urges" and that they were going to beat them out of him. They pounded him pretty good, too, until he got one smack in the nose and made a run for it. Never went back. Never saw his father again. Always wondered if the cop lost his sense of smell. Seemed only fair.

He was fourteen then and he'd been on his own ever since. He'd done pretty damn well for himself, all things considered. But he never forgot the cats. He never forgot what it felt like to hold someone's life in his hands. He still did a cat every now and again, or a puny little poodle. He dreamed of greater things. But he never knew how to fulfill those dreams, how to make them a reality. He never had an excuse—no, a reason—to use his God-given talents. To do what he did best. He had nothing to live for. Until, at long last, by means he never could have anticipated, his destiny was revealed unto him.

Now he could do all the things he had always wanted to do without guilt or penalty. Even better, he could sleep soundly with the knowledge that he was doing something good, something that was meant to be. That he was doing it for love.

At long last he arrived. Exactly twenty-one miles from the epicenter, the central axis point. 0,0. He slid the headless corpse off his shoulder and fell back against the brick wall of the alleyway, breathing heavily. The body was bundled in painters' sheet wrap, but it wouldn't be long before it was discovered by a homeless person or wino or vagrant. Fine. He wanted the body to be discovered.

He was still tired, even with his burden lightened, but he had to move on. Couldn't risk discovery. At home, he could sleep. A carefree, dreamless sleep.

Until tomorrow night. When, thanks to the magic of the calendar, he would have the blessed opportunity to exercise his God-given talents once again.

5

I SPOONED another helping of the marvelously creamy and undoubtedly fattening frozen custard into my mouth. "Have you tried it yet, Darcy?"

"I—I—"

"Try it, Darcy."

"But, today is Thursday, and on Thursday, I—"

"Yes, I know. You have Praline Lovers' Delight on Tuesdays and Vanilla Toffee on Wednesdays and Strawberry Mash on Thursday, unless there's a new flavor, in which case you substitute the new flavor for whichever flavor on your list has the most letters in its name. If there's a tie, you cross out whichever one comes last alphabetically, unless the Thursday falls on the last day of the month, in which case you reverse the alphabetical order and . . . I forget the rest."

"So you will understand why—"

"The Peppermint Pop is a seasonal special, Darcy. It won't be here next week, and it's delicious. So even though Praline Lovers' Delight has more letters in its name, you need to try it today."

"But—"

"Darcy." I looked at him, not harshly, but firmly.

And to my happy surprise, he took a bite.

It may seem like a small thing, but it reminded me just how far Darcy had come in the relatively short time since I met him. Darcy was diagnosed at age three as an autistic savant, but his father—Police Chief O'Bannon—had undertaken constant therapy and consultation with behavioral intervention experts at the Lovass Center in L.A. and had worked wonders. Slowly but surely he'd left his autistic world and entered our own. In time, his compulsive obsessions began to fade, though they were never extinguished, and he developed relatively normal speech ability. His inflection was askew, unless he was imitating someone, which he could do flawlessly, and he often didn't understand what people were saying, particularly if they spoke euphemistically or idiomatically or sarcastically, but he was still light-years ahead of most autistics, even other savants. His problems with language were understandable; he didn't understand why one word should have multiple meanings and had difficulty gathering which one to apply in context. Metaphors were beyond him; tell him that the sun was a glistening incandescent orb and he would politely tell you that the sun was a thermonuclear reactor processing helium and hydrogen. Jokes—especially wordplay—similarly escaped him.

His appearance was perfectly normal; autistic kids are renowned for their angelic appearance. He was sweet as a baby and kind and incurably gentle. He hated to see people in pain. He had a genuinely sympathetic nature and cared for others. But you didn't have to be around him long to know there was something different about him. Part of it was his reaction—or lack of reaction—to what went on in his environment. He never made eye contact, couldn't read facial expressions or take cues from them. Nonverbal language was a form of expression he would never master. Some theorists believe autistic persons don't really see faces at all, which would explain why Darcy was often confused about whether he had met someone before, unless he was able to pick up on some other clue—the sound of their voice, a scent, even the familiar squeaking of a shoe. He didn't understand people, their motivations, what made them do the things they did. But that was okay. Because I did.

After his father was shot—and my niece, Rachel, was taken into a foster home—we began to spend time together. He enjoyed the company, I think—you can never really be sure of anything with Darcy. He had profound tactile defensiveness; he didn't like to be touched and shunned signs of affection. Even though you suspected he wanted them, something inside just wouldn't let it happen.

"I think that actually this is kinda good," Darcy said, as he gobbled the custard down.

"Five stars?"

He stopped eating and reflected a moment. "Two point seven five."

"And that makes it . . ."

"Number seventeen on my list. Just beneath Rocky Road Almond with Skittles. But that is still very good."

"I'd say so. Especially since your list includes . . . how many flavors?"

"Two hundred and seventy-four. Would you like me to list them all for you in order?"

"Thanks, I'll pass."

On the other hand, his savant gifts were astounding. He remembered virtually everything he had ever read—sometimes he could even tell you what page he'd read it on. Probably because he saw the world from such a different viewpoint, he had a penchant for noticing things everyone else missed. He'd come up with telling pieces of information all the crime tech and forensic experts had missed. I couldn't begin to measure his mathematical abilities, since I personally can't even balance my checkbook. He could solve puzzles, cryptograms, codes, almost instantaneously. His brain was an overcrowded hodgepodge of information that made it difficult for him to focus, but I tried to teach him to sift through all the concurrent and conflicting thoughts and stay on task. Every day he took another baby step out of his obsessive autistic prison. It may not seem like getting him to try a different flavor of custard on the wrong day was a major triumph. But it was.

"So tell me—how are you and your father getting along?"

His face always changed whenever we talked about his father, or whenever his father was around. It wasn't that Darcy didn't like him. I knew perfectly well they both loved each other. But Darcy was his only child and . . . well, obviously not what O'Bannon had expected. His wife died when Darcy was seven, and raising him alone had been an incredible burden.

"My dad is fine. He walks much better now. With his cane, he gets around almost as well as he did before the Bad—you know."

I did know. Before the Bad Man shot him. Which Darcy didn't like to talk about.

"You're not answering my question, Darcy. How are you and your father getting along?"

He shrugged lopsidedly, then flapped his hands together. "My dad never lets me do anything, not unless you are with me. He thinks I cannot do anything."

"He just wants to make sure you're safe, Darcy. That's what parents do. It's like their job description."

"But I am not a baby anymore. I can do lots of stuff."

"He knows that."

"He does not know that! He will never let me do anything. I—I—" Darcy looked up at me, as if wondering if I could be trusted. "I am thinking about running away from home."

It took some effort, but I managed to suppress my smile. It's not often you hear a twenty-six-year-old talk about running away from home. "But Darcy—how could you support yourself? You don't make enough working part-time at the day-care center to even afford a crummy apartment, much less food and transportation and—"

"I know. I know." He finished the custard, then licked the spoon. "I—I was—was w-wondering . . . Do you think maybe . . . you and me . . . would it be possible? . . ."

"Spit it out, Darcy."

"Would you adopt me?"

I bit down on my lip, hard. "What?"

"I would be good. I promise I would. And I would help you with your police work, just like I do sometimes now. You said I was helpful, right?"

"You're always helpful. But I can't—"

"And then maybe we could share money. And we would share your apartment, since you adopted me."

"Darcy." I laid my hand gently on his shoulder. He flinched, but let it stay. "You are very dear to me, and I love being with you. But I can't adopt you. And frankly, half what I make wouldn't be enough to get you a bus ticket to Caesar's Palace. I can barely pay my own rent."

His head fell. "You don't want to live with me."

"Darcy, it's not—" I stopped short. What exactly were we talking about here?

Fortunately, my cell phone vibrated, saving me from having to do any deeper thinking. "Pulaski."

"This is Chief O'Bannon. I've got a case for you. Are you available?"

"You know I am. What is it?"

"It's . . . I don't want to talk about it on the phone."

"Homicide?"

"Definitely. Looks like it's right up your alley."

Meaning not just your average, everyday run-of-the-mill murders. Something weird. Something that called for a consultant in aberrant psychology.

"Just come out to the Burger Bliss on Fremont, okay? Granger will fill you in. And Susan?"

"I'm still here."

"Don't bring Darcy."

"Are you sure? He's with me now."

"Drop him off."

"But—why? He's proven—"

"Are you listening to me, Susan? Don't bring Darcy." He paused a moment. "You'll understand when you get here."

He rang off, and I snapped my pocket cell closed. "Looks like I've got a case."

Darcy's eyes brightened. "Are we going to catch another crook?"

I sighed heavily. This wasn't going to be pretty. "I'm afraid there's no *we* this time, Darcy. You can't come."

"But—But—" He ran his fingers through his hair. "You said that I was helpful. And—And—that casino man who took the money. No one else knew how tall he was. And the lady who lost her wedding ring—"

"I know, Darcy. I know. I'm not saying I don't want you along." I paused, considered, then atypically opted to just tell the truth. Sort of. "They, uh, say I can't bring you with me."

Darcy lowered his voice to a whisper. "Then we will not tell them."

"Sorry, Darcy. I'll have to drop you off at home."

I knew he wasn't happy about it, but he was too nice to argue, too sweet-hearted to cause me any grief. He threw away his empty custard cup and headed toward my beat-up Chevy.

"I just hope I can manage," I said, trying to bolster his spirits. "It's been a long time since I went out on a job without you by my side. I probably won't know what to do."

"It will go very well. You will be very wonderful," he said, sliding into the passenger seat. His eyes looked as if they were brimming with tears.

"And how can you know that?"

"Because we had custard together today," he replied, beaming that goofy, beatific smile. "And any day we have custard together is a Very Excellent Day. It's a rule."

IT TOOK ME four months to stop stuttering and not be nervous and ask Susan to adopt me and then when I did she said no and she laughed at me I mean she did not really laugh at me but her voice did I could hear it because it was just like when I ask my dad if I could be a policeman or when the ladies at the day care watch me change a diaper and why would anyone laugh because no one wants to change a diaper I remember when my mother was alive and she used to—

Stop. Susan says I have to learn to stop and slow down and focus and put more periods in my thinking and I like Susan so I am going to try. To do. What she says. It is hard when there are so many ideas going on inside my brain all at once I wish I could block some of them out but I cannot they just keep coming and I have a hard time remembering what I am supposed to do because my head is like a computer trying to do too many things at once and then the CPU gets blocked and it crashes and I don't remember to stop and—

Reboot. Windows is loading. One thought at a time.

Being with Susan is always interesting. I like being with Susan but she would not let me be with her today and it is my dad's fault it is always his fault he never never never wants to let me do anything he does not think I can do anything he just scowls at me and acts all disappointed and I wish I did not look so much like my mother I think it would be better if I did not look so much like my mother because then maybe my dad—

Stop. Blinking hourglass symbol. One thought at a time.

I am disappointed that my dad would not let me go. With Susan. Because I love Susan and I want to be with her always. I knew she would never marry me because I am so stupid and weird but I thought that maybe if she adopted me then we could live together and we would not have to be married. I do not care if we do sex because I do not know how and I think it has a lot of touching so I probably would not like it and probably would not be any good at it anyway. I do not care about anything except that I want to be with Susan and I love her. I like babies and babies usually like me and if we had babies that would be very nice I think. Babies are easier to understand than big people.

I still see the Bad Man sometimes at night when I am sleeping or just before I am sleeping. Susan says I should not let him scare me because he cannot hurt me now but he does he does he hurts me and I don't know what to do about it. I think that if Susan would adopt me then the Bad Man would go away forever just like my mother did but she said no so now I am alone with my father and I am not happy and he is not happy and what is the point of everyone not being happy?

I wish that I were with Susan. I hope that she does not meet another Bad Man.

6

YOU'LL UNDERSTAND *when you get here,* O'Bannon had said, and those words were still echoing in my head when I reached the Burger Bliss fast-food joint as per his instructions. *Don't bring Darcy.* O'Bannon had initially been resistant to my involving Darcy in police investigations but over time had become gradually, if guardedly, accepting of it. Despite his protestations to the contrary, some part of him must've enjoyed seeing Darcy's phenomenal gifts put to good use. For the past couple of months, it had been automatically understood that anytime he gave me a consulting job, Darcy would be tagging along. Until today. Which told me that either he had undergone a dramatic change of heart . . .

Or there was something in there he really did not want Darcy to see.

I gave a shout-out to the two uniforms posted at the door, who smiled and waved me inside without a word. I can still remember, just after I was released from detox and got myself booted off the force, when I practically needed a hall pass to get onto a crime scene. And O'Bannon would sniff my breath the moment I arrived. This was better.

It wasn't hard to figure out where the action had taken place. The videographer was making a detailed record of the entire kitchen, everything behind the cash register counter. At least a dozen other crime techs were swarming around in their coveralls, protective coverings on their shoes, always careful not to step off the butcher paper that had been laid on the tile floor. I loved watching these guys (and gals) work. It was like when you're a kid and you can spend hours staring at an ant farm, observing all the specialized tasks as the creatures scurry across one another's paths but never collide. Some of the crime techs were using forensic oils and chemical swabs, some were shining fluorescent lights, some were crawling on their hands and knees, scrutinizing the tile floor for anything that might've been missed. It was no accident they decided to set that TV show in Vegas; according to the FBI, we had the second best CSI unit in the country, here in a city that ranked only thirty-second in terms of population.

On the far left, one of the stainless steel countertops was covered with blood spatter. Didn't take empathic powers to figure out what must've happened there.

I hopped over the countertop and was heading in that general direction when I felt a strong arm yank me backward. It was Barry Granger, the man who filled the gap I left when I lost my job and who had recently been promoted to chief homicide detective. He'd been my husband David's partner; he was very close to David and took his death hard. Over the past few months, we'd learned to coexist, but we weren't friends and I couldn't imagine that we ever would be. Fair or not, he blamed me for David's death.

"Just so you know," Granger said, "I was opposed to bringing you in on this case."

I smiled. "Top o' the mornin' to you, too, Barry. How are the wife and kids?"

"Don't get smart with me. Just listen and understand what I'm saying. We have a good homicide department and we will crack this case. You've been asked—against my wishes—to give us some psychological insight on the sicko who did this. That's all. The men here respect me, and I don't want you parading around with your smart mouth and superior attitude and undermining my authority. It's my case. You work for me. Understood?"

"Loud and clear. Now let go of my arm before I have to embarrass you in front of all these men who respect you." He did.

"I mean it, Pulaski. Are you going to cooperate?"

"Hmm. Magic 8 Ball says: Outlook Not Good."

"It would be different if you were a team player. But you never are. While my men are out pounding the street, you're off in your own little world, doing your weird stuff."

"I'm a behaviorist, Granger. I don't street-pound."

"If you really wanted to help, I could assign to you some of the hundred or so people who need to be interviewed. You could hit the back alleyways, talk to contacts, see what you can stir up. Show the street scum that we mean business."

"Thanks, but that sounds a little too Starsky and Hutch for me. Who was the first responder?"

"MacNeill."

"Thank God." Meaning, thank God it wasn't you. The first officer on the premises has the critical job of securing the crime scene, making sure it isn't contaminated. If it had been someone as sloppy as Granger, there'd be no clues left to find.

I turned back toward the blood spatter. Even at a glance I could see the arching pattern that suggested a single blow from behind. And although the quantity was plenty enough to turn my stomach, there was very little blood outside the arch. No pooling on the floor.

"DRT?" I asked Granger. This is hip cop slang for Dead Right There.

"No question."

"ID?"

"We're working on it. My men just arrived. The body is not on the premises."

"That adds to the challenge."

He made a mock salute. "That's why you're here." His voice rose. "Now get to work, lieutenant. Er . . . former lieutenant. Whatever. Hop to it."

Granger walked away, having accomplished his mission. Which was not to put me in my place. He knew that was useless. What was important to him was that he stage a scene that everyone present would see—with him reading me the riot act, reminding everyone that no matter how smart I was or what cases I had solved in the past, I was not in charge.

I'd be seriously mad at him—if I didn't know deep down that it *was* important for the head of the department to be in charge, to be seen to be in charge, to keep upstarts in line. He didn't want to lose his job any more than I had wanted to lose mine.

In the back of the kitchen, I spotted Tony Crenshaw. I knew he'd be useful. He'd come on board as an expert in dactylograms—that's what he insisted on calling what you and I call fingerprints—but had proven himself so darn smart that O'Bannon let him do pretty much anything he wanted to do. What's more—he liked me, and he had stuck by me, even in the tough days following David's death. Being single and good-looking didn't hurt him any, either.

Tony smiled as I approached. "Me and the boys were betting on how many seconds would pass before you showed up."

I guess that was a compliment. Of sorts. "That weird?"

"Oh yeah."

"Slit the guy's throat?" I paused.

"Right."

"Looks like he did it in a single blow."

His eyes widened appreciatively. "Very good. So you *were* awake during my blood spatter seminar."

Well, off and on. "Do we know what weapon was used?"

"Not exactly. Any big knife would do. Lots of them here in the kitchen. I don't really know yet. But we can safely assume it was something strong and extremely sharp. Look at the pattern of the arch." With a finger in the air, he traced the path of the blood across the stainless steel counter and then onto the wall behind it. "It's one thing if your victim is beneath you and you can swing the weapon executioner-style, like you're swinging one of those hammers to ring the bell at the county fair. But if that had been the case, the blood would've spattered across the floor. These two, killer and victim, were standing one behind the other. Meaning the assailant had to reach around his throat, while holding him upright."

"So we're looking for a guy. A very strong guy."

"I don't want to sound sexist, but given the upper-body strength requirement . . ." He shrugged. "Either it's one of those chicks from the Worldwide Wrestling League, or it's a guy. A barbarian."

"Tall, dark, and brutal?"

Tony shook his head. "Again, look at the main concentration of the blood spatter. Over six feet off the floor, and forming an upward elliptical arch. Our assailant was shorter than his victim, probably shorter than average."

"A homunculus."

"Well, I don't like to make value judgments about strangers. But I wouldn't set him up on a date with my sister."

I nodded my agreement. "I'm surprised the victim didn't struggle more."

"Oh, God, didn't anyone tell you?"

Just the way he said it gave me a severe case of the jim-jams. "Just give it to me straight, Tony. What happened?"

He pointed to the stainless steel gizmo to the left, obviously uncomfortable. "Do you know what that is?"

"Tony, the only thing I cook is Lean Cuisine."

"That's a deep fat fryer. It's where they make french fries and onion rings."

"I feel certain the victim wasn't killed by onion rings."

Tony swallowed. "The killer pushed the vic's face down into the fryer. Into the boiling oil. While it was on."

I felt an intense surge of nausea rising up my stomach like a surfer on the big kahuna. "So the temperature was . . ."

"Approximately three hundred and fifty degrees."

I took several quick short breaths, trying to steady myself. "How—"

"First," he continued, "the skin would melt off your face. Then you would go into shock. Your brain would literally begin to cook. It would feel like—"

I held up a hand. "I don't need to know what it would feel like."

"Okay." He looked away, then muttered: "Having his throat cut afterward was probably a mercy."

I fought back the nausea, the shaking in my knees that oh so desperately wanted a quick snort of something with a very high alcoholic content, and asked, "But—*why*?"

Tony laid his hand on my shoulder. He was looking a bit ashen himself. "And with that question, Susan, you have officially moved out of my realm—and into yours."

7

I STEADIED MYSELF against the counter, doing my best to stay out of the way of the scientists who had real work to do, and thought. Or perhaps more accurately . . . I listened. To the kitchen. What had happened? What went on here?

Could there possibly be a rational motive behind boiling someone's face? It was hard to imagine. Was this planned or spontaneous? The killer used his brute strength and the tools at hand—in this case, one that fried potatoes at three hundred and fifty degrees Fahrenheit. But he might've also brought a weapon for the decapitation. Premeditated? Every instinct told me he wasn't killing for love, money, jealousy, revenge, hatred, or any of the usual motives. Everything I had seen so far pointed to a psychopath.

Which led to the second question: Why here? Why commit a murder in a fast-food restaurant? Just to take advantage of the deep fat fryer? It hardly seemed likely. A private location would be better. Even the victim's home would be better. Perhaps he didn't live alone. Still, subduing a family would be easier than luring someone to a downtown eatery late at night, wouldn't it? No, the only possible explanation was that the victim worked here. Maybe the killer didn't know where he lived, maybe the victim was just in the wrong place at the wrong time. But he worked here. Which meant there was about a ninety percent chance he was young, thirty or under. He was here late, after hours, presumably alone. So he must be on the managerial staff, the poor chump with the job of turning everything off and locking up. Except this time, he didn't lock up fast enough. Or the killer was too determined to be deterred by a locked door.

"Granger," I said, doing my best to feign politeness, "find out who was the manager of the late-night shift yesterday, okay?"

"We're methodically reviewing all the employee records—"

"Forget that. Just find out who was last night's late-shift manager. Then call his home."

"Oh yeah? Why?"

"Because I have a hunch he won't answer."

I left Charlie Chan wondering what I knew that he didn't and approached my best friend on the force, Amelia Escavez. Over the past few months—after my childhood friend Lisa moved to Los Angeles—we had become very close. We palled around at the office and off-hours, too. She helped me get through some rough times and I loved her dearly.

Amelia was standing by the patty grill, her trusty field kit close at hand. She was an impressions examiner. Over the years, I'd seen her taking impressions of tire tracks, footprints, fingerprints, even teeth marks. But this was the first time I'd seen her plying her trade with a greasy grill.

"Trying out a new oven cleaner, Amelia?"

She glanced up for barely a moment, then returned her attention to her work. She'd coated the surface of the grill with a white substance and was now hardening it with a handheld hair dryer. "Yup. Figured I could sell it to Dow and finally make some real money."

"New car, new house, speedboat on Lake Mead?"

"I'd be content if I could just get a date."

Girl talk. The older we get, it never really changes. I used to be so obsessed with work that I almost never socialized with anyone else in the PD—well, not counting David, obviously. But after Lisa took off, I made a real effort to get to know some of my colleagues, especially Amelia. Turned out we were very compatible; we were both smart, funny, and utterly sans a love life. Although staring at her slim figure and perfect height (meaning she didn't tower over and intimidate three-fourths of the male population like yours truly), I couldn't imagine that date-getting was really that much of a problem for her. My theory was, for whatever reason, she just wasn't trying. "Don't tell me the perp left a tire track on the grill."

"Oh, it's ever so much stranger than that. Someone—we're assuming the killer—left a message in the grease."

"What message? Stop me before I kill again?"

"No."

"His name and address?"

"You wish." She glanced at her watch. "Two more minutes and I'll show and tell."

"What's that weird goo you've poured all over everything? It doesn't look like dental-stone casting or any of your usual fixatives."

"My own special recipe. Not an easy thing, lifting an impression off cooking grease."

"I would imagine not."

"We took pictures, of course, but there's always a chance that an impression will reveal something not apparent to the naked eye. A fingerprint, a swirl pattern. A minute hair or fiber. You never know. Problem was, all my normal casting agents would've dissolved the grease."

"So what did you come up with?"

"Hard to describe. Kind of a combination of plaster of Paris and cotton candy."

"You're joking, right?"

She winked. "Great scientists never reveal their secrets." The buzzer on her wristwatch sounded. "It's soup."

With anyone else, I would've had my doubts, but Amelia knew her stuff. Carefully, Amelia put a gloved hand on each corner and lifted the cast. To her evident delight, it all held together in one perfect piece. Her secret recipe had worked. With an elegant flip, she showed me what was on the other side, what had been finger-painted into the grease.

It was reversed, of course, but I could still read it. As it turned out, it wasn't a message at all, at least not in the conventional sense. There were no words. Only . . . numbers. And symbols. And it wasn't a sentence, it was an equation:

$$\frac{(a+b^n)}{n}=x$$

"What does it mean?"

Amelia gently slid her impression into a plastic evidence bag. "As if I would know. I gave up on math after my second semester of algebra."

"Uh, yeah. That was a tough one for me, too." I hadn't taken a math class since junior high school. "If this was left behind by the killer, it might be important. There must be someone on staff who knows math."

"My understanding is that O'Bannon is trying to round up experts but not having much success. You know anyone who's good at math?"

As a matter of fact, I did, but he had been barred from the premises. I jotted the equation into my notebook and started to move on, when Amelia said, "By the by, Susan—it's really good to see you here."

"Because of my sunny personality?"

"Because the person who did this . . ." She grimaced. "Needs to be caught. As soon as possible."

"Amelia, dear. Have you no faith in our distinguished chief homicide detective?"

"I wouldn't want to say anything that might lose me my job . . ." She paused. "So I won't. But as I said . . . I'm really glad you're here. And most of the gang in Forensics feel the same. So don't let Granger get you down, okay?"

"Deal," I said, not feeling nearly as much confidence as I pretended. But when you had someone as sweet as Amelia trying to give you a happy shot, it would be churlish not to cooperate. The reality was, I was already feeling edgy, nervous. I knew Granger didn't want me on this case. He was content to let me handle minor matters—property theft, embezzlement, and whatnot. But this was something else again. If I didn't produce, and fast, Granger would be pushing O'Bannon to get rid of me. The first time I slipped up, any way at all, he'd have my consulting contract yanked and kick my butt back to the suburbs. That kind of pressure I didn't need. That kind of pressure made me instantly flash on my uneraseable mental map of every liquor store in the city, made me calculate the approximate distance to the nearest of them and plan a route.

Granger, Tony, Amelia—all of them had said the same thing, in one way or another. This was my kind of case. They were counting on me to bring this monster in, to stop him before he mutilated someone else.

The only problem was—I didn't know if I could.

8

CHIEF ROBERT O'BANNON found his son, Darcy, lying on the floor in his library, as usual. Darcy didn't look up, didn't say hi. But then, he never did. Why would he? In his mind, there was no reason to offer a common greeting. What purpose did it serve?

The library also doubled as O'Bannon's home office, but he always preferred to call it the library. Because he loved books. Three walls of the room were lined with high-quality mahogany shelves—he'd done the carpentry work, as well as the wood-staining, himself. And all the shelves were full. Full and then some—they'd had to put overflow shelves in the garage. He had all kinds of books—dictionaries, encyclopedias, fiction, nonfiction, books on every topic imaginable. He was curious about almost everything. He often said the best cure for being lonely, or depressed, was to learn something new.

He had scores of criminology texts; every time something at the office was replaced by a more current edition, he took the throwaways home. But he rarely read them. That was what he did during the day. At night, he indulged his first love: novels—the best of everything, from classic literature to current bestsellers. But his favorites had always been nineteenth-century British fiction: Hardy, the Brontë sisters, Dickens, Trollope, and perhaps his personal favorite, Jane Austen. Not exactly the conventional image of what a tough-as-nails cop read in his spare time. But he was not a cliché; he didn't go to monster truck shows or watch NASCAR races and he was content to keep it that way. It hadn't held him back any so far. And there had been benefits, he thought, as he gazed down at his hapless autistic adult offspring, who was thumbing through the pages of *Wuthering Heights,* a book he'd read so many times he could probably recite it from memory.

Forget the *probably.* He could recall every word, like one of those living books in the last chapter of *Fahrenheit 451.* The image brought a small smile to O'Bannon's face. Darcy was his boy, after all. At least a little piece of him.

O'Bannon placed his sterling steel cane against his desk and eased into his chair. He'd spent every day for the past several months pretending he wasn't having any serious trouble getting around. What was a gunshot wound in the gut to a tough old cop like him, anyway? Barely worth mentioning. Except that it still hurt, even half a year later, every hour of every day, even with the medication no one at the office knew he was taking. It was much more difficult now for him to get around, to take care of business. More difficult to take care of Darcy. And Darcy typically required a lot of care.

"Have a good day, son?"

"Okay," Darcy said, not looking up from the book on the floor, his chin propped up on both elbows. "Not Excellent. Certainly not Very Excellent."

"Did you go to the day-care center?"

"For three hours and forty-six minutes. But they do not really let me do anything with the children. Not by myself."

"And I guess there was no time for custard. Because of course then it would be a Very Excellent Day."

"Susan took me to The Custard Factory." He rolled over onto one elbow and, although he didn't actually make eye contact with his father, did look in his general direction. "But she got a call before we finished. I had to take Bus 14, then Bus 36B home."

"She, um, didn't take you with her?"

"No. Not this time."

"Did she say why?"

"She said they would not let her."

"Did she say who *they* was?"

"No."

"Did you ask?"

"No."

Well, that was a relief. "Why didn't you?"

"B-B-Because I already knew." He twisted back onto both elbows and resumed the adventures of Heathcliff and Catherine.

Oh. Well, of course he did, damn it. The kid was scary sometimes, the way he knew everything. Except the common sense and social skills normally acquired by a five-year-old. Looked like O'Bannon was in for a chilly evening. Unless maybe . . .

"Darcy, you wanna play a game? Maybe chess? It's your favorite."

"But you hate it," he said, mumbling into his hand. "It is not fun to play with someone who is not enjoying the game."

"Okay, what about Scrabble? We both enjoy Scrabble."

"I always beat you at Scrabble."

Yes, that would be because you know every word in the whole damn dictionary and can anagram letters like a code-breaking computer. "I still enjoy playing."

"I would rather not, if you do not mind."

"Well . . . what would you like to do?"

Again he turned, if only for an instant. "I would have liked to have gone with Susan."

O'Bannon sighed heavily and closed his eyes. He knew better than to perpetuate a discussion that could never reach a satisfying result. They couldn't talk to each other. They just didn't know how. And much as he might like to, he couldn't blame it all on the neurological disorder. Darcy did much better with Susan. Some of the young women at the day-care center. Even small children. But not with his father.

He still remembered sitting in that child psychiatrist's office, twenty-three years ago, hearing the devastating news for the first time. He hadn't wanted to go at all, but the administrators at Darcy's nursery said there was a problem, a serious one, and that he wouldn't be allowed to return unless they sought some professional help. So they did, and the great man in the glistening white coat returned after half a day of observation and informed them that their child was autistic.

God, he barely knew what the word meant back then. But he learned soon enough. What, he'd asked, can we do about this? Basically—nothing. Get your kid in a "special" school. Accept that he will never be normal, that he will never be emotionally satisfying in the way parents want their children to be. Be prepared for a lot of work. And be forewarned that it will never end, because Darcy will never be able to leave home, can never hope to take care of himself, no matter how long he lives.

O'Bannon read all the books on the disorder, such as there were. Then as now, no one really understood what autism was. They called it a "spectrum disorder" to disguise the fact that it took so many forms, that no one could come up with a consistent description (much less diagnosis) that fit all cases. His wife, Connie, who seemed to cope with the bad news much better than he did, took Darcy to California for a month of intensive training and behavioral intervention therapy with Dr. Ivar Lovass, while simultaneously administering a barrage of diet and drug therapies. It drained every penny they had in savings, but that was okay, anything to get their boy fixed. Which was, of course, impossible. By the time the money ran out, she had learned enough to continue the program at home, to train other volunteers to work with him.

Her efforts made a profound difference. Slowly but surely, Darcy became more communicative, more disciplined, easier to control. But fixed? Hardly. Cured?

For autism, there was no such thing.

A few years later, Connie died and left him a widower, Darcy motherless. Her heart had given out. Many people thought she had worked herself to death. But that wasn't O'Bannon's theory. Oh, she'd worked diligently all right, more than any woman in the history of the world ever worked, his Connie. But what hurt her most was the emotional vacuum where her firstborn son was supposed to be. The child who never said "Good night," much less "I love you." The boy who never gave nor returned a hug, who shied away from displays of affection. That's what hurt Connie the most. That was what killed her.

Since that time, O'Bannon and Darcy had muddled on in their own way, coexisting, but never truly living together. Friends had suggested that he put Darcy in some kind of home, but he couldn't. Darcy was his boy. His only son. He knew Darcy was frustrated. He knew he thought his father was holding him back. But the truth was—he was protecting him. He'd watched this boy for twenty-six years. He knew what he could do and what he could not do. He was not going to set him up for disappointment. He would not put him in a position where he would be belittled, made the object of a sniggering freak show. He had been very reluctant when Susan first started involving him in her casework. But Susan looked after him, protected him. She had a gift for taking what seemed like inane autistic ramblings to everyone else and turning them into pertinent investigative information. She made him useful.

But could Darcy function on his own? No, not now, not ever. Without Susan his directionless observations would be worse than useless. He could never hold a position of real authority, a job where people depended upon him. A job that forced him to interact in the real world, to try to understand people's minds and motivations. It was absurd. Impossible. He was an innocent, a child. He couldn't possibly allow Darcy to visit the scene of a crime where some maniac had melted a man's face off with boiling hot cooking oil. He was the boy's father, damn it. Darcy had been through so much, had borne so many struggles normal boys never had to face. He would not set him up for failure. Not like that.

He glanced at his son, still lying on the carpet. He turned a page every now and again, but O'Bannon didn't think he was really reading. For a kid who supposedly didn't grasp emotion, he did a pretty damn good version of the cold shoulder treatment.

"Darcy," he said, clearing his throat, trying to carefully choose his words, ". . . are you . . . interested in the case Susan is working on?"

Darcy's head turned ever so slightly in his direction. "Y-Y-Yes," he said.

The stuttering again. Whenever Darcy was around him. "Can I show you something? Something to do with the case?" Even as he'd stuffed the document into his satchel, he'd had misgivings about showing it to Darcy. He didn't need to be involved in anything this ugly. Still, as long as he kept Darcy away from the crime scene . . . maybe . . .

Susan was always able to find a way to make Darcy useful.

"Here it is." He slid a photocopy of the imprint Escavez had taken off the grill. The mysterious formula:

$$\frac{(a+b^n)}{n}=x$$

"Can you read it?"

"Yes."

"Do you know what it is?"

"It is . . . an equation."

"I know how good you are in math. Can you, uh, tell me what it means?"

Darcy tilted his head to one side. "What it means?"

"Yeah. We think it must have some significance. It was found at the scene of the crime. Do you know what it means?"

"Are you asking me . . . can I solve it?"

As if he knew. "Okay, can you solve it?"

Darcy took it into his own hands and stared at it. "What does *n* stand for?"

"I don't know. Why?"

"It is used twice. If I knew what *n* was, then I would be able to maybe narrow the range of possible solutions."

"Well, we really don't know what—"

"What does *a* stand for? Or *b*?"

"Darcy, we don't know what any of the symbols stand for."

"Then it is impossible for me to solve it. I could give you a list of possible solutions in algebraic form. But there would be an infinite number of numerical answers. Unless I know at least one of the integer substitutions, I cannot narrow it down to one solution."

"We don't know what the formula stands for, or what it means, or what you do with it. Maybe it's something theoretical. Like $E=mc^2$. I mean, that has some meaning"—or so he'd heard—"but you don't know what any of the numbers are."

"I do not have to. I know that E is energy and M is mass and c is the speed of light. Even if I do not have any of the numbers, the equation is still true."

"Well, then—"

"But without one of the numbers, I cannot possibly give you any of the others, so I cannot solve it." He laid the paper down.

O'Bannon blew air through his teeth. Every conversation they had always turned out like this—with both of them totally frustrated. He thought Darcy would jump all over this—a clue to a crime involving mathematics, his strongest subject. At school they used to call him the human calculator. He could multiply five-digit numbers in his head. So why couldn't Darcy help now?

"Well, thanks for trying, son."

"I-I-I did not try, because it was not possible. Why would you ask me to do something that was not possible?"

"Well, I didn't know—"

"Y-Y-You don't think I can do anything. Y-Y-You wouldn't ask me to do anything that was possible."

"Darcy—that's not true!" O'Bannon protested, but it was too late. Darcy was already back on the floor, his eyes glued to the book, either reading or not. Damn it all. He should've known better. He shouldn't have come home asking for trouble.

Or maybe, just maybe, he should've recognized what everyone else already knew.

Susan could work with his son. But he couldn't.

9

JULY 13

"I HOPE YOU DON'T MIND meeting me so early in the morning, Rachel," I said, as I passed her the Krispy Kremes. "I'm on a new case. And I'm supposed to be in the office at nine o'clock sharp."

"I don't mind. Which one's cream-filled?"

I pointed. She wolfed. Rachel is my beautiful, effervescent, clear-skinned, sixteen-year-old niece, who is good for a smile even at this god-awful time of the morning. How I loved her. She was the only real family I had now, but there was a lot more to it than that. Everyone who knew her loved her. I certainly did. Which was why I finally abandoned the custody battle and left her in foster care.

She licked a dollop of cream out of the center with a quick flick of her tongue, an Ingrid Bergmanesque move, if Ingrid Bergman had been as lovely as my niece. "I get up this early every morning anyway. Basketball practice."

"Ah. Of course."

"City league. I was on the school team before, but since it turned out I wasn't half bad, I thought—why not?"

That was my girl. Well, David's late brother's girl, but still. Mine. Initially I had been hostile to the idea of her playing basketball, not to mention joining a youth group and a church group and everything else that was her foster parents' idea and not mine. But they had worked wonders with her. They were sweet old folks, straight shooters. Honest as the day is long. Boring as hell. But you could see where there might be some value in that, when you're raising a teenage girl.

"So," I said, as I started my second coffee. I know, I shouldn't, but cut me some slack—it's my last remaining addictive substance to abuse. "Anything new in little Rachel's life?"

"Not really." Her head turned down, her face shrouded by her gorgeous auburn hair. "I mean, nothing important. Nothing worth, you know, nothing—"

I decided to put her out of her misery. In a little singsong voice, I said, "*Ra* . . . chel's *got* . . . a *boy* . . . friend . . ."

"I do not!"

"Do so."

"Do not. Not really."

"Meaning, Rachel wants a boyfriend?"

"No! Ugh! I mean, okay, not ugh, but, you know, yuck."

Fortunately, I speak fluent teenager. "So there is a guy and you like him but you're not sure if he likes you yet."

She stared back at me. "You know, you're really amazing."

"Well, I am a trained psychologist. So is this that—what was his name—the skateboard guy?"

"Bobby? Oh, God no. He is so yesterday."

"Just as well." I smiled and snarfed the last cruller. "Look, Rach, if you really like the guy, just tell him."

"Easy for you to say. What about you? Have you been out on a date lately?"

"No. But Amelia and I have been running around some. Keeps me off the streets. Look, I'd better get you back to the Johnsons."

"There's no rush."

"Rachel, it took that man three months to trust me enough to let me take you out of his sight. I'm not going to blow it now by being late."

"I know. But—" She hesitated, and this time I really didn't know what was on her mind. "I—I wanted to give you something."

"Unless I've really lost track of time, it's not my birthday."

"No, I meant—" She swallowed hard, then plopped it down on the table. "I saved this when Lisa moved you out of your apartment, while you were in the clinic. It's—"

"I know what it is." No explanation required. I carried the thing around for almost nine years, till I started getting so drunk every day I forgot to put it in my pocket. It was a good-luck charm, a tiny four-leaf clover, a real one, encased in translucent acrylic.

"Guess I used up all the luck it had for me," David said, while he was lying in a hospital bed in the recovery room. "Why don't you take it? Maybe it'll still work for you." And it did, a least for a little while. I got David.

David's father was not pleased. Not about David giving away the charm he'd given his son when he was twelve or, for that matter, anything else. Or more specifically, anything relating to his son and me being together. I could see where David's father might be overprotective—he'd already lost one son, Rachel's father. So when David was wounded during a 405 pursuit—armed robber, gunshot to the upper thorax—his father went on twenty-four-hour orange alert.

"I guess I haven't been shy about my thoughts regarding this relationship," his father had said.

"That's all right," I replied, lying through my teeth. "I think it's best to be up front with each other."

"Well, I've done some checking up on you, miss. And most of what I've learned I haven't liked. You're not exactly . . ."

"Donna Reed?"

He took it in stride. "The image of what a man sought in a woman when I was courting." He paused, choosing his words carefully. "David is very vulnerable right now. He needs someone who can look after him. He needs a woman who really cares about him."

"I would not lie about this," I said, looking his father straight in the eye. "I love your son. More than I've ever loved anyone in my entire life."

He met my gaze for a long, long time, then finally nodded. "Take care of my boy, Susan."

Light filled my eyes, and I felt them watering of their own accord. "I'm so sorry," I said, not even realizing I was speaking aloud. "I'm sorry I let you down."

"What?" Rachel said. "What are you talking about? You've never let me down in your entire life."

I blinked, then dragged myself back to the present. "Sorry. Daydreaming. That good-luck charm—"

"See, that's why I kept it for so long. I was afraid if I gave it to you, it would just bring back memories . . . that maybe it was better you forgot."

"No, you did the right thing. This is a treasure. This . . . will always be a treasure to me." I clutched it tightly in my hand. "Thanks, Rach. You're a hell of a girl."

"Susan, if you start swearing, Mr. Johnson will revoke your visitation rights."

"Good thing you know how to keep a secret." I gave her a squeeze on the shoulder. "Get in the car, you squirt. I've got work to do."

LADY DANIELLE HAD TO MOVE quickly, before her captors returned to the ship and discovered that she had escaped. This was the pirates' first chance to go ashore for months, and they jumped at it, the whole scurvy lot of them. They were certain to take advantage of the pleasures to be had: the grog, the gaming, and the lusty wenches all too ready to serve. But she couldn't count on them all staying gone, not for long. Captain Longsword knew he was carrying valuable and potentially dangerous cargo. He wouldn't be absent any longer than necessary. Once he'd paid for the necessary supplies, he'd likely return in the first transport that rowed out from the shore. Which made it all the more important that she hurry. It was not easy, maneuvering through the hatches of a ship, up and down ladders, through the narrow passageways, all while wearing a full petticoat. But she had to discover where they had imprisoned Mason. Before it was too late.

"I don't have time for modesty," she muttered, as she loosened the fastener and slithered out of the petticoat, leaving herself in a tight laced bodice and white frilly bloomers. Now she was able to move quickly. She brushed her golden curls behind her shoulders and threw open the door to the captain's private quarters—

Mason was hanging from two chains suspended from the ceiling, his head bowed. Was he asleep, unconscious? Or worse? He was naked from the waist up, his muscled hairy chest marred by the scars from his recent flogging. (Once again, Mason's pride had interfered with his judgment.) She should have realized he would be in here. Longsword wouldn't risk having him anywhere else. Plus, this gave the vile captain the opportunity to torment him all day long if he liked. To eat like a pig right under Mason's nose, when he had been given nothing but stale biscuits and water for days. To luxuriate in his plushly appointed quarters—the end result of his ill-gotten gains—while Mason hung like a slab of meat in constant agony.

The sound of the door closing brought his head upright. "Lady Danielle?"

"It is I."

His face reddened. At first, she thought it must be

from the pain, but then she realized—"I hope you will forgive my indecent appearance. Female attire is not well-suited for pirate vessels."

"Indeed not," he said, nobly averting his eyes. "But—you should not be here, my lady. If the pirates return—"

"I could not leave you at their mercy."

"My lady, I am but a humble stable boy. Unworthy of your notice, much less—"

"You saved my life. You defended my honor when Longsword threatened to make me his by force. I will not leave you in your time of need."

Mason's chin rose. "He keeps the key to the chains in that desk drawer."

Lady Danielle found them. The lock was old and rusted and turning it required great effort. To get at the lock, she was required to stand on a chair and lean against Mason, her bodice pressed forward. They were both all too aware of the physical contact. Her breathing accelerated. His chest heaved.

At long last she managed to spring the lock. Mason fell to the deck, but quickly righted himself. He stretched and massaged his arms, flexing his magnificent muscles, slowly restoring his circulation. She stepped down from the chair. They were still very close to each other.

"My lady . . . I do not know how I could ever repay this kindness."

"By staying alive. By . . . by . . ."

An instant later, their lips were pressed tightly together. He wrapped his strong arms around her in a tight embrace.

"My lady," he repeated, as he lavished kisses up and down the side of her neck, "this is wrong. If your family learned—"

"Family be damned," she said, seizing the waist of his trousers and all but tearing them loose. "Perhaps I have lost all reason, but my heart is inflamed and I cannot resist you. From the moment you were brought on this boat, I've done nothing but think about you, dream of being with you. And I am a woman accustomed to getting what she wants." Once his pants were gone, she removed her own remaining clothing with intense speed. They stood naked before each other, their hands in erotic exploration, their kisses reaching a violent intensity.

"But the pirates," Mason said, even as he maneuvered her toward the captain's bed. "They could return—"

"Not before the sea change. This is our time, Mason. Time for you to give me what I have craved all these long, lonely days at sea. My heart aches with desire for your throbbing manhood—hey, wait a minute!"

A face appeared from behind the camera. "Problem, Danny?"

"Yeah. Where's his throbbing manhood?"

Everyone on the set broke up. Everyone, that is, except the actor playing Mason.

"What do you think we pay you studs for, anyway?" Danny said, removing her wig. It itched and after too much exposure to the klieg lights, it started to smell. "The Vegas standard for studdom is definitely declining."

"Cut me some slack. It was a long scene. And this is the third take."

"Yeah, yeah. Excuses, excuses. Where's the fluffer?"

"Right here." A young woman in a pink halter top stepped forward. In the adult film business, it was the fluffer's job to keep the male studs looking studly. Take after take.

The man behind the camera pointed at his watch. "It's almost quitting time, Danny."

"Not till we get this scene in the can. Then the boys can set up for the captain's bed/bondage scene and we can start fresh on that first thing in the morning."

"As you wish, my lady," he said, grinning. "And you still want Mason to be the one who gets tied up? Usually it's the other way around."

She smiled as Gina, her personal aide, handed her a robe and a cup of Yorkshire Gold, her favorite hot tea. "Not in my movies."

10

I FELT THE HEAT the instant I walked into downtown police headquarters—the heat emanating from a hundred pairs of eyes bearing down on me. Perhaps I was exaggerating—maybe it was only seventy-five pairs—but I didn't think so. Everyone in the shop had heard about what happened the other night at Burger Bliss; for that matter, an article reporting the incident, though happily unaware of the goriest elements, ran on the front page of the *Courier.* No doubt there had been speculation, perhaps even a betting pool, regarding how long it would be before I walked through the front doors.

Here I was. And they all expected me to solve the mystery, to make some sense out of something that was so patently senseless. They were counting on me to stop the madness before it happened again.

I felt an aching in the pit of my stomach, a desperate desire to flee, to run back to the parking garage and speed home. There was a twenty-four-hour liquor store on the other side of the block; I could be there in minutes. I wouldn't overdo it—just a little swallow to settle my jangled nerves so I could perform, function at peak efficiency . . .

Which was all crap, damn it. If I gave in once, it would all be over. I wouldn't stop with one drink. I wouldn't function at peak efficiency; I wouldn't function at all.

I clenched my fists and plowed a trail to my desk.

Yes, my desk. My own little cheap plywood desk, but it wasn't positioned in front of the men's room like the last one. O'Bannon had tossed enough work my way during the past months to justify giving me a tiny corner of my own on the upper level. He'd kept me fairly busy, but I knew in my heart that he was going easy on me, tossing me softballs so I wouldn't be too stressed, too pressured. So I'd have time to recover, to see my doctor, to get my life together again. He'd been good to me. I bet he thought about it a good long while before he brought me into this mess. But in the end, he'd had no choice. I was his behaviorist, and this case demanded one. He either called me or replaced me.

So here I was, pretending I was up to the challenge, pretending that everything was normal, pretending that I couldn't see the ripples on the surface as I carried my Styrofoam cup of jamoke back to my desk. I was a wreck. And they expected me to catch some goddamn maniac. Isn't life great?

Before I even had a chance to finish my cuppa, I saw Granger making his way to my desk, and for once, he wasn't smirking. As if that wasn't strange enough, instead of the usual caustic epithet, he muttered a very pleasant "Good morning, Susan."

I hardly knew how to respond. "And to you, Barry," I replied, waiting for him to spring a trap.

"Here's the preliminary info we've gathered on the victim. I've got detectives searching his apartment as we speak. You were . . . umm . . ." He coughed into his hand. "You were right."

Ah. Now I understood. I glanced at the file. "Mohamadas Amir. Indian immigrant. Age twenty-eight." I looked up at Granger. "Night-shift manager at the Burger Bliss."

"Landlord says he didn't come home night before last,

hasn't been seen since. And," he added, dropping another file on my desk, "we found the body."

I lapped up the file like a toddler with chocolate ice cream. "Really! Where?"

"An alley on the north side of town. About twenty miles from the Burger Bliss."

"And we're sure it's the right body?"

"What, you thought it might be some other faceless corpse?"

What I was thinking, of course, was that it was possible this might not be the first time our killer had struck. Only the first to be discovered.

Granger continued. "The coroner's office is being typically tight-lipped until all tests are completed, but I can't imagine that it would be anyone else."

I just hoped he was right.

"Look, can we clear the air?" Granger obviously had something he wanted to say, so I let him say it. "We both know I didn't want you on this case. But whatever you may think, it really isn't personal. Since I became head of homicide, I've poured hours and hours into building a tight, strong team. I don't think we need outside help. In fact, I think it's a slap in the face. But I was overruled by O'Bannon, and here you are. I can live with that."

"Appreciate it," I mumbled.

"And I appreciate the assist you gave us." He drew in his breath. "But what I said yesterday still goes. If I feel that you're being unproductive—" He paused ominously. "—or if I get one whiff of a hint that you've returned to your old bad habits, I will be in O'Bannon's office demanding that you be removed so that I can apply the money he's paying you in a more useful fashion. Understood?"

"Loud and clear," I said. "Mostly loud."

He blew air through his teeth, sighed, then walked away. My eyes fixed on the back of his head, thinking how neat it would be if people really did have heat vision. While I was trying to calm my jagged nerves, Granger dropped in and practically pushed me off a cliff.

And into a bottle. Jerk.

I read the ID file first. It was very preliminary, mostly stuff they'd gotten off the Internet and city records, but there didn't appear to be any distinguishing characteristics about the victim, much less anything that might inspire someone to have him boiled in oil. He didn't finish high school; never went to college. He lived in a crummy apartment in a crummy neighborhood and made about ten bucks an hour watching other people sling burgers. He'd been married and divorced once, had four children. There was no evidence of large withdrawals or a connection to drugs or gangs or organized crime or anything else that might cause him to die such a gruesome death. He was, at least on paper, a perfectly average lower-class Gen-Y slacker.

Why did the killer single him out? Why, given the host of options at his disposal, did he choose to kill him in such a hideous way? Why was it necessary to push his face into the fire? And what was the point of the equation on the grill? I suppose it was possible someone else did that, an employee with a math fetish or something. But that didn't ring true to me. It was the killer. It was all part of . . . something. But what?

I was desperate to call Darcy. He was the math savant, after all. He stood a far greater chance of deciphering that message than anyone on Granger's detective squad. But I had promised O'Bannon I'd keep him out of it, and I certainly didn't want to give anyone an easy excuse to grant Granger's fondest wish and can my ass. I'd have to think of something else.

The second file was even stranger than the first. The body had been discovered early this morning by a homeless man in an alley between two department stores on the north side, more than twenty miles from the restaurant where the murder took place.

What the hell sense did that make? Why not just leave the corpse where it was instead of dragging it twenty miles across town? There didn't appear to be anything special about this alley. It wasn't even a good hiding place; the body was bound to be found. And it was just off a busy street that had nightclubs and bars and other places with heavy nighttime traffic. Somebody took a hell of a risk depositing the body there.

Why? Why go to all that trouble and incur so much danger just to leave the body . . . nowhere special?

I hadn't a clue. I stared at the photo of the victim, then closed my eyes and let my mind wander, but nothing came. It just didn't make any sense.

But it must've made sense to the killer. He must've had a reason. And my instincts told me that if I could figure out that reason—then I could figure out the killer. And if I could figure out what made this guy tick, maybe I could catch him.

But so far, I was at square one. Maybe not even there.

LIKE SEVERAL other young women in Vegas, Danielle Dunn made porn films; in fact, she'd been doing it for twelve years. But she wasn't the usual statistic, the pathetic drug-addicted nitwit who gave the camera one humiliating pose after another just to get a little chump change from the man. She was the man.

It hadn't always been that way, she reflected, as she sat in her private office in the studio she owned, sipping tea from bone china. She'd left home when she was sixteen, pregnant, a social pariah. Her own parents would have nothing to do with her. Those had been tough times, and some of the things she did back then still haunted her. But she had survived. She was too young for most of the legitimate work on the Strip—cocktail waitressing, dealing cards. She was young and skinny and more than once some pervert tourist had suggested ways she could make a little money. And she'd thought about it. But fortunately, she was able to resist, although some might think her next job—stripping at a downtown club—wasn't much better. That led to working as a nude model, which in a short time led to an encounter with one of the top direct-to-video porn producers late one night at the Sahara. In less than two years, she'd gone from high school cheerleader to porn queen. But those porn movies saved her from prostitution. And a host of other evils even worse.

She knew that, in some people's minds, there wasn't much difference. Taking money for sex was taking money for sex. But to Danielle, there was a Grand Canyon of a difference. She might be having sex (although most of the time penetration was simulated), but it was no squalid twenty-dollar back alley transaction. She was on a set, playing a part, following a script. She was acting. And when she did get paid, the money didn't come from the man with whom she'd had sex. It came from the producer, who was compensating her in a legal and legitimate way because she had performed a valuable service.

She was good at it. Not just at being naked—the whole job. She learned lines quickly and rarely stumbled, and that meant a lot to a producer working on a limited budget. What's more—she could actually act. The flat delivery that characterized so many porn actresses (either because they were high or barely able to read, or both) was light-years from Danielle's performances. She not only could deliver a line, she could assume a character. As a result, the producers started investing more time in the plot, costumes, music, spending an extra penny here and there to make it better. If they had a real actress, why not make a real movie? With a sex scene every eight minutes, of course.

That's when her career began to really take off. She became a name-recognized asset, something rarely accomplished in this industry where too often the women seemed interchangeable (and disposable). Her name appeared above the title. She got offers to make live appearances. She made decent money. But she still didn't like the way they treated her: "Just lie on your back and kick up the high heels. Okay, bring the camera in closer between her legs." And she noticed that, at the end of the day, it was those cigar-chomping producers, the talentless money men whom you might pay to put their clothes back on, who were driving the Caddys and playing high-stakes poker at the Sands.

So she decided to do something about that, too.

"All right," Gina said, breaking her out of her reverie. She had a coat over her arm and purse in hand. "The captain's bed set is ready to shoot. Everyone's been told to be ready to do 42B at nine o'clock sharp."

"Excellent. And Gina?"

"Yes?"

"I don't want to have any more problems with John's . . . . mmm, problem. Time is money. Let's have a stunt double ready, okay?"

Gina arched an eyebrow. "A stunt member?"

"Exactly. We haven't cast Longsword's mate yet. Get someone who can perform both functions; we won't have to pay him any more than scale, no matter how many parts we give him."

"I think I know someone who'll do it. I can send him over tonight if—"

"I'll be here. Still got mounds of paperwork, and I want to check the set. Don't want any eleventh-hour mistakes tripping us up. If we stick to our schedule, we could be filming the money shot by Friday." The money shot was industry slang for the climactic on-camera ejaculation, the scene most viewers seemed to live for.

"Shaving a week off the shooting schedule. That'll make your investors happy."

"That's how you keep investors. Make the call, then give yourself a rest. You've earned it."

"Will do. See you in the morning, boss."

Boss. Now that was a word she liked to hear. As long as it was in reference to herself.

When she formed her own production company—the first porn actress ever to do so—the hooting and hollering could be heard all the way to the Hoover Dam. But she knew she could do it. If those slimy silk-shirt stogie-chomping slobs she'd been working under for years could do it, why couldn't she? She was smarter than all of them combined, and she'd managed to bank enough savings to make it happen. Well, to make one film happen. Like a high roller at the Flamingo, she put all her chips on one number on the roulette wheel.

She gave it a lot of thought before she spent a penny, which again put her head and shoulders above most of the porn producers out there, who thought if you just got some guy with a prodigious member and a woman who'd invested heavily in silicone, put them in a room together with a shoddy video camera, then packaged it with a title parodying the latest Hollywood hit, or playing on some cliché male fantasy (sorority girls, cheerleaders, nurses, women behind bars . . . the banal list was endless) and shipped it off to the usual distributor, that was good enough. And in truth, it was good enough, apparently, to make some bucks and keep the boys in business. But she wanted to do better than that. She wanted to make real movies. She wanted to be the Louis B. Mayer of skin flicks. To bring that off, she needed . . . something different. Some gimmick. A fresh approach. A new . . . something. But what? She spent months contemplating—until she finally figured it out. She knew she couldn't eliminate porn movies—and she didn't really want to. What she wanted to do was to make them her own.

The traditional view of porn movies was that they were made by men, for men, that they existed solely for the purpose of male gratification. Frat houses, bachelor parties, lonely guys in hotel rooms. According to statistical studies, the average pay-per-view hotel porn movie is watched for twelve minutes. Yes, that's how long it took viewers to get what they wanted out of the film. That's why the flicks almost always started with close-up oral sex—before you even knew who the characters were or what the story, if there was one, was about. These films usually put the female characters in demeaning roles that suggested that they lived solely for the purpose of gratifying the always dominant male. What if just once, Danielle thought, someone made a porn movie for women? A movie that showed a woman in the dominant role, taking her carnal pleasures whenever and however she wanted them? A porn movie made by the women, of the women, and for the women. That idea appealed to her.

The question was: Would it appeal to anyone else?

Every investor she approached thought it was far-fetched. Impossible. She didn't give up. She'd talked to women who worked in adult gift shops and they told her that increasingly it was couples, not grimy unshaven brutes, but *couples,* who were coming in to rent porn flicks. The mail-order people told her the same thing: more and more, watching porn was a couples activity. Almost fifty percent of all erotic films were rented by women or couples.

That knowledge gave Danielle power.

She set up her studio, DannyDunn, on the south end of the Strip, outside the City of Las Vegas limits, because the nebulous anti-prostitution laws in the city raised the possibility of legal trouble if some court ruled that the actors were really prostitutes because they took money for having sex. Sort of. The first film from DannyDunn Inc. was set in the wilds of the Congo. It was a Tarzan riff—she played a Jungle Girl, a latter-day Nyoka who was raised by wild animals after her explorer-parents were killed. Tom Matheny, one of the hottest new hunks on the circuit, played a shipwrecked archeologist, washed onshore near the Jungle Girl's home and thrust into a series of dangerous and sexy adventures, culminating in his capture by Tra, the Queen of the Lion People, who tried to force him to become her mate, the sire of a new generation of stout-hearted men to rule her lost kingdom.

Role reversal? Yes. But at the same time, Danny was careful not to put the hunk in demeaning roles. She didn't want to trade one half of the potential audience for the other; she wanted everyone. The male lead might be the one getting rescued, but he wasn't portrayed as stupid, weak, or subservient. And when sex happened, it was gloriously passionate. Maybe *Congo Conquest* was still a low-budget skin flick, but it was a low budget skin flick with a story and characters. For the target audience, it was an ideal fantasy.

And it was fantastically successful.

Now, six years later, Danny had produced twelve films running the gamut of fantasy themes—Sinbad, WWII spies, science fiction—and now, the pirate movie. She had captured a dependable secondary market via two of the top cable channels, where the sexual content was slightly abridged and the films found an even greater audience. She didn't always star in the pictures these days, but whether she did or she didn't—her name was always above the title. She was well known in Vegas, often offered opportunities to speak to the more liberal-minded groups or to serve as a resident celeb at poker tourneys and such. Not bad for a girl who'd been desperate, almost suicidal, at sixteen.

Which was more than ten years, and about four million dollars, ago.

Enough reminiscing. She had a set to inspect. She pushed out of her chair and—

Did she imagine that she heard something? A squeaking? She listened hard but didn't hear anything more. That actor Gina was sending, or any other visitor, would've rung the bell, especially this late at night. Must be her imagination.

Wasn't it? She froze, listened again.

Of course it was. She didn't have time for this foolishness. She had a set to inspect. She walked onto the soundstage and gave it a once-over. This would not be the major sex scene between the protagonists of the picture; the pirates would return too early and passion would be exquisitely delayed for another twenty minutes or so of screen time. But she still wanted it to be an arousing scene. Something to work the emotions of the viewers into such a fevered pitch that they could barely restrain themselves from hitting the fast-forward button when the dastardly pirates returned. Happily, everything seemed to be in order. Now all she had to do was deal with that paperwork and she could—

"Excuse me? Are you Ms. Dunn?"

Danielle was startled by the sudden voice out of nowhere. Standing on the set, still lit by the bright overhead lights, she found it impossible to see anything beyond the perimeter.

"Who's there? Are you the actor Gina called?"

After a moment's pause, the man replied, "Yeah. That's me."

Danielle walked off the set, shielding her eyes. Slowly, the male figure took shape before her.

Gina called this guy to be in the movie? Had she totally lost her grip? He was a big man, strong, but much too short. Burly, rather than the thin-hipped lean look women seemed to favor today. Not to be cruel, but he was not remotely attractive: a big pug nose that looked as if it had been broken at least once, pocked skin, short black hair that draped his head like a mop. Mean eyes. Why on earth would Gina pick him unless . . .

Two possibilities occurred. Gina might be going for a change-of-pace look, something to differentiate him from the rest of the male cast. He was probably a more realistic incarnation of what a pirate's mate would look like than the rest of the pretty boys in the cast, not that this film had anything to do with reality. Or it was possible Gina had some . . . inside information. And her choice of this lug had focused more on the need for an impressive stunt member.

"There will . . . I'm sure you understand . . ." She was stumbling for words, and she didn't know why. It wasn't as if she hadn't been through this a hundred times before. Something about him . . .

Suddenly she was wishing Gina was still around. "Anyway, you're going to have to audition for the part. For . . . both parts. If you know what I mean."

Even though she didn't really want to, she took a step closer, hand extended. "I don't think we've worked together before, have we? I'm Danielle. And you're . . ."

The man smiled, a crooked lipless sneer that was truly chilling to behold. "Tucker. Everyone just calls me Tucker."

11

I IMMEDIATELY FELT a surge of sympathy for Mrs. Asparagita Amir. Just one look at the shabby apartment where she lived and raised four children was sufficient to accomplish that goal. Her three daughters were in school at the moment, but her son, barely eleven months old, was in a cradle on the floor, sleeping soundly. She rocked the cradle as I asked my questions.

"Do you have any idea why anyone might want to hurt your husband?" I asked as gently as possible.

"My former husband." She looked at me, her brown eyes small but direct. "No. As I told the detectives, I cannot imagine any reason for anyone to do him harm."

A natural response. I wasn't surprised. "Did he have a life insurance policy?"

"I do not think so. If he did, it is unlikely that I would be the beneficiary."

"But your children—"

"He did not have contact with the children, after our marriage was discontinued."

I frowned. "His choice, or yours?"

She glanced down at the infant in the cradle. She was a petite woman, fragile-looking, and each movement sent a tremor through her entire body. "It is the way of our people. Once a marriage is over, it is over."

"But you're not in New Delhi anymore. You're in Las

Vegas. The United States of America. We have laws about parental responsibility."

"You must understand . . ." She paused, her eyes moving downward to the cradle and the silent figure sleeping within. "My husband has been through a very difficult period. Back in our country, he was a civil engineer, an important man with responsibilities. Engaged in important work. But he sought even greater challenges, so he came to the United States to pursue them."

"It didn't work out?"

"No. The prejudice against our people was too strong. Even though we have never been enemies to the United States and have never associated with those who were. The tragedy of 9/11 occurred almost immediately after we arrived in the States. The job that my husband thought he had secured here in Las Vegas disappeared. No one ever said why, but we knew. It was too . . . how you say? . . . *controversial* to have someone from the East in a position of power and prestige while politicians were on television every night, demonizing the third world. He worked very hard to find work in his field, but none was offered to him. Eventually, he was willing to take any job just to support his family, but even that was difficult. Finally he found work at that restaurant."

So one of the top engineers in India ended up as an assistant manager at a burger joint. Pathetic. "I imagine that put quite a stress on your marriage."

"Yes," she said simply. "But I was his wife and I remained loyal to him. Such is my duty." I noticed that, although she was conservatively dressed, she was not in the traditional garb of women from her country. A plain dress, no robe, no headdress.

"He must've been very frustrated. Wracked with guilt."

"True. But such shame as this can be borne by any marriage with a firm foundation in faith."

She wasn't giving me much to work with. I decided to push the question, and watched her face very carefully as I did. "Then—why the divorce?"

Her facial expression was a strange combination of helplessness and unwillingness to defend what seemed self-evident. "He could not care for us. I was not able to earn an income, especially not with my many dependent children. I also could not appeal to the state for support so long as my husband was working, however minimal his income."

"Divorce was economic survival," I said, swearing once again at how stupid the law could be. "Did he visit often?"

"No. Although I believe that he wanted to do so. He was . . . filled with shame."

"Because of the divorce?"

"Um . . . yes, because of the divorce," she said, but what interested me most was her hesitation. There was something she was not telling me.

"Anything else?"

"Such as what?"

A direct approach wasn't going to work. So I tried a page out of Psych 101—change the subject. So you can abruptly return to it later and try to catch her off guard. "Any problems with his coworkers? His boss?"

"I do not believe so. They knew they were very lucky to have a man of his quality to work for them. He was so . . . what's the word? . . . overqualified. Such a contrast to most of the other young people working there."

No doubt. "Do you suppose some of his coworkers might have been jealous of him?"

Her eyes diverted downward. As if in recognition of what she had done, she lifted the still sleeping baby into her arms and laid him against her chest. "I believe he was given to some . . . abuse as a result of the color of his skin. But certainly nothing that would rise to the level of inspiring anyone to do something such as what was done to him."

But then, what *would* inspire someone to dip another human being's face into a vat of boiling oil? "Did your husband have much money saved?"

"None. Most of our savings were spent traveling to America. The rest was used to survive during his long months of unemployment. To feed so many mouths—much money is required. He tried taking a second job, even playing in games of chance. But nothing worked."

All right, enough with the small talk. The time had come to cut to the heart of the matter. "Ma'am, I don't mean to be rude, but—what was the real reason he was too embarrassed to visit his children?"

"There is no reason. He was simply a proud man. He did not want to . . . to seem small before his offspring." But as she said it, I noticed her eyes darting to the left. Which clinched what I already knew—she was lying to me. Hiding something.

Unlike some behaviorists, I never put all my chips behind NLP—Neuro-Linguistic Programming—a theory based on the fact that we all depend upon an artificial construct—language—to express ourselves. Language centers have specific locations in the brain, and when we access different sections, our face and body language reflect it. This gave rise to the visual lie detector test often bandied about in television and movies. If a person's eyes move to the right, they are accessing memory banks. If a person's eyes move to the left, they are engaging their imaginations. In other words, they're lying.

In reality, of course, it's never that simple. A person might look to the left because they're lying, or it could be a personal tic, or they could have something in their eye, or something could attract their attention. They might be nervous, fidgety. Many people find it hard to maintain eye contact for long. I wouldn't draw any conclusions from a single occurrence. On the other hand, I had a distinct feeling that Mrs. Amir was holding something back. And a gut instinct coupled with a little NLP was more than enough for me to go on.

"Forgive me, Mrs. Amir, but you're hiding something. I don't know what it is. But I have to insist that you tell me. It could be vital."

"There is no . . . no vital."

"I have to be the judge of that."

"He—He—He—" Again her head turned away, but this time I had more of a sense that she was struggling for words, perhaps struggling with her conscience, more than she was trying to be deceptive. "He was a proud man."

"That's a reason why he would insist on seeing his children, not a reason for avoiding them." I stared at her; she seemed to shrink before my eyes. What was it? I thought about her, how she was living, trapped up in this dingy apartment, never seeing the father of her children, making do on whatever the government sent and—

Or was there an *and*?

But why would she hide that? More likely she'd be raising the roof, complaining bitterly that—

No. I was reading her like a born-and-bred American, which she wasn't. Her culture came with an entirely different set of guidelines. I needed to get out of my usual mind-set and access the proper owner's manual. This divorce hadn't been born of any adultery, disharmony, wanderlust, or even selfishness. By all appearances, it had been mutually agreed upon for the welfare of the children.

That was the key. The children.

"Mrs. Amir, how long has your ex-husband been delinquent on his child support payments?"

She looked up, startled, her eyes riveted to mine. "But—I never—how did—"

"It doesn't matter. I know. And I'd appreciate it if you'd tell me the truth. How long?"

"It has been . . . almost two years now. But—"

"Have you brought any legal proceedings against him?"

"No. But those people—the DHS—they harass him, dunning him for the money he owes."

"How did the DHS even know?"

"At the time of our divorce, the court appointed a lawyer to represent the children as their legal guardian."

Made sense. The judge probably realized this woman would never take action against her ex-husband. So the court appointed someone who would. Even after all she had been through, this woman remained loyal. To a fault.

Or was there a more practical reason for her reluctance to speak? The fact that he owed her could make her a suspect, particularly with a bobblehead like Granger leading the investigation.

"So the DHS was hounding him for past child support. Any success?"

"No. When he had money, he would give it to me. As it was, he barely made enough to keep himself in a room at the YMCA. He walked to work each day. He ate so little he has lost more than thirty pounds since we came to America. He worked double shifts, worked late, worked holidays and all the most inconvenient times, anything to earn more money. He was constantly looking for better positions. But he found nothing."

I nodded. I had an idea who this man was now—and who his wife was as well. What I didn't understand was what would bring anyone to kill him—particularly in such a horrendous way. This was a point of interest, but clearly not a motive—this poor woman wasn't my sadistic killer and neither were her underfunded children. Whatever the motive—or perhaps I should say, mode of selection, so as not to suggest a rationality that didn't exist—it had to be something else.

"Did your ex-husband have any . . . hobbies?"

"He was much too busy for that."

"Any places he liked to go? Things he liked to do?"

"I do not know what you mean."

"Well, I'm trying to figure out how he met the killer."

"I do not know. He worked in that restaurant for long hours. The clientele is . . . not what you would find at the Bellagio."

Point taken. So is that all it was? A psychotic customer came in for a burger and decided that poor Amir was going to be his victim? Something about that didn't ring true. The elaborateness, the bizarreness of the murder, all spoke to something larger at work.

"Was your ex-husband particularly interested in . . . math?"

"He was an engineer. He was a gifted mathematician." She lightly touched her hand to the base of her neck. "Me, not so much."

"Me neither," I said, smiling. "But we found what looks like some sort of mathematical equation scrawled in grease at the crime scene. Did your husband . . . doodle?"

"Not that I ever saw."

"Did he pal around with other people who were mathematicians or math enthusiasts?"

"Amir did not have time for, as you say, palling around. He was a devoted, hardworking man."

"Yes, I can see that." This was going nowhere. Better to wrap it up, maybe leave an opening to return when I had more information. "How are you doing, ma'am?" I asked.

"I am . . . well."

"This can't be easy for you. Taking care of four children, all on your own, one of them still in diapers. And now you're confronted with this tragedy. Are you going to be all right?"

She lowered her baby back into the cradle, then looked directly at me with penetrating milk chocolate eyes. I didn't need NLP to perceive her guileless honesty. "Where is it written that life should be easy? Not in our sacred texts. Certainly not in your Christian Bible. I know nothing of easy, certainly not since we came to this country. But I know this. I have a duty. To my family, my children. And I will honor that duty. It is perhaps not so much that I do. But I will do it."

SOMETHING WAS WRONG. Danielle understood that immediately. Something about the man's manner, the brutish expression on his face. Even if Gina were trying to avoid typecasting, she knew that ultimately their films had to be entertaining. And not in any way . . . frightening. This guy intimidated without even speaking.

"Look," she said, "it's late, and I'm tired. I really don't have the energy for an audition right now. Could you come back in the morning—"

"I'm not here to be in one of your filthy films," he said, and before he had even finished the sentence, he sprang forward like a bull terrier released from his leash. "I left your actor lying in a heap in the parkin' lot." Danielle tried to back away, but she wasn't nearly quick enough. He grabbed her right arm by the wrist and twisted it behind her at an extreme angle.

Danielle cried out. "You're hurting me!"

"That's why I'm here," the man growled.

"Why?" she whimpered, fighting back tears of pain. "Why are you doing this?"

" 'Cause you earned it," he answered, snarling. " 'Cause you were chosen."

All at once, he shoved her onto the bed, decked out in crimson silk sheets for the next day's shoot. He slammed her back against the brass headboard, making her head spin and her eyes flutter.

"Earned . . . it," she managed. She had to fight unconsciousness. If she fell asleep, there was no telling what this maniac might do to her. He might be a crazed fan, bent upon raping his favorite actress. But she didn't think so. The look in his eyes didn't suggest sexual lust. It was just . . . evil.

She tried to speak again, but before she could, he had jerked her arm up and snapped a pair of prop handcuffs, dangling from the bedpost, around her wrist. But no, she thought, her brain still scrambled, those are for the guy. Mason. I'm supposed to be the dominant one. "I—I haven't earned . . . anything. I'm a respectable businesswoman."

"Really? Is that what your daughter would say?"

A cold chill spread through Danielle's already almost insensible body. How could he know?

"Maybe we oughta ask her how she felt, lyin' in that basket, cryin' for a mother who wouldn't come."

Danielle didn't understand, couldn't follow. The throbbing in her head became more intense. A moment later, her other arm was locked into the cuffs. She was pinned down, spread wide and vulnerable, unable to escape.

"A mother like you doesn't deserve to be no successful businesswoman, if you can call it that." He straddled her, but made no move to remove her clothing. Again, despite his position, Danielle sensed no aspect of sexuality in anything he did. All she sensed was violence, rage. A fiery determination to do harm.

"That was . . . so long . . . ago . . ."

"Sometimes justice is slow. But it always finds you in the end," he said, as if reciting something he had heard but only barely understood. "It's in the equation." He reached under his overcoat and, to Danielle's horror, produced a long-handled axe.

The shock was enough to jolt her system and force her into action. She thrust her body upward. Weak as she was, it was enough to throw him off balance. The instant his grip weakened, she raised a knee with all the strength she could muster, straight into his groin. He fell off the bed howling, clutching himself.

She knew she had to act quickly. These handcuffs were just props, not the real thing. After all, they didn't want any of their actors to be inadvertently hurt. You were supposed to be able to shake them loose at will. All you had to do was pull hard. And so she did. She yanked down with her right arm as fast and as hard as she could.

Nothing happened.

She pressed her lips together and tried again. She was not going down without a fight, not after so much time, so much work. Danielle pulled again with enough force to shatter a wooden plank.

But nothing happened. Her arms were still trapped.

And a moment later, she felt another set of handcuffs snap around her left ankle.

The little monster stood beside her, his face flushed and full of rage. "I brought my own handcuffs," he said simply, nostrils flared. "I replaced yours before you came in here." He locked the fourth and final handcuff onto her other leg, and Danielle knew she was helpless. Unable to resist. At the mercy of a madman.

He recovered his axe and resumed his position on top of her. With a swipe of his left fist, he knocked her across the face.

Her head once again slammed against the brass railings. Her eyelids fluttered. She was almost gone now, she realized. In so many ways. Almost gone . . .

"Are you . . . going to kill me?" she asked.

"Is that what you think? That I'm just some—some crazy killer? That I'm doin' this because I want to?"

"Then . . . what . . . are you going to do?"

"What the numbers dictate. The branding iron is still heating. But we don't have to wait for that."

"Wh—what?"

"You are Binah, the Godhead. You have dishonored your connection to the Sefirot. So I must remove your identifying feature. Your aspect of the primordial human form."

Her eyelids were so heavy; this time, she let them fall. "I still . . . I don't understand . . ."

"It's really very simple," he said, as he grabbed the front of her hair. Danielle felt the cold sharp blade at the base of her neck. "I'm going to remove your head."

12

JULY 14

THE ALARM CLOCK was like a shrieking banshee, relentlessly shattering every nerve in my body. It had taken me hours to fall asleep. I'd stayed at the office way too late, in part to show O'Bannon I was working hard, in part because I was so desperate to come up with something useful, some kind of lead. But I didn't. Soon they would be expecting me to give them a profile, and I had nothing, nothing but the most obvious well-known profiling constants that would hardly justify my salary. I'd come home a wreck, pacing the floors, desperate for a drink. Tried to watch junk television but couldn't concentrate. Turned out the lights, but my eyes wouldn't shut. The LED on my clock told me it was three in the morning long before my body finally succumbed to sleep.

This case was getting to me, in the worst possible way. And I knew where this was going to lead. How long could I resist? How long could I keep my face out of a bottle when I was feeling this kind of stress?

I finally stumbled out of bed, eyes blurred, and forced myself into the shower. That helped a little. At least enough to get me going. I remembered all the stuff they told me back in detox. I quietly recited my personal mantra. I know I have a problem, I said, over and over again, as the water cascaded down my hair, my face, my long flat stomach. But I will not give into it. I want to be a better person. I am trying to be a better person.

I said it over and over again. But I didn't believe it.

I stepped out of the shower, wrapped a towel around my head, and heard the doorbell ring. Who the hell was that? Couldn't be anyone from the office; I wasn't due for another hour. Darcy? He'd dropped by unexpectedly before, but never this early.

I threw on a robe and made for the front door. All I had to do was glance through the peephole before I unchained, unlocked, and threw my apartment door open.

"Amelia!"

"Hiya, sweetie."

"What are you doing here this time of the morning?"

"Just checking on you. How're you holding up, sweetie?"

"Oh, fine. Why?"

She gave me a long look. "To tell the truth—you looked a little shaky in the office yesterday."

"Me?" I glanced at myself in the mirror over the faux fireplace. "I don't see anything."

She squeezed my hand. "I know when something's wrong. What is it?"

I shrugged. "I don't know if I can really explain it. It's just . . . I'm feeling a lot of pressure. This killer . . ." I shook my head. "He's seriously twisted. The type who's likely to repeat. And we've got no logical leads. So everyone is expecting me to do my little empathy magic trick and point them in the right direction."

"And?"

I gave it to her straight. "And so far, I've come up with nothing. It's making me crazy. My hands are shaking. I can't concentrate. I can't sleep. I'm a nervous wreck."

The corner of her mouth turned up. "Good girl."

My forehead creased. "Have you been listening to this conversation?"

"Yes," she said with a laugh. "And it tells me one thing for certain. You aren't drinking." She gave my hand another squeeze. "You're just having an anxiety attack. Believe me, I've been there."

"You have?"

"Of course. Who hasn't?"

"Then—what did you do?"

"Well . . . if you really want to know . . ." She picked up her purse and fished around in it for a few moments, finally producing a small smoked plastic bottle. A pill bottle. She opened the lid and popped out a tiny blue pill, then put it in my hand. "Here. Take one of these."

I stared at it like it was a dead fish. "What is it?"

"Valium. Nothing major. But it will ease the strain a little. You'll feel better."

"I don't know. I don't want to get started on drugs."

"This is harmless."

"Will it make me sleepy? I'm going to put in a long day."

"Possible. Maybe you should break it in half. See how it goes. It's easy to do; it's perforated down the center."

"Well . . . I'll give it some thought."

"You do that." She headed for the door. "I'll call you tonight. Maybe after the police dogs let you go, I can pick you up and we'll do the town."

"That would be so wonderful." And I meant it. I felt better already.

"Just remember one thing, kiddo." She turned and placed her index finger against her nose. "Chasing sickos is your job. Not your life. When I pick you up tonight, I expect you to leave all that behind. In fact, every night, whether I'm there or not, I expect you to leave it behind.

I know how obsessed you can get. I don't want to see it happen again. You are a wonderful person. So take care of yourself."

I felt my eyes getting itchy and was immediately embarrassed. "Why are you so nice to me?" I asked, my voice breaking.

"Don't you remember? My first day on the job. You complimented my plastering technique." She winked. "See you tonight, girlfriend."

She gave me a kiss on the cheek. And then she was gone.

I WAS DRIVING downtown when I got the call on my cell phone. It was Chief O'Bannon, who gave me an address and told me to meet him there immediately.

"What's up?" I asked, as I pulled into a driveway and turned back in the opposite direction.

"There's been another killing."

I felt a lightning bolt race up my spine. "By the same killer?"

"Can't say for certain. But . . ."

"Yes?"

He paused. "I think so. I hope so."

"You *hope* so?"

"Yes. Because if there's more than one creep running around doing this . . . God help us all."

OF COURSE I knew what DannyDunn Studios was, although I'd never been here before. Its proprietor was almost a legend in town, the former porn star who took control of the whole shebang. The uniform outside the front door waved me in and I climbed a flight of stairs to the main soundstage, which had been roped off by yellow crime-scene tape. All the usual suspects—the coroner techs, the forensic CSI crews, the videographers—were busily going about their appointed tasks. I spotted Granger standing in the middle of the action supervising, which is a nice way of saying he wasn't actually doing anything.

I crawled under the crime-scene tape and boldly approached. "Before you throw a fit," I said, "O'Bannon told me to come out here."

"I know." His voice was odd—sort of . . . distracted. And absent of the usual malice.

"So what happened?"

"Another murder."

Oooo-kay. We'll do it the twenty questions way. "Do we know who the victim is?"

"No positive ID. But we're pretty sure it's Danielle Dunn. She hasn't shown up for work, and she isn't at her home. Didn't come home last night."

I couldn't believe it. It was like hearing that someone had offed Steven Spielberg. In a Vegas sort of way. "And you think it was the same killer?"

Granger still sounded odd, and he wasn't looking at me. "Very possible."

I rolled my hands around themselves. "Because . . ."

"There's no body. Again. Just . . ." He swallowed. "A head."

"Excuse me." I was breathing heavily and my heart was palpitating. I looked around till I found the nearest bathroom, then closed the doors behind me.

I knew what the men would think and I hated it. They would assume that I was about to be sick, that I was going to throw up. But that wasn't the reason. I ran some cold water, then fished around in my pocket until I found what I wanted. The little blue pill.

I put the whole thing in my mouth, then swallowed. I sat down on the toilet with my head between my knees and waited until I felt better. Or at least until my knees stopped knocking.

Chopped off her head. Mary, Mother of God. What

kind of person was this killer? How could I possibly hope to catch him?

WHEN I FINALLY felt ready—and able—I walked back to the crime scene as if nothing had happened. I had no idea how quickly that little pill was supposed to take effect but—maybe it was just the placebo effect—I did feel better. Calmer. More level-headed. Better able to do the job everyone was expecting me to do.

I closed my eyes and took a personal inventory. No—it wasn't any placebo effect. I *was* calmer. And thank God for it.

I had no idea where to start, and no one was crying out for my attention, so I approached the crime scene the way I liked to do it—dead reckoning. Hard to explain, at least to anyone who wasn't born with this gift or curse or whatever it is. In the old days, when adverse weather prevented sailors from using their standard navigational devices, they resorted to dead reckoning. They put away their toys and relied on their gut. They used their accumulated wisdom, talent, and experience to guide the ship to its destination. And that's what I did, in my own way, at crime scenes. There was no way, intellectually, to sort through all the possible sources of information and deduce what was important and what was not. So instead of killing myself trying, I closed my eyes, let my mind drift, and navigated by instinct rather than information. It was almost like having a sixth sense, but it was real, not some nonsense like ESP. It was why they paid me the big money. Or a tiny stipend, at any rate.

I considered what I knew so far. What were the salient elements? Decapitation. Face . . . removal. Assaults at the workplace. What could I deduce from these facts? What psychological likelihoods could be determined?

The killer is obsessed with certain facial characteristics. . . . The killer is collecting faces. . . . The killer denies his victims' identities by making them impossible to identify. . . . The killer is making a protest against certain industries or businesses. . . . The killer is harvesting organs. . . . The killer gets a sexual charge out of mutilation. . . .

No. None of it sounded right. Or to be more precise, none of it *felt* right. It didn't explain everything. Deduction was getting me nowhere. What could I induce? That is, what probabilities could I assume from what was known?

Not many. Because not much was known. Except this: Signature murderers never stop until they are caught. And this creep had a hell of a signature. So it was safe to assume that he would strike again. And again. Until he was stopped.

I opened my eyes. This was getting me nowhere. I couldn't even find a pattern in the selection of the victims. What on earth did a successful star and producer of adult films have in common with some young immigrant working fast food?

I strolled across the room to the oversized brass bed; it appeared to be the center of attention. Tony Crenshaw was hunched beside it, scraping a sample of something into a test tube.

I couldn't help but notice that the sheets were a dark blackish red. "So this is where the deed was done?"

"Probably. What I'm seeing suggests a blood loss so enormous that the victim couldn't possibly have survived."

I walked away, shaking my head. I really didn't want to hear any more. I spotted Amelia crouched on the floor about ten feet from the bed, near the top of the stairs. She was taking an impression off the floor. Guess she got the call from O'Bannon, too.

"Footprint?" I asked.

"Bingo. Good one, too. Looks like the perp stepped in some mud somewhere."

"Anything useful?"

"Well, I'm not as accurate as your friend Darcy, but it looks to me like about a size seven male. Wide. Wearing tennis shoes. Cheap ones, well-worn. Once I get this back to the lab, I can run it through the computer and tell you exactly what brand of shoe it is."

Which was good work, but not likely to be helpful in finding the man. "Does it look like there's . . . anything unusual about it?"

"No. This footprint isn't going to be all that helpful in finding the guy." She looked up. "But it will be a means of confirming ID, proving he was here. Once you've caught him."

Once I've caught him. That's what they were all expecting, what they were counting on.

Before I could respond, my cell phone rang. I stepped to the side of the room and took the call. "Hello?"

"Has there been another murder? Because I think that maybe there has been another murder."

"Darcy? Is that you?"

"Yes. Are you at the crime scene? Did something bad happen?"

No way was I going to lie to him. Among other reasons, he was bound to find me out. "I am. What makes you think there's been another murder?"

"I talked to my dad just now."

"And he told you?"

"No. He did not tell me. He did not tell me anything. That is how I knew. I want to come to the crime scene."

"Darcy—"

"I want to be useful. That is the most important thing in the world isn't it even my dad says so. To be useful."

"Darcy, if it were up to me, I'd have you out here in a heartbeat. But it isn't."

"My dad says no."

I hesitated. Last thing I wanted to do was turn the chief into a villain in the eyes of his son. But it was the truth. And I think Darcy already knew it. "Yes."

"Will you please talk to him?"

"Darcy—"

"He will not listen to me. He does not think that I know anything and he never listens to me. But he will listen to you."

"Darcy . . . I can't risk getting thrown off the case."

"Please!" he cried. "Please, please, please, please, *please*!"

"Okay. I'll talk to him. But I can't promise anything."

"You can promise you can try. That is all anyone can promise."

"Okay, I'll try. Promise."

The line was silent for a few moments. "Do you want to go for a custard tonight?"

"I want to, but I can't. I've made other plans. Soon, though."

"Okay, soon. I think that we should do it soon. I would enjoy it." Another strange pause, then: "And I think you could use a Very Excellent Day."

How right you are, I thought, as I snapped the phone closed. How perfectly right you are.

13

TUCKER HATED doing this while it was still daylight. But as luck—or math—would have it, the body had to be deposited in the heart of the nightclub district, an area where, ironically enough, here in the *real* city that doesn't sleep, it would be busier in the middle of the night than it was now.

If the delivery position had been calculated properly—and he knew it had—his destination was in the center of a parking lot. Unfortunately, it was a private, paid parking lot roped off by chains barring both entryways. There was a guardhouse, but as he drove slowly by, it appeared to be empty. He parked as close as he could on the side of the street, just across from the appointed destination.

He walked to the back of the car, made sure no one was looking, then popped open the trunk. There she was, bundled in painters' wrap, just as he had left her. She'd fought harder than he'd expected, even while restrained; certainly she made a better showing than that punk at the fast-food joint. But in the end, it didn't matter. What he was doing was foreordained; he was following a plan that had been carefully and scientifically selected. There was no margin for error.

Hadn't been a bad-looking woman, either, but he guessed that was to be expected, given what she did for a living. Under different circumstances, he might've been interested . . . But who was he kidding? Women like her never gave him the time of day. They looked down at him with contempt. They taunted him with their female smells and teased him and then never gave him anything. No one had ever loved him. Not until—

But he was allowing himself to be distracted. There was no time for this. Every moment he stood here, exposed, out in the open, he took a profound risk. He reached down, hoisted the bundle, and flung it over his shoulder.

Tucker crossed the street, moving at a brisk pace, but she was heavy—dead weight, literally. He crossed into the parking lot, calculated the proper position, then laid the body down to rest on the asphalt surface.

"Hey! Whatta hell you doin'?"

Damnation! There was someone in that guardhouse after all. The door swung open and an elderly man, seventy if he was a day, in a threadbare security uniform, came running in his direction.

The man didn't bother Tucker; he knew he could take him out, even without the axe or the knife, even if the guard was armed. Probably just by blowing hard. But he was carrying a radio. No telling who he might be able to contact. Or how quickly. If the guard got a good look at him, there could be serious complications.

Tucker ducked behind a car, then started moving, lowering himself to the ground. He was bluffing the guard, doing what the man would expect—running away—then doubling back. He watched carefully under the cars until he saw the guard's slow footsteps move past him. Then he circled around the car and came at him from behind.

He tackled the old man like a linebacker, knocking him over face forward. He heard the man's head crack against the pavement with a sickening thud. After that, he didn't get up. Didn't even move. Which should prevent him from using that nasty little radio.

Tucker checked the guard's pulse. Still breathing, although he probably wouldn't be reporting in for work anytime soon. But that was good. Unauthorized kills might be a problem. He had to stick to the pattern. The work had to form a perfect unity. Any flaw might damage the whole. Any mathematical statement with a random variable inserted would not produce the proper result.

He crossed the street hurriedly, careful to make sure the noise hadn't attracted any additional attention, then climbed into his car and sped away. That had been a close shave. Much too close. In the future, he would have to be more careful. There was too much at stake. And too much left to be done.

Only three more days, and then he would complete the next component in the equation.

IT WAS A LITTLE after ten before I called Amelia. I kept hoping that if I worked myself to death, if I kept poring over each file and report as it came in, eventually I would have an epiphany. Some useful insight. But it never came. I saw the preliminary coroner's report—just as gruesome as I'd expected it to be. The coroner found an increase in histamine and serotonin levels, which told us Amir had been terrified for a good long time prior to his death. Big surprise. The photographs were unbearable, gut-wrenching. Why was the letter *K* branded on his body? The forensic reports were thorough, detailed, and completely unavailing. They had vacuumed and grid-searched and checked the vents and plumbing and even peeled up the tile but found nothing of use. They'd even gotten an expert to run handwriting analysis on the mysterious formula, but he couldn't tell them anything. How much personality could you deduce from a finger scrawl in grease? I went online and searched the FBI's database for psychological profiling of serial killers maintained by the Behavioral Science department, but it wasn't helpful. We just didn't know enough.

The more time passed, the more anxious I was. The

more aware I became of my own incompetence. Of how much everyone was counting on me. And sure enough, by nightfall, my stomach was doing flip-flops again, my hands were shaking, and I could hardly talk without an embarrassing tremolo in my voice. That Valium had been great stuff, but evidently it didn't last forever.

Amelia arrived to pick me up in record time. "Where are we going?" I asked, as we zoomed off, top down, into the blazing neon.

"There's a dinner theater magic show theme park thing going down at Caesar's Palace." I admired, not for the first time, how good she looked when she got out of the white coat and dolled herself up. "I thought it might be a kick. Get your mind off things."

I had to smile. I happened to know for a fact that she despised magic shows, but she also knew that I despised gambling, rarely went to movies. And she wasn't taking me to a nightclub or any other place where booze was too visible and tempting. The sacrifices of a good friend. "That sounds great. I'd like to unwind. I'd . . ." I shook my head.

"What? What is it?" Her eyes stayed on the road, but all her attention was on me.

"Oh, I just feel . . . wretched." I paused. "That new victim we found today."

"Yeah. Gruesome stuff. Is there anything I can do?"

"I don't know." I paused long enough to give the impression this idea had just popped into my head. "Do you have any more of those little blue pills?"

Her neck immediately stiffened. "Susan . . ."

"Is there a problem? You use them."

"I use them occasionally, when I'm having a serious anxiety attack. And even then sparingly."

"What's the big deal?"

"The big deal is, if you start taking too many, they saturate your bloodstream and pretty soon your body craves them. They can be addictive."

I held up my hands. "Okay. Never mind. I just—I feel so stressed."

Amelia frowned. "I know. I can see it. Even without looking at you." Her right hand darted into her purse, then she pulled out the pill bottle and tossed it to me. "Just take one so you can relax a little at the show and you'll be sure to sleep afterward. But that's it. No more."

"Understood, mon capitaine." I unscrewed the bottle, popped one in my mouth, then put the bottle back in her purse. I hate to admit it, but almost immediately I felt better. Just the thought that help might be on the way had an enormous calming effect.

"All right then. Are you ready to have fun?"

"I sure as hell am. You promise not to heckle the magicians?"

She gave me a thin, sly grin. "I make no promises." She turned her head slightly my way. "After all, I want to have some fun tonight, too."

14

JULY 15

IT IS NOT RIGHT it is not fair it is not right it is not fair it—

Stop. But it is not right. I am the one who is good at puzzles and I am the one who is good at math and they will not even let me help I could help I know I could help but they will not let me none of them will let me not even Susan will let me.

Are they punishing me because I could not solve that equation? My dad said It's okay Darcy but he said it with that voice that same voice he always uses that tells me what a disappointment I am to him and he probably never thought I could do it anyway because he doesn't think I can do anything. I couldn't solve his equation but that was not a fair test because it was not possible I cannot no one can reduce an equation to a numerical solution without knowing any of the variables all you can do is restate it or simplify it or maybe it has some sort of scientific specialness but how could I know that how could I possibly know if they will not tell me what any of the letters stand for?

Maybe they will not let me help on the case because there is another Bad Man and they know I do not like bad men and I did not like what happened last time and I might not like this too but how can I ever be with Susan how can I ever be a policeman how can I ever get her to adopt me if we never spend any time together it is not right it is not fair it is not right—

Stop. Reboot. I wish Susan were here. I am always better when Susan is here. I always feel better when I am being useful because John Adams said it and he was right the most important thing in life is to be useful.

I know I could be useful. If they would let me.

I miss Susan. I want to see her again.

I will find a way.

BEFORE I EVEN got to my desk I saw that Granger was standing nearby, waiting for me. Stalking me, more like it.

I wished I hadn't wasted that Valium last night. I should've saved it for now, when I really needed it. How the hell was I going to get through the day? Without resorting to old bad habits. The kind you don't need a prescription for.

Hell. I sucked it in, steadied myself, made sure I looked calm and secure and ready to tackle anything. In other words, my usual brassy obnoxious self. But kind of loveable in a way. Or so I like to think.

Granger didn't even wait for me to sit down. "Have you figured out yet who our guy is? Or what our guy is?"

"I'm working on it," I said, faking supreme unrufflability. "I'm still collating all the information we gleaned from the second crime scene. In many ways, it changes everything, or at any rate, illuminates the dark corners. And by the way," I added, kicking my feet up onto my desk, "you shouldn't assume it's a guy."

"Give me a break."

"You shouldn't make any assumptions, not with a killer this weird."

"Only three percent of all multiple murderers are female."

"That's true, but—"

"Ninety-five percent of all serial and signature killers are white males between the ages of twenty and forty."

"That's also true. And I agree, most likely, the killer is male. I'm just saying, don't assume anything. It's dangerous. And potentially embarrassing."

"I'm confident it's a guy."

"Stop saying that, you pinhead. You don't know that you're right."

"Actually, I do." He flipped around the paper he'd been holding. "Eyewitness report. The killer was spotted dropping off the body. And it was a guy." He smirked.

I snatched the report out of his hands. Stupid son of a bitch. Why didn't he just tell me?

My eyes scanned the pages, drinking in the font of information therein. This body had been branded just like the first one, only with a different letter. "He left the body in a parking lot? In broad daylight?"

"Yes," Granger replied, "*he* did." He was still smirking.

"That's just . . . bizarre."

"Yeah. And stupid. Which makes me think we'll be able to catch him. Without the help of the vaunted behaviorist."

I gave him a look.

"Which is just as well," he continued. "At the rate you're going, the man will die of old age before you give us a profile."

I turned my eyes back to the printed page, fighting an aching combination of panic and rage. "He was spotted by a security guard?"

"Right. He worked the parking lot, made sure everyone paid their fees and kept an eye on the cars. Tough old bird, too. He's pushing seventy and he took a hard blow to the head. But he wasn't down long. He crawled back to his guardhouse, called an ambulance, then called the police. Gave his statement just as soon as the docs would allow it."

"Did he get a look at the guy?"

"Only from a distance, before he ducked behind a row of cars. Said he was short, thick, but not overweight. Solid."

"Strong," I murmured.

"Yeah. Has dark hair, was wearing blue jeans with a rip in one knee. That was all he got. Well, plus confirming that it was, in fact, a guy," Granger added, rubbing salt in my gaping wound one more time.

"But why?" I said, changing the subject. "Why dump the body in a parking lot on the northeast side of the city? That must be, what, ten miles from where he left the last one?"

"Twelve."

"And why do it in the middle of the day, when he was bound to be spotted?"

"Maybe he wants to be caught. Deep down. He did go to the trouble of leaving us a clue, after all. That crazy equation."

I shook my head. "That was a tease, not a clue. Meant to show how superior he was to us, that we would never be able to catch him. There must be some other explanation."

"Well, I don't know what it is. And apparently you don't, either. But I do know this." He leaned in close. "If you don't give us something soon, not even O'Bannon—or his son—will be able to keep you on this case."

I rose out of my chair. "You stupid, ignorant son of a—"

"I'm your superior officer, Pulaski."

"I don't care if you're Mother-fucking-Teresa."

"I'll put you on report," he said, voice rising.

"You try it," I said, matching him decibel-for-decibel, "and I'll put my fist up your—"

"What the hell is going on here?"

It was Chief O'Bannon, standing right behind Granger.

"Do either of you alleged officers understand that this is a police station? We're supposed to suppress civil disturbances, not create them."

We both kept our mouths closed.

"My officers should set an example."

Granger turned to face O'Bannon, stiff as a board. "Sir, I formally request that former Lieutenant Pulaski be removed from the case. Her services are not needed."

O'Bannon leaned forward against his cane. "Denied."

"Sir, speaking as head of the homicide department, now that we have an eyewitness report, I believe those funds could be better spent on manpower—"

"Speaking as the chief of police, your request is denied."

"But—"

"Denied!"

Jeez Louise—he was getting into with it with Granger worse than I had. I decided to try to salvage my rep by playing the peacemaker. "Hey, everybody. Let's calm down here."

Granger turned a fiery eye in my direction. "Don't tell me what to do, Pulaski!"

O'Bannon was on his heels. "Keep your flap shut, Granger!"

"Whoa, whoa," I said, holding up my hands. "What are we gonna do here? Solve a murder? Or have an Alpha Male Smackdown?"

O'Bannon blew air through his teeth. "Granger," he said quietly, "I need to speak to Susan. Privately."

Granger pivoted and walked away with a supremely irritating swagger. Of course, he was aware that by this time, half the office was watching us. He wanted it to appear to the casual observer that, by some contortion of reality, he had come out on top.

O'Bannon put his hands on my desk and leaned forward, obviously trying to calm himself. "Got something for you."

And what could that be? More bad news, most likely.

He reached under his coat and, to my enormous surprise, pulled out a weapon. The gun and shoulder holster landed on my desk with a thud.

I didn't know what to say. "Is there . . . perhaps . . . a badge coming with this?"

"You're not being reinstated, Susan."

"And why not?"

"Because you're not ready."

"Sir, I've been clean and sober—"

"I know. I can tell. Plus, I get reports from your doctor. But a few months on the wagon doesn't mean you're ready for full-time duty. Ready to be someone's partner. Ready to have someone's life depend on your performance."

"Then . . ." I gestured vaguely toward the gun between us. ". . . why this?"

"Because it's damn clear that this killer I've asked you to catch is dangerous. I don't want you hurt." He picked up his cane and jabbed it down on the linoleum for emphasis. "Don't make me regret it."

"I won't," I said quietly, but he was already walking away, one careful step at a time, acting as if he was just as strong as ever, as if nothing was wrong or ever had been.

Just like me.

I DON'T KNOW why I didn't think to call Colin before. Probably because he'd been a college friend of David's, and all the experts kept telling me I had to put my memories of David behind me, to compartmentalize them, so I could move on. And I tried to do what they said. But this mysterious equation business was so more up his alley than mine. He'd helped me before, on the Edgar case, when I needed a code breaker—until I discovered Darcy, who could decode more in ten minutes than Colin—or to be fair, any normal person—could do in ten years.

Colin is a self-styled cruciverbalist, or to put it in English—he makes puzzles. For a living. That's his job, if you can imagine. He works out of his home and creates brain teasers for *The New York Times* and *Games* magazine and similar publications favored by people with too many brains and too little to do with them. He wasn't rich but he made enough to get by and make his house payments and not have to wear a tie and go to an office and, all in all, especially when I observed Granger glaring at me, it seemed like a pretty good gig, even if I do think people who work mind-numbing puzzles for entertainment are all a little whacked in the head.

"Susan!" he said when he opened the door and ushered me in. "Great to hear from you!"

"You too, Colin." He'd always been the nicest of David's college buddies. Even if he was a little whacked in the head. "Everything going well?"

"Can't complain." I cleared a place on the sofa and sat. The room was a mess and, for that matter, so was Colin. I thought, not for the first time, how badly this man needed a wife. "And you?"

"Fine and dandy." Except for the perpetually shaking hands, the cold sweat on the brow . . . "You got a girlfriend yet?"

"No. For some reason, chicks just don't dig puzzlemasters." I thought it probably had more to do with the fact that he rarely dressed, groomed, or left his house, but I kept my opinion to myself. "Why don't you ever send a friend my way?"

"Hey, I offered to set you up with Lisa, my oldest friend in the world."

"Yeah. And that was tempting. I loved that Porsche she drove." He sighed. "But I could never get serious with a woman who hasn't mastered cryptic crosswords."

What*ever.* "Look, Colin, I'm calling because *I've* got a puzzle. In a case."

"Think I hadn't figured that out already? Pitch it to me."

"It's weird."

"That's all right. I can handle anything."

So I gave him the formula.

"Hold on, Susan. You didn't tell me this was going to involve math."

"Is that a problem?"

"I'm a word boy. Left brain. Math freaks are a whole different breed. And this doesn't look like a real puzzle anyway. How can you possibly solve an equation if you don't have any of the numbers?"

Which was exactly what Granger's experts were saying. "I'm sorry. I just hoped you might be able to help."

"Sorry, I'm not your man." He paused. "But I know who might be. The distinguished Dr. Goldstein. At UNLV."

"He some kind of math expert?"

"Susan. Shame on you for your sexist assumptions. It's a she. And she's an expert in weird math."

Which would explain why Colin knows her. "What's weird math?"

"Oh my God, you have no idea. Mathematicians are so twisted. You wouldn't believe some of the stuff they get into."

Like maybe melting people's faces? "Sounds like someone I should talk to. Do you have her number?"

"Sure. Better yet, I'll call her. They keep her pretty busy out there and her rep is huge, so she may not take every call she gets. But we were both on the U.S. team in the International Puzzle Olympics two years ago. She'll talk to me."

"That would be great, Colin. Ask if she'll see me as soon as possible. Tell her it's very important."

"Will do. And Susan?"

"Yeah?"

"You think if maybe I sent you a cryptic crossword, you could pass it along to Lisa? I know she's in L.A. now, but—you never know. I mean, that is a really hot car."

"My pleasure, Colin."

This hardly solved any of my problems, but it at least gave me hope. If a specialist in arcane mathematics could shed light on these bizarre murders, so be it.

Seconds after I returned to the office, Amelia sidled up to my desk. "Have you seen my report?" she asked.

"On the sneaker? Converse, size seven-and-a-half."

"No."

"The forensic report? Sounds like the hair and fiber boys got next to nothing."

"No. On the impression I made of the grill." She rolled her eyes in the general direction of Granger's office. "Figured as much." She surreptitiously slid a three-page stapled report onto my desk.

"Learn anything?"

"Not much. There were some swirls in the mix—whoever wrote the equation did it with his finger. But grease isn't a particularly good surface for lifting prints. We've tried several procedures on the grill and my cast of the head and the corpse. But all we've come up with are a few frustratingly incomplete partials. Not a solid print in the bunch."

"Any partial enough to work with?"

"We've created a composite, based on several of them. It's speculative. But it's enough to run through FINDER."

That was the FBI's automatic fingerprint reader and processor. If the print was in their database or that of several affiliated agencies and nations, they'd be able to provide an ID.

"And?"

"Nothing."

"So our man has never been printed."

"I can't say that with absolutely certainty. We're working with pretty low-grade material here. But I can tell you who you can eliminate."

"Rage on, girl."

"The victim. And everyone else who worked at that restaurant or had access to that grill."

"So the killer left the equation," I murmured. Just as I thought.

"Looks that way. But I'm a scientist, you know. I don't make theories. I just report the facts."

"And look damn good doing it. Thanks, Amelia."

"Anytime." She laid her hand on my shoulder. "I mean it. And that goes for everyone else in the basement." Meaning the forensic department. "We're all behind you."

Talk about a sweetie. If she only had some clout around here, my hands might even stop shaking. "Thanks, Amelia. That means a lot."

But not enough to keep my hands from shaking. Not nearly enough.

I CHECKED WITH GRANGER and confirmed that the coroner's office was still staying tight-lipped. No leaks. No confirmation that the head and the corpse were a match. Which was pretty damn frustrating, because if I was going to come up with a profile, I really needed to know how many dead people we had on our hands. Granger told me he'd tried to pry something out of Patterson, our chief coroner, but without success. Told me not to waste my time trying.

But I have some resources that were not at his disposal. And the greatest of these is girl power.

I hovered in the corridors of the coroner's office, trying to make it look as if I were waiting for someone or something, until I was certain she was alone. When she was, I slipped into her office and closed the door behind me.

Jodie Nida, one of the coroner's techs, was seated behind her desk. She was initially startled when she saw me standing there and checked the window in the door to see if anyone had observed my entrance.

Coast was clear.

"I know we don't have much time," I said, leaning over her desk. "So spill."

She adjusted her cat's-eye glasses and gave me a wry grin. "I assume you're talking about the Burger Bliss corpse and Danielle Dunn. And all their pieces."

"Dead on. Do we have a match?"

"Well, Patterson still wants to run about a day and a half of additional tests but . . ." She grinned. "It's a match."

"You're sure?"

"Positive."

"Any info on the weapon used on Danielle Dunn?"

"Again, more tests need to be performed. False positives could be created by—"

"Cut to the chase. What did he use?"

She inhaled deeply. "Well, the slash follows a diagonal arc which, when matched with the head, forms a slight wedge shape. Like a tiny triangle. Also, we found particles of rust on the head."

"Which means . . ."

"A wedge-shaped weapon made of iron. I'd bet on an axe. A long-handled axe, something that would give you the power you'd need to chop off a head in one stroke."

"And you would find such a weapon . . . ?"

"In any hardware store in town. In every other garage in town."

I nodded. "Appreciate the help. You know, if you'd get a phone, this would be a lot easier."

She sighed. "Coroner techs don't get phones. Only Patterson has a phone." She lowered her voice. "Control freak."

"My condolences," I said as I made my way to the door.

"Don't bother," Jodie replied, waving a hand in the air. "At least I don't have to take orders from Granger."

It was all I could do to keep from laughing as I ducked out of her office and slipped away, sight unseen.

15

I RETURNED to my desk, tried to block off the outside world, and mentally constructed a rough draft of what everyone in the department was clamoring for—a profile of the killer. It was hard going, and I couldn't exactly put my finger on why. Top-notch FBI behaviorists had been known to construct a profile based on the evidence found at the scene of a single murder. I had two to work with, but somehow, that made it harder, not easier. There was very little I knew for certain about this killer. Narcissistic personality? Probably. Antisocial personality disorder—the current jargon replacing *psychopath*—almost certainly. According to the standard outline for profiling developed first by Roy Hazelwood at the FBI, my approach should be to, first, identify what noteworthy actions had occurred, second, construct a theory about why they occurred, third, retrace and understand the events that led to and occurred during the crime, and finally, determine what kind of person would do such a thing. I had a problem even getting started. What was important about what this killer had done? Or even consistent? Despite the similarities between the manner in which the crimes were committed, on a psychological level, there were contradictory indications regarding this brutal maniac we were chasing.

For instance, in the old-school profiling technique, the threshold question was supposed to be: Is the killer organized or disorganized, or to use the current terminology, is he impulsive or ritualistic? Usually the answer was simple—but in this case, there were indications of both, which is supposed to be impossible. Certainly there were signs of organization—the consistent modus operandi regarding the branding, the transportation of the body, the absence of trace evidence, the selection of the murder site, the mysterious formula left behind to tantalize his pursuers. On the other hand, there was significant evidence indicating a disorganized mind at work—having mud on his shoes, a rip in his jeans. You wouldn't've caught Ted Bundy running around with a hole in his pants.

Any profiling analysis that stumbled on the threshold question was inherently flawed, but just for the sake of trying, I mentally assumed that despite indicators to the contrary, the killer was essentially ritualistic and attempted to soldier on to the next question. There are five distinct components common to all ritualistic murderers, or more specifically, to the fantasies that drive them to commit their crimes: relational, paraphilic, situational, victim demographics, and self-perceptional.

The relational component addresses the question of what the murderer imagines or fantasizes the relationship between his victim and himself to be. And in this case—I had no idea. I had to eliminate all the usual sexual fantasies, since we had victims of both genders and no signs of sexual assault. The paraphilic component assumes some sort of sexual deviancy. I couldn't absolutely rule that out—a bisexual serial killer?—but it didn't seem likely. The situational dimension explores what setting or environment the killer is trying to create. Bundy was trying to create a fantasy family domestic home life—a sharp contrast to his own real one. John Wayne Gacy was trying to create a torture chamber. And this killer . . .

Again, I just couldn't answer the question. True, both victims had been killed in their place of work, but what did that tell me? Nothing—except that it was probably the simplest place to find them. Victim demographics were even more confusing. Here I could detect no pattern at all. The first victim had been male, the second, female. The first victim had been young and poor, the second, more mature and considerably more wealthy. They looked nothing alike; they were in totally different lines of work. What was the connection?

The last building block in the profile relates to the killer's self-perception—How does he see himself? What role or function does he fantasize that he is performing or fulfilling? Did he dominate them? There was no evidence that he saw himself as a sexual master, or that he was attempting sexual gratification, or domination, or bondage. I really had no business even addressing this question, given my inability to answer All of the Above. And yet, at the same time . . .

Both times I stepped onto the crime scenes and closed my eyes and tried to dead reckon myself into the killer's head, I got a sense that he . . . he . . .

My mind groped for words. It wasn't exactly that he was deluding himself about his actions. He knew he was a killer. Maybe even knew he was a brute, a monster. But at the same time . . .

I didn't get the impression that the killer perceived himself as a bad person. Just the opposite, in fact. I think there was a reason that he did what he did, a reason so strong that in his mind it justified the maiming, the decapitating, the murder.

And how twisted was that?

NEVER WAS ANY WOMAN on earth more pleased to see another than I was when Amelia pulled up to the curb to pick me up.

"You caught me by surprise," she said, as I hopped into her convertible. "Knocking off early? By your standards, anyway."

I shrugged. "I wasn't getting anywhere. I've hit a brick wall. It's pathetic."

"Sorry to hear that. But the good news is—I've been shopping. For you."

"Really? What did I get?"

"Not telling till we're back at your apartment."

"Amelia!"

"It's for the apartment, Suze. Besides, I want to build up a little suspense. You like that, right?"

Sure I do. She was as good as her word, too. Didn't give me so much as a hint all the way back to my place. She strategically took the crosstown expressway, theorizing that the usual congestion might be reduced this time of night. She wasn't right, but she still managed to make good time.

She parked on the street, walked around back, then popped open the trunk. "Ta-da!"

I stared into the trunk. "You bought me a coffee table?"

"For the living room. I couldn't help but notice that you're still using that ratty old thing you've had since the dawn of creation."

"I like that coffee table."

"It's got, like, teeth marks or something. All up and down the legs."

"I like the teeth marks—"

She held up a finger. "Susan, I've been to the Venetian. You know, where Michael Jackson bought all his crap. This isn't just a table. It's a Brancusi knockoff."

"Is that a good thing?"

"It is. I'm moving you up in the world."

"If you say so."

I reached down to get it, but she stopped me. "You've

been working all day, and this was my idea. I'll get it. You just carry my stuff."

So I did. While she struggled to maneuver the table up the stairway to my second-story apartment, I got her purse and her sunglasses and her iPod.

And when I was absolutely certain she wasn't looking, I dipped into the purse and retrieved the Valium. The entire bottle. Shoved it in my coat pocket before she noticed.

The strange thing was, just having it in my pocket made me feel better. Help was on its way.

16

THE PILLS must've done their pharmacological duty; I was deep in the throes of the best sleep I'd had in weeks, certainly since I got assigned to this twisted face-melter case. I don't even think I was dreaming, or if I was, it must've been something so pleasant that it left me feeling tranquil and content. Talk about a sea change to the system. I might have known it wouldn't last. My blissful idyll was interrupted by the sound of seagulls, whistling winds, crashing water. The alarm clock was whooshing relentlessly, turning the increasingly loud white noise surf sounds into a thunderous tidal wave threatening to carry me and my sanity away with it.

"Can you get that? You're closer."

He didn't answer, which only irritated me all the more. I pushed up from my pillow. "Look, sugar bear, I know you're faking and—"

There was no one there. Of course there was no one there. I'd done it again. How long was it going to take before I got it through my head that I wasn't married anymore? That I lived alone. That David . . . wasn't here anymore.

All at once I felt the calm and tranquility falling away like a shedding skin. I reached across the end table, knocking over the alarm clock in the process, and clutched the good luck charm Rachel had so thoughtfully provided. I squeezed it tightly in my fist, then pressed it against my chest, as if somehow I could crush the solace out of it. Sure, I knew David wasn't going to appear to me anymore—he told me he wasn't—but if I could just access some tiny piece of him, some memory of what it was like when he was still there on the other side of the bed . . .

Yes. There it was. Bless Rachel for saving what I had so carelessly left behind. I could feel him. Even though I knew he wasn't there. I could feel what it was like to have his arms around me, holding me, whispering in my ear, telling me everything would be all right.

It's okay, he would whisper, his sweet breath warming the side of my face. Whatever it is. It'll be okay. We have each other.

I will, Mr. Pulaski, I promised, looking his father straight in the eye. *I'll look after your boy. We'll look after each other.*

The four-leaf clover was good, but at the moment, not good enough. I raced into the bathroom, upended the pill bottle, and swallowed a little blue pill, not even waiting long enough to pour a glass of water. In fact, I reflected, I should probably have two. Hell of a way to start your morning, and I didn't want it ruining my day. I had things I needed to get done. I stepped into the shower and immersed myself in near-scalding water, but by the time it was over I still didn't feel much better, so I swallowed a third.

Finally I felt a tiny amount of the—well, if not calm exactly, then stability—I'd experienced before returning to me. My hands were steady. I had a strong temptation to crawl back under the covers, but I managed to resist.

I brushed my teeth and got dressed and even experimented with a tiny amount of makeup, not my usual face, but it couldn't hurt to shake up the boys at the office a little. Besides, today I was going visiting.

Okay, three pills was too many, I knew that. The label

on the bottle said NO DOUBLE DOSING and I'd just violated that prohibition and then some. But it wouldn't happen again. Last thing I needed was to become dependent on a new chemical. I trudged into the kitchenette and put on the coffee. I wasn't sure which I liked better about coffee, the taste or the smell. Or the warm sensation as it trickled down my throat. Come to think of it, caffeine was a chemical, too, wasn't it? What the hell.

It was only this once. After today, I'd give Amelia her pills back or flush them down the toilet. This wasn't going to happen again. No way. I wouldn't let it.

"HELLLLO?" a tentative voice on the other end of the line said.

"Howdy, heap big chief," I said brightly. "How are things at the O'Bannon residence?"

"Gooood," O'Bannon replied. "In a quiet sort of way. Umm . . ."

"Yes? Something wrong?" There was no immediate answer. "You seem perplexed."

"Well . . . I'm torn. I am impressed to know that you're up this early in the morning. But I don't know why the hell you're calling me!"

"You know what traffic is like during rush hour. I wanted to get an early start."

"Okaaaaay . . . that explains the first part of the questionnn . . ."

"And I'm calling to see if I can take Darcy with me."

"Susan, I already told you—"

"Hey, I don't want to drag him to a crime scene. I'm just going out to talk to an expert who might be able to shed some light on that equation we found at the first crime scene."

"I don't care what you're doing, the answer is—"

"Yes. Yesyesyesyesyesyes!" a slightly higher voice interjected.

"Darcy!" O'Bannon bellowed. "Are you on the extension?"

"Please say that I can go with her, Dad. Please. Pleasepleaseplease—"

"I thought you were reading."

"I was, till I looked at the caller ID and I saw that it was Susan. Please let me go, Dad. Pleasepleaseplease-pleasepleasepleaseplease—"

"Would you stop that already!" He blew air into the receiver. "Pulaski, I can't believe you're doing this to me. I already made it clear—"

"Chief, I'm driving out to UNLV. To talk to a mathematics professor."

"I'm very happy for you. Is there a point?"

"I flunked high school trig. I'm not going to understand a word she says. Your son, on the other hand, has more math knowledge than every member of the LVPD combined."

"Be that as it may—"

"Please, Dad, please!"

"Darcy, would you get off the phone!"

"Please, Dad. I promise that I will be good. I will stay out of trouble and not get in Susan's way. And if there are any murders, I will not look."

I didn't have to see O'Bannon's face to know that his frustration level was climbing fast. And he probably hadn't even had his morning coffee. "Look, Darcy, it's just not a good idea. We have detectives who are trained to handle this kind of work. You're not going to be able to do anything that—"

"That is what you said when you were looking for the Bad Man," Darcy said, cutting him off. "But I did help. I solved the puzzles no one else could solve."

"That was totally different."

"It is not different. It is exactly the same. Someone has left us a puzzle. I want to help solve it."

I could imagine the range of expressions crossing O'Bannon's face—none of them pleasant. The silence was probably less than twenty seconds, but it seemed interminable.

"All right, then, damn it. You can go."

"Yippee! Thank you, Dad. Thank you so much. Thankyouthankyouthankyou."

"But this is the only time, understand me, Pulaski?"

"Loud and clear, sir."

"Nothing else. And especially no crime scenes!"

"Got it. Darcy, I have to stop by the office first, then I'll come for you. I'll be there around noon. And Chief—have a nice day."

He slammed the receiver down without comment.

I SAW GRANGER standing near the top of the stairs at Central Headquarters reading a report, so I braced myself for the usual onslaught of threats and criticism, fortified by Valium and the knowledge that even if he was my superior in rank, I was his superior in, well, everything else.

He barely looked up. "Morning, Susan."

Now that was just weird. "That's . . . all you have to say? No pounding me for a psych profile? What's the deal?"

He did that shrug again, the one that made me want to disconnect his head from his shoulders. "Personally, I've always thought psychological profiling was overrated. Good solid detective work—that's how you solve a case."

Like hell. I peered into his beady little eyes. "You've got something, don't you?"

"In what way?"

"You know damn well. You've found something. Something you think is so brilliant and insightful that you don't need me. You think you've got it all figured."

"Well, that is my job."

"Come clean, Granger. What do you know?"

He continued talking with that insufferable indifference, but from the corner of my eye I could see that we were beginning to attract attention. In other words, once again, he was playing for an audience. Building his rep by trashing mine. "I know the killer is male. Right?"

My eyes widened. "Wow! You must have a Ph.D. in psychology or something."

"I know he's motivated by some kind of sexual obsession or deviancy."

"And how did you decide that?"

"Almost all serial killers are, right?"

"There are exceptions. Aileen Wuornos—"

"But most of them are sexually motivated, right?"

"So far, there's no indication that the victims were sexually molested."

"Which, as we both know, does not in any way rule out the likelihood that his crimes are sexually motivated. He's probably impotent."

"You can't keep making assumptions in the absence of evidence—"

He held up his hand. "But statistically speaking, I'm probably right, aren't I?"

I tried to penetrate a little further into that titanium-reinforced skull. "You wouldn't be playing so high and mighty with me in my own ballpark unless you knew something. Spill."

Granger stared at me for a long moment. Eventually, he turned around the paper in his hands so I could see it. It was a victimology report from one of his investigating officers, one who had been interrogating the friends of Mohamadas Amir. "Amir was a porn freak."

I snatched the report out of his hands. "How do they know?"

"It's more like, how could anyone not know. Everyone who knew him knew. Except his wife, apparently."

I scanned the report as quickly as I could input the data. "So what wild and utterly unsupported conclusion are you drawing here?"

He spread his arms wide. "Isn't it obvious? It's Jack the Ripper all over again."

I squinted. "Jack the Ripper killed prostitutes."

"Jack the Ripper was obsessed with everything he perceived as sexually obscene. Prostitutes were the easiest to get at, in nineteenth century London, but his notes to the police show that his sexual obsession didn't stop with ladies of the evening. He didn't have access to porn queens or those who favored them. But if he had, I'd be willing to bet he'd have gone after them with that great big knife of his."

"How does this explain the equation? How does this explain the face peeling?"

"Didn't Jack the Ripper mutilate his victims?"

"Yes, but in a clearly sexual manner, at least most of the time. You're extrapolating too much from two bits of information that may or may not indicate a pattern. We need more empirical data before we—"

He held up his hands. "Susan, Susan, Susan. I'm not trying to get you kicked off the case. I'm really not. But I think you'd be more useful if you worked with the evidence, instead of fighting against it." I could've lived with that, but he had to add: "Just because you didn't find it yourself."

"I'm not—I just—" I tried to concentrate, get my head straight, but I was having a hard time focusing. "I can't explain, Granger. It just doesn't feel right."

He smiled again and this time, just for good measure, added a little chuckle. "Like I said, I think psychological profiling is overrated."

"You sorry son of a—"

"Which reminds me." He pulled another document out of his pocket. "This is a consulting contract. I knew everything was all loosey-goosey and handshakes with O'Bannon, but now that you're working directly under me, I want a formal signed contract on file spelling out the terms of the employment—and grounds for termination."

I snatched it out of his hands and read. "I agree to follow all instructions given by my superior officers. I promise to observe the chain of command and show respect to my superior officers." I pushed it back into his face. "I'm not signing this."

"If you want to go on working on this case, you are."

"I don't care how important you think you are. O'Bannon won't fire me. And I'm not signing this."

He took a step closer. "So help me, Pulaski, if you don't—"

I shoved the contract into my mouth and ate it. Chewed it up and swallowed it, the whole thing. The office spectators began to laugh. Granger fumed, swore under his breath, then pivoted on one heel and stomped away.

Okay, so that probably wasn't the smartest thing to do. I still don't really know why I did it. Well, I suppose I do, in a way. But I knew it would come back to haunt me. Granger would be in O'Bannon's office first chance he got, trying to get me booted, and now he even had a decent excuse.

I decided to make tracks. They couldn't fire me if they couldn't find me, right? Besides, if I wanted to stay on this case, I needed to find out something they didn't already know. The faster the better.

"DID YOU KNOW that the Eiffel Tower has exactly 2,500,000 rivets?"

"What, like, exactly?"

"Exactly."

"I don't believe it."

"It is true. Gustave Eiffel planned it that way."

"Wow. That Gustave must've been . . ."

"A master engineer?"

I smiled. "A man after your own heart."

I was driving Darcy to UNLV by way of the Spaghetti Bowl, what the locals call the loop formed by I-15 and US 93-95 as they circle around downtown Vegas, which seemed to be jammed with commuter traffic around the clock. Fortunately, I had Darcy to keep me company. I'd told him we were going to meet an eminent mathematician, so he decided to entertain me with more of his seemingly inexhaustible supply of numerical trivia.

"Do you know how many Elvis impersonators there are in Las Vegas?" he asked.

I couldn't hazard a guess. "Way too many."

"Twelve thousand, six hundred and ninety-two."

"No!"

"Yes. The growth rate over the past decade has been exponential. If this pattern continues, by the year 2020, one in every six people will be an Elvis impersonator."

I couldn't resist a hearty belly laugh. "Darcy, you're cracking me up."

"What do you mean?"

"You—That—" I kept my attention on the gridlock traffic, but glanced at him out of the corner of my eye. "That wasn't a joke?"

He stared at me blank-faced.

What was I thinking? Darcy didn't even understand the concept of jokes.

"Have you had lunch?" I asked him. "We've got time to stop, if you haven't."

"Thank you, but I have already eaten. I had leftover chicken from our dinner last night. From KFC. Do you know what KFC stands for?"

"Yes!" For perhaps the first time ever, I actually knew the answer to one of Darcy's questions. I felt as if I had won the *Jeopardy!* Tournament of Champions.

"I had double helpings of coleslaw," Darcy added. "Although now I am thinking that maybe I shouldn't have. Do you know how many times the average adult passes gas each day?"

"Uh, no, and what's more—"

"Nineteen."

"That—can't be right."

"It's true. There was a study done at Cornell University."

I wondered what lucky graduate student got to write that grant application. "Nineteen?"

"On average."

"Well," I said, veering onto the exit ramp. "I've never done it. Ever. In my entire life."

His forehead creased. "Then you would be a statistical anomaly."

I made a hard left and passed through the campus gates. "I've always suspected as much."

I WAS SO HAPPY and it was so good to see Susan again it has been so long since my dad let me be a detective with her and I missed being a detective with her. I like being with her. I do not know if she's decided whether she will adopt me I wanted to ask but I was afraid to ask and I thought that if the answer was yes she would tell me so maybe I should not ask. I am glad that she wanted me to be with her but I hope I can help her I like math and math likes me but it is not always easy. At least numbers are better than words. Words can mean so many different things and you never can be sure what they mean because you have to know which meaning is right and you have to know how someone is saying it or see their expression when they are saying it and I can never understand how someone is saying it or why that should matter. Numbers are always the same. One is always one. Two is always two. And one and two are always three. Unless you are not in base ten. But that would be different.

Susan smells good today and she seems okay and her hands are not shaking and that makes me happy. But she is talking funny and that makes me worried. She is talking funny like she used to talk funny except not like she used to talk funny and I don't really know what I mean but something is not right and I do not like it when something is not right for Susan. For Susan everything should be right because I love Susan and I love Susan and—

Stop. Insert period. Start again. I do not like the way her words are running together, but she does not have that funny smell she used to have when I first met her and as long as she does not have that funny smell everything will be okay. I think. I wish I understood the world but I do not and I never will. That is why I need Susan to adopt me. She could help me. She could take care of me. And I would always try to take care of her.

17

I GUESS we got there early, because when we arrived, Professor Goldstein was still teaching a class. It was one of those multitiered amphitheater classrooms with enough seats for at least a hundred students, and there wasn't an empty seat. What's more, there wasn't a bored face in the room; she seemed to have her students absolutely mesmerized, which was amazing, because I didn't understand a word she was saying.

"Darcy," I whispered, "are you getting any of this?"

He was staring at the problems written on the chalkboard, which looked to me sufficiently complex to create an atomic bomb. "I am working on it."

"Is that a yes or a no?"

"I . . . I have never seen anything like this before."

"Does that mean you don't get it, either?"

He continued staring straight ahead, eyes fixed. "I am working on it."

I tuned into Dr. Goldstein's lecture. "The important thing to bear in mind about continuing fractions is that they're fundamentally no different from simple fractions—except that instead of being able to reduce them in one, perhaps two steps, it's going to be more like, oh, fifty or a hundred steps." There was a low ripple of laughter from the classroom. "But never fear—it can be done. And it's worth the effort. Continuing fractions made it possible for men to go to the moon, for us to send probes to Mars and beyond. They made it possible for us to decode the human genome, to understand the natural process of crystallization. And Tupperware. Never forget Tupperware."

The bell rang. She laid her chalk back on the tray and brushed her hands together. "Class dismissed. Try to complete all three problems on the board. See you next time."

I CAUGHT HER as she was packing up her materials and introduced myself. "Thank you for seeing me, Dr. Goldstein."

"Oh, it's no trouble. Colin and I have known each other for years." She offered me a chair. "Are you all right? You seem tired."

"Do I?" Damnation. "Did you catch me yawning during your lecture?"

She laughed. "No. Everyone does that. But your eyelids seem droopy."

"Sorry. I've been working double shifts on this case. Didn't get much sleep last night." I was lying through my teeth, of course. Three little blue pills was definitely too many. "I was impressed by your lecture. I don't believe I've ever met a female mathematician."

"Well, times are changing. Even if we haven't come that far in two thousand years."

"Two thousand years?"

"Since Hypatia. In ancient Egypt. History tells us she was the first female mathematician. Also kept the great Library of Alexandria. Very radical figure, in her time. Many people considered math—all the sciences, actually—a male enclave. Didn't like having a woman intrude on their turf."

"What happened to her?"

Dr. Goldstein pursed her lips. "Hypatia was attacked by a mob and dragged from her chariot. Her skin was flayed from her body with seashells. Then they burned the library. As a result, innumerable works of science and literature were lost for all time. Most of the work of Ptolemy. Most of the plays of Sophocles. An immeasurable loss."

"And, I bet, an end to women wanting to be mathematicians."

"For a time, yes. But enough about math history. How can I help you?"

"I'll be happy to explain that, although I warn you, it may take a while. And some of the details . . . aren't too pleasant."

"Why don't we step into my office?" She gestured toward the door on the left.

"Sure. Darce?"

"Huh?" He stared at the blackboard.

"Let's go into Dr. Goldstein's office."

His head tilted at an odd angle. "If it is okay—I mean if you do not mind or anything—I would like to stay out here."

I was puzzled. He'd practically begged to come with me, and now he didn't want to hear what the woman had to say? Still, I wasn't going to force him.

"Okay. I'll pick you up on my way out."

I followed Dr. Goldstein down the corridor into her office. For someone who held the Laura K. McClain Chair in Mathematics, she had a damn small office. Life in academia, I supposed. Of course, I myself had no office at all, so perhaps I shouldn't be criticizing.

"What can I do for you?" she asked, taking a seat behind her desk. I guessed her to be in her mid- to late thirties, with platinum blond hair and a few tinges of gray. She was not tall, but she was reasonably attractive. She wore a loose-fitting dress that gave no hint as to her figure, but even so, I could see this woman was capable of attracting male eyes.

"Well," I answered, "Colin tells me you're an expert in . . . I'm sorry, I don't know how else to put it. Weird math."

I was relieved to see she didn't take offense. In fact, she laughed. "In the scholarly world, we call it cryptomathematics. It's a discipline that combines elements of mathematics and philosophy. We apply the fundamentals of mathematics not simply for the more common ontological purposes but to pursue teleological inquiries as well." She must've noticed the blank expression on my face, because she added: "We apply math not simply as a way of solving problems but of understanding the mysteries of the world in which we live."

I nodded as if I understood; I was processing information much more slowly than usual. I tried to shake myself out of the cloud and force myself to function. "Well, I suppose that beats doing calculus."

"Funny you should say that. Differential calculus was invented by Isaac Newton, you know."

"May he burn in hell."

"He was a seriously strange dude, not at all the Sunday school genius you learn about in science class, sitting around waiting for an apple to fall on him so he could invent gravity, a story he probably made up."

"You're joking."

"I'm not. I did my dissertation on Newton. Sure, he experimented with gravity and light prisms and optics and higher mathematics, but as it turns out, he spent far more of his time dabbling in alchemy."

"You mean, trying to turn lead into gold?"

"Exactly."

"But isn't that . . . totally cracked?"

"That would be a nice way of putting it. Worse, in his day, it was illegal and perceived as anti-Christian, so he did all his alchemical work in secret. Most scholars today believe his thoughts on gravity arose from those alchemical experiments—although he couldn't admit it—not any apple-falling epiphany. For that matter, he also dabbled in sorcery and astrology and biblical prophecy; he had this whole timeline worked out of not only the history of the universe but the future. All the way from Adam and Eve—which by the way only occurred about six thousand years ago—right up to judgment day."

I gulped. "Dare I ask?"

"You can relax. According to Newton, the Second Coming is scheduled for 2060."

"Yikes."

"Yeah. He believed it, even though he never published it in his own lifetime. At the end of his life, Newton compared himself to Christ; he believed he was the only person able to interpret this divine knowledge. He wrote far more about the Bible than he did math; his future-history analysis is ten times as long as the *Principia Mathematica.*"

"And this is the world's greatest mathematician? Sounds more like the profile of a serial killer."

"You're not far wrong. He was neurotic, suicidal, anti-Semitic." She took a deep breath. "And then in his spare time, he revolutionized the world. He built the best refracting telescope. He made the Industrial Revolution possible."

"Even though he was wicked whacked."

She smiled. "Even though."

"And you chose to do a paper on this guy?"

She shrugged. "Hey, I got my Ph.D. You gotta do something to get academia's attention. It made a good dissertation, even if the man was mad. Ingenious, but mad. A dangerous combination."

Yes, that much was becoming clear to me. And I very

much suspected that combination had made its way to beautiful downtown Vegas.

"I'M TELLING YOU, Chief, her speech was slurred."

"I don't believe it."

"Why would I lie?"

O'Bannon looked up at Granger, one eyebrow cocked.

Granger pressed his fists against O'Bannon's desk. "Look, I'll admit that Pulaski and I have had our differences. But we've also worked together—remember?"

"I just talked to the woman this morning. And she wasn't drunk."

"She could've been faking it. You can't be sure."

He looked at his detective with a steely eye. "I've been on the police force for thirty-four years," he said levelly. "I can be sure."

"Then maybe she stopped off someplace on her way to the office. I don't know. All I can tell you is, when she came in here, she wasn't right. She was too loose, too . . . I don't know. Un-Susan-like. Calmer. Relaxed. And she was definitely slurring her words."

"Personally, I think a calmer, more relaxed Susan might be a pleasant change of pace."

"Assuming she's sober. But she wasn't."

"She's been clean for months. Why would she start drinking now?"

"Because for the first time in months, you're actually asking her to do something!"

O'Bannon didn't respond.

"You think I don't know you've been going easy on her, making sure she didn't encounter anything that might put her under stress? Everyone in the department knows!"

"So you're saying you want me to hire a different behaviorist? Take on a second expert consultant?"

Granger paused. "I'd rather scratch the psycho-profilers and redirect that money to manpower. Let me beef up my detective squad. Hell, we've got a description on the guy. We just need to fan out, hit the streets, track him down."

O'Bannon pushed away from his desk. "Look, you want extra manpower, fill out the forms and I'll see if I can get it. I'll back you one hundred percent. It's not an either/or deal."

"You know as well as I do how strapped the budget is in this crappy economy. No way the city council will let me increase spending unless I can show them where I'm going to get the money."

O'Bannon didn't bother arguing with him. "Nonetheless, as long as the perp remains at large, it would be irresponsible to fire our best psy—"

Granger slapped a newspaper on O'Bannon's desk. "Have you read this yet?"

He unfolded the morning edition of the *Courier* and glanced at the under-the-fold headline. FACE KILLER STILL AT LARGE, and beneath that, POLICE BAFFLED. The article was by Jonathan Wooley, one of the top crime reporters for the paper, one O'Bannon knew all too well. He skimmed the article quickly. Wooley was unstinting in his criticism of the police department. Even though they hadn't released all of the gruesome details of the case, Wooley was still basically telling his readers they weren't safe on the streets.

"Prepare a statement. Tell them as little as you can. Pretend we're following up on a lot of serious leads."

Granger paced back and forth, his frustration mounting. "You know what I think? I think you know how risky Susan is. I think you know she'll start drinking again, sooner or later. You're just protecting her because you used to be her father's partner!"

"And you know what I think?" O'Bannon replied, matching his volume. "I think you're still pissed because of what happened to her husband—*your* partner—even though you don't know a damn thing about it."

"That's such bull—"

"Or maybe it's because she didn't melt in your mouth when you came on to her the first day you transferred over here. Which is it?"

Granger's face crinkled with rage. "I am just trying to help you! All I want is what's best for the department!"

"Then get out of my office and solve this case!" O'Bannon shouted.

Granger slammed the door on his way out.

O'Bannon fell back in his chair, exhausted. He pressed his fingers against his forehead, trying to fight off an incipient migraine.

Of course, Granger was right, at least about many things. He was protecting Susan. He couldn't forget her father—or what happened to him. For that matter, he'd known Susan all her life; he couldn't stand by and let her go down the tubes without trying to stop it.

Was she really slurring? He hadn't noticed it this morning on the phone. But as much as Granger might hate her, he couldn't imagine that the man would just make it up. If she was drinking again, Granger wouldn't be the only one who noticed, no matter how practiced she was at hiding it. Her career as a police officer would be finished. He would've let her down. Again. He would've dishonored the memory of her father, who—even though no one knew it but him—gave his life for O'Bannon's.

And Darcy would never forgive him.

He closed his eyes and said a silent prayer, something he had gotten more used to doing during the months of recovery and rehabilitation following his gunshot wound.

Please God, whatever it is she's doing—tell her to stop. Tell her to stop now, before it's too late.

He tried to return his attention to the two dozen other files on his desk, but he couldn't really focus; he might as well have been reading James Joyce for all he comprehended of it. His mind was on Susan.

Please, Susan, be smart. Just this one time. *Be smart*!

"I'VE READ about the murders in the paper," Dr. Goldstein said. "Horrible. But what do they have to do with my field of study?"

I handed her a photocopy. "This was found scrawled in grease at the scene of the first murder. It appears to be a mathematical equation, although by all accounts, an impossible one. Does it mean anything to you?"

She had looked at it for barely two seconds before a broad smile crossed her face. "Oh, yes. That again."

"That—what?" I craned my neck. "Have you seen this before?"

"Of course. Many times."

"But—what is it?"

She laughed, then passed it back to me. "It's a joke."

"A joke? What do you mean?"

She settled back in her chair. "You've heard of the Swiss mathematician Euler?"

To hedge or not to hedge . . . "The, uh, name sounds familiar . . ."

"He was a major figure in the history of mathematics. Is credited with being the first person to apply calculus to physics. Was the first to use the term *function* in a mathematical context."

"And this equation has to do with his work?"

"No, this has to do with his joke. As the story goes—and I warn you, it may be entirely apocryphal—Euler was a guest in the court of Catherine the Great at the same time as the great philosopher Diderot. Diderot was an atheist—or to be more accurate, he refused to believe in anything that couldn't be proven by rational, logical, or deductive principles. Anyway, he was making a big scene in court, offending everyone, declaring loudly that, 'I will believe in God when you prove to me that He exists.' So Euler hands him this formula and says, 'There.

$$\frac{(a+b^n)}{n}=x$$

hence God exists, reply!' " She laughed. "Q.E.D."

I really wished Darcy had come in with me. It might've saved me so much embarrassment. "And . . . was he right?"

Dr. Goldstein gave me a long look. "Do you really think a mathematical formula could prove the existence of a divine maker? It was a joke. But Diderot didn't know. So he takes the formula and mumbles something like, 'Oh.' And crawls back to his room and stays there for the rest of the week, not bothering anybody. Euler becomes the hero of the court."

"Great story," I said. "But a little obscure. Most serial killers aren't, you know, students of little-known moments in the history of French philosophy."

"Oh, this theory gets around more than you know. Your killer may read the Mathematical Games column in *Scientific American*, or books on famous practical jokes. Maybe he's addicted to the History Channel."

I nodded. "I've always been suspicious of people who are addicted to the History Channel."

She laughed. "My point is, it wouldn't take a mathematical genius to scrawl this formula. This equation may have been intended as a joke, but hey, all the world loves a joke. And as you said before, without more information, it is totally insoluble."

"So when the killer left this behind at the scene of the

crime, he was . . ." I held up my hands. I had no idea how to finish the sentence.

"I'm no detective," Dr. Goldstein replied. "But my guess is he was doing the same thing to you that Euler was doing to Diderot. Pulling his leg."

I nodded slowly. "Leading us on a wild goose chase. Proving how much smarter than us he is." Which was a common trait of the narcissistic personality disorder. And much as I hated to admit it, it would fit well with Granger's sexual obsessive theory, too. "And this has nothing to do with your work? That . . . crypto . . . thingie."

"No. There have been some serious efforts to link theology and mathematics, but this isn't one of them. Have you heard of Pythagoras?"

Darcy, of course, could've recited the entire encyclopedia entry on Pythagoras. I was stuck with: "Didn't he have some kinda theorem or something?"

"Very good. You remember your high school geometry." Was that a compliment? I wasn't sure. "Pythagoras proved

$$a^2 + b^2 = c^2$$

as applied to the sides of a triangle. One of the most important discoveries in the history of mathematics. What you may not know is that Pythagoras was also the leader of a secret society."

"The ancient Greek version of the Elks lodge?"

"You're not far wrong. They called themselves the Brethren of Purity. They believed there was a connection between math and the cosmos, that all existence was predetermined by mathematical laws, and that God must have a mathematical form, since the universe He created does and always has. They swore to keep to themselves, safe from the public, one mind-shattering secret."

"And that was?"

Dr. Goldstein leaned forward and whispered. "The square root of two."

"Wow," I said, trying to keep a straight face. "That was a biggie."

"To them, it was. See, they didn't have an answer for it. They didn't have irrational numbers, or algebra or calculus. The square root of two was a problem with no solution, and therefore, it undermined not only their theory of mathematics but their very understanding of the cosmos. So they kept it to themselves."

I shook my head. "No wonder I never trusted math geeks."

"Of course, today we have ways of expressing the square root of two, even if we can't exactly solve the problem. But the Brethren of Purity started people thinking along certain lines that linked math with philosophy and theology. It is true that math is everywhere in the universe. The orbits of the planets follow predictable elliptical paths. Leaves expand at a predictable exponential rate. Gravity can be measured. The speed of light can be quantified. All these discoveries inevitably led to the question: Did man invent math in order to understand the universe, or did man simply discover what God created and made the basis of His universe?"

"And you . . . cryptos try to answer that question?"

"In a way. The famous mathematician Canzoni believed math had its own consciousness, which was evidenced in its physical manifestations in the world. Aristotle claimed to have proven the existence of God through logic based upon his theory of objects as we know them and their relationship to first causes. The first cause must be God, he argued, to avoid the logical inconsistencies of an infinite regress of possible causes for the creation of the universe. Avicenna, an ancient Muslim philosopher, made much the same argument. Only a few years ago, the mathematician William Hatcher, an adherent of the Baha'i faith, based upon the teaching of the prophet Baha'u'llah, proposed a logical proof that God exists, using relational logic. There have been others. Some of them brilliant, some of them totally insane."

"Like that guy in *A Beautiful Mind*?"

She nodded appreciatively. "John Nash. Yes, that's a very good example, actually. Math has been riddled with positively brilliant madmen."

"In school," I reflected, "we were taught that the line between genius and madness was thin. And too often transversed."

"That's true, but it occurs far more often in those disciplines that are centered in the right brain—like math. Or music—which of course is fundamentally based upon mathematics. Remember Mozart—writing symphonies when he was four, antisocial narcissist unable to function in society by the time he was an adult. Or chess. Poor Bobby Fischer went from being the greatest chess player in the world when he was fifteen to hiding from the law, spouting conspiracy theories and anti-Semitism—even though he himself was partly Jewish."

"But isn't this true in all artistic and intellectual fields?"

"Not so much, no. Because when you get to the disciplines that are centered in the left brain, you don't get prodigies of this nature. Literature, for example. Sure, Tolstoy was a brilliant writer, but he didn't write *War and Peace* when he was four. That kind of dangerous precociousness doesn't exist in the left brain fields."

So I was looking for someone very smart. And dangerously precocious. Swell. "Thank you for your time, Doctor. I'm sure you need to get back to . . . the unified field theory, or whatever."

She laughed. "That's a little over my head. Actually, I'm trying to posit a solution to the Reimann hypothesis."

"Come again?"

"It's the greatest unsolved mathematical puzzle, at least many of us think so. Hard to explain to a layperson, since it involves complex numbers. Basically, if the Reimann hypothesis is false, then the occurrence of prime numbers is essentially random. But if it's true, it implies that the occurrence of prime numbers is far more orderly than we are currently able to prove. That there is a pattern, even if we are unable to discern it."

"In other words, that there really is a mathematical meaning to the universe."

"Some would say so. One of the top mathematical theoreticians who ever lived, David Hilbert, said that if he were to awaken after sleeping for a thousand years, his first question would be: Has the Reimann hypothesis been proven?"

I suspected I would be more interested in the growth of my IRA account, but that's why I'm not a mathematician. "Thanks again, Doctor. You've been an enormous help."

"Have I? I feel as if all I've done is take your clue and prove it doesn't lead anywhere."

"Perhaps. But that too is useful. Now we can move on to other things." I held out my hand. "Thank you for your time. And good luck with your work on that . . . hypothesis. I have a feeling you're going to end up a lot better than Hypatia did."

She smiled. "Well, I could hardly end up any worse."

DR. GOLDSTEIN escorted me back to the empty classroom, where we found Darcy still staring assiduously at the equations on the chalkboard.

I slapped him on the shoulder. "Having any luck, champ?"

Darcy did not look at me. "Twelve," he said.

I glanced at my watch. "No, it's almost two."

He ran his fingers through his hair and bucked his head toward the chalkboard. "That one. Twelve."

Dr. Goldstein picked up a clipboard lying on the podium and flipped through the pages. "My God," she whispered. "He's right."

"Huh?" I turned back and looked at her notes, which were totally meaningless to me. "What do you mean?"

"I mean twelve is the ultimate answer—the ultimate reduction, if you will—of this continuing fraction." She shook her head in amazement. "Do you mind if I look at your work?"

Darcy stared at her. "Work?"

"Your process. How you solved the problem."

Darcy's expression was still uncomprehending. "I did it in my head."

Dr. Goldstein's eyes fairly bulged. "In your head? That fraction requires more than thirty-two steps of reduction."

Darcy shrugged. "I did it in my head."

"Well, I don't mean to be rude, but—I find that very difficult to believe."

Darcy pointed at the other two problems on the blackboard. "Eighty-seven. Six point four two nine."

Goldstein's lips parted. "He's right!" She looked at me. "I doubt if I have a single graduate student who will be able to solve all three problems in a week. And that's using paper, pencil, and calculators. Where did Mr. O'Bannon go to college?"

I couldn't help but grin. "He's never been to college."

"You're kidding. Where did he study continuing fractions?"

"I don't believe he ever has."

Goldstein appeared stunned. "Are you sure? I've never seen anything like this in my entire life." She laid down her clipboard. "He must be a math savant. Incredibly gifted."

"I think so, yeah." I gave Darcy another nudge. "C'mon, champ. Let's go get some custard."

Darcy beamed. "Then I did good?"

"Very good. Thank you again, Doctor."

"Lieutenant—" She held me by the arm. "I don't want to seem forward, but if your young friend ever does decide to go to college, please have him come here. I would love to have him in my department."

"Well, thank you, but I don't think he has any plans—"

"If it's a matter of money, I'm sure I could rustle up a grant for someone with his gifts. I'm talking about a full scholarship."

"Really?" Now that was a thought. "I'll mention it to his father."

"Thank you. You have my number. Tell him he can call me at any time."

"I'll do that, Dr. Goldstein."

"Please, call me Esther." She handed me a business card, then excused herself. Darcy was still staring at the chalkboard, but I steered him toward the door. "Well, you made a heck of an impression. What do you think, Darcy? Wanna be a college man?"

He tilted his head at an odd angle. "If I went to college, could I be a policeman?"

"Well . . . possibly. Some of our detectives have college degrees. Although they don't usually come from the math department."

"Would they give me a place to live?"

I peered into his eyes. What was he thinking? It was so impossible to tell with him. "I assume room and board would be part of a full scholarship."

"Would it be a place where . . . where . . . you would want to live?"

"Huh?" I frowned. "Darcy, I've already been through college. And I already have a place to live."

"Oh." He pushed open the outer doors and stepped into the sunlight. "Can we at least get the custard?"

I didn't know what he was talking about, and I knew I wasn't going to figure it out now. My foggy little Valium-coated head was already throbbing from all the talk about mathematics, so I took the easy way out and didn't try to understand. "Custard it is. And this is the second Wednesday so . . . English toffee, right?"

His eyes lit. "You understand!"

I squeezed him around the neck. He pulled away, but not too hard and not too fast. "I'm learning, Darce. Slowly but surely, I'm learning."

TUCKER HANDCUFFED the woman to the bed, tightening the screws until he was certain her hands were immobilized. When she struggled, he grabbed her dark black hair and squeezed her head with his strong, massive hands.

"I could crush your skull if I wanted to," he growled, his expression leaving no doubt that he could or would. Nor disguising how much he would enjoy it. "Is that what you want?"

The woman looked up, her face masked with terror. She was practically naked, wearing nothing but a bright crimson teddy with white lace at the bodice. "No, sir. I'll be good. I promise I'll be good. Just—don't hurt me any more, okay? Please don't hurt me."

"Are you tryin' to tell me what to do?"

"No, of course not. I wouldn't—"

He whipped his hand around and slapped her ferociously. His brute force knocked her face sideways against the headboard.

"Get the message?" Tucker growled. "You'll do as I say. You're my slave."

"I'm—I'm your slave," she repeated, working her jaw as she spoke, trying to expunge the soreness.

He sat beside her on the bed. "Now for your legs. It'll

make things a lot easier when . . . when we do what we hafta to do next. So don't fight me."

"No, sir," she said, eyes wide. "I won't fight you."

"Good, we'll start by—"

Without warning, her knee shot up into the air, making a line drive toward his chin. But he was ready. He caught the knee with both hands, then pushed it downward at a bone-twisting angle. She screamed, then squirmed, trying to readjust her weight to ease the strain on her leg muscles.

Tucker pushed her legs apart and thrust himself on top of her. "Do you want me to be mean?" he shouted. "Do you? Because if that's what you want, that's what you'll get!"

"No, sir!" she said, her eyes wide and desperate. "Please, no!"

"You will not get away. The only question is whether we do this the quick way, or whether I have a little fun with you first." He grabbed her by the throat. "You understand what I'm sayin'?"

His grip was so tight she was barely able to speak. "Yes, sir. I understand. I'll do whatever you say."

"I just hope for your sake that's true." He tightened his fingers, choking her, giving her a brief taste of death. "You will not resist. Or I will hurt you."

"Yes, sir." She lay on the bed, sobbing, passive, as he snapped the cuffs around both of her ankles, leaving her helpless, pinned down on the top of the bed like a butterfly in a mounted collection. He ran his fingers up her left leg, making her shudder.

Then he got out the knife.

"I want you to understand that I have no choice about this. It's like—" He paused, as if trying to think. Or perhaps, to remember. "It's like we're all part of this big equation, see? We don't choose what we do, it's planned out in advance. But there are clues, and we hafta follow them." He pressed the knife against her forehead, just at the baseline of her scalp. "I guess you know what happens next."

"Please, sir. Please don't. I can give you money, if that's what you want. Lots of money. You want me to suck you off? I'll do it. I'll do it right now. I'll do anything. Just don't hurt my face."

"Too late."

She screamed, a high-pitched piercing wail, but it didn't stop him, didn't even slow him down. She tried to thrash back and forth, but the handcuffs left her so little room to maneuver that she barely moved. She gnashed her teeth, trying to bite him, but he was careful this time.

"Hellllp!" she cried, so loud Tucker winced. "Someone please help me."

With lightning speed, he reached into her mouth and grabbed her tongue, pinching it between two fingers. "Do you want me to cut this out, too? Do you? 'Cause I wouldn't mind a bit!"

She shook her head no.

"Can you keep your damn mouth shut? You think?"

A slow nod.

"Good." He released her tongue, then once again started at his work, while the woman on the bed dissolved into helpless, hopeless sobbing. He placed the knife once more on her forehead, then, with his other hand, grabbed her hair at the crown . . .

And yanked it off. All at once. The black wig pulled free, revealing the platinum locks beneath.

"Enough with the faces," Tucker said, grinning. "This time I decided to go for the scalp."

"Very funny," the woman said. Her entire demeanor changed. The fear was gone. The terror-stricken expression had vanished. "Now unlock these cuffs."

Tucker did as he was told. As soon as she was free, the woman gently massaged her wrists and ankles, everywhere the cuffs had chafed.

"Man. Those things hurt."

"I told you," Tucker said. "I wanted to use the plastic ones."

She shook her head. "No. If you're ever going to learn anything, we have to do it the right way." She looked up, smiling. "And by the way, you handled that fairly well."

He beamed. It was obvious that even such little praise as this was immensely important to him. "Really?"

"Really. You corrected your previous mistakes. I pulled all that slut's tricks and a few more of my own, but you never lost control."

"I—I was trying to be careful," Tucker said, head bowed.

"And you did a nice job of it. Which was the point of the whole exercise. To correct mistakes that might bring the whole thing crashing down on us before we have a chance to complete the pattern. Practice makes perfect. A little more work on the disposal of the corpses and I think we'll be ready to move again."

"On schedule?"

"Of course on schedule. What's to stop us?"

"I love you, Esther."

"And I love you, Tucker."

Her confidence was no façade; after all, her plan had worked perfectly thus far. Tucker would never understand why he had been instructed to leave those equations at the scenes of the crimes, nor did he ask. He simply obeyed. She needed to know her opponent, without exposing herself to suspicion. She needed to bring the opposition to her—and she did. Those clues brought that psychologist to her office so she could evaluate her, calculate the variables and compute the odds. And the final result? That woman and her associates had no chance of stopping her. They were as far from understanding her as Ptolemy was from understanding Einstein. "So we move forward, as planned. Remember, God is in the numbers."

"God is in the numbers," he repeated, as he had learned to repeat so much of what she had taught him. He lifted his left hand, revealing a tiny blue star tattooed at the center of his palm. She raised her hand and pressed it to his. "We are the Brethren of Purity," he murmured. "And I did good?"

"You did so well—I think you deserve a reward." She crawled on top of him, then pushed him back against the bed. She took his T-shirt by the collar with both hands, then ripped it down the center.

"Why did you do that?"

"I know how you like it." Esther gripped him by the arms, pressing her sharp fingernails into his flesh. She crouched over him, then slowly drew a soft line with her tongue from his navel across his stomach and chest.

"Oh, God," he murmured. "Oh, my God!"

"You have been a good boy. You have compensated for your errors. Will you continue to be a good boy?"

"Oh, yes," he said, feeling the intense heat of her body enveloping him, carrying him away. "I'll be good. I'll be careful."

"And you'll do whatever I tell you?" She straddled his groin, brushing herself back and forth against him. She grabbed his nipples and twisted them savagely. "Are you going to be a good boy and obey me?"

"Oh, yes. I'll do anything. Anything at all."

18

JULY 17

I ASKED MY DAD if I could go to one of the crime scenes and he said that the first one had already been cleaned so I asked how about the second one and he said no he did not think it was a good idea so I asked Susan and she said she did not think it was a good idea but I think she was just saying that because my dad wanted her to say that I think she likes to have me around she likes to call me and invite me and she took me to meet the math lady with the funny look in her eyes and the run in the heel of her hose and the Band-Aid on her left wrist and the blue star on the palm of her hand.

I have to carefully plan my way of getting there because I cannot drive but I know I could drive but my dad will not let me and I do not have a license or even a car but the buses can get me there if I plan it right and I go while my dad is at work so he does not notice that I am gone.

I liked it when Susan asked me if I wanted to go to college because I know smart people go to college and I would like to be a smart person and if I was a smart person maybe Susan would adopt me and we could have babies. Maybe I could learn to do more of that hard math but I do not think I would want to learn it from that lady because I did not really like that lady but I liked her math. I can understand math but I can never understand people. People would be easier if they were equations. I thought that maybe I could make people into equations, like Funny Smile plus Jokes I Don't Understand plus Shaky Hands plus Smart plus Pretty equals Susan. But I cannot always tell if she's joking or not and last time her hands did not shake but her voice was funny and maybe I need to factor out the way she smells because it changes so much. But she's always smart and she's always pretty. Those are constants. I like constants because they are always the same. You cannot do math without constants. I cannot do Real Life without constants.

My mother used to say I love you and I never knew what it meant and she would get upset so I started saying it back but I still did not know what it meant. My dad tried to explain that when people love each other they want to take care of each other and make each other happy and maybe he's right but all parents do that so I think there must be more. When Susan is around I get all strange and squishy feeling and my stomach hurts and I really try to be smart and not so weird. Maybe that's what love is. I wish there was a formula for love but there is not I know because I opened the encyclopedia and looked.

I know I will be in trouble with my dad when I do this, but it will be worth it if it makes Susan happy.

WHEN I GOT to the office that morning, everyone was acting strangely. Not to say they were unfriendly. Just the opposite. It was as if they were going out of their way to be friendly to me. Gave me the shivers.

Granger practically beamed when I passed by. "Morning, Susan." That was it. No griping about my report, no insults, no attempts to show his superior psychological know-how. "Sleep well?"

"I did, actually."

"I read your report on your interview with the math nerd. You really think it has anything to do with this case?"

"Well, that formula didn't draw itself into the grease."

"Good point. You're a sharp one, that's for sure. Congratulations on a nice piece of work."

Okay, so at this point, there were two possibilities. Either Granger had been taken over by one of those pods from *Invasion of the Body Snatchers,* or he was setting me up. You can imagine which I thought was more likely. While I tried to puzzle it out, O'Bannon sailed up behind him.

"Hey, Susan."

"Hey, Chief."

"Hear you and Darcy had a fun expedition to the university yesterday."

"Yeah. Actually, I'd like to talk to you about that."

"I read your report."

"No, about Darcy. Apparently his math skills are off the chart. Dr. Goldstein was ready to recruit him on the spot and enter him in the Math Bowl."

O'Bannon smiled a little. "Of course, she doesn't know about his . . . difficulties, right? I expect her eagerness would fade if she knew the whole truth, don't you?"

"I don't know. I don't think anyone who can do math problems that require over a hundred steps is what I'd call normal." I was watching them both very carefully, or more accurately, watching to see what it was they were watching for. Six months ago, I would've suspected this obviously forced conversation was for the purpose of sniffing my breath, but neither of them were close enough to do that now. For some reason, they just wanted to hear me talk.

That was it, of course. Darcy told me my voice sounded funny. The Valium must've been slurring my speech. Granger picked up on it, so today they were all out to see if he was right. Thank goodness I'd stopped at one pill this morning. Although the aching in my stomach and the knocking in my knees told me it wouldn't be long before I had another one. But I didn't want to get like I was yesterday—so doped I could barely stay awake, barely assimilate information. Sure, I was an old pro at faking sobriety. But it didn't help me do my job.

"Well," O'Bannon said, "let's talk about it later." In other words, no way in hell.

"As you wish. But the woman was even talking about scholarships. This could be a golden opportunity." I turned toward my desk. "Was there anything else?"

Granger and O'Bannon looked at each other without saying anything.

"Okay, look." I took a deep breath, then started. "Peter Piper picked a peck of pickled peppers . . ." I went through the whole thing at lightning speed, then did it again, just for good measure. Didn't trip up once. When I'm good, I'm good. "Satisfied?"

Granger frowned. "How did you know?"

"How did I know?" I took a step closer and peered into his eyes. "Because I'm a trained psychologist and to me the human mind is an open book. In your case, a comic book. I know everything you're thinking, planning, considering, every seedy, greasy little contemplation." I leaned in closer. "I even know what you were doing in your apartment by yourself last night."

Granger pulled away, staring at me as if he were ready to re-inaugurate the Salem witch trials. "I—don't know what you're talking about."

"That's all right," I answered, eyes narrowed. "Because I do. *Bwah-ha-ha-ha-ha!*"

IT'S ALWAYS A PLEASURE to see Darcy. Except perhaps on those rare occasions when he gets so excited he throws himself across my desk.

"Ooof!" I said, dodging, narrowly avoiding a collision of skulls. All the papers on my desk, not to mention my In/Out box, went flying. "Darcy, what are you doing? Are you blind?"

"You moved your desk forward!"

"I most certainly did not."

"It is at least seven inches closer to the top of the stairs than it was yesterday."

"Look, Spock, I didn't move anything. I—" But of course, I had to look. I stared at the linoleum on the floor and saw square impressions, remnants of where the legs of the desk once had been. About seven inches away from where they were now. Cleaning people, probably. "Do you calculate your trajectory on your way up the stairs?"

Darcy blinked. "Sorta."

I didn't bother asking because I knew I wouldn't understand. "What're you so excited about?"

He leaned across my desk. His face was lively in a way I'd never seen it before. "Can you keep a secret?"

Darcy had secrets? Since when? "Sure."

"Scout's honor?"

I gave him a long look. "Were you ever a Scout?"

"For two meetings. Till the Scoutmaster got mad at me and threw me out. My dad said it was my fault but it was not my fault because this other boy was making fun of me and he said that Saturn was larger than Jupiter bu—"

I held up a hand. "Periods, Darcy. Periods."

He took a deep breath. "Right."

"So tell me the secret before I burst already."

He came so close his lips brushed against my ear, which was pretty unusual for a kid with severe tactile defensiveness. "I went to the crime scene."

I pulled away, my eyes wide. "Darcy, I told you—"

"I know. But I thought that I should so I went anyway."

"I—But—" I didn't know where to begin. "Which scene?"

"The movie studio."

I looked him straight in the eye. "Darcy, I know for a fact that CS is still restricted. How could you get in?"

Darcy looked to his right, then his left. When he was certain no one was watching, he pulled something out of his underpants and flashed it at me. Something shiny. A badge.

"Where did you get that!"

"I borrowed it from my dad's desk."

"You—*borrowed* it! What's going to happen if he notices it's gone?"

"He already did. He thinks he lost it. He got tired of looking and went back to making pottery ashtrays."

"But—he's bound to suspect—"

"He will not suspect me. He does not think I am smart enough to do anything smart."

"And he never will if you keep doing crazy stuff like this! Darcy, your father told you to stay away!"

"But I wanted to go." His face sagged. "I wanted to help you, Susan."

I closed my eyes and blew out my cheeks. What could I say? It was impossible to be mad at him. "The uniform posted outside must've recognized you."

"I think that he did. But who is going to stop the son of the chief of police?"

Good point. "But Darcy—why did you want to go there?"

"Because I wanted to find something that would help you, so you could solve the case and not be so nervous and shaky."

"Darcy—"

"And I did."

My mouth closed. Then reopened. "You found something?"

He shook his head wildly up and down. He looked both ways, making sure no one was watching. Then he reached inside his coat.

It was only a scrap of paper, but Darcy'd had the foresight to enclose it in a plastic evidence Baggie. I held it up to the light.

It was another equation:

$$\frac{(P-1)!+1}{P}$$

"Swell," I murmured. "What's this one do, prove the existence of Santa Claus?"

"Wrong!" Darcy said. He made a snorting noise, then began jumping up and down. "I know what this one does! I know what this one does!"

He was bouncing like Tigger on speed. "So, does that mean you know what this one does?"

"Yes! It's a test for determining primes!"

"Huh?"

His voice changed. I'd been around him long enough to understand that this meant he was in his mimetic recitation mode. "The theorem for determining primeness was discovered by Cambridge mathematics professor Edward Waring, the author of *Meditations Algebraicae,* in 1784. He named it for his good friend John Wilson, who left mathematics to become a lawyer and later, a judge. He was knighted in—"

"Stop. I get the idea. Periods, remember." Maybe it was the mellowness induced by the Valium, or maybe I've just lost all self-respect, but I didn't try to pretend I understood. "What the hell is primeness?"

"Prime numbers! Numbers that are only divisible by themselves and one."

"Oh, right, right. So you use this to find primes?"

"No. To test a number to see if it is prime. There is no way to find primes."

"Really?" I tried to act cool and nonchalant. "What about the Reimann hypothesis?"

He couldn't mask his surprise any more than he could mask any of his other emotions. "Y-Y-You know about the Reimann hypothesis?"

"Of course," I said offhandedly, declining to mention that the only reason I knew anything about it was that Dr. Goldstein had mentioned it and I'd written it down in my report. "What do you take me for, some kind of stooge?" I stared at his new piece of evidence. "Why would the killer think this was important?"

Darcy might be able to sniff out evidence, but when it came to questions that required an understanding of human motivations, he was useless. "I do not know. Maybe the killer thinks math is fun. I think math is fun. Lots more fun than killing people."

Personally, I didn't care for either. "Where did you find this?"

"In the dead lady's computer."

My forehead creased. "I remember watching the computer CSIs scanning the hard drive."

"Not inside the computer's memory. Inside the computer. In the hard shell case of the CPU."

"You opened the computer itself?"

He nodded eagerly. "And I found this!"

I assumed this scrap of paper was too small to prevent the computer from functioning. "What on earth would inspire you to open the computer case?"

"Because the bad man did."

"You mean the killer? How did you know?"

"I could see the traces of him on the outside. When I got close, I could smell them."

"Are you talking about blood? Because I know that Tony went over everything in that studio with luminal and ultraviolet light."

"Not blood. Sweat. He sweated on the computer."

"And you could tell? No way." But I had the evidence in my hand, didn't I? And I knew darn well Darcy was not capable of lying. "Why would he be sweating? The studio was at normal room temperature. All the big camera lights were shut off."

"I think that maybe he did not like what he was doing or he knew he should not do it or the lady made it hard for him and it made him upset so he started sweating. Do you sweat when you are doing something you do not want to or you know you should not do? I know I was sweating when I snuck into the crime scene and I remember once when I was five that—"

"Periods!" I fairly screamed. "What makes you think the killer didn't want to do what he did?"

"The blood. In all the wrong places."

As usual, I had no idea what he was talking about. I opened the file on my desk and pulled out the crime scene photos. "Show me."

Darcy rifled through the photos like a computer scanning its files. He pulled one out and thrust it toward me. "See the blood?"

"Yeah, I see tons of blood. The man chopped off her head."

"No, there." He pointed away from the main pool, near the top of her pillow. "See?"

I didn't. I had to pull out a magnifying glass. Eventually I was able to spot two drops of blood that were distinct from the pool. "Splatters, I suppose."

"Splatters would be elongated," Darcy said. "These drops are round. That means they fell straight down."

I didn't have to be a forensic scientist to know he was right. "When did it happen, then?"

"When he started to hurt her the first time. This—" He raced through the pics till he found the one he wanted. "And this is from where he tried to hurt her the second time."

I examined the picture and nodded. "And the third?"

"There is no third. So it must be covered with the other blood."

"So after two false starts, he finally managed to do it." Was it possible? The victim put up a fight? Our homicidal maniac was reluctant to kill? If that was the case—why do it? It didn't make any sense. What's more, it was totally at odds with the typical profile of a serial killer. And it threw my narcissistic personality disorder theory out the window.

"This is good work, Darcy. Very good work." If only I knew what it meant.

"But you will not tell my dad, will you?"

I pulled my nose out of the pictures. "I think he should know. If he understood how good you were at this, maybe he wouldn't be such a pain in the butt every time I want to take you somewhere."

Darcy rubbed his hands together, as if he were washing them with invisible soap. "I do not think that you should tell him."

"Why? Are you afraid he might punish you?" But even before I said it, I had already sensed that wasn't the problem. But if not—

Of course. This was Darcy we were talking about, not every other self-centered male on the face of planet earth. He wasn't afraid his father would punish him.

He was afraid his father would punish me.

"Darcy, I've got to bring this evidence to the attention of the detective squad."

"Tell them you found it."

"Take credit for your work? That's just wrong. Goes against everything I believe in."

"Would you do it . . ." His awkwardness was so apparent it was painful. "Would you do it for me?"

Well, if you'd been looking at his pathetic puppy dog face, you would've agreed too, right or wrong. "All right, Darcy. For now. But as soon as I think it's . . . safe to give credit where due, I will."

"That's okay." He cocked his head to one side. "Are you going on more interviews today?"

"I sure am."

"Can I . . . Maybe . . . I was thinking . . ."

I clapped him on the shoulder. "I'd be honored if you'd come with me."

His face lit up like the spotlight on the Luxor. "Oh, boy. Oh boy oh boy oh boy!"

"Hey," I said, grabbing my coat, "you're the one who's doing a favor here. At the rate you're going, you'll have the case cracked by midnight."

19

DANE SPENCER WAS almost afraid to look at his watch. He knew he was working well past midnight; it was only a matter of how much. It was always like this, the night before a big trial. No matter how early he started, no matter how hard he worked, there were always a million things left to be done at the last moment. This time was no exception. Now it seemed clear he wouldn't be going home at all. That, too, had occurred before, which was why he always kept a spare suit and a grooming kit in his office. He didn't even need to call. Jenny knew he had a trial coming up; she wouldn't be expecting to see him anytime before she went to bed. And when she woke up and saw the other side of the bed still empty, she would just shrug and say, "Good luck."

Least it paid the bills.

Karen Dutoi was still sitting at her desk outside his office, typing each new revision of his witness outlines as soon as he slid them into her box. It was an endless process; every time he went over them he thought of something new. Thank God trials had a start date; otherwise, you could revise your strategy until the end of time.

"Go home, Karen," Spencer said, leaning against her desk. "It's late. You have a family that needs you."

"Oh, no," she replied. "If you can stand it, I can."

"I have to do this. You don't."

"But all these revisions . . ."

"I don't mind going into court with a little ink on my outlines. It's not as if anyone's going to see them but me."

"I appreciate the offer, Dane, but I know there'll be more work than this before you get to the courtroom. You're going to need me. I'm staying."

"But your kids—"

"Are fine. I'm staying. Besides, aren't you still waiting for that expert witless?" It was a little joke they'd told each other at least a dozen times.

"Yes, but that still doesn't mean you have to be here."

"What kind of joker wants to meet in the dead of the night?"

"The kind who doesn't want his employer to know he's turned quisling until he's in a room surrounded by federal marshals. Seriously, Karen—"

"Forget it. I'm not going home."

He sighed, pretending to be annoyed. In reality, it was impossible to be annoyed with her. Among other reasons, because he went for her pageboy cut and button nose in a big way. If she weren't married, he would've made a move weeks ago. Of course, technically, he was married himself. Not that he'd ever let that stop him before. Who knew? Maybe if he finally got all this work done before the sun rose, and they weren't both unconscious . . .

"Well," he said with resignation, "if we're both staying, someone's going to have to make another pot of coffee. And the unsexist, egalitarian thing would be for me to make it. The only problem with that being—I don't know how."

She laughed. "I'm right on it, boss. Just let me finish—"

Karen was cut off by a pounding at the door, so sudden it made her jump. She slipped out from behind the desk, peered through the peephole.

Must be the expert witness. A short burly man in torn jeans and a tight T-shirt. What field could possibly be his expertise? Karen wondered.

"You gotta help me!" the man said after she let him in. He was wide-eyed and panicked, looking from one of them to the other. "I spotted one of my bosses' goons in the parking garage. They know I'm here!"

Spencer stepped forward. He wasn't sure what to say. This witness could be crucial to winning a multimillion-dollar case. But looking at him, it was hard to believe he had ever been part of a professional industrial firm. "I'll call Barney, down at the security booth on the first floor lobby. He'll make sure no one gets in who isn't on the list."

"There's three of them," the man said, "against one old guy? They'll slaughter him."

"Please. Try not to be melodramatic."

"You don't get it," the man said, flailing his arms. "I left my girlfriend in there."

"What?"

"I'm not kiddin'. She's sittin' in my car. They're gonna kill her!"

"But why—"

"Please, mister, I'll explain later. But first we gotta get her out of there."

Spencer didn't know what to do. He did not trust this man, not at all. But if there really was a woman in danger, he had to help. He'd just make sure he collected Barney before he followed the man into the garage. And make sure Barney was armed.

Karen was frantically rummaging through her top desk drawer. "I know I put my passcard in here somewhere," she muttered, forehead creased. "Why is it you can never find things when you need them most?"

"I'll get mine," Spencer said, disappearing into his office. No way he was letting Karen go off with this man by herself, anyway. He walked back to his office, took his coat off the hook on the back of the door, retrieved his passcard, then returned to the lobby.

Karen was sprawled on the floor, her legs bent back, her dress bunched around her waist, a white cloth across her mouth.

"What in the hell—" But before he could finish the sentence, much less understand what was happening, he felt his left arm being jerked behind him.

The man from the hallway was holding a pair of handcuffs, and before Spencer knew what was happening, he had slid the cuffs over one wrist and snapped the other end to the doorknob.

"What is the meaning of this?" Spencer barked. "Are you working for the defendant? Because if they think they're going to bully me into giving them a settlement, you can just tell—"

"This ain't got nothing to do with your case, mister. Your number came up, that's all."

"Number? What are you talking about? Did you hurt Karen?"

"Nah. She was just in the way. Tough girl, though—knocked me up against the wall but good till I got my hands on her. She'll wake up in a hour or so. Worse she'll have is a headache. You—now that's different."

"Wh-What do you mean? What are you going to do?" He paused, the horror of his situation slowly dawning on him. "Are—Are you going to burn off my face? Like those people I read about in the paper?"

"Course not. You ain't Keter."

Spencer was terrified, but he knew better than to let that show. Even after all these years, he still went into a courtroom scared to death that he would embarrass himself. But he'd learned to cope. Indeed, he thought that perhaps the fear gave him an edge, gave him the impetus to succeed. Maybe it could do the same here. He had to look firm and strong—even if he felt anything but.

"This is your last chance. Unlock these cuffs or I will scream for help."

"Scream all you want. There's no one else on this floor. I checked. That's why she—I—made the appointment for this hour of the night."

"You—" Spencer could feel his heart racing. "You planned this."

"Yeah," the man growled. He returned from the outside hallway with two heavy implements, one of them an axe, the other a long iron rod. A branding iron. "I would've rather done this earlier. I'm not really a night person, you know? But it was important to get you in your place of work. Your primal habitat."

"Me? Why me?"

"You are Chesed. You represent a part of the primordial human form. A piece of the divine."

"I haven't done anything to you."

"You have taken God's greatest gift and tossed it away like it ain't worth nothin'."

"I don't know what you're talking about."

"Really? How is your child doing?"

"My—daughter? What? Have you done something to my kid?"

"You've done somethin' to her, not me." He looked up. "Where's the kitchen?"

"The kitchen?" Spencer twisted back and forth, trying to get close enough to slug the man. But the handcuffs held him back like a leash. "Why do you want the kitchen?"

The man balanced the branding iron in his hands, measuring its weight. "Gotta heat this little baby up."

"Oh my God. Oh my God. You *are* the one." He stopped short, his throat suddenly dry. "Look, I've got money. Tons of it. Look around you. You think this office was built on peanuts? I could make you a very rich individual."

The man shook his head. "So you've got tons of money for me. But not a dime for your own flesh and blood."

"What are you talking about?"

"How much money have you been sendin' that kid of yours?"

Spencer swallowed. There was something very strange going on here. This man knew too much, knew things no one could possibly know. "In the final divorce decree, the court did not require me to make any support payments to my wife or daughter. At the time, I was flat broke."

"On paper. Not in real life. You have a house worth more than a million bucks."

"The law does not require you to sell your home. And since it was a gift in trust from my father, my wife did not own half of it. So—"

"Lawyer talk." The man waved a hand in the air. "You abandoned your child."

"She's with her mother—"

"Did you know your Jenna was diagnosed with juvenile diabetes?"

"What?"

"Yeah. But her mother can only afford the most basic health care, and it won't cover all the insulin and other stuff she's gonna need if she wants to live past thirty."

"But—then—why didn't Abigail call—"

"Because she knew you didn't give a damn. She knew it would be a waste of time. You'd turn her down, just like you did every other time she came to you for help."

"You don't understand. Abigail is very manipulative. She uses the child—"

"I understand everythin' I need to understand." All of a sudden, Spencer realized Tucker was crouched on the floor. A second later, before he could react, another set of handcuffs had chained his right ankle to the leg of

Karen's desk. Spencer flailed back and forth, but it was no use. He was trapped.

The man disappeared again, but this time, when he returned, he was carrying a video camera. And wearing a ski mask.

"What the hell are you going to do with that?" Spencer bellowed.

"Make a movie," he replied. "Don't worry about it. You're never gonna see it." He set the camera on the desk, pushed the Record button, then picked up the axe.

"Do you think you're going to cut off my head, you bastard?" Spencer shouted, his voice rising. He tried to tell himself there was an errant hope that someone might hear, but he knew that in reality his panic was surfacing. "Well, you're not. I may be tied down, but I'm not helpless. I won't just stand here and take it! You'll never get my head!"

"That's all right," Tucker said. He pinched the blade of the axe between his fingers. A spot of blood rose to the surface. The blade was sharp—very sharp. "That's no problem at all. 'Cause I don't want your head." He raised the axe high above the arm stretched out from the desk to the doorknob, then lowered it.

20

JULY 18

THE MADDENING INSISTENCE of the doorbell finally got my eyelids open a centimeter or so. I hoped it would go away, like maybe it was just some kid selling magazines so he could go to Bible college or something, but it was unrelenting. So I eventually pushed myself out of bed, threw on a robe, and stumbled to the door.

"Amelia!" I said, doing a darn good job of acting as if I was glad to see her, even though the clock over the oven told me it was barely seven in the morning. With friends and associates like I've got, why do I bother setting an alarm? "What are you doing here so . . . unexpectedly?"

"When else am I going to catch you?" She didn't need an invitation; she pushed past me and headed into the living room. "I called all last night, but you never came home."

"Oh, sorry. I was working late. I had to do some catch-up."

"I can imagine. You don't want the killer to get a head." She paused. "That was a joke."

"I got it."

"You didn't laugh."

"It wasn't funny." I instinctively groped toward the kitchen and started the coffeemaker. When I returned to the living room, she had her fists on her hips and a scowl on her face. "Something the matter?"

"Where is it?"

"Where's what?"

"You know perfectly well what."

And I should, too, since I am Little Miss Empathy. But my gifts didn't work this early in the morning. "Can you give me a hint?"

"The coffee table! The Brancusi knockoff! You've still got this . . . this . . ." She gestured toward the offending pine object. ". . . this chewed up banged up piece of—"

"Oh, did you want me to replace this table?"

"You know perfectly well I did."

"I thought it made more sense to put it somewhere I didn't already have a coffee table."

"And that would be?"

I held up a finger. "I think the coffee's ready."

"Don't run away from me, you coward. Where is it?"

I shuffled my bare feet. "It's, um, in the bathroom."

"The bathroom! You put an expensive Brancusi-like coffee table from the Venetian in the bathroom!"

"You know how much trouble I have reaching the top shelves in there. I thought—"

"Susan Lynn Pulaski, you march up there right now and bring down that coffee table!"

"Amelia, I—"

"Susan, this thing you've got is a piece of junk. I'm going to have it burned. Go get the new table!"

"Amelia . . ." *Sure, I was mad at the time, but I got over it. Because I loved him.* "I'm really too tired to do any heavy lifting. I didn't get much sleep last night."

Her demeanor changed immediately. "You didn't? Why not?"

"I don't know," I lied. "I just . . . couldn't let go of the case, I guess. Everyone is counting on me to lead them to the killer."

"I know. When the detectives are floundering, they always start blaming you. When are you going to quit this lousy cop shop and get an office job? Help losers patch up their marriages for a hundred dollars an hour."

"Oh, I'll get over it. But in the meantime . . ." I looked down at the carpet. "I know you said no more, but I thought if you gave me another one of those little blue pills . . ."

She frowned, then started rummaging through her purse. "That's funny. Must've left them somewhere." Of course I knew she wouldn't be able to find her Valium bottle, since I was the one who took it. But I also knew that eventually she would notice, and I would be her prime suspect. Unless I threw her off the scent by asking for some. After all, if I were the thief, I wouldn't have asked, right? This is the way you learn to think in the police department. I had deviousness down to an art. "Just as well. You don't need any medication. Just try . . . running around the block or something. Soak in a hot bath."

"Yeah, okay."

"So once you've imbibed some caffeine and gotten yourself together, wanna go play around?"

"Can't. Work."

"On Saturday? They don't even expect me to come in today."

" 'Fraid so."

She grunted, then headed for the door. "Get that overpriced piece of pseudo-art out of the bathroom, understand, girlfriend?"

"Understood."

She blew me a kiss and disappeared. I grabbed some

java and fell in a heap on the sofa. I hated to disappoint Amelia. Hated stealing from her and lying to her even worse. But that table . . .

You can't imagine how I felt when I found out. But he didn't mean any harm. And I loved him.

I headed for the bathroom, but not for the table. For two of those little blue wonder pills. And then I held my head under a spigot of cold running water for about half an hour. It did not make me feel better. But it did, at least, sort of deaden the pain.

SINCE IT WASN'T A SCHOOL DAY, I called Rachel on my cell during the drive out. She was in good spirits, but busy. Basketball season. We gossiped a little and exchanged terms of endearment, but it made me realize how dramatically things had changed. It wasn't that we'd grown apart so much as just . . . separated. I suppose this was what all empty-nest parents experience. I just didn't expect it to happen while she was still in high school.

I agreed to meet Darcy at a bus stop, rather than picking him up at his home, as I normally would do. He didn't specify why, and I didn't inquire, but I could guess. We had to leave early to get crosstown by nine, so his father was probably still at home. And since Darcy wasn't supposed to be a part of this investigation, he just acted as if it were any other ordinary kind of day, leaving to catch the bus for the day-care center.

Eventually, O'Bannon would figure it out. He was a detective, after all. But if I wanted to catch this killer, I'd be crazy to refuse Darcy's help. We just had to keep it under the radar. And hope it didn't cost me my job.

When he saw me coming, he wiggled his fingers, put on that goofy grin of his, and climbed into the passenger seat.

"Morning, Darcy."

"Allegro Vanilla Bean Espresso!"

Only took me a minute. Maybe two. Slowly but surely, I was learning to speak Darcy. "That's very good. I suppose you smelled it on my breath. Shouldn't have grabbed that last cup on my way out the door."

"Or brought it in the car," Darcy added. "Or spilled it on your blouse."

"Where?" I said, looking down, and practically having a wreck in the process.

"I think that you should look at the road and I should look at your blouse," Darcy said excitedly, his hands flapping. "Does that seem like a good idea?"

"Reasonable enough."

"Did you know that more car accidents occur because women are putting on their makeup while they drive than because people use cell phones?"

"Then you're in good hands. Since I rarely wear makeup."

"It's probably hard to look at the road while you are putting that black stuff on your eyelashes."

"I'd imagine."

"Why do women put that black stuff on their eyelashes?"

How to explain. "Some men find it attractive. Or at least women think men find it attractive."

"Does it make them want to make babies?"

"Whoa now." I put my foot on the brake. "Where did that come from?"

He looked away, fidgeting with his hands. "I just . . . wondered."

"Well, it has nothing to do with that." Actually, it did, in a way, but I wasn't going into it with Darcy. "Kid, did your father ever have that . . . talk with you?"

"Talk about what?"

"You know. Birds and bees."

"I know lots about birds and bees. Did you know that it is aerodynamically impossible for a bumblebee—"

"No, I mean about men and women. About how babies are made."

His face turned blood clot red. "You mean about doing sex."

"Umm, yeah."

"We talked a little. He gave me a book with lots of pictures."

I suppressed a grin. Better than nothing, I suppose. Especially for the kid who remembers everything he reads. "Darcy, have you ever . . ."

"What?"

I shook my head. "Never mind. None of my business." What was I thinking? When would he? And with whom?

"I got a kiss from a girl once, in the sixth grade. Beatrice McKenzie."

Damn mind reader. "That was it? A kiss?"

"No. She, um, she let me . . ."

"Yes?"

"She let me touch her top part. Just for a second."

Aha. A little childhood playing doctor. "And did you . . . get anything out of it?"

"Yes. I got thrown out of school for the rest of the semester. I had to go to a special school for kids with problems. Most of them were in wheelchairs."

"And since then?"

"I do not want to get thrown out of anything. So I am very careful."

"Of course you are." When we stopped at the next light, I leaned over and gave him a quick peck on the cheek. "There. Now you've had a second kiss."

"Am—Am I going to get thrown out of something? Does this mean—?"

"It doesn't mean anything, Darcy. Except that you and I are friends. Right?"

"Right. Friends." He paused. "I like being friends with you, Susan."

"Feeling's mutual, kiddo." I saw the house and parked next to the curb. "All right, Sherlock. Showtime."

"ALL DONE?" Esther asked.

"Yeah," Tucker said, scrubbing his hands in the sink. "Done."

"No mistakes?"

"None. Hell, the porn actress fought harder than that miserable lawyer. What a crybaby he turned out to be."

"And you left nothing behind."

"Nothin'. I wore gloves. Put paper on the floor. Didn't leave any blood or anything else. Brought back the weapons. Left the secretary tied up in the closet. Just like you told me."

"And the arm?"

"Still there. Tonight I'll take care of the body."

"Perfect. Just perfect. You've done very well, Tucker. Very well indeed."

With a speed that startled her, he spun around from the sink. "How much longer is this gonna go on?"

Esther stepped back, surprised by this sudden display of emotion. "You know the plan, Tucker. You always have. The Sefirot has seven divine components. Disassembling those components will complete the act of summoning. It's a simple equation."

"Simple. Yeah. You're not the one who's out there killin' people."

"Are you saying . . . you don't wish to continue?"

"I'm sayin' it ain't that easy, killin' people."

"I know that, Tucker," she said, gently laying her hand on his shoulder. "That's why you were chosen. You are my instrument."

"I'm your hired killer! And—And—" His face crumbled into his hands. "It's hard."

"Of course it is." She stepped closer, letting him feel the body heat radiating from her. "It's a test. We approach the divine by destroying it, a daunting task. If it were easy, it would have no meaning."

"I know that," he said, not looking at her, staring at the floor. "I just—I don't know how much longer I can go on doin' this."

"I'm still your guide, aren't I?"

"Of course you are."

"And we are the wandering angels, are we not? Like those cast out and left behind in the Book of Enoch?"

"Yes, but—"

She pressed her cheek against his and held it there, very still. "You want to please me, don't you?" she whispered.

"You know I do."

"Have I been good to you?"

"You've been—like no one else ever was before. No one ever treated me good. No one ever made me feel wanted."

"And I've done . . . things for you, haven't I? Just like you've done things for me."

"I know that. I know all that. But it's . . . different."

She forcefully pushed him away, abruptly breaking contact. "You want it to end. Is that what you're saying?"

"No! I mean, I don't want *us* to end. I want—"

"Make up your mind, Tucker. You can't have it both ways."

"I want—I just—" His head fell. "I don't know what I want."

"I know what I want." She reached out and ripped open his shirt, sending the buttons flying. "I want you."

She pushed him back onto the bed. While he lay there, helplessly, she brought her tongue to the side of his face and licked it. "You love me. I know you do."

"I do," he echoed softly.

She pulled off his pants with as much violence as she had the shirt. "And you want me just like I want you?"

"More," he murmured. "More."

"Then come to me." She pulled him up by the arms and pressed herself against him. She dug in with her long fingernails and dragged them down the length of his back. Blood rose to the surface.

"Oh, my God, yes," he said, weak, helpless. "Oh, my God!"

She shoved him back against the bed then straddled him.

"This is what you wanted, isn't it?" she said, rocking her hips.

"Oh, yes."

"You earned this. By what you did tonight." She moved faster, rhythmically. His eyes lit.

"Oh, God. Oh, God, yes!"

She accelerated her thrusts. "We're a team, Tucker. In every possible way. We are one person. Two primordial forms reunited. We have what no one else has, what no one else has ever had. We represent the Aleph."

His eyes ballooned. His head swung back and forth. "Oh, God. God God God God God . . ."

She knew this wouldn't last much longer. She crouched down and bit his earlobe, hard enough to draw blood. "And you want us to continue to work together, don't you? In every possible way? The next prime is fast approaching. You don't want to disappoint me, do you?"

"Noooooooo . . . !"

When it was over, she lay beside him for a long time, stroking his hair until he fell sound asleep.

He was good. At least for now. He would be faithful to her. If she had to proceed without him at some point, so be it. But until then, he was her slave. This powerful brutish muscleman. Her willing slave.

She gathered her belongings and slipped out the front door.

I LEFT DARCY outside to scout the grounds. Probably not the best use of his talents, but I couldn't take him inside a porn studio, even if they weren't filming at the moment—especially after that last conversation.

Inside, I was greeted by Gina Berend, the woman who had served as Danielle Dunn's top aide and vice president of her company. Her face was perfect—as far as I could tell, it never moved—and her attire was immaculate, but for all that, the stress emanating from her was palpable. After the loss of Danielle, she was running the business. Moreover, I also got a distinct feeling that she was mourning the loss of a close and dear friend, someone she not only admired but loved.

"Thank you for agreeing to see me," I said, shaking her hand. I tried not to stare at her face. She was obviously a master at the art of makeup, what my mother used to call "putting on her face," a talent at which I was so inept that I rarely tried. All hail the natural girl, right? "I know this must be difficult for you."

"It is," Gina said softly. There was no trace of the martyr in her voice; it was a simple statement of fact. "But I want the man who hurt Danielle caught."

"I understand. We all do. That's why I've been brought in on the case."

"So I gathered. Although I don't know what I could tell you that I haven't already told the detectives."

It isn't a matter of you telling me something you didn't tell Granger's troops, I thought. It was a matter of asking the questions they wouldn't think to ask. "How long had you known Danielle?"

"Almost seven years now. I came on board about a year after she formed her own company."

"So you weren't the first vice president."

"No. Or the second, for that matter. A series of men who had considerably more experience in the straight-to-video world preceded me. But none of them stayed long."

"Why is that?"

"Pick your own explanation. Most of them complained that Danielle was difficult to work with, which is ridiculous. She was a perfectionist, true. She had a vision of what her films should be and she remained true to it. But she was never difficult. I think those men just had a problem accepting a woman as their boss. Perhaps you've had some experiences along that line yourself."

"Once or twice." And I didn't have the added credibility problem of having worked as a porn actress. "The two of you hit it off?"

"Almost immediately." She gestured toward a chair in the front lobby. The furniture was functional but not plush. The only items hanging on the walls were clippings and magazine covers featuring the deceased president of the studio. "It was more than just personality. It was like . . . I don't know. I understood what she was trying to do. So many women have a negative attitude toward porn that they simply couldn't comprehend, much less embrace, what Danielle was trying to do. But I got it, right off the bat. At DannyDunn Studios, our productions aren't about female subjugation. They're about female empowerment."

"So I've read."

"Have you seen any of Danielle's pictures?"

"I'm afraid I haven't." And wouldn't admit it if I had.

"You might be surprised. The scripts may follow a formula, but they're smart, witty. She looked for actors based upon their ability to actually act, not the size of their genitalia. Even when she shot straight-to-video, she insisted on top-flight lighting, quality sound, elements that might be invisible to the average viewer, but made a huge result in the final product. That's why people are able to distinguish a DannyDunn film from others, why people became devoted fans and repeat customers. After you've been to Disney World, the school carnival just isn't all that exciting anymore."

"I can appreciate and admire anyone who tries to do their best work," I said. Even if I still thought the work was of dubious merit. "I know you've been asked this before, but can you think of any reason why someone might want to kill Danielle?"

"I wish all they'd done was kill her." Gina's face hardened. "You're asking if I know why anyone would want to torture her. Mutilate her. And the answer is no."

"Did she have any enemies?"

"She had competitors." Gina walked behind the desk just beside the front door and pulled out a ledger. "More than one small film studio bit the dust because Danny-Dunn commanded such a huge market share. And it was well known in the industry that she was the heart and soul, not to mention the brains, of the company."

"If she went down, so did the studio."

"So they might think. I'm going to do my damnedest to keep it going. To keep Danielle's dream alive."

"Good for you." I couldn't believe I was cheering for a woman to keep churning out pornography. But such was the depth of Gina's feeling; it oozed sincerity. "Can you give me a list of some of these competitors?"

"I can. But how does that explain the—the—" She could hardly make herself say it. "The torture. The . . . decapitation?"

It didn't, and I didn't believe for a minute that this crime was committed by some stogie-chomping porn-meister. But I had to at least consider the possibility. "Did Danielle ever receive any threats?"

"Sure. All the time. It was inevitable. Every time she got a little publicity, every time a magazine did a feature piece on her, some of the desert rats would come out of their caves and send her hate mail. Some of it was from women—you know, Take Back the Night types who still clung to the tenuous link between pornography and sexual assaults. But most of it was from men. Very religious men. People with bad penmanship and worse spelling who called her the Whore of Babylon or the Witch of Endor or whatever trite and misapplied biblical allusion first popped into their heads. Of course, it was always clear from the letters that the authors had watched her films. Probably several of them. Probably done the solo nasty while they conducted their research. And then, rather than facing up to their own guilt, blamed it all on Danielle."

Disturbing. Mostly because it made me wonder if Granger's lame "sex prude" theory might possibly be correct. "Did you report these letters to the police?"

"No. What good would it do? It wasn't as if they were signing their names. We thought they were all impotent mother-fixated nutcases. Vile but harmless."

"And yet, someone did come after Danielle. Someone who clearly was . . . not entirely sane."

"Yes," she said, her chin lowering. "I know. But I still can't believe it was any of these whack jobs. At the end of the day, they'd be more likely to bad-mouth Danielle at a tent revival meeting than commit an act of violence."

I had to admit that the enormity of the event, the amount of planning and detail—weird detail—suggested that something else was at hand. But there had to be more to this than fervent sexual prudery. I didn't know why this man picked Danielle for his next victim. But it wasn't because of the movies she made. "Could I get copies of the letters?"

"Your detectives already took them."

I nodded. "Anything else you can tell me?"

"Just this." Gina sat beside me on the sofa, about as close as two women could sit without one of them getting nervous. "Danielle was a good person. A genuinely good-hearted person. Don't let anyone convince you otherwise. She came from a very difficult background. Kicked out of her home when she was sixteen."

"Why?"

"I don't know. She wouldn't tell. I know her mother was an alcoholic and abusive, but Danny didn't talk about it. From that age on, she made her own way in the world. And there weren't that many opportunities for a sixteen-year-old girl on her own in Vegas. She did the strip joints, then the adult films, but she never let it get her down. And she never stopped planning, never took her eyes off the prize. She knew she was capable of doing bigger, greater things, and when the opportunity came, she seized it. She built something wonderful—more than that. She built something important. How many people can say the same?"

A good and valid question. But if I was going to find her killer, I couldn't afford the luxury of canonizing her. "Did Danielle have any . . . secrets?"

"No." A beat. "Not that I know of."

I've had so much experience at this that now, I'm not always sure what I'm listening to—my inner instincts or the telltale traces that even the most gifted liars couldn't erase. But I was definitely getting some flashing lights from the seemingly guileless Gina. None of the obvious signs like her eyes drifting to the left; after all, she wasn't inventing, she was denying. On the other hand, I had detected a hesitation, slight, but the first I'd encountered yet in a conversation that she'd had at least twice before with other detectives. For whatever reason, her subconscious had to think a nanosecond before she gave her answer. She blinked, and now, as I stared at her without answering, she shifted her crossed legs and began to tap the floor with her left toe. Her breathing remained steady, her face didn't flush. She held her hands together in her lap.

"Do you suppose there were some secrets you didn't know about?"

"I—don't have any reason to think so."

"Ma'am, I urge you not to hold back anything that might conceivably—"

"I'm not." Her voice rose with the denial, both in pitch and volume. She shrugged, not very convincingly. She smiled, but it was lopsided, asymmetrical. "I mean, there's hardly anyone in town who has had more written about her than Danielle did. Everyone knows her past, her troubled childhood, how she rose from bit actress to major industry player. What secrets could there possibly be?"

That I didn't know. But every word Gina spoke convinced me that there was something. "Once again, I have to emphasize the importance of not withholding any information that might help us find the link—"

"I assure you, I'm not. Danielle was the most up-front person I've ever met. She had no secrets."

"A boyfriend, maybe?"

"Not at present. She had dated here and there, but . . . it never really took."

"A girlfriend, then."

"The characters she played in the movies were just that. Characters. Fictional."

"So she wasn't dating anyone on a regular basis?"

"Not to my knowledge."

"I'd imagine she would be an intimidating partner. Someone that confident. Self-assured."

"True. And I think . . . well, to be blunt, she was just too smart for that. She didn't need a man to make her life complete. Don't get me wrong. I'm not saying she was gay. I'm just saying . . . her life was already whole. Do you understand?"

"I think, perhaps . . ."

"I notice you're not wearing a ring. Are you married?"

I felt my back stiffening. "Not anymore."

"I guessed as much. You've got a full life. You don't need a man to tell you who you are."

A full life. I felt a powerful aching at the pit of my stomach. If only it were so. I didn't need a man to tell me who I was. I needed a man to tell me why I should get out of bed every day. To tell me why I shouldn't order a double scotch and pour the whole bottle of Valium into it and—

No. I had to stay on task. "Could I see Danielle's office?"

Gina shrugged. "I guess. But the detectives have already gone over it with microscopic scrutiny. I don't know what you could see that they didn't."

"It's not a matter of seeing something different," I replied. "It's a matter of seeing it with a different set of eyes."

"All right. But I'll warn you." She tilted her head slightly to one side. "Her office is not what you might expect."

21

GINA HAD BEEN RIGHT; Danielle Dunn's office was not what I expected. I imagined a professional environment—mahogany tables and desks and large windows and eighteenth century maps hanging on the walls. A lawyer's office, or an accountant's. What I found looked more like a pre-adolescent girl's dream hideaway.

"She didn't entertain clients in here," Gina explained. "This was just for her."

"I can see that," I said quietly.

"Is there anything else . . . ?"

"No. If you don't mind, I'd prefer to be left alone. It's easier for me to listen."

Gina blinked. "Listen? To what?"

"To the room," I said, closing my eyes.

The soft click of the door told me Gina had exited. I let my mind wander, burrowing down into deep contemplation of what I had seen. This office was a little too obvious to be the secret I'd sensed Gina was withholding. But it was a start in the right direction. At least, I hoped it was.

The predominant color was pink. Curtains, wallpaper, mostly plastic furniture. Pink. There was no desk as such, but the center of the room had a round plastic table, low to the ground. More a playground than an office. Someplace to play pretend games with your Barbies.

Though to be fair, I spotted no Barbies, or Kens, but an entire wall of the room was covered with stuffed animals. Bears, giraffes, koalas, dogs, and cats. Lots and lots of cats.

I opened my eyes. Why would she do this? Even if it was restricted from unfamiliar visitors, there was always a chance someone might stumble in. How could this place help her maintain her reputation in the business world? What was its purpose?

Its purpose, I realized, was to make Danielle happy. To recapture the innocent childhood she never had. To give her a place of retreat. Escape. Based on what I'd read, that seemed to be the theme that permeated all her films. Sure, they were sexual fantasies, but they also had strong strains of escapism. Pirate stories, outer space tales, Jane Eyre–like sagas of strong women finding a place for themselves in the Victorian world. None of them involved little girl fantasies; catering to that fetish would've been too controversial. So why did she indulge in it herself? What was she trying to accomplish? What need did this satisfy? What had she lost that she was trying to reclaim?

I wasn't going to find the answers to my questions just standing around. I strolled through the room, brushing my fingers on the artificial surfaces, looking for anything out of the ordinary (that is, more so than the entire room), anything that might give me a clue to who Danielle Dunn really was. I opened a closet door and found a toy collection that would be the envy of the richest kid in Summerlin. But there was no Trivial Pursuit, no Monopoly, no Scrabble, nothing a self-respecting adult might play. It was Careers and Mystery Date and Talk to Me Girlfriend. A huge collection of dolls, I think they were from that woman's collection, Madame Whatever. Or maybe Marie Osmond. And American Girls. I wasn't sure. What I knew about dolls you could fit in a thimble.

There were bead kits for making jewelry. Crafts kits for making homemade bookmarks, valentines, calendars. Tons of books, but all of the same sort—*Little Women, Anne of Green Gables, Z is for Zacharias, Black Beauty.*

My first impression was that she was trying to recapture her lost childhood, but she left home when she was sixteen, an age when I would've expected her to be well beyond most of this stuff. Rachel had been through a bead jewelry phase, too, but that was a good long time ago. No, there had to be something more going on here. If only I could figure out what it was.

I closed the closet door and examined the pictures hanging on the wall. They were all of Danielle. Sometimes she was paired with other people, but she was always present. There were no family photos, no pics of mom and dad, no siblings. Most were promotional photos taken from the sets of various films. In one, her blond hair was tightly tied, giving her a youthful, almost innocent look. She was either very young or skillfully using makeup to convey that illusion. In the next, her face was surrounded by blond ringlets and she was wearing a low-necked Regency costume. I could only imagine what the film must've been. *Pride and Prejudice,* with explicit sex. Did Elizabeth get it on with Darcy, or perhaps one of her sisters? It made the mind reel.

The only photos I found that didn't appear to be stock shots, either taken on a set or by pros at celebrity events, were on a table in the corner that presumably functioned as Danielle's work space. The top of the desktop was almost the antithesis of my own—tidy, organized, and devoid of paper. Was Danielle a neat freak, or had Gina done some after-the-fact expurgation? At any rate, in one corner, she had framed a series of pictures that showed Danielle surrounded by large numbers of small children, hordes of them. Dorothy surrounded by munchkins, except the munchkins adored her.

How did a notorious porn star manage to make public appearances with children without being inundated by objections from the PTA? Where were these taken? Public schools? YMCAs? In some, she appeared to be handing out gifts, the same type of fuzzy fluff that filled her office. What could be the purpose? Usually, when celebs choose their charities, they target groups that might create goodwill that would lead to business opportunities. But there was little chance that these toddlers were going to become porn flick aficionados anytime in the near future. Every appearance must be fraught with controversy and a million hoops to jump through. Why did she do it?

And how did that relate to her secret? If it did. Maybe it was the Valium coursing through my system, but I had the distinct feeling I was not in top form. My antennae were not firing like they should. I was missing something. I knew it. And I hated myself for it.

I found one more photo, tucked on the wall behind an elaborate two-story dollhouse, one big enough to house Barbie, Skipper, and their entire extended family. She was holding a stuffed animal and dressed in a rather skimpy undergarment and—

Wait. I was missing the obvious. I didn't need Colin to point out the punning that was going on here. She was holding a teddy; she was wearing a teddy.

I peered at the photo, once again letting my mind wander. What did it mean? Why had she allowed this one anomalous photo in this child's paradise? Granger and his team must've spotted it, and I could imagine the snarky macho remarks it must've engendered. But I saw it as something more. Like maybe the key to the puzzle.

I turned back to the shelf inundated with stuffed animals where E.T. could've easily hidden. Took me almost five minutes to find the one I wanted. The bear she was holding in the picture. I wasn't certain, but I believe the distinctive cap and attire identified this furry gentleman as Paddington Bear. I think. Like I said, I was more a stickball and riding-my-bike-with-no-hands kind of girl.

I held the little ball of fluff in my hands. There was nothing extraordinary about it. I was glad no one else was in the room, because if they were, I felt certain I would become an instant object of ridicule. At the same time, there was something . . .

I squeezed the teddy bear, hard. I don't know what I expected—maybe it would cry "Mama" or something. It didn't. No sound at all. But inside, I felt something crunch.

Zipper in the back. I opened it up and found a long envelope. Stuffed with cash.

Now I was cooking with gas. A slush fund. Payoffs. Bribes. The stuff murder motives were made of. I pulled the envelope out and stared at it.

Only four words on the front: CLARK COUNTY CHILDREN'S HOME.

The money was going to a children's home? An orphanage for wayward children or something? What would be the point of making a charitable contribution in cash? You wouldn't even get the tax deduction. I'd never heard or read anything about this, and Gina didn't mention it, so it couldn't have been for publicity purposes. What was going on here? A quick riffle through the cash suggested that there were several thousand dollars tucked in there.

I bagged it, marked the bag, then tucked it inside my jacket. I had no idea what it meant. But I was certain it was important. Not that I had any illusion that this was the big elusive secret I had been seeking. But perhaps, with a little luck and intuition, it might lead me to it.

I FOUND DARCY outside the studio—far outside, actually. I was afraid I had lost him. I did find him eventually, almost a quarter of a mile away, walking around an old water tower in an uncultivated dusty strip of desert behind the studio.

"Find anything of interest?" I asked him.

He was pacing in circles, staring at the muddy ground. "I did not like the studio. I think that is a place where they do sex." His hands began flapping with the utterance of the last word.

"Well . . . perhaps. Mostly simulated, I think."

His head tilted at an odd angle; the inflection of his voice, though questioning, was all wrong. "Simulated?"

"Yeah. You know. They fake it."

"They were doing sex but not really doing sex?"

"Yeah, they just—look, I don't really know that much about it."

"About doing sex?"

"About—" I pressed my hand against my forehead. I was not getting dragged into this. "Look, let's get back in the car and head downtown. I'll tell you what I learned. Maybe you can make some sense of it."

He looked up at me, hands still flapping. "Do you know how many water towers there are in Las Vegas?"

I gave him a long look. "Two hundred and twelve."

His eyes widened as if he were impressed. "That was true in 1971. You should update the books in your library."

"Yeah, well, I'm on a tight budget." No way I was going to tell him I just plucked that number out of the air.

"Today there are four hundred sixty-six. And twelve more are being planned."

"Do tell."

"We need lots of water towers. Las Vegas is in the middle of a desert."

"That fact I actually knew."

"This one leaks." He pointed up at the base of the water repository, then down to a wet patch on the ground.

Apparently it had been dripping for some time because the muddy area was quite sizeable.

"Well, when we get back to headquarters, we can report that to the city officials. Don't want our tax dollars going to waste."

"The leak makes mud."

"Water and dirt will do that."

"The killer tracked mud into the crime scene."

I stopped, pivoted. "And how did you know that?"

"I saw where the tracks had been fixed and lifted when I—"

"When you broke into the crime scene. Yes, don't remind me." I crouched down on the ground. "So you think this is where the mud came from?" I placed a finger in the sticky ooze. That would explain the presence of mud when we hadn't had rainfall for about two months. But why would the killer be hanging around the water tower?

Darcy grasped a rung on the ascension ladder on the east side of the tower. "Do you know that this ladder has one hundred and forty-two rungs?"

"Does it? I wouldn't have guessed a rung over one-forty. But why would anyone want to—"

I looked up to the top of the ladder, and the answer to the question was so obvious I didn't even need to finish asking. Not so obvious that any of us had noticed it before, mind you, but obvious once Darcy led you to it. "If he climbed to the top and used a pair of field glasses," I said, "he could see straight into the studio's second-story soundstage."

"If he was not afraid of heights. I do not like heights. I like for my feet to be on the ground. Do you like—"

"And that would explain how he knew so much about what was going on in there. How he knew that handcuffs—real ones—could be useful. How he knew everyone else had left and Danielle was alone. How he knew where to find her. He'd been spying on her from this water tower, waiting for his opportunity."

Darcy looked up at me sheepishly. "Have I been useful?"

"Of course you have. This confirms that she wasn't chosen randomly. That the killer was waiting for an opportunity to get to Danielle. And perhaps, that it was important that he confront her in her workplace."

"Do you think that maybe he wanted to do sex with her?"

"No." I batted a finger against my lips. "No, I don't think that has anything to do with it."

"Then what does?"

"I don't know." Teddy bears. And that formula for testing prime numbers. Not that any of that makes the slightest amount of sense. I squeezed him on the shoulder. "I suppose I don't need to mention that this investigation has become a custard event."

He jumped up and down. "Very Excellent Day! Very Excellent Day!"

"An overstatement, perhaps. But I'm starving. What flavor are we having today? Wait, don't—"

But it was too late. "Today is Thursday, and it is the third Thursday of the month, so that would mean whichever flavor is third in the alphabet, unless they have Pumpkin Crunch, because Pumpkin Crunch always wins on Thursdays, unless it is spring, because in spring they have fruit flavors that they do not have in the fall, like . . ."

WE HAD ALMOST MADE IT to the custard joint when O'Bannon rang me on my cell phone. "Where are you?" he asked, without even bothering with niceties like "hello."

"I'm on my way back from DannyDunn Studios," I

said, not exactly answering the question—but close enough to get by, I hoped. "Why?"

"We have a third victim."

"God." I felt my heart sinking to the base of my chest. "Are you sure?"

"Well, we haven't found the corpse yet—at least not the majority of it. But all signs point to the same guy. How soon can you get to the Legal Arts Office Complex on Sanders and 47th?"

"About ten minutes. I'll just have to drop off—" I stopped myself just in the nick of time. "My dry cleaning."

"Huh?"

"I'll be there before you know it. So . . . I suppose you're working off what was left behind? Another head? Or just the face?"

"Neither."

"Then how do you know—"

"This time the bastard chopped off his left arm."

"His—" I felt my blood pressure rising. "What sense does that make?"

"That's what we keep hoping you'll tell us. See you soon." He rang off. I'd have to be deaf to miss the seriously gruff tone in his voice.

"Darcy, you'll have to give me a rain check on the custard. Got to visit another crime scene."

"I want to go with you!"

"I know you do. And I wish you could. But it's not a choice. And don't go stealing any more badges from your father." I gave him a wink. "I'll sneak you in myself. As soon as I can."

"Promise?"

"Swear to God and hope to die."

"Could I—Can—Maybe—Can I wait outside in your car?"

"Oh . . . . I suppose. But keep your head down. Especially if your father shows up. As soon as I know something, I'll come tell you." And I meant it.

That's what we keep hoping you'll tell us.

But . . . first maybe I'd stop for gas, maybe a vanilla Coke. Anything to wash a pill down. No way I could face this without a triple dose. At least. And as I swallowed the pill, I tried not to think about the fact that I was getting dangerously near the bottom of Amelia's bottle. I didn't know how I could survive without this stuff.

"ALL TAKEN CARE OF?" Esther asked him, as she slid the key into the lock.

"Perfect. No problems. This was an easy one."

"Thank goodness."

"From now on, I think we should leave all the bodies at places that don't have people swarmin' around. Makes it a lot easier."

"Unfortunately, that choice is not for us to make."

She pushed open the door and entered the deserted office. The cluttered cubicles, the desks stacked high with paperwork, the flickering image of computer screen savers, all gave notice that this was a busy office during the day. But now, in the dead of the night, they had it to themselves.

"This computer seems to be operational," Esther said, as she slid into one of the barely functional chairs in a tiny cubicle.

"Why do you use a different one each time?"

"Just to be cautious. Computers leave a trail that can be followed. If someone knows where to look." She punched a few keys and brought up a large database formatted in Microsoft Excel with the speed of someone who had done this many times. "And now, to determine who comes next."

"I brought the calculator," Tucker said.

"You're a dear. But let me see if I can do without." She mentally processed the calculation, entered the variables. Once she had a list of names, she ran them through the numerology algorithm she had devised herself. And a few minutes later, she had a name.

"Did I get it right?" she asked.

Tucker had been using the calculator to check her work, hovering over her shoulder. "Perfectly. You're a perfect woman. You make me wanna—"

"Yes, yes, we'll talk about that later. For now, let's keep our focus on the matter at hand. See who this person is."

A few more keystrokes and she had a picture with a condensed biography.

She let out a slow whistle. "Tucker—do you know who that is?"

"Nah. Should I?"

She smiled to herself. "I suppose not. Joshua Brazee is one of the most successful performers in Vegas. He headlines at the Florence. I wonder what he did." A few more keystrokes, then she scanned the screen that appeared. "It seems even fame and fortune cannot immunize you from . . . cruelty. The sin of ingratitude. This will be a pleasure. A difficult operation, to be sure. But a pleasure. I don't know any situation that better could have served our purpose." She blanked the screen, then turned to face her accomplice. "I know this must all seem random to you, Tucker, but I have a strong feeling that our destiny is somehow . . . being guided."

"You're my guide."

"I know. But there's more to it than that."

"The numbers?"

"Indeed. The numbers. With a consciousness of their own." She printed out the essential information, then tucked it into her pocket. "Come, Tucker. This will require a lot of preparation. The next prime is tomorrow."

"Whatever you say. Whatever you say." Like an obedient puppy, he followed her, careful not to make any unnecessary sound, as they left the office and closed the door behind them. The door that read, in large black stenciled letters: DEPARTMENT OF HUMAN SERVICES.

22

I DON'T KNOW—maybe I've watched too many episodes of *Boston Legal.* I just expected to find something a little snazzier when I stepped onto the sixteenth floor of one of the highest of high-rises in downtown Vegas and entered the front offices of Hucalak & Llewellyn, a top Vegas law firm. Instead, I found a lobby that looked as if Godzilla had used it for a piñata. The front window by the door had been smashed; shattered glass lay all over the floor. Chairs were upended; files were strewn everywhere. Almost every piece of furniture had been dented or damaged in one way or another. But the worst was the receptionist's desk. It had a huge gash in the outside right corner; unless I was very much mistaken, the signature of the executioner's axe. Attached to the leg of the desk, a dangling pair of handcuffs. And attached to the other end of the handcuffs—a severed arm, surrounded by a pool of blood.

"What the hell happened in here?" I asked Granger, who as usual, was standing around the crime scene "supervising." I guess once you're promoted to head of the detective squad you can let your minions do all the work.

"That's what we were hoping—"

"Yeah, yeah, I know." I scanned the room, standing on tiptoes so I could see over the heads of all the criminalists buzzing around the premises. "Cause of death?"

"No official word. But look." He pointed to the immense stain on the carpet. "Rennard tells me there's maybe seven pints of blood on the floor. And the average joe only has ten to twelve."

He bled to death. Swell. "When did it happen?"

"Last night."

"I saw a security desk downstairs. Have you checked the Admit list?"

"We will. But it looks as if the perp broke in." He pointed to the glass shards by the door. "Shoved his hand through the tinted glass, then opened the front door from the inside."

I nodded. "Is there a head somewhere that goes with this arm?"

"Yes. But it isn't here."

"Then where—"

"Still attached to its neck. Got a call a minute ago, while we were waiting for you to show up. Found the body in a rock quarry about ten miles north of here."

"And you're sure it's the right one?"

"Unless there are multiple corpses lying around town missing their left arm, yes. Think it's the same killer?"

"Hard to say. The *modus operandi*—or rather—the *murderus operandi*—is somewhat different, cutting off an arm instead of the head or the face, but . . ." I paused. "Have you heard whether the body was branded?"

Granger nodded. "Letter C."

"Then it's the same creep."

I closed my eyes and let it all soak in. I didn't know why the killer had taken the chance of coming to a high-glitz palace like this, or why he took an arm instead of a head, or why he branded them, or really, anything else. But just the same . . .

"Any witnesses?"

"Sort of. A secretary was here. Karen Dutoi. Tried to shove him out of the way and make a run for it. He was too strong for her. She only saw him for an instant before he chloroformed her. Her description matches what we got from the parking lot attendant." His eyes got all squinty, which I knew meant he was thinking, always a dangerous prospect. "What's wrong with you?"

"What do you mean?" I said, arms akimbo. The best defense is a strong offense, right? So I tried to be seriously offensive. "There's not a damn thing wrong with me, except that there's some maniac running around hacking off people's body parts for no apparent reason."

"You sound . . . funny."

"Are you going to start that crap again? Because I've had it up to here with these false accusations."

"Did you hear that? 'Cause if you didn't, I did."

"Hear what?"

"There's only one *s* in the middle of accusations. But you made it sound as if there were ten."

"You're full of it."

"It's not as if you don't have a history."

"I haven't had a drink in months, asshole. This is just your way of trying to get me off the case."

"No. This is just my way of protecting my investigation. But since I can't fire you—not at this moment, anyway—why don't you get to work?"

With pleasure. I pushed past him and scanned the room, trying to decide who I wanted to tackle first. I saw a sketch artist working with an elderly man—probably last night's security man describing everyone he saw come into the building at or around the time of death. Kestner, the department's accountant, was going over some ledgers; Granger was probably chasing the angle that the murder might relate to some financial impropriety. It didn't. Crenshaw and a chemist I didn't know were working over the glass shards by the front door while someone else sprayed for fingerprints. Spotted a CSI geologist scrutinizing a brownish stain on the floor;

my guess was our killer still had mud on his shoes. Rennard, the serologist, was working on the copious bloodstain on the beige carpet. Everyone seemed to have something to do—everyone but me. My specialty was supposed to be the criminal's mind. Pity he didn't leave it behind for me to examine.

I decided to start with Crenshaw. He'd never failed me in the past. "Anything of interest, Tony?"

"What have I taught you, Susan? At a crime scene, everything is of interest."

"Yeah, yeah, but—"

"Have you met Sean Latham? He's a chemist. Specializes in glass."

He was a short man, bespectacled, slightly balding, toothy smile. Reminded me of Wally Cox. "Nice to meet you, Sean. What can you tell me about the glass?"

"Well," he said, clearing his throat. Did I make him nervous? I seemed to have that effect on people sometimes. I have no idea why. "Glass is actually not a solid but a liquid that has been cooled to such a degree that it solidifies and is held together between two outer layers. That's why it breaks so easily."

I saw Tony behind him, grinning. "That's fascinating, but what I really meant was—what can you tell me about the glass in this room?"

"I am telling you about the glass in this room. Like all glass, it breaks in a predictable manner. Every shard from a broken pane will have the same intrinsic properties as every other piece."

"I still don't see—"

Tony decided to be merciful. "Tell her about the hackle and rib marks," he said, cutting in.

"Oh, that." Latham cleared his throat again. "Those are the fracture marks—envision them as strands in a spider's web, if you will. By studying them, we can tell whether the glass was broken from the inside or the outside."

"And here?"

"The glass was broken from the inside."

"The inside? But then shouldn't the glass shards be on the outside?"

"Yes. And since they aren't—"

"We know our killer isn't an idiot. He moved them."

"Bingo."

"But how does that help us?"

"Two ways. We can dust the glass shards for prints—although I'll admit that's a long shot. More important, if you bring us a subject, and we find a trace of glass caught in the cuff of his pant or the sleeve of his shirt—"

"We can prove he's the one who broke the window! Because every shard of glass from a broken pane has the same properties as all the others."

Latham glanced at Crenshaw. "You were right. She is smarter than Granger gives her credit for."

"What?"

IN THE MANY YEARS I've worked with the LVPD, I've seen a lot of strange stuff. Worse, I've seen my friend Amelia do a lot of strange stuff. Hunched on all fours over tire tracks. Testing a footprint for silica content with her tongue. And most recently, trying to lift a mathematical equation off a cookstove. But somehow, none of that prepared me for finding her spread-eagled and pressed flat against the wall, her head turned to one side. Like she was listening to the walls. While under arrest.

"Please tell me you don't hear rats," I said. "Because, tough girl though I am, if this place has rats, I'm outta here."

I saw Amelia smile—okay, it was more like a twitch,

because her face was pressed up against the wall so she had the look of an astronaut traveling at several Gs, but still, I felt certain she appreciated my humor. "I'm not listening," she said, out of the corner of her mouth. "I'm experimenting."

Okay, I'll bite. "You're . . . trying to find out if hugging a wall can substitute for hugging a man."

"No fair bringing my abysmal love life into this." She stepped away from the wall, then shined an infrared spectrometer on the spot where the side of her face had been. "Voilà!"

"Should I be impressed?"

"No. My ear is impressed."

"Your . . . Okay, like, I have a master's degree, but I'm just going to be bold and admit that I don't know what the hell you're talking about."

"My ear left an impression. And it only took about a minute. See?" She pointed to a spot on the wall about five feet up and, sure enough, under the glow of the light, I could see faint traces of the outline of Amelia's ear. "The skin covering the cartilage of the ear secretes just like fingertips. And the shape of each person's ear is distinctive."

"You're making this up."

"I'm not. In 1999, a Washington State D.A. got a conviction based on an earprint. I'm not saying they're as good as dactylograms—" She hesitated. "—that means fingerprints—"

"I know what dactylograms are!" But only because Tony frequently reminds me.

"—but they're more than good enough to confirm a potential suspect's identity."

"If you have an earprint. So I'm hoping we do."

"We do." She walked me around to the wall on the opposite side of the dividing corridor. It was basically the same as the other—same surface, same paint. She shined her little light and, sure enough: earprint. "It's going to be tricky lifting this off the wall. There's a conflict among authorities as to the best procedure. But I'll get it for you."

"It's probably the victim."

"I think not. One of the officers who found the body photographed the ear and faxed it to me. They look very different. Doesn't match the secretary, either. I believe we have the killer's ear."

"But why would the killer press his ear against the wall?"

"He wouldn't. My guess is it happened when the secretary gave him a shove and made a break for it. Bad guy gets flung against the wall, leaves aural impression."

"But he wouldn't have been there for a full minute."

"No, but he would've hit the wall with great force. That makes the difference. Look." She pointed toward the earprint. "You can even see a slight depression in the wall. He hit it hard."

"I don't suppose the FBI has a database of earprints."

"Would that they did. But no. This will still be useful, though, to tie the suspect to this crime. If you catch him."

If you catch him. If *you* catch him.

"Susan? You all right?"

I snapped myself out of it. "Sorry. I'm fine."

"Well, actually . . ." She made sure no one was listening, then leaned in closer. "You're not. Look, I know you're going to want to work all night on this, but that won't accomplish anything anyway. What say you and I go out tonight and party?"

"What did you have in mind?"

"One word: Chippendales."

I gave her a long look. "Boy, it has been a long time since you've been out on a date."

She giggled. I was so lucky to have a friend like her.

"I'll call you at the office around nine. I won't take no for an answer."

I KNEW WE'D FIND a formula somewhere in this place. Or if we didn't, Darcy would. I just didn't expect to find it in the carpet. Written in blood.

"Holy shit!" Dr. Rennard said.

I should explain that Dr. Rennard, our chief serologist, is in his sixties, extremely prim, proper, and conservative. He calls me Miss Pulaski. He wears a hat. And worse, he takes it off when I enter the room. He always wears a tie, speaks in proper formal English, and has never to my knowledge said the word "Gosh," much less any stronger expletive. So you can imagine my reaction when I hear this sweet old geezer suddenly ejaculate "Holy shit!"

He was standing above the immense bloodstain, where the dismembered arm had been dangling before the coroner's team packed it in ice and took it away. He was staring at the floor as if he'd never seen blood before in his entire life.

I inched beside him. "What is it?"

He pointed downward, his arm shaking. "The . . . blood."

I couldn't for the life of me figure out what he was talking about. "Doctor? I . . . know there's blood. We all saw it when we came in. One of those funny facts of criminology—where you find severed arms, you usually find blood."

"But—but—" His face was awash with confusion. "We always . . . microscrutinize. We take samples. We fix the stain, then lay paper to preserve it. I never thought to look at the . . . the . . . big picture."

"The big picture? Of blood?"

"I mean, who would?" The man looked so shaken, if I'd had any Valium left, I would've given it to him. "And it wasn't really apparent until the fixative set in."

I grabbed him by the shoulders. In the movies, people always shake and slap guys who are acting like this, but I resisted that temptation, since he already looked as if he were about to come apart at the seams. "Dr. Rennard, have you found something that could be useful to the investigation? If you have, please tell me."

He nodded shakily, then removed the remainder of the protective butcher paper and stared at the stain as a whole. The big picture.

It took me a minute. It was like staring at one of those Magic Eye puzzles where you have to let your eyes go into deep focus until the hidden reverse three-dimensional image finally appears. For the longest time, I saw nothing.

And then it came to me. What else could it be? Mathematical equations. Two of them. Scrawled in the bloodstained carpet.

23

I TOOK the equations down, best I could make them out, scrabbling for position while Amelia and the videographers and maybe half a hundred other criminalists fought for access.

I didn't understand these equations any more than I had any of the others, except that these did not appear to be quite so complex. Perhaps it's hard to get anything complex down in blood. Even seven pints only goes so far.

I stared at them, but it was pointless; all it did was remind me of how poor my SAT math score had been. I wondered if this might be an opportune moment to slip out to the car and show them to Darcy . . .

"Good to see you hard at work, Lieutenant."

His voice was so loud and so close that I almost jumped out of my skin. "Chief O'Bannon." He was standing just behind me, leaning heavily on his metal cane. "What are you doing here?"

"What is the chief of police doing at a homicide scene?" His eyes screwed upward. "Maybe Granger's right about you."

I didn't dare ask what that meant. "How's everything going? How's Darcy? I haven't seen him since—"

"Cut the crap, Susan. I spotted him outside in your car."

Oh. Well, that did change things.

"Care to explain what he's doing there? Since I expressly forbade you to involve him in any part of this case other than the interview of your weird math specialist?"

"Well, I, um . . ." Words, come on, words! "I had an interview with a difficult witness earlier today, someone about his age, so I thought he might be able to give me some psychological insight."

"Darcy? Psychological insight?" He appeared somewhat less than convinced. "And what are you doing?"

"Me? I'm . . ." I showed him the paper I was holding. "I was working on these mathematical equations we just found in the carpet."

His eyes squinted. "Let me see if I understand this. You're working on complex math problems, while Darcy is out in the car working on a psychological profile. What is this, Freaky Friday?"

I cleared my throat. "If you have no objection, I'd like to pass these equations along to Darcy."

"Absolutely not."

"Chief, you don't know how good he is at these math problems!"

"I don't?" He leaned into my face so close I could smell his breath, not that I wanted to. "May I remind you that I've been living with that boy all his life? When he was three years old, he was obsessed with numbers. Everything was about numbers. If we went on a drive, he counted the fire hydrants. If we went to see his grandparents, he called out the mile markers. Sometimes he counted down seconds as they passed, aloud. He would count aloud to a thousand—then start crying, because he thought that's all there was. So I showed him how you could always add one to any number and keep on going into infinity—a lesson I learned to regret, believe me. His math OCDs were out of control, till we finally got some help from Dr. Lovass's behavioral modification team. But there's no such thing as a cure. You understand what I'm saying?"

"I . . . think so."

"In other words, the obsessive-compulsive behavior could return at any moment. Especially if he's given incentive."

"But I would never—"

"For instance, if he thinks obsessing on numbers will get him in tight with this bubble-headed behaviorist he's got a huge crush on."

"Oh, now you're being ridi—"

His face was so angry I was afraid he was going to hit me. "I know my son, Susan. Better than you."

"But, Chief—" I pressed my forehead. My stress levels were rising like a thermometer in a sauna, and I had no chemical additives left to combat it. "This could be important. And Darcy might solve the equations immediately, or at least tell us what they are. Please. Just this one last time."

He grunted. "Well, I'd be pretty stupid to say no, wouldn't I? Since he is here and all." He turned toward Granger, then stopped and pivoted back on me. "But this is the last time, Pulaski. The absolute last time."

I didn't waste any time. I ran outside, brought Darcy inside, found him a quiet corner at a conference table in the lawyer's office, and handed him the equations.

"Hurray!" he cried, almost immediately after seeing them. "Hip hip hooray!"

Well, I knew he liked math, but this seemed a bit much. "May I ask the reason for this sudden display of exuberance?"

"I can solve these!"

I slid into the chair next to him. "You can? Why?"

"Because these can be solved."

"And the answer is . . . a number? Life, the universe and everything?"

"A letter."

"A letter? But why—"

"Because it is algebra. Shhh."

Excuse moi.

"The common denominator is fifteen, so I multiply this one by five and this one by three . . ." He was doing it all in his head; he didn't even ask for a piece of paper. ". . . the twos can cancel each other out, so that leaves us with *T.* The second one is almost the same, but with different letters. I wonder why the killer would use different letters?"

"What do you mean? What do letters have to do with this?"

"They are variables. Unknowns. The problems do not tell me enough that I can give you a number for them. All I can give you is a letter."

"And they're different."

"Right."

"Well, I don't see how that helps us."

"The answer to the first one is *T,* and the answer to the second one is *V.*"

"Well, maybe it's not meant to mean anything. Maybe it's just—" I froze, closed my mouth and gave my brain a momentary opening. "The answers are *T* and *V*?"

"That's right!" he said, beaming as if he'd just saved a baby from a burning car. "And I know now that this is a custard day because—Susan?"

I was already out the door. I remembered seeing a television in the front lobby.

I turned it on. Nothing unusual happened.

"Hey, Pulaski," I heard Granger yell. "Oprah doesn't come on until four."

Asswipe. The television had a built-in videotape

player. I punched the Eject button and a tape popped out. I was secretly hoping for *Finding Nemo*, but I was sorely disappointed. It wasn't a commercial tape. Something homemade.

It had already been rewound, so I popped it back in the tape deck and pushed Play.

And was almost immediately sorry I had done so. By the time the killer was swinging the axe, I was so sick I had to leave the room.

I DO NOT KNOW why they will not just let me work on this case and get it over with when it seems like I do all the best stuff anyway. My dad does not think I can be a policeman and he will not let me try but who was the one who found the second equation? That was me. And who was the one who found the water tower? That was me. And who was the one who solved the equations that helped them find the tape? That was me. And what was my reward for helping them? My dad gave me bus fare and told me to go home. I think maybe Susan wanted me to stay but I cannot be sure because I cannot exactly see people's faces or understand their feelings so maybe she was sad or maybe she was still messed up about what they saw in the videotape. They would not let me watch the videotape but I do not know why because I watch videotapes all the time and nothing could be worse than *Pocahontas*.

Last night I had a dream and when I was sitting in Susan's car all by myself it came back to me except then I guess it was a daydream except maybe I fell asleep again I do not really know. I dreamed that I woke up and my father was gone, and Mrs. Bellows was gone, and the pretty lady with the red hair at the custard shop was gone, and before long I realized that pretty much everyone was gone. The whole population of Earth had disappeared. And at first this was a good thing because I could play Rayman Arena longer than I am supposed to and I could watch *Futurama* which I am not supposed to and I could get into that closet my dad does not think I know about where he keeps his magazines with the ladies who forget to put on their clothes and the really strange videos and the gun that he does not want me to know he keeps at home because he is afraid I will put out my eye or something. But after a few days—I guess it was not really a few days because this was a dream and not like real time—I started to get bored. I liked not having my dad say Don't Don't Don't Don't but without anyone else around there was not really anything to Do.

And then I remembered Susan. I ran all the way over to her house thinking Susan Susan Susan Susan Susan should still be alive and she was still alive and I think she was happy I was there and she explained why she could not come see me but she was glad I came to see her. And that is when I realized—she did not have to adopt me anymore. She did not have to marry me. I could go to the police academy, if there still was one. We could do anything we wanted if we wanted and she wanted and it did not matter what anyone else thought. We could have babies, and even if Susan was not crazy about the idea she would want to because you need babies when everyone else has suddenly disappeared. We could even do sex if she wanted to but if she did not want to that was okay because I do not really care if we do sex all I want is to be with Susan.

I wonder if Susan would want to be with me. If everyone else suddenly disappeared and I was the only person left on the face of the earth.

ESTHER SAT beside Tucker in the living room of her apartment, reading the newspaper to him. He could read a little, but only with difficulty, and he much preferred being read to. Just as he liked it when she cut his meat. And rocked him to sleep (after wild twisted sex during which she acted as if this clumsy oaf were The Sheik of Araby). He was like a child in so many ways. Which, she supposed, was why they got along so well. And why he was so easy to control.

"This reporter," Esther explained, "this Jonathan Wooley, has almost every detail of any importance wrong. He thinks you broke into the office, but you didn't, did you?"

"No," Tucker said, looking up at her with subservient eyes. "The secretary let me in. I broke the window afterward, like you told me to do."

"You're a good boy," she replied, patting him on the top of his head. "And he says that the secretary was knocked out—but you used the chloroform, right?"

"Yeah."

"And the suggestion is that you were after money, which even this shabby journalist must know is balderdash. They're just trying to comfort the populace. Trying to assure them that there is a motive they can understand, that we are simply operating out of greed." She took his chin and raised it. "But we're not, are we? We have a much higher purpose in mind."

"Yeah. A sacred purpose."

She quickly scanned the rest of the article. "Pathetic. This man doesn't even know that you severed the lawyer's arm. The police are probably intentionally withholding many details. So they can weed out crank confessions. Perhaps we should leave the next body on the monorail. Then everyone could see the truth for themselves."

"I—I don't think I would be able to get a body onto the monorail without—"

"Shhh." She pressed a finger against his lips. "We don't have to worry about that. The deposit spots have all been preordained. And none of them is anywhere near the monorail track." She laughed. "Just as well. If you tried to get a corpse on it, it would probably break down."

Tucker chuckled, but with little enthusiasm.

"I think we should go to bed now, my darling. I have class tomorrow. And you have a very big day. You understand that, don't you?"

"Y-Yes."

"Trying to get to a C-list celebrity backstage at the Florence—that's going to be a good deal more complex than catching a workaholic lawyer in his lair. Not that you can't do it. I know you can. But you're going to need your strength. So why don't we toddle on upstairs—"

"Esther?"

She stopped, brushed the hair tenderly out of his face. "Yes, Tucker, dear?"

"I—I am doin' the right thing, aren't I?"

"Do you doubt it?"

"No, I just—I just—"

"You understand what I've told you, don't you? Why we're doing this? Why our work is so important?"

"I . . . try. But it's hard for me . . ."

"And you know I can't do it myself. Not in my condition. I need a big strong man, someone I trust." She took his face in her hands again. "Someone I love."

"You . . . love me?"

"You know I do. Don't I show you that? Don't I show you every night?"

"Yes." He straightened. "Then I don't hafta . . . understand it all. All I hafta know is what you want me to do."

"Dear boy. Dear sweet boy." She took his hand and stood. "Now let's go upstairs, shall we?"

"Okay. And—"

She turned again. "Ye-es?"

"Are we gonna have time for—for—you know."

She smiled beatifically. "Do you think we should? I don't want to deplete your energy. Not when you have so much work to do."

"I'm sure I could manage both."

"Very well then." She took his hand and laid it gently on her left breast. "I want you, too, you know. I crave you. When you're not around me, I burn."

"You—You do?"

"Oh, yes. Come my love, let us go upstairs and give our bodies what they so urgently require. Just—try not to get too violent this time, would you?" She led him up the stairs. "We must be careful of the baby."

24

JULY 19

"JOSH, JOSH, JOSH," the chubby man in the bolo tie said, his arms up in the air. "Calm down. It's not good for your heart, baby. You want I should get you a scotch and tonic before you go on?"

The tall thin man in the satin tuxedo whirled on him. "No, I do not want any damn scotch. I want some butts in all those empty seats."

"Josh, you know what the economy is like."

"I know what my bank account is like!"

"It's hard times. People don't have disposable income like they used to."

"That's bullshit. Vegas is filled with disposable income. It's the goddamned kingdom of disposable income!"

Charlie Halliwell mopped his brow, wishing to God he hadn't made the mistake of meeting his client backstage. Sure, he'd been doing it for over twenty years now, religiously, before every show. But Joshua was in one of his moods, usually induced by a combination of booze, phentermine, and the odd glance at the no longer young face in the mirror. When he got in one of those moods, he could not be reasoned with. Best just to stay clear. Worse, there were about twenty stagehands watching, hearing every ugly word his client ranted.

"Look at that crowd," the man continued. "Pathetic! There was a time when the name Joshua Brazee meant something. I was the first performer to sell out the Sands for three months straight. Did you know that, Halley? Did you?"

"Of course I knew it, Josh. I was the one who booked those gigs at the Sands, remember?"

"Yeah, I remember. Back then, you knew how to be an agent. You knew how to rustle the bushes. Now you're a has-been."

Halliwell bit back the obvious reply. "Vegas has changed, Josh."

"Bullshit."

"It has. They don't turn out for crooners the way they used to."

"You're wrong, Halley. There's always an audience for talent. And that's what I am. Real talent. Not some bimbo teenager lip-synching and thrusting her navel into people's faces. Real talent."

"You're not a teen idol anymore, Josh. Your audience is aging."

"So is the competition! I'm probably the greatest standards man left alive today."

Halliwell suspected Tony Bennett might have some thoughts on that score, but he kept his mouth closed. "You know, Josh, I have tried to get you to liven up your act. Bring it into the twenty-first century."

"People don't come to Joshua Brazee to see flashing lights and hydraulic sets. They come to hear a man sing."

Halliwell mopped his brow. Where to begin? "Have you looked around lately, Josh? Take a look at the Strip. The new Strip. Giant video displays. Escalators that cross highways. Roller coasters. A monorail, for God's sake. Times have changed."

Brazee thunked his manager on the chest so hard it

knocked him back a few steps. "There's always an audience for a good show."

"Good show!" Halliwell knew he should keep his mouth shut, but the anger was building inside him with such intensity he feared he might burst an artery. Why had he gone into show business? Why hadn't he stayed home and run the family farm in Dill City, Oklahoma, like his mother wanted him to do? "You wanna know what a good show is, Josh? Then why don't you go see one? I got you tickets!"

"I don't need to see some hyped-up gimmicky—"

"You need to know what you're up against. Céline Dion doesn't just warble. She puts on a show! Dancers! Acrobats! Stagecraft!"

He rolled his eyes. "The woman can barely sing. And that accent—"

Halliwell slapped his forehead. "The woman plays to four thousand people every night! Because it's a *show.*"

Halliwell was bouncing up and down. At his height, he looked like a leprechaun. "Did you go to the Mirage? Did you see 'O'? They got a stage with more water than a swimming pool. They got people descending into the water and disappearing. I don't know how they do it. But I know that's a show!"

"Not for my audience. My people grew up when Liberace and Wayne Newton owned this town."

"Even Liberace knew how to put on a show! You think people came to hear him play piano? They couldn't care less about the piano! He wasn't even that good at it. If they craved piano, Van Cliburn would've ruled Vegas. They loved Liberace because he knew how to put on a show. Hell, people still love Liberace. He's been dead for years, but his museum is the top non-casino tourist attraction in town!"

With a sudden calm that bordered on the eerie, Brazee

stepped closer to Halliwell and grabbed him by his wide lapels. For a split second, Halliwell thought the man was going to kiss him. As it turned out, his intention was considerably less affectionate. "Let me put this to you in words that I think you can understand, Halley. You're fired."

"What? What!" Halliwell shook himself free. "You can't fire me, you son of a bitch. I made you!"

"See, that's where you're wrong, Halley. *I* made me. You were helpful, in your day. But that day is long past. We both know your agency contract expired years ago. So now I'm making it formal. You're fired."

"Think for a minute, you ass. You'll never find anyone who can replace me!"

"Actually, I already have."

"But—you can't—you—"

"And now, if you'll excuse me, former manager of mine, I believe I hear my entrance music."

"You can't do this to me!"

"Halley—I already did it!"

"You can't treat me like this, Brazee. Not after all these years. Not after I worked my butt off for you!"

"As I believe I just said—I already have."

"I'll get you for this, you bastard. I won't take this lying down. You don't work with me, you don't work with anyone. You're dead in this town, understand me? *You're a dead man*!"

Brazee smiled and fluttered his eyelids. "Love to stay and argue with you, Halley, but I can't. My audience is waiting for me. What's left of it."

"You slimy son of—"

But it was too late. Brazee was already onstage, playing to somewhat less than thunderous applause. "Las Vegas, Las Vegas, that toddlin' town . . ."

Halliwell turned away from the stage, his fists balled, his face white.

And saw about twenty stagehands. Watching. Miracle they had remembered to turn on Joshua's spotlight.

Halliwell stared at his shoes and marched off the stage. If that bastard thought he'd take this lying down, he was very much mistaken. He'd had bigger and better clients than Joshua Brazee, at least at one time, back in the good old days when the mob ruled this town. He'd deliberately chosen to slow down, winnow his list, ease toward retirement. But now, what with the gambling debts and the paternity suit . . .

He had to get Joshua back. He had to.

So he'd just talk to the man. Once the show was over, and the pill buzz had faded, and he was once again basking in the better-than-sex afterglow of a room full of applause. Then Joshua would be reasonable, and he'd rehire the man who'd put him where he was today. And maybe they could start making some real plans for the future, find some way to broaden the audience. Maybe Joshua would listen. Maybe for once he'd be reasonable.

He had to. There was no choice about it. He had to.

"ALL RIGHT," Granger said, trying to keep his wits about him, which for him I suppose took some doing. "Let's try to get organized here. Go over what we know. This investigation needs some direction. And I guess we'll have to go with the forensic experts. Since we don't have a psych profile."

"How can I write a psych profile when the whole damn case changes every day!" I screamed. Which was a mistake. You should never start a meeting screaming. Leaves you nothing to build up to.

"First," Granger said to the staff gathered around the conference table, "we know the killer broke into the office."

I wasn't in the mood to give him a break. "Actually, he didn't."

"We all saw the glass on the floor."

"Guess you haven't bothered to talk to Forensics." Granted, this was obnoxious, even by my standards, but it's not exactly as if he was trying to be my friend. "The glass was broken from the inside."

"Th—Then how did he get in?"

"Obviously, they let him in. Like the secretary said."

"You're saying the expert witness was the killer?"

"Ding-ding," I said, touching my nose. "So instead of running all over the sign-in sheets at the security desk, you should just look in Spencer's appointment book."

"He would've used an alias," said one of Granger's detectives, Holly Laird.

"Yeah. But logically Spencer would've asked for some way to contact him. Maybe you can find a phone number or address somewhere in his office."

"It's worth a try," Laird said, gracefully saving her boss from having to admit the obvious—that I was way ahead of him.

I looked at Granger. "Want me to tell you what else we know about this murder?"

"Oh, would you be so kind," he said, his voice dripping.

"I could be persuaded. Amelia found an earprint that could be useful to establish a positive ID, if we catch this guy. Dr. Rennard found two formulae which, when solved by Darcy—"

"Who shouldn't have even been there," Granger growled.

I ignored him, one of my favorite pastimes. "—led us to a videotape in the TV. In which we see the killer—wearing a mask—hack off that poor pathetic lawyer's arm, while the killer makes . . . taunting remarks to the police." Which would be a nice way of putting it. I watched the whole thing in grisly detail, not once but twice. He toyed with Spencer for a while, babbling a lot of rot about numbers, most of which was too whispered for me to make out. And then I got to hear him say, in a voice so loud he obviously wanted the tape to get it: "And there's nothing the police can do to stop me. Not that windbag Lieutenant Granger. Not that bitch Pulaski. No one." And then: "Next we venture into the wonderful world of showbiz. And after that—the next victim will be someone you know very well."

He knew us by name. He'd been following the investigation on television, in the papers. And we didn't scare him in the least.

Then I got to watch Dane Spencer scream and plead for his life, for the well-being of his daughter, for the clients and others who depended upon him. With the mask on, it was difficult to tell what was going on with the killer, but I didn't get the impression he was enjoying this. No psychopathic pleasure. No hysterical laughing, like The Joker or something. Just as if he were a man on a mission.

And then he sliced Spencer's arm off, just below the socket. Right before my eyes.

I was glad I was in the video room by myself. Because I couldn't stop crying for half an hour.

"I assume someone has performed a stress analysis test on the videotape," I said, careful to keep my voice steady.

"To determine what?" Granger asked. "Whether he was telling the truth when he called you a bitch?"

I almost lost it. So almost. But I couldn't afford to, not now. "I'm more concerned about the part where he threatens that the next victim will be someone we know. Especially since he knows at least two of us by name."

Granger waved it away. "The *Courier* is constantly printing our names. That doesn't mean he's coming after us."

"He didn't say it would be us. He said it would be someone we know, Granger. Like, maybe, your mother?"

His head jerked up.

"Or my niece. Or—anyone. No one is safe. Not one of us. Not anyone we know."

"The video team ran a PSE—a psychological stress evaluator on his voice," Laird said. I was familiar with the gizmo. The basic concept is that when someone lies, the pitch of their voice rises, ever so slightly. The recorded voice can be printed in graph form that allows them to detect even the tiniest gradations in pitch. It's the next generation of the CVSA—Compressed Voice Stress Analyzer. Problem is, neither of them was generally considered entirely reliable—less reliable even than polygraphs. And there still weren't any courts that would accept polygraph evidence, much less this stuff. "They think he was telling the truth. About his future plans."

I thought he was telling the truth, too, but it wasn't because of that analysis. I couldn't even claim I saw it in his eyes, since he was wearing a mask. I just . . . knew.

"Anything else?" Granger asked. Now he was the one who sounded as if he were begging. "There must be something."

"Purcell's team found some hair and fiber," Laird said, "but nothing that's going to help us catch him."

"The only way we're going to catch him," I said, "is if we can figure out what his methodology is, no matter how twisted or irrational it may be. So we can be waiting for him the next time he tries to strike. We have to get inside his head."

Granger grunted. "Which is what you're—"

"Yeah, I know already, okay?" Yes, I snapped at him. But I didn't call him an asshole, which I thought showed remarkable restraint.

"Pulaski, I want a preliminary profile on my desk tomorrow morning."

"I can't—"

"I don't care how rough it is, or how many spaces you

have to leave blank. I want something." He glared at me. "Unless you're not capable of doing it."

"I'll do it." You bastard. "I'll give you everything I've got." I only wished it could be with my fist. But I probably would've missed my target. My hands were shaking even as I thought about it.

25

"Mr. Brazee?"

He didn't look away from his bulb-studded mirror. "That you, Halley? Come to grovel for your old job back?" He chuckled. "Ain't gonna work."

The sound of the door closing was followed by the deadbolt sliding into place.

"Hey, what's the big—" Brazee swiveled in his chair. "Who the hell are you?"

The short stocky man behind him did not answer. He heard the jingle of a pair of handcuffs, and a second later, felt the snapping around his left wrist. The other end of the cuffs clamped onto the arm of his chair.

"What the—" He tried to stand, but the cuff chain jerked him back into his seat. "I don't know what you think you're doing, but all I have to do is say 'Boo' and there'll be people crawling all over—"

"I don't think so." Calmly, Tucker opened his overcoat, withdrew a long-handled axe, and placed the blade against Brazee's throat. "First, near as I can tell, everyone else has gone home already. Like rats from a sinkin' ship."

"My act is not—Anyway, even if the crew has left—"

"I told your driver you wanted to walk home. Clear your head. Said you had some thinkin' to do."

"He wouldn't believe you."

"He did. Got the impression he didn't mind leavin' early all that much. Got the impression he doesn't like you so much. Tell the truth, Mr. Brazee, I get the impression no one likes you much."

"That's insane."

"I remember when you were somethin', when you had that song on the radio, what was it called?"

"I've had many hits." He sniffed. "But the one you're remembering is probably 'I Miss You So in Springtime'?"

"Yeah. That's the one. That was a good song. Damn good song."

Brazee's eyes moved slowly from Tucker's face to the blade still pressed against his throat. "So . . . are you an . . . enthusiastic fan?"

"No. But I liked that song."

"Then why don't you let me go?"

"Can't do that."

"If you free me, I could . . . sing it for you."

"Nice offer. But nah." He grinned a little. " 'Fraid your number is up. And I really mean it."

"I don't understand. If you like my song, why don't you let me—"

"This has nothing to do with your songs. You were chosen, that's all."

"Chosen? But—" His eyes slowly widened, the horror dawning. "You're that man. The one I read about in the paper. You killed two people."

"Three."

"And then you—" His head fell. "Oh, my God. Oh, my God."

"Like I said," Tucker replied, looking away, "it's nothin' personal. Well, it is, in a way. But it's still all about the numbers."

They both heard the creaking sound outside at the same time. "Halley!" Brazee shouted. "Halley! Help!"

Tucker dropped the axe, ran to the door and flung it open.

No one was there.

"Just the house settlin', I guess," Tucker growled. "But that was stupid. I coulda killed you."

"Then why didn't you?"

"Because there's supposed to be a . . . a procedure." He spoke each syllable slowly, as if it were its own word. "A pattern." He put the blade back against the man's throat. "But don't get the wrong idea. You screw up again, I'll kill you right here and now and do the rest of the stuff later. It's not the best way. But I'll do what I gotta do."

"Other stuff? What . . . other stuff?"

Tucker spoke as if it were the most ordinary thing in the world. "The brandin'."

"Why would you possibly want to . . . to . . . hurt me? I've never done anything to you. I've never done anything to anyone."

Tucker's eyes narrowed. " 'Zat what they say back in Terre Haute?"

Even with the blade against his throat, the stiffening of his neck was noticeable. "W—Why would you ask me about . . . about that city?"

"What kinda man doesn't take responsibility for his own kid, huh?"

Brazee could feel the man's hot breath on his face. He pulled back, as far as the cuffs would allow. "There were . . . practical considerations . . . Career . . . You wouldn't understand."

"Try me."

His voice dropped. "His mother was a groupie. Met her backstage at a concert. We weren't married."

"You coulda married her."

"Yeah, and killed my career. I couldn't disappoint the little girls, man. I'm sure you know how that is. The chicks had to think I was available. I was a teen heart-throb."

Tucker placed his free hand atop Brazee's head and slowly turned it to face the mirror, bringing the blade right along with it. "Been a long time since you've been a teen, huh, mister? Bet it's been a long time since you had a teenager in your audience, too."

"That's not my fault. It's just bad management."

"You haven't been makin' your payments."

"I haven't been pulling in the scratch like I used to. But I got a plan. My new manager, he's gonna make my show bigger, better. Maybe bring in the guys who did the act for . . . for . . . those two German guys with the cats."

"Too late." Tucker reached under his overcoat and this time withdrew a branding iron with the letter *N* at the end.

"What—What are you—Oh my God—"

"You are Netzach. You must make the sacrifice."

"The sacrifice. What does that mean?"

"Well," Tucker said, as he pulled out his acetylene torch and began heating the branding iron, "it means you won't be doin' any more singin' anytime soon."

I COULD HARDLY ASK Amelia to refill the prescription I swiped from her, could I? And I sure as hell couldn't get through all this, Granger breathing down my throat, having to cancel on Amelia, feeling lost, feeling alone.

Watching that videotape. Twice.

I know why he made it, and why he left it behind. At least in my mind I did.

He left it for me. He left it because he knew how badly it would screw me up. And he was right.

Thank God for the Internet. In less than twenty minutes, I found some shady outfit that could have Valium at my doorstep tomorrow afternoon, if I was willing to pay the outrageous shipping costs. But for that matter, as I hyper-clicked around, I found all kinds of options. Why stop at Valium when there was Xanax, and Effexor, and for that matter, even better stuff. Vicodin. Prozac.

I ordered a wide assortment. A smorgasbord of relief. I was going to need it.

Might as well stay up all night working on this preliminary report. I knew I wouldn't sleep, not with two lousy Valiums left. But tomorrow would be different. If I could just get through the next twenty-four hours. So I logged off the Internet, logged onto the FBI's BSI database, and went to work. It would be a hard night. But I knew I could make it.

Help was on its way.

26

Behavioral profile—The Math Man
by Susan Pulaski, *M.A., LVPD*

. . . is complicated by conflicting psychological indicators. The investigators have uncovered data suggesting an orderly personality as well as a disorderly personality, a narcissistic personality as well as a sympathetic personality, an antisocial or poorly socialized personality as well as a keen understanding of social conventions and social strata. One possible explanation is that the serial killer's *modus operandi* and rationalizations are still developing; however, the fundamental fact pattern and extremely stylized and complex methodology have remained consistent from the start. Another more dangerous possible diagnosis would be dissociative personality disorder, that is, the existence of multiple personalities, one dominant and controlling, one submissive and compliant, and both extremely dangerous. The prototypical Jekyll-Hyde split allows one alter-personality to assume the qualities which the central consciousness recognizes to be the most socially unacceptable, while the submissive personality, however regretfully, carries out the plans mapped by the other. This is a particularly dangerous combination, because it creates an outlet for rationalization and release that allows even personalities that have not progressed to full sociopathy to commit the most heinous deeds.

Despite the conflicting indicators and the paucity of concrete information, there are some facts we can state affirmatively about the killer. The killer is:

1) a white male between the ages of twenty and forty. (Although this information cannot be ascertained by psychological profiling, eyewitness reports have indicated that he is short, only somewhat over five feet tall, stocky, strong, dark-haired);

2) from a low income bracket, probably only marginally above the poverty level. Most likely he finds his menial job unfulfilling because it provides no outlet for his intelligence, or at least his aptitude for mathematics, creating a desire to do what his delusional mind conceives as "greater things" to show his worth;

3) fond of, or at least able to tolerate, acts of extreme violence. It is possible that he has convinced himself that the merit of his acts is so great that it justifies deeds he would otherwise find repellent. It is remotely possible that he finds acts of violence to be sexually arousing, that his usual impotence is overcome by acts of extreme brutality;

4) the product of a broken home and a troubled childhood. He probably was raised by only one parent, or neither. The fact that he has chosen both male and female victims, however, makes it difficult to determine which influence he was missing in childhood. He probably mistreated

animals or smaller children. He may have been a late bed wetter. All factors likely to produce an ongoing frustration with the UNSUB's lack of impulse control; and

5) very fond of and very good at mathematics.

Detectives should be looking for an adult who is lonely, isolated, angry, and violent, someone who spends long hours alone, obsessively working on problems of his own creation, or indulging in an aberrant but well-developed fantasy life. As classified by the DSM-IV, he suffers from antisocial personality disorder and may have sought or been given psychological therapy in the past.

The key to locating this killer will almost certainly be understanding the mathematical clues he has left at the crime scenes, as well as the videotape of the most recent assault. Some part of his complex psyche wants to be caught, or perhaps wants us to appreciate the "majesty" of his design, or to be awed by his superior intellect, hence the mathematical equations. Even if we are unable to perceive it, in his mind there is a rationale, a pattern to his crimes. If we could understand that, we could anticipate his moves. If, for instance, we understood how he selects his victims, we could protect them and lay a trap for him.

It has been suggested that he possesses a prurient mania against pornography or sexual sin, but that does not seem consistent, does not explain his seemingly random and diverse selection of victims, and does not appear to link the most recent victim. The selection process is almost certainly mathematical, but how the determination is made is still unknown. There is a strong indication that all his crimes "add up" to something, some ultimate goal, some purpose, but that too is unknown. In some respects, the killer almost seems driven to commit his crimes, as if somehow he is compensating for past wrongs, perhaps those done to him, or trying to punish others who have committed like crimes, or trying to prevent future incidents from happening. In his self-deluded, narcissistic mind, some such rationale justifies the violence. The exact process, however, remains unknown. When we understand that, we will have taken the most important step toward understanding this killer. If this is, for him, a numbers game, we must try to comprehend, however bizarre they may be, the rules of that game . . .

I YANKED the last page out of the printer, stared at it, then with more than a little reluctance, passed it to O'Bannon's new assistant Amanda David for photocopying. Just as well I was out of the little blue sleepy-bye pills. I was tense as hell, but I had been able to stay up most of the night, working and reworking this report, until it was as good as I could make it, given that I really didn't know squat about this killer and writing this report was pitifully premature.

This should have been simple, but somehow, I just couldn't get my head around it, couldn't get my usual empathic ability to see inside someone else's head. The key to finding an UNSUB is Why+How=Who. And I'd worked it. I'd written a report that was consistent with the facts and made best use of the information in our possession. But deep down, I knew it sucked. A total waste of taxpayer paper. I didn't know enough about Why to get to Who. And I couldn't shake the feeling that somehow, somewhere, I'd gotten something fundamentally wrong. It was just a hunch, an instinct. But profilers worked on instinct—or at least they should. They had to be able to sense what could not yet be proven.

They had to be able to crawl inside the killer's mind, or perhaps more accurately, reconstruct it on a piece of paper. But my instincts had gone to hell, and I was stuck here, banging at the keyboard like a monkey, putting words together that didn't say much and wouldn't help anyone, much less Granger. Well, they might help him prove my utter worthlessness, but nothing else.

The worst of it was, if Granger came after me again, now, I'm not sure I'd fight him. Maybe it was just the stress weighing down on me while I waited desperately for the pharmaceutical FedEx. But somehow, I couldn't shake the feeling that despite my best efforts, everything I'd written was critically, tragically wrong.

"FOR GOD'S SAKE, can't you hold still?" Tucker bellowed. "Do you have any idea how hard it is to cut a leg off?"

He wiped his brow, then took aim again with his axe. It would be so much simpler if she weren't so particular. Everything had to be done just right—removal at precisely the pinpointed place, the body carried to a predetermined location, most of them incredibly inconvenient. And it had to be on the right day. All according to the numbers. Maybe when the baby came she would relax a little. Even though she wasn't showing that much, the doctor said her time was a lot closer than they had previously imagined. Maybe her health was a factor—he didn't know. Unfortunately, between now and the blessed arrival, there was still much work to be done.

"Please don't do this," Brazee cried. His hands were restrained behind his back, his right leg was handcuffed to a table, but unfortunately Tucker hadn't brought anything to close his mouth. Next time he would invest in some heavy-duty duct tape. It would be worth the investment. "What are you, a critic or something?"

Tucker didn't honor that one with a reply. He had

hoped that after the branding, after the searing pain of an *N* imprinted on his leg, he might be somewhat subdued. That was how it had worked before. But not this guy. No matter what Tucker did to him, he just kept on talking. Like, thanks for the essay, but you're still losing your leg, okay? It was as if the man thought he was still on the stage and the adrenaline rush was immunizing him against the pain. He worked mindlessly through the same old patter, as if his purgatory was being forced to run though an endless lounge act, over and over again. And Tucker's purgatory was to have to listen to it.

"I mean, I know some of the patter fell flat tonight. I was having troubles, you know, with my manager. I was distracted. But I can do better. I promise. What'd'you want? A song? A joke? I know some great ones. Hey, how many Republicans does it take to screw in a lightbulb?"

Tucker tightened the rope that held the man's right leg to the card table. "I'm not interested in jokes."

"What then? You wanna song? You wanna hear 'I Miss You So in Springtime'? I mean, I hate that old song, never wanted to record it in the first place. But for you—I'll make an exception."

"This may come as a shock to you," Tucker said, balancing the axe in his hands, "but this isn't really about you. Certainly not about your stage act."

"Then—what is it?"

"It's about fate, destiny. God is in the numbers," he said, with a self-evident air of pride. "Brace yourself. I imagine this will hurt."

"Wait!" Brazee cried. "What about—everything you said. About my daughters."

"What about it?" Tucker glanced at his watch impatiently. He knew he had only so much time before others would enter the theater. Plus, he wanted to get to the delivery spot before the sun rose and his chances of being detected multiplied.

"You . . . you gotta understand what really happened."

"No, actually, I don't."

"But you're punishing me—"

"I don't make the decisions."

"It wasn't my fault. There was nothing I could do. The kid's mother wanted it this way. And I've taken good care of them."

"The Department of Human Services has a different opinion."

" 'Cause I was late with the money a few times? I'm an entertainer, for God's sake. An artist. I don't get a check every two weeks like the mundanes. I pay when I can. But I've always made it good in the end. Hell, with the manager I got, it's a miracle I work at all."

Tucker shrugged, then focused his attention on the man's leg. The dismemberment had to occur at just the right point, the juncture between the pelvis and the thigh. He needed to remove the leg, but nothing more and nothing less. He raised the axe—

All at once, Brazee thrust his upper body forward, as if performing a monumental sit-up. He head-butted Tucker in the abdomen, sending him reeling backward. Tucker was tempted to bring the axe down on his neck, but he knew that was not what Esther wanted. While Tucker was trying to think what to do next, Brazee brought his free leg around and kicked Tucker.

Tucker hit the wall with a thud.

With an impressive display of strength, Brazee balanced himself on his free leg, using it as a pivot point to twist around. Although he was still dazed, Tucker saw to his horror that the man had managed to get his hands free. He dove forward across the room.

He was trying to get the axe.

Tucker forced himself into action. He raced forward, knees still wobbly, and stomped on the man's hand with all the force he could bring to bear. Brazee shouted in pain, pulling his hand back and cradling it against his body.

Tucker grabbed him by the hair and slung him roughly back to where he was supposed to be. He raised his fist toward the man's face—

Then stopped. There could be no extraneous bruising. She had made that clear. They must stick to the plan. If we indulge our violent passions, we are animals. If we hew to the plan, we become creatures such as even God must sit up and take notice.

He cuffed the man's hands, this time making certain there was no chance of his escaping. He wiped the sweat from his brow, wiped his hands dry, and recovered his axe.

"You shouldn't've done that," Tucker muttered, low and gravelly.

Brazee was amiable and nonchalant. "Hey, can't blame a man for trying, right?"

Tucker's glare was sufficient to communicate his feelings.

"Okay, look, I'll come clean," the pinioned man said. "I got some money. You don't need to be telling the little lady in Terre Haute or nothin', but I do got a little something stashed away. A Cayman Islands account. You know how it goes. Not a fortune, but every penny of it is yours."

"I don't want money."

"Then what do you want?" The strain was evident in his voice. Beads of sweat streamed down the sides of his face. "Girls? Is that what trips your trigger?"

Tucker hesitated for a fraction of a second.

"Aha! Well, let me tell you, mister, you've come to the right place. I got girls out the wazoo. I'd be more than happy to throw a few your way."

"I—I don't—"

"And we're not just talking any girls here, buddy. We're talking Grade A prime cheesecake. Showgirls. Strippers. Hometown homecoming queens looking for their first big break. I mean, you've never seen boobs like the boobs on some of those wheatfield wonders."

"I—I'm not interested—"

"You wouldn't say that if you saw them. These girls will do anything, my friend. Anything. Let your imagination run wild—you still won't come up with everything these girls will do. And they're limber—there's no position they can't make work."

"I—"

"Threesomes, what about that? I bet you've never been the crème filling in an Oreo cookie, huh? This is your big chance. A once-in-a-lifetime."

"I'm—not interested."

"I know—you're worried about . . . the way you look. Listen to me, bud—these girls don't care. They aren't gonna be looking at your face, if you know what I mean."

"I—am not interested!" Tucker bellowed. "I have a girl. A beautiful, smart wonderful woman. I love her. I love her and she—she—" Tucker cried out, something between a growl and a battle cry, and the axe swung downward, precisely on target.

It was just as well there was no one else in the theater. Some of the diners in Monet's, almost three hundred feet away, heard something strange, faint, but still possessing its distinctive character—an agonized cry of unendurable pain. They assumed there had been an accident in the kitchen and went about eating their asparagus mousseline.

27

JULY 22

"AMELIA!" I SAID, GLANCING up from the papers that spread across my desk like an asexually reproducing organism. "What brings you to my pathetic workstation?"

Amelia smiled a little, but it struck me as a pretty weak effort. "Doing the friend in need bit. Thought you could use a little cheering up."

"I guess you've read my report."

"Umm, well, actually, no. Should I?"

"Not really. Won't tell you a damn thing. So if it's not the report, what brings you to—"

"I have it on good authority that you're about to receive a visitation from Granger."

"You say that like he's an archangel or something."

"Maybe one of the ones who got booted out and had to take up new residence in H-E-double-hockey-sticks."

"What makes you think—"

"He stomped though the crime lab, trying to get a fix on what little evidence we picked up at the last crime scene, griping all the way."

"He wasn't impressed by your ear impression?"

"Oddly enough, no. The problem is, every time he groused about what sorry shape this case is in, he dropped your name."

"Well, it is all my fault, of course."

"Yeah. And I figure he'll be here soon to tell you about it. So I just wanted to make sure you were . . . umm . . ."

"Make sure I was what?" I said, my eyes narrowing.

"Just to . . . make sure you were okay. You seem to be okay."

And I certainly was, ever since the morning FedEx packages arrived. I shoved mine in my desk and was still waiting for an opportunity to open them. Amelia obviously suspected something. I must be slurring or looking drowsy or . . . whatever. That was the problem with switching substances. I had mastered the fine art of being a high-functioning drunk. Pharmaceuticals were a whole new world.

"Well, don't drink too much coffee. Makes you jittery."

"Too late. I was born jittery."

"Speaking of coffee—put in the new coffee table yet?"

I squirmed. "Well . . ."

"But you will. Soon. Right?"

"I . . . Yes. Sure. Soon as I can."

"Great." She lifted an eyebrow. "I think I hear His Master's Footsteps. Good luck. Try not to piss him off."

"That would be a first." Almost the instant Amelia scurried away—taking an alternate route so she wouldn't have to explain why she wasn't handcuffed to her microscope—she was replaced by the mustachioed ruddy face of my arch-nemesis. Okay, so maybe the killer should be my arch-nemesis. Granger was a lesser one of the . . . nemeses? Try saying that three times fast.

Without a word, Granger flung a copy of my report onto my desk.

"Thanks," I said, "I've already read it."

"That is without question the most useless, unmitigated waste of time I have read in my entire life."

"You had to look up the three-syllable words, didn't you?"

"Don't be smart with me."

"I won't. Being smart would put you at a distinct disadvantage."

His ruddy cheeks were getting ruddier. "There's not a single thing of use to my detectives in that entire report!"

"I did warn you that it was premature."

"You didn't warn me that you were incompetent!"

I felt the short hairs on the back of my neck stiffening. In an attempt to display my moral and intellectual superiority, I tried to remain calm. "I am not incompetent. I have been of great use to this department for over nine years. I solved the Wyndham killings."

"Ancient history. I want to know what you've done for us here, now. On this case. Because if there isn't anything, I can think of about a dozen more productive ways that your salary could be put to use."

I breathed in deeply, then slowly released it, silently chanting a mantra involving several words you couldn't say in front of your mother. "If you're quite finished—"

"I haven't even started. I want you to stop dragging the chief's boy to these godawful crime scenes."

"Actually, I haven't taken him to any—"

"Don't do yourself any favors. Everyone in the department thinks he carried you through the Edgar case, then let you take the credit for it."

"*What*?"

"And what does that say, when you can't solve a case without some brain case in tow?"

"He is not—"

"Whatever. He's the chief's son, and the chief doesn't like it, so neither do I."

"If he's so damn smart he solved the Edgar case single-handedly, don't we want him working on this case, too?"

"No. He is not a member of the department. He has

not had the proper training. Every time you take him out into the field, you put his life in danger."

"I would never put his life in danger!"

"You already have."

I know I shouldn't let Granger get my goat like that, damn it. But he managed to work me over but good every time we talked. That was the flaw in knowing someone for too long, especially if that someone is a total asshole. He knew all the right buttons to push. And he pushed them with impunity.

"I will amend my report," I said, making some attempt at civil reconciliation, "as soon as we have more information from the new crime scene."

"That may not be good enough. Have you seen the morning paper?"

I hadn't, since I hadn't left the office all night. He spread the morning *Courier* on my desk. The double-size bold headline read: POLICE STYMIED BY MUTILATION KILLER.

"I got the mayor breathing down my back," Granger said, and for a brief moment, I almost felt sorry for him. "Strange as this may seem, he doesn't think coverage like this is going to be good for the number one tourist city in America. He wants this creep caught. So do I."

"When we have more information—"

"Great. At the rate you're going, it'll only take twenty more murders for you to catch him." He tossed a stack of paper onto my desk. "Here are the preliminary reports."

"And do they support your brilliant Jack the Ripper theory?"

Granger straightened. "To be honest, no. All indications are that this lawyer was pretty much a straight shooter. Wife, kids. Haven't found any porn in his home or office." He paused. "I'm thinking maybe he was diddling his secretary."

"And that puts him on the same level with a kid wanking off to *Playboy* and a porn star?"

"It's something."

"It's nothing. It's a dead-end, dead-wrong theory."

"Perhaps," he said, leaning into my face, "but have you got anything better?"

A lethal silence descended upon the immeasurable space between us.

Asshole, I mouthed silently, as I watched his outsized butt recede from my desk. Double-dog-asshole. I excused myself, ducked into the ladies' room, and tossed back several of the new pills that had arrived in the mail. I wasn't sure what they all were. Did it matter? Anti-anxiety, antidepressants—God knows I needed them all. I splashed some cold water on my face and almost instantly felt my heartbeat returning to normal. A pleasantly drowsy umbrella of calm settled over me. Felt a bit nauseous, but that was a small price to pay for the calm. Probably because I hadn't eaten. I grabbed a couple of doughnuts from the kitchen and returned to my desk.

I looked through the new information that had arrived overnight. Most of the forensic data I already knew. Turned out the vic had been a plaintiffs' tort lawyer, but contrary to what I kept hearing from Rush Limbaugh, this was not a quick ticket to Easy Street. He'd almost always had to take cases on a contingency fee, which usually meant he had to pay millions of dollars in expenses up front before he even got to trial. And since plaintiffs' cases were only successful about one time in ten, that meant the other nine times he was stuck holding the bag for all those bills. When he did score a success, he was lucky if it paid the bills for all the cases that didn't go his way. In his own way, this distinguished member of the bar was one of the highest rollers in Sin City.

His home life seemed perfectly normal. A stay-at-home wife of seven years, two kids, a girl and a boy, ages five and three. He had a shop in the garage where he did some amateur carpentry. He played basketball with friends on Friday mornings. He still drove a perfectly regular car, but he had allowed himself one splurge last year—a backyard hot tub. Even though Granger had desperately wanted to do so, they hadn't found a trace of porn in his house, nor any evidence of out-of-the-norm sexual activity. No criminal record. No tax problems. If he was messing around with his secretary, he'd managed to keep it under wraps.

My eyelids were getting heavy—too many drugs taken too quickly, I suppose—but I managed to force myself to turn to the next page. Someone in Granger's team—not Granger, obviously—had the sense to run a full computer sweep on the man, including government agencies. Turned out he was known to my old friends the DHS, the kindly folk who took Rachel away from me and placed her in a foster home. Seemed he had an earlier family, a woman and a daughter. They had never actually been married, but the woman claimed common law marriage based on living and procreating together. Court awarded child support, but he had been difficult about it. They'd constantly had to drag him to court and he finally agreed to pay it only on the condition that they move out of Nevada. He wanted to be able to make a fresh start without being pulled down by the barnacles of his past. The DHS hadn't liked the idea, but the wife was amenable, and they eventually signed off on it. Family One moved and he hadn't seen them since. Not even a phone call.

I closed my eyes and let my mind do its thing, let it wander, take me where it wanted to go. Instinct, that was the key to being an effective behaviorist. Taking a liminal sketch and turning it into a person. Taking what seem to be irrelevant details and turning them into a motive.

Hadn't the first victim had a family, once upon a time? The fast-food kid? Granger kept harping on his porn collection, like that was really unusual for a single guy in his twenties living alone. But he had a wife and . . . weren't there children? I dug deeper into my memory. Yes, three girls and a baby boy, and he had been repeatedly called to task for failing to make child support payments.

So one victim is a deadbeat child support dodger, another shoved his children into another state and acted as if they no longer existed.

I wondered if maybe the people at the DHS had some information on Danielle Dunn. She'd had a troubled youth. It would be less than shocking to learn that she had something . . . something almost no one knew about . . . the secret she was hiding . . . what was it her assistant had said . . . and all those stuffed animals . . . it wasn't her childhood she was trying to re-create but . . . but . . . something else and . . . that money for the charity . . . untraceable . . . in cash . . . why would anyone making her kind of income want to make a charitable contribution in cash? . . . it just didn't . . . didn't . . . ddddd . . .

I WOULD NOT SAY it if I did not mean it. I never say things if I do not mean them. I do not understand why other people say things they do not mean but I never do it anyway. That would be like telling a joke but I do not get jokes and I do not like them so I do not tell them. No one should tell jokes. Jokes are evil, like big dogs, and I think they should be outlawed. But yesterday when I told my dad that the bad man was going to kill someone today, he thought it was some kind of joke. I do not like this bad man. He messes around with numbers and he should not do that because numbers are good things and sometimes I think they are the only things you can depend on because they are always the same and they always do what they are supposed to do.

But this bad man uses them all wrong, he uses them to kill and he is going to do it again and I told my dad but he did not take me seriously. Did he think I was joking? Or did he think that I did not know what I was talking about? Or maybe he thought I was saying that I was going to go out and kill someone. That would be just like him. He never understands anything I say or anything I want. He does not think I can do anything and he does not want me to try.

So I took the bus downtown and came to see Susan. Susan would listen to me she always listens to me even when I can tell she is tired or funny in the head or talks and acts funny like she has lately but even still she always listens to me. She might not believe me, at least not at first, but it is so obvious! Why am I the only one who can see it? Why would the bad man have left that formula behind if he did not want us to use it?

When I got to Susan's desk, I saw that her eyes were all closed and she was not moving. I was afraid she was dead. That would be awful if she were dead because I love Susan and if she is dead she cannot love me and we cannot have babies and I cannot go to live with her and get away from my dad, not ever. I do not want her to be dead. I do not want to be in the world if Susan is dead. Please God, do not let Susan be dead. Please please please please please. I promise to be good and I promise to go to church and I promise not to do anything naughty when my dad is not around. I would even give up reading if it would mean that Susan was not dead, and that is almost the only thing I like, except being with Susan. Please God no. Please please please please no!

DAVID WAS KISSING ME. He was a fabulous kisser. He was a fabulous everything. Maybe it was all a show, but it was a damn good one. He would wrap his arms around me and squeeze so tightly I couldn't catch my breath, then his lips would swoop down onto mine and I felt like Lois being super-smooched by Superman, and I got this heady rush that made me feel like I was losing it, everything, not just my memory but my head, my body, my soul. Everything I had was his. But this must've been during that time when he made an abortive attempt to grow a mustache, because he was tickling me on the face, and even though I was trying to be romantic, it was really annoying . . .

I sputtered and coughed and grimaced. There was hair in my mouth but it wasn't from any smooching. Someone had his head in my face.

"What in—" I pushed the head away, blinked several times, tried to focus. "Darcy! What the hell were you doing?"

"I was wanting to see if you were breathing. You looked like maybe you were not breathing so I put my ear up to your nose to see if you were exhaling."

"Don't put your face next to mine when I'm sleeping! I mean, not that it's likely to happen again, but—"

"I watched you for a long time. You did not move."

"I didn't?" I looked all around. No one was watching, but that didn't mean they hadn't been earlier. I must've fallen asleep. "I was just catching forty winks, Darcy. I stayed up late last night."

"You should not do that. Statistics show people live longer if they get at least seven hours of sleep every night. But a study in Stockholm said that too much sleep—"

"Yeah, that's okay, I don't really need to know. I'll sleep double long tonight to make up for it."

"It is not possible to make up for lost sleep. Your body adapts, but the potential damage—"

"Darcy, did you come here for a reason?" I wiped the sleep from my eyes and tried to look bright-eyed and bushy-tailed. God, I hoped I hadn't drooled. " 'Cause if your dad or Granger sees you here with me, my ass will be—"

"Someone is going to be killed tomorrow. Maybe they already have been."

"Well, I suppose statistically, several people are murdered every day."

"I mean here, in Las Vegas. By the math man."

The corner of my lips turned up. Was Darcy intentionally being funny? Punning *math man* for madman. Nah. "How do you know the killer will strike again?"

"The formula. The one I found in the computer."

"You told me that was for checking prime numbers."

"Exactly. And why do you think the killer would want to check prime numbers?"

A more telling question would be: Why would the killer want us to know that he's checking prime numbers? "I give up. Why?"

"Today is the twenty-second day of July. Twenty-three is a prime number."

I arched an eyebrow. "And that means the killer will—"

He pulled a wadded-up scrap of paper out of his jeans pocket and passed it to me. "I made a list."

I took it from him and gave it a quick once-over. It was a list of all the murders so far, and the dates on which we believed they occurred. Victim one, the eleventh, victim two, the thirteenth, victim three the seventeenth . . .

"Those are all prime numbers, aren't they?"

Darcy nodded enthusiastically, then ran his fingers through his hair. "All of them."

"And that means someone died on the nineteenth. We just don't know it yet."

"And the next one is—"

"Twenty-three. Tomorrow." I pushed out of my chair, trying to wake myself up. "Gotta hand it to you, Darcy. You're on to something."

"Can we stop him? I think that we should try to stop him."

"But how can we, when we don't know where he is or who his next victim will be? Or who his last victim was? No murder has been reported since the lawyer was killed." I snapped my fingers. "Missing persons. If there's someone who hasn't come home from work on time, or never returned from a coffee break, it could be the next vic."

"But—the police receive hundreds of reports about people missing in Las Vegas every day."

"Yes," I said, clicking through the databases on my computer terminal, trying to find the one I wanted. "But I think I know how to narrow the field."

"Do we . . . do math on the missing persons?"

"No, thank goodness." I raised a knowing eyebrow. "We cross-reference with the database they keep at the DHS."

28

DAMN THE BUREAUCRATS, anyway. Took almost two hours to get clearance to tap into the DHS database. What did they think I was going to do, plant a virus to rescue all the deadbeat dads? Actually, I was tempted to eliminate everything they knew about me, but I knew data left traces even after it was erased—electronic skidmarks, Darcy called them—so I didn't bother. While we were at it, we uncovered Danielle's dark secret—an out-of-wedlock child born many years ago, before she found success, and whom she had put up for adoption at—you guessed it—Clark County Children's Home. The one she gave all the cash contributions—in a way that couldn't be traced back to her.

Once we had access to the DHS records, the process of cross-referencing the DHS database against all the missing persons reports for the past twenty-four hours was daunting. Darcy wrote some kind of subroutine—whatever the hell that is—that sped up the process, but it was still slow going, especially since Darcy had to duck every time his father or Granger emerged from their offices.

While he worked, I excused myself to the bathroom. I'm sure Darcy wondered why I had such a small bladder today, and as smart as he was, he probably suspected I was up to something. But I would think I could be forgiven this minor non-impairing indiscretion when

I was in the midst of trying to save someone who was sure to be dead before midnight tomorrow.

Darcy finally produced a list of three names, all male, who had been reported missing and who also had histories with the DHS. It didn't take me long to know which one was the likely target.

"Joshua Brazee," I said, without blinking.

"Why him?" Darcy wondered.

"He's a celebrity, and twenty-five years ago, he had a pretty good following as a teen heartthrob and recording artist. These other two guys—who knows why they haven't come home? Probably stopped off at a bar and lost track of the time. But when a celebrity misses a show, and there's no press release suggesting that he's collapsed from exhaustion or checked himself into the Betty Ford clinic . . . something's wrong. Besides the killer told us on that tape that he was moving into showbiz next." I grabbed my coat. "I'm going to check it out."

"Can I come?" Darcy said, his eyes wide and imploring.

I looked both ways, made sure the coast was clear. "Okay. But lay low till we're far away from headquarters."

He giggled. "Are we going to act like we are spies? I think that it would be fun to act like we are spies."

"Something like that."

"What if they will not let you backstage?"

I smiled. "I have a friend at the Florence. He owes me one."

THANKS TO my healthy relationship with Frank Olivestra, I had no trouble getting backstage. Joshua Brazee was still missing, but his manager was on the premises. I entered Brazee's dressing room, instructed Darcy to stay out of the way, then started talking.

"Charles Halliwell?" I asked. He was sitting in a chair before a dressing mirror with about a hundred lightbulbs, a handkerchief pressed against his brow.

"Oh, my God, don't tell me. Has something happened to Joshua?"

"That's what we don't know, sir. What we're trying to find out."

I took a seat on an ottoman near him, close enough to smell his breath, which was laced with a certain scent I knew all too well. "Mind if I smoke?" he asked.

I didn't really want him to; I just wanted him to look up at me. It worked. "No, go right ahead."

"That's okay. Probably against the building code." His face was flushed and lined. Coupled with the booze on his breath, I got the impression he'd been through a tough patch. Concern about losing his cash cow? Or was there something more?

"I gather Joshua is still missing?"

"Yes. I don't know what's going on. Joshua has never been anything but trouble, not from the moment I first took him on as a client, when he was just a snot-nosed nobody from Queens. Nothing but trouble. Disappears, never tells anyone where he's gone."

"And you don't know what has happened to him?"

"No idea. None at all. I wish I did."

He was lying. But why? He wasn't the man who had killed the previous victims. Maybe this killing—if it was a killing—was unrelated. Or maybe he had some other reason for playing dumb. "Forgive me, sir, but I've been told by some of the other workers in the casino that you and Joshua had quite a row recently."

Halliwell waved the suggestion away dismissively. "Show people. They're all very high-strung. Like spoiled children, really. Doesn't mean anything."

I plowed ahead. "In fact, some witnesses have suggested that he actually fired you."

"Josh has probably fired me a thousand times. But I'm still his manager."

"Can you think of any possible explanation for his disappearance?"

"Only the obvious one. He disappeared himself."

"Surely he would've told you. Or someone?"

"No. He's taken a powder before without giving anyone so much as a boo. Like I said, show people are like children." He snapped his fingers. "Now that I think about it, he did mention that his mother was in poor health. I thought maybe that was why he was so grumpy with me. It would explain a lot."

"You're saying he took off to see his mother?"

"Well, now that I think about it, it does seem the most likely explanation."

"But—if he's not in danger, why would you call in a missing persons report?"

"I didn't. Olivestra did. I thought we should wait until we knew more. But Frank has his reasons. If he doesn't make a report, he can't file an insurance claim for the loss of income."

True enough. But somehow . . . "Can you give me Joshua's mother's name?"

"Sorry. I don't know it."

"Where does she live?"

"Don't know that, either."

"You've managed him for twenty years and you don't know where his mother lives?"

"He was my client. Not my friend."

That much was clear. "So I've got to search the country looking for a Mrs. Brazee?"

"Actually, Brazee is Josh's stage name."

Someone would choose that for a stage name? "What's his real name?"

"Smith."

I felt my head throbbing. This was impossible. I would be boiling over with frustration—if I believed anything the man was telling me. But I didn't.

Behind me, I heard Darcy clear his throat about as subtly as a bulldozer. I looked back.

He was pointing at the television set. What about it? Darcy made sure Halliwell wasn't watching him, then pantomimed plunging a dagger into his chest.

What the hell?

"Oops!" I said, doing my best to act frantic. "I lost an earring!" Of course, I wasn't wearing earrings. I should've said I lost both earrings, but somehow, that lacked verisimilitude. I just hoped he hadn't noticed the unadorned state of my lobes when I came in.

"Sorry," Halliwell said. "You'll never find it in this shag carpet. Must be a million years old."

I crouched down and pretended to search. In the process, I put the side of my face down against the carpet, next to the television. "You're right. I can't see a thing. Oh, well. They came from Target, not Tiffany's." I scrambled back to my feet and resumed the interrogation. "You say you weren't his friend—would you have any reason to want to get rid of him?"

"Excuse me? What are you saying? Should I call my attorney?"

"Relax. I have to ask everyone these questions."

"I have never hurt anyone in my life, and even if I were going to start, I wouldn't go after one of my own clients. How stupid would that be? Joshua Brazee pays my mortgage."

I shrugged. This interview was going nowhere. Obviously, a different approach was required. I passed him my card. "If you learn anything else—anything about Joshua, or his mother, or anything else that might possibly be of relevance, please call me immediately."

"Of course."

"Thank you for your time, Mr. Halliwell. And speaking as a psychologist, may I recommend that you take some time off? You look as if you could use it."

"Well . . . thank you."

I headed for the door, careful not to betray what I was really thinking. "C'mon, Darcy. There's nothing to find out here."

IT WAS ALL I COULD DO to get Darcy halfway down the hall before he started spilling over.

"But—"

"Not now."

"But—"

"I said, not now."

"But I think—"

"I know what you think. Not now."

"But—"

I found an empty side room—looked like someplace the showgirls got into costume—and pushed Darcy inside, shutting the door behind us.

Darcy couldn't hold it another second. "I do not think that man was telling us the truth."

"Yeah, me neither. Shifty eyes. Went left way too often."

"Shifty . . . ?" And then I remembered—Darcy didn't see faces. "Was there something wrong with his eyes?"

"No, not—I mean not like—" I sighed. "Why don't you believe him?"

"There was blood on the television set. The speckles were very small. But I saw them."

I nodded. "When I put my cheek down on the carpet, it was damp. Like maybe he spilled a drink. Or something."

"I think that maybe he cleaned up most of the blood. But he didn't see the little bitty drops on the television."

I batted my finger against my lips. "Well, if he missed those traces, he must've missed something else."

"We can find the evidence even if he did clean up. Many substances, such as luminol, will reveal traces of blood under ultraviolet light even after the blood has been cleaned and is no longer visible to the naked eye. Blood is absorbed—"

I held up my hand. "End of lecture."

"I was just trying to be helpful."

"And you were." I put my hand on his shoulder and squeezed. "Now we have to figure out what we're going to do about it."

ESTHER LOOKED up from her calculations. She had been working feverishly into the night. This time, she was almost certain she had it. It wasn't finished yet, but all the proofs added up, even the ones that lived only in her head. It was going to work this time. What had once been mere hypothesis would now be acknowledged as fact.

The slamming of the door downstairs jolted her from one mode to the next. The prim intellectual researcher must now give way to the seductive, sex-starved mathematical mystic. Tucker, like any instrument, had to be played with care and precision if she wished to produce the desired effect.

She pushed herself out of her chair, and at the exact same instant that she did, the baby kicked. Kicked like he was going for three points, she thought, as she clutched her tummy and allowed herself to fall back into the chair. The time was fast approaching. The child's time, and her time, and His time. The time when all accounts would be reckoned.

Tucker strode into the room and, without stopping or speaking, went to the bathroom. He was washing his hands, she knew. He always did that, even when he hadn't a thing on him. Pontius Pilate syndrome, she supposed, even though that brute probably had no idea who Pontius Pilate was.

After he finally finished, he came to her, his face ashen, his step hobbled, uncertain and trembling.

"How are you?" she asked, as she cradled him in her arms.

"Not . . . so good," he said, snuggling his head into her shoulder. "It gets harder every time."

"If it were easy, Tucker, anyone could do it. You have been chosen because of your strength, your courage. And your conviction. You do believe in what we're doing, don't you, Tucker?"

"I—" He closed his eyes and dug deeper into her shoulder. "I believe in you."

"As I do you. We are so close. Only a few more and the deconstruction of the primordial form will be complete. The spiral will be finished. The time of the final questioning will be upon us."

"And—And then we can get outta this place?"

"If you wish," she said, not meaning a word of it. Her work was here, her future. She wasn't going anywhere. But then, neither was he. "After that, there will only be you, and me, and the child. No one else. Not in our world. We will live in a universe of three."

"That—That'd be nice. But I worry . . ."

"About what, my love?"

"I'm worried that . . . after I've done all the stuff you want me to do . . . you won't be interested in me anymore."

"That's ridiculous."

"I know what I am. I'm—"

"My hero!"

"A monster. A short, squat monster."

"Tucker! Why would you say these horrible things? You know that I love you."

"You—You do?"

"Haven't I said so? Haven't I said it a million times or more? And if words are not enough . . ." She fiddled with the top button on his shirt. "I'll be happy to show you."

"Does the next one have to be so soon?"

"I'm afraid it does. The numbers control our destiny." She ran her fingers down to his belt and slowly removed it. "But think what a pleasure that job will be. To strike at someone so close to our pursuers. While they remain helpless to prevent it."

"But what if they don't? What if they start to cause trouble?"

"Have they caused any trouble?"

"Not yet. But—"

"Why do you think we left that videotape behind? It's a distraction. It will distort all their attempts to profile, all their attempts to understand. Just as you do."

"I guess. But . . . oh, God." He clung to her like a child, his hands gripping the fabric of her sleeves. "I couldn't go back to the way things were before. Bein' alone all the time. I couldn't live like that. I couldn't live without you. You're . . . everythin' to me."

"And you to me, my love. I trust you, depend upon you." She paused. "And at the moment, I lust for your flesh." She removed his shirt and leaned in closer, sucking and biting his nipples. "Come to me, my love."

"But . . . the baby."

"I'll be on top. You stay just as you are. Be the man I want you to be. Penetrate my soul and fill me with your strength." She wondered if this was a bit over the top, even for a stupid troll like him. Apparently not. She could feel his interest swelling.

"But—you don't have to—"

"I want to," she said, quickly removing her loose-fitting dress and undergarments. "I want to make you happy. I want you to feel things you've never felt before. We are one person, Tucker, you and I. We are meant to be together." She pulled off his pants and lowered herself upon him. His head rocketed backward as if he'd been jolted with an electric current. "Together, Tucker," she said, "you and I. Together always."

29

JULY 23

I WAITED UNTIL well after midnight, until he was almost right beside me, to allow him to bask a few moments in a totally misleading sense of security. Then, just as he exited the elevator and entered the underground parking lot, I grabbed him by the collar, flung him down on the hard stone floor in a storage closet, and locked the door behind us.

"What the—" Halliwell rolled around in the dark, his short roly-poly body resembling nothing so much as Humpty Dumpty after the fall. "You! What are you doing? Why are we in here?"

"I wanted to continue our conversation. And I was hoping that this time maybe you'd tell me the truth."

"The truth! I am offended beyond measure. I know who your superiors are. And don't think I won't contact them. I may even file suit. Flinging me around by force. That's battery. And false imprisonment. I have a very good lawyer, lady. You'll never work in this town again."

"Whatever." I gave him a little kick in the side, not too hard, just enough to let him know I meant business. "Can we continue our conversation now?"

"Absolutely not! And if you don't unlock that door immediately, I'll scream."

"Spare me girlie theatrics." I pulled my weapon out of the holster under my coat. "Because if you try it, I'll shoot you."

"You won't. You can't! I've done nothing wrong."

"I tried to get him to stop, Chief, but he kept resisting arrest. Then he pulled a knife on me. I had no choice."

"I have no knife!"

"I'll lend you one." I cocked the hammer on the gun and aimed it toward his head. "You're only useful to me if you can help me find out what happened to Joshua Brazee. Otherwise, as far as I'm concerned, you can be dead."

"I told you before—I know nothing about that."

"Yeah, but you were lying."

"I was not!"

"Then why did you clean up the blood?"

"I—I did nothing of the sort."

I wagged a finger. "Liar, liar, pants on fire. The carpet was damp. When I returned to Joshua's dressing room, after you left, I found out why. I lifted the carpet in the corner near the television set. Blood had seeped through. You cleaned up the mess topside. But you didn't think to check the carpet pad underneath, did you? Allow me to answer for you. You didn't."

"You conducted an illegal search. An offense to my civil liberties."

I sighed, then stretched out my arms, gun in hand. "Last chance. Tell me what really happened to Joshua."

"I have a right to remain silent. I'm exercising it."

"Listen, Buster Brown—"

"Don't try to do the bad cop routine on me. And don't bother playing any head games, either. You're not gonna crack me, got it? I heard how you took out one of Frank's security nerds. Let me just tell you that I may not look like much, but I got a brown belt in karate, and if you come anywhere near me, your pretty face won't stop me from taking you apart. Try anything with me and I'll put you in the hospital."

"You need to talk to me, Halliwell."

"I'm not telling you a damn thing, you stupid bitch."

So I shot him.

In the upper thigh, barely creasing his leg. I knew (from experience) that a wound like that would hurt like hell, but it wouldn't do any lasting damage. Probably wouldn't even bleed that much. But he didn't know that.

He screamed, but I could hardly fault him, given the circumstances. I just had to hope no one was around to hear. Of course, if someone did try to intervene, I'd just do my Peace Officer routine and shoo them away.

He bellowed, clutching his leg. "I can't believe you shot me!"

"Well, feeling is believing. Want to tell me now what happened? Or should I do the other leg as well?"

"No! God, no!" He held up one hand, then immediately returned it to his wound. "Don't hurt me. I didn't kill Josh. I didn't!"

"I know that," I said, towering above him, gun still in both hands. "No one ever thought you did."

"But—I thought you'd suspect me. Everyone saw us fight. Everyone heard him fire me."

I rolled my eyes. "I get it. You two juveniles had been fighting, so in your egomaniacal way you thought you'd be the prime suspect. You hid all the evidence of murder and told me Joshua was off visiting his mother with the untraceable name. Very smooth." I tilted my head. "It would've been smoother if my research people hadn't discovered that Joshua's mother died ten years ago, but still. You did what you could with your limited resources. Mental resources, I mean." I paused. "Was a part of Joshua's body left behind?"

His face widened, and it wasn't just because of the hole in his leg. "How—How did you know?"

Confirmation. It was our killer. "What part of the body?"

His eyes scrunched closed, as if trying to block out a painful memory. "His right leg."

Ouch. "Tell me that you kept it."

"It's in the basement."

"Don't suppose you know where the rest of him is?"

"No. All the killer left behind was the leg and a lot of blood."

"Tell me about the crime scene, before you screwed it up. Was there anything unusual about it?"

"I need medical attention!"

"So answer my question, and maybe I'll remember that I have a cell phone."

His eyes were watering; his face was losing color. He didn't like any of this, but I really wasn't leaving him any choice, was I? "There was just blood, a huge pool. And that ghastly leg. There were no weapons, no footprints, at least none that I could see. And so many people go in and out of there every day, I can't imagine that you could get any fingerprints."

"We already have the killer's fingerprints. I need something more."

"There was one other thing. A piece of paper." Even though I could tell every movement hurt him, he reached into his pants pocket and pulled out a white scrap covered with pencil scribblings. I wasn't surprised to see it was mathematical. I didn't understand any of it. But I knew someone who would.

"Anything else?"

"No. I promise. Nothing. Now please call an ambulance."

"I will. But remember—you can't tell anyone what happened in here."

"Are you insane? You shot me! I'm going to tell your superiors and everyone—"

"And when you do, I'll tell them how you tampered with a crime scene and lied to a police officer and obstructed justice, all felonies. I'll lose my job, but you'll go to prison. Gee, I wonder who comes out worse?"

"But—"

"No buts. You keep my secret, I'll keep yours. I'll tell them an overzealous maid tried to clean up the blood."

"But—there's a bullet in my leg."

"No, there isn't. Just a graze burn. Tell the docs you were cleaning your pistol and didn't realize there was a bullet in the chamber."

"I don't own a pistol!"

"You do now."

"But—But—"

"Look, it's your own fault. If you'd told me the truth in the first place, this wouldn't have been necessary."

"You still didn't have to shoot me!"

"Actually, I did. Because I don't have time to screw around with your sleazy little showbiz games. This man has killed four times, and has threatened to kill someone linked to the police department. We think he plans to strike today. I can't let that happen. I won't."

30

I EXPECTED the forensic team to show up at the Florence as soon as I reported what had happened, but I didn't expect to see Darcy sitting in the backseat of his father's car. Of course, I'd wanted to check in with him anyway, to see if he was making any progress on the equations I got from Halliwell and read him over the phone. I just expected to have to do so surreptitiously.

The window was down, so it was easy to get his attention, despite his intense concentration. "Hey, Darce. Got those equations solved?"

"Yes. They were easy. I cannot believe you could not solve them." Somehow, when he said it, it wasn't an insult. Just a statement of fact regarding relative intelligences. "The equations are easy. What I do not understand is what good they are."

"Are equations normally good for something?"

"Of course. Do you know about the Enigma machine?"

"Umm . . ."

"It was a code-making and -breaking machine the Germans used during World War II. It was based on mathematics. Most good codes are."

"Well, I suppose—"

"The atomic bomb is based on equations. Numbers put into use."

"Tell me the killer hasn't left us the formula for an atomic bomb."

"I cannot tell what it is."

I put my hand on his head and tousled his hair. "You'll figure it out. I have confidence in you."

I went inside, determined to remain low-profile, but alas, O'Bannon spotted me before I had a chance to duck for cover.

"Pulaski. I got three questions for you. And the answers had better be the right ones."

"Fire away," I said.

"This business of someone cleaning up the blood—that was really the manager, right?"

"Right. But I promised not to tell."

"And the fact that he's currently in the hospital because he accidentally shot himself in the leg—that has nothing to do with you, right?"

"Absolutely."

"Good answer. And you're the one who gave Darcy the latest secret formula, right?"

"You said it was okay to involve him in the math part."

"As if that was all you've done. But you haven't answered the question."

"Yes. 'Twas I."

"Figured as much. You see him outside?"

"Sure."

"He got it solved yet?"

"No. But he will."

A voice from behind me: "Well, that beats doing your own work, doesn't it?"

Granger, natch. "I really resent that, you stooge."

"Hear that?" he said, glaring at O'Bannon. "You hear it?"

"Hear what?" I asked.

"There's only one *s* in resent and stooge. At least, when you're sober."

My eyes flared. "You son of a bitch!" But I couldn't help listening to myself. My *s*'s did seem exceptionally sibilant. Guess I overdid the medication. "I've been sober for six months."

"Bullshit. You've been slurring since this case began."

"You don't know what you're talking about."

"I know your eyes are at half-mast."

"You pathetic dickless wonder. You're so scared of me you'll try anything to get me off the case before I show you up by solving it."

"So far, there hasn't been much danger of that. Your report was the most—"

"Both of you, stop it!" O'Bannon bellowed. "Now!" He turned his head away. "David would be so ashamed. Of both of you!"

"Chief, I have not been drinking."

"Fine. There's an easy way to prove it. I'm sure every trooper outside has a Breathalyzer in his glove compartment. Are you willing to take the test?"

Granger folded his arms, gloating with pride. I hesitated, just to make it good. Finally, feigning nervousness, I said, "Okay, I'll do it. But we do it out of sight and if I'm clean—" I jerked my thumb toward Granger. "You have to promise to keep this ape off my back."

"Done."

"That means I don't take orders from him and my employment is not dependent on his approval."

"Wait a minute!" Granger said.

"What's the matter, big boy? Not willing to put your dick where your mouth is?"

His eyes flared, enraged. "Fine. It's a deal."

So Officer Tompkins was called in, the test was given and—surprise!—I passed. Not a drop of liquor in me. Happily, benzochloriphine doesn't show up on a Breathalyzer. They couldn't possibly know what I knew. That I'd traded one drug of choice for another. Granger's problem was that he couldn't keep pace with the changing shape of my dependencies.

Nonetheless, I smiled defiantly at Granger. "Gosh, you must feel like . . . what's the phrase? . . . a total ass right now."

His fuming was so strong I could smell it.

"Maybe we should run the test on you. You have been acting rather erratic of late."

"Go to hell."

"What are you afraid of?" I cried to his back as he stomped away. "I proved I was clean and sober."

"You proved you were sober," O'Bannon said, in a quiet voice. He gave me a quick look—I didn't even want to contemplate what its meaning might be—and then he returned to the crime scene.

"YOU UNDERSTAND what you have to do?"

"Yes."

"You know the target?"

"Yes."

"You recognize the risks involved?"

"Course."

Esther took Tucker by the arms and held him firmly. "You know this will be harder. Harder than anything you've done yet."

Tucker looked away. "I . . . try not to think about it."

"But you will have to think about it. This will require all your attention. All your strength."

"I know that. Are . . . Are you sure this must be done?"

She touched his sleeve. "I've performed the calculations. I've checked and double-checked them. It is the Way, the Truth, the Pathway to the Eternal. It is written in the Tree of Life. It is illuminated in the Letters of Light."

He nodded gravely. "I understand."

"Do you? Really? Do you understand how important this is?"

"I . . . you told me . . ."

"But do you understand?"

Tucker inhaled deeply, as if purging his inner self. "I don't have to. You understand. That's good enough for me."

As if swept away by the moment, Esther pulled him close, hugging him tightly against her breast. "My God, Tucker, I love you so much. You are so . . . so good."

"I'm not. Good."

"You are. You're good to me." She pulled him away again, holding him at arm's length. "Are you sure you can do this?"

"I could do anything. For you."

They each raised their left hands and pressed the blue stars together. "We are the Brethren of Purity," they chanted. "We preserve the mysteries of the cosmos. We hold the universe in our heads. We know the secret names of God."

Their elbows bent and they drew closer to each other, then closer still. She kissed him, long and passionately, pushing against him as if with a driving need, only separating when it seemed evident any further continuation might lead to an encounter that would delay her plans.

"I'll be waiting for you when you return," she said, her meaning unmistakable.

"I can't wait," he said breathlessly, turning toward the door.

"Darling!"

"Yes?"

She smiled. "Don't forget your knife." She held it out to him.

He took it from her and turned back toward the door, his steps a fraction heavier than they had been before.

"Remember," she said, calling as he headed toward his quarry. "This is the turning point. This is when we make our intentions unmistakable." A thin smile spread across her face, invisible to him, but satisfying to her. "This is when we get to the heart of the matter."

"HE'S LOSING IT," Amelia pronounced, with a certainty that made my heart swell. "This was the killer's sloppiest job yet."

"How can you tell?" I asked, unable to come up with a more intelligent question, mostly focused on making sure my *s* sounds only had one syllable. "Especially after Halliwell screwed up the crime scene."

"Talk to Tony. So far, we've come up with hair samples, fabric fuzz, blood not belonging to the victim—we think he cut himself when he was severing the leg—and epidermals that are almost certain to be good for a DNA match. This is a CSI feeding frenzy. If your killer had a record, we'd have him by the short and curlies."

"But he doesn't."

"Evidently not. Still, surely we'll find something we can trace back to him. There are more tire tracks outside and we have an eyewitness who thinks he saw the UNSUB's car. Combine the two, make a call to VIR, and we should be able to significantly narrow the field. I need to get some of these samples back to the lab. Meet you back there after a bit to compare notes?"

"The sooner the better. Remember—this is the prime number day."

"I haven't forgotten. But take care of yourself, okay? These murders aren't your fault. You're a good person. We need you healthy." I had to smile. Amelia was not only unpredictable—she was damn nice. And she loved me, even though I didn't deserve it. "Tonight then."

I heard Darcy bounding through the door of the dressing room, almost bowling over the plainclothes posted there. He was flying toward me in great sprawling leaps, like Nureyev on acid. "Suuuuuu-sannnn!"

Amelia watched him, more than faintly amused. "This is where I check out. Later, amigo."

"Yeah. See you," I said, just as Darcy all but crashed down at my feet.

"See you?" he said, his head tilted as if he were processing new input. "Where will you see her?"

"Umm, later tonight. At the crime lab."

"Can I come, too?"

"I . . . don't think so." Crestfallen didn't cover it; he looked as if he'd just lost his brother. "But tomorrow, if I can get off work, I'll take you for Shrimp Limone at Zio's. What'd'ya say?"

"Custard afterward?"

"Natch."

He bounced like a pogo stick. "Very Excellent Day! Very Excellent Day!"

"Yes, yes." I held him by the shoulders and tried to calm him. "I'm guessing by the way you came in here that maybe you had something you wanted to tell me?"

"I know what all that algebra is for!"

I inched closer. Could this be the break I'd been waiting for? The one that let me catch this killer? "Give it up, Darce."

"It's for numerology!" Even if he didn't see faces, he must've noticed the decided lack of reaction from me. "Do you know what numerology is for?"

"I don't even know what it is."

He cleared his throat, and the odd, almost mechanical tone of his voice gave way to his recitation voice. "Numerology is the ancient occult belief that numbers influence the lives of people. It is based on the premise that numbers produce harmony throughout the universe. Thus, numbers can be utilized to acquire harmony in personal and professional relations, ranging from a successful marriage to a successful business. It is related to the ancient practice of gematria, the interpretation of scripture by examining the number equivalents of letters or words in the Hebrew or Greek alphabets. Even today, many people—"

"Stop already!" I said, holding out my hands. His eidetic memory was nothing short of amazing. I knew he'd gotten it word-for-word; I knew he could tell me what book he read it in and could probably tell me what page it was on. But recitation wasn't the same as explanation. "Are you saying people use numbers to . . . predict the future or something?"

Darcy nodded with excitement. "All you need is the person's name and their birth date. There are four methods. These formulas use the Birth Path procedure. You take your name as it appears on your birth certificate, excluding titles or qualifiers, give each letter its predetermined value, add them up, divide, and the remainder is your number. You do the same sorta thing with your birthday, add the two, average them, and get your final Destiny Number."

"And that's supposed to tell you something about yourself?" I scanned the room; I didn't want O'Bannon to see me talking to his son. And I especially didn't want him—or anyone—to eavesdrop on this wacky conversation. "So this is about as reliable as, say, astrology?"

"Many famous people have believed in numerology," Darcy said, returning to recitation mode. "It was frequently employed by the ancient alchemists as a substitute for real science or mathematics."

"Algebra and alchemy," I muttered under my breath. "So this crap was cooked up by the same kooks who thought they could turn iron into gold?"

"Most of the basic precepts were formulated by Pythagoras and served as the foundation for his Brethren—"

"But why is this so complicated?" I asked, staring at the arcane formulas written in crimped handwriting on the scrap of paper. "You make it sound as if it's all adding and averaging. Hell, I can do that."

"That is because these formulas do not do it right."

I tried to twist my head around that. "I thought you said—"

"Usually, you would start with a name and apply math to get a result. But these equations start with the result."

"I don't follow."

"These equations are for putting names and birthdays into a mathematical formula and seeing which ones come up as ones. One is the primary and most desirable number in numerology. Anyone who liked numerology would want ones."

Including anyone looking for a victim? I knew that this killer was obsessed with numbers, math. And there didn't seem to be any rational pattern to the selection of the victims. Could that be because he wasn't really picking them? They were being randomly selected by this formula?

"What if you have more than *one* one, Darcy? You'd have to, wouldn't you, if your list of names was large."

"I do not know how the ones are ranked. Maybe in order of birth?"

I thought a moment. No, Danielle Dunn was older than Spencer.

"Maybe in the order the birthdays fall in the year, not counting the year."

Maybe; I didn't remember every victim's birthday. No normal person would—

"No," Darcy announced, "that doesn't work. Amir was born after Danielle. So was Spencer."

"This is hopeless, Darcy. Are you sure there isn't anything more?"

"There is nothing I can do unless I know what list of names is being put into this formula to—"

"Names? Darcy. If I gave you that list of names, do you think you could use this formula to figure out who the next victim is?"

He barely paused a second. "I think that maybe I could do that. Do you have the list of names?"

"Not exactly. But I have an idea—a hunch, anyway—how we can get it. Come on. We're going back to my office."

"But—my dad told me to wait in the car. If you go to your office, he will see me."

"We'll have to sort that out later," I said, tugging on his collar. "You're coming with me, big boy."

NOT HERE, Tucker realized, as he stepped through the glass-paned doors, wearing a long overcoat to hide the knife within. As if this wasn't sufficiently complicated already. He didn't want to linger. Too conspicuous. There were likely hidden cameras that had already captured his image; he didn't want to make it any easier for them than it already was. He couldn't go away, either; too great a risk of missing his intended. What was he supposed to do? She hadn't prepared him for this. She had said the target would be there; his challenge would be to create a diversion to get everyone else out of the building. As it turned out, the diversion was unnecessary. Everyone was gone.

He checked his watch, noticed that his hands were shaking. Every second he delayed was a second off schedule, a number lost, an inevitable subtraction. Too many and the plan would be off-kilter.

She wouldn't love him anymore.

Something had to happen. Something. Maybe if he got down on his knees and prayed—

But that was what she wanted him to do, wasn't it? In her own way.

He had the phone number. He could call, make up some story. But he knew from experience that every diversion from plan entailed a risk. Phone lines could be recorded, traced. A record would be made of who called whom. The person he sought might become suspicious, might not come alone.

What should he do? He was desperate with anxiety. He touched the tiny blue star tattooed on the inside of his palm, his physical reminder of her, what she had done for him. And all that he had done for her. Even the parts that gave him nightmares. The nightmares still continued. But he could live with that. He could live with anything. As long as he had her.

What could he do? What could he possibly—

And then he saw a face behind the glass doors. A face that matched the picture in the computerized database. The target.

He stepped forward. "Uh, 'scuse me."

"I'm sorry, sir. I'm very busy."

"Oh, I know, I know, but, see, I got information."

"What kind of information?"

" 'Bout that guy you've been lookin' for."

A beat. "All right. Follow me."

And he did. As he followed downstairs into the acrylic-walled chambers below, he marveled at how truly easy it could be to penetrate the inner chambers of the Las Vegas Central Downtown Police Department.

"CAN'T YOU MAKE that thing work any faster?" I didn't mean to shout. I would never dream of shouting. But I couldn't help myself. I knew this was the day. The magical mystical prime number day. It was barely an hour till midnight. Any delay would mean we were too late. "It can't have taken the killer this long."

"I think that maybe the killer had an algorithm or program set up to crunch these numbers," Darcy said, never once removing his eyes from the screen. "I have to make one up."

"Then do it already."

He stopped, turned. "I was doing it. Was I doing something wrong?"

"No! Just—don't stop! For God's sake—" I wrapped my arms around him, but at the same time, pushed him gently back toward the computer. "Do you realize how important this is? You're the one who told me the killer would strike again today."

"Yes."

"And the only chance we have of stopping him is to find the name of the next victim."

"That is what I am trying to do."

"But you're not—" I pressed my hand against my forehead, pushing long strands of black hair out of my face. I knew I wasn't helping. Every moment I spoke I distracted Darcy from what he needed to be doing. But I couldn't help myself. Because I knew one detail Darcy didn't. I wasn't simply sure the killer would strike today. I knew he'd promised to hurt someone close to one of us.

I had called the Johnsons, strongly suggested that they get Rachel somewhere safe, someplace no one could get to her, no matter how smart they were. Thank God they listened. I told Granger he should do the same and pass the message on to his detectives. At the same time, I knew it was all probably futile. This creep wouldn't have given us that information if he thought there was any way we could stop him from doing whatever it was he planned to do.

I'd gotten us back to my computer terminal as quickly as possible and re-entered the DHS database. This was playing a hunch in the extreme, but I felt certain the DHS records were the connection.

Unless I was wrong. Unless the killer really was Granger's pathetic anti-porn crusader. In which case, the next victim was dead.

"Maybe this is not the answer to the puzzle," Darcy said, frowning, obviously frustrated.

"It has to be," I insisted. "The man is a signature killer. We just have to uncover the signature. He's not going to change, any more than most people can change the way they sign their names. His signature gives him a feeling of power. He may be a loser in real life, but controlling others allows him to feel better about himself."

"The computer is being very slow. Do you like it when the computer is slow? I get tired of looking at that silly hourglass."

"Tell me you've got something, Darcy," I muttered under my breath. "Come on. Tell me you've got something."

"I have got something."

"No, I mean—" I blinked, then crouched over his shoulder. "Really?"

"Yup. See the names the computer is spitting out? It is making a list. The same list it made for our killer."

"But how could you do it so quickly?"

"I added a few parameters, like I limited the search to people who live inside the city, since all the victims did. And I screened out all the complaining parties. These are just people who had complaints made against them."

I squeezed him tightly. "You are so damn . . . smart!"

"Is that a good thing?"

"Of course it is."

" 'Cause sometimes, my dad says, 'Don't be smart with me, young man,' and I think, what's wrong with being smart? Why is that a bad—"

"Darcy, pay attention to the computer!" I physically adjusted his head to face the screen.

"See!" he cried enthusiastically. "There's the first

name. Amir. That is why he was the first victim. It *is* all in the numbers."

I watched as the computer added names to the list with what seemed painfully slow speed. "Danielle Dunn. Dane Spencer. Joshua Brazee. My God, Darcy, you cracked the code!" The computer was still thinking. I could barely breathe, waiting. It was the next name, I told myself. All we had to do was wait for the next name. And then we'd know.

What must've been seconds seemed an eternity. I could hardly stand it. Come on! I wanted to shout at the damned thing. Give me what I want. Give me what I—

And then it did.

"Oh, my God." My hands clutched at the base of my throat. "Oh, no. God, no."

"I do not know that person," Darcy said. I do not think—" A picture appeared on the screen with a concise bio. "Oh! I do know that person! I do know that person! I just did not know her name. But now I do!" He turned to me. "She is your friend! Do you know where she is?"

"I sure as hell do," I said, already racing away from the desk. How could I not know where she was? She told me. She said she'd be there till I showed up.

Amelia was waiting for me. But the killer was waiting for her.

31

"PLEASE DON'T HURT ME!" Amelia screamed, struggling against the handcuffs. "Please! I don't know anything!"

"You're not here 'cause of what you know," Tucker said, calmly heating the branding iron with an acetylene torch, part of the lab's standard equipment. "You're here 'cause of what you did."

"Do you mean what I did for the investigation? Because if so, you've got the wrong girl." Veins throbbed on the sides of Amelia's smooth forehead. Sweat dripped from her as if she had been out in the rain. She watched as he heated the iron, knowing all too well what he planned to do with it. "I don't know anything. I've been no use to them at all. Useless."

Tucker held the iron up to the light to see if it was hot enough. It was. "You sold your own child."

"What?" She stopped, stunned. It took a moment to catch her breath. "You're—wrong. I—"

"You traded your own flesh and blood for bucks."

"You don't know anything about it. I—I was just a child myself. I didn't know what else to do."

"God gives us brains so that we can know the right thing to do."

"Does God know what you're doing?"

Tucker froze. Even when he resumed movement again, he was slower. Some of the certainty had drained from his eyes. "Course. That's the whole point. To make God . . . understand."

"Then why can't you understand what I did? Why can't you at least try?"

"I didn't choose you. The numbers did. You're Tiferet, a part of the sacred Sefirot, a part of the holy body."

"I'm not! My name is Ameila! I'm a scientist! I don't even believe in—" She stopped herself.

Tucker came closer, holding the iron aloft with its red hot *T*, moving all too certainly toward her. "You will."

"GODDAMN IT, why can't I get the door open?" I pounded on the entrance to the basement crime lab, but it wouldn't give. It was locked and deadbolted, and I didn't have the key. I threw all my weight against it, but it wouldn't budge.

"Is anyone down there?" I screamed. There was no answer, and I knew why. Everyone but Amelia was on duty or at the goddamn crime scene, that was why. Had he planned this? Don't be stupid, I told myself. He couldn't know that sleazy manager would hide the crime. He couldn't know Amelia would be the first to return. He probably had some alternate plan if he needed to get rid of everyone. This was just dumb luck. Blind dead dumb bad luck. That could cost Amelia everything.

I called her on my cell phone, but she didn't answer. I screamed again, and this time I thought I heard something in response. I pressed my ear against the door.

That wasn't a response. It was more screaming. Painful screaming.

Amelia. I was certain of it.

I threw myself against the door, crying out her name. Nothing happened.

"I do not think you are going to get through the door that way," Darcy said. "Not unless you have superpowers. Do you have superpowers?"

Yeah, actually, but none that would get me through that damn steel-reinforced door. I rubbed my sore shoulder and said: "Give me a boost, Darce."

"Huh?"

I pointed upward. There was a small window, probably designed to let in a little light. Definitely not designed for human beings to crawl through.

"I do not think that you will fit. And the glass—"

"I'm going to try!" I shouted.

Without another word, Darcy got down on his hands and knees. I had thought he might lock his hands and let me step into them, but whatever. He got me head-level with the window. I didn't have a proper tool and I wasn't going to waste time searching for one. I balled up my fist and busted out the window. Hurt like hell; my hand came back bleeding, but I ignored the pain. I put both hands through the opening, knocked away the remaining glass, and tried to haul my carcass through. Cut myself but good in the process, but I ignored that, too.

It might be the first and last time, but I thanked God I was a long, skinny flat-chested thing. Thanked God I've been so tranquilized by anxiety medication I've forgotten to eat most meals for the past two weeks. Thanked God my senses were so dulled I didn't notice the shards of glass cutting into me as I slithered through that window.

Even after I'd pulled myself through, I was still about ten feet off the ground—headfirst. Tough. No time for delay.

I let myself drop. Somehow, my usual catlike reflexes failed me. I hit the floor—the very hard tile floor—landing on my right shoulder.

I clambered to my feet, pulled out my gun, and tried to figure out which way to go first. The CSI lab space was enormous, almost half a block, all of it underground. I listened—and heard nothing. That could be good, I tried to tell myself. Or very, very bad.

In each past instance, I reminded myself, the killer had attacked his victims at their place of work. I knew where Amelia's work space was, so I made a beeline for it. I shot down the iron staircase, taking steps two at a time, landing at the bottom with a thud. So much for any chance of surprising him, which was probably shot the instant I broke the window. I had to get to Amelia in time. I had to.

I raced to her desk, then slowed. No one was sitting in her chair. The computer was on, but no one was working with it. I saw a sterling silver tray with all her instruments laid out: the calipers, the scalpel, the tuning scissors, which to me looked all the world like a big fancy pair of garden shears. I saw no people. But the chair was swiveling, ever so slightly. Someone had been there recently.

Behind the desk, I spotted something on the floor. White, or mostly so. I took a step closer.

He must've climbed up on one of the other desks, because when he came down on me, he came from above and he came down hard. I fell forward. My chin hit the desk and you can imagine what that did to my state of mind. My gun skittered across the floor.

I turned around just in time to take one in the stomach. Never in my life have I been hurt like that. I felt as if his fist had gone all the way through me, had rent me into pieces.

And then I saw his face. We were right when we called him a homunculus. There was something inhuman about his strength, his determination. His expression never wavered, never showed the slightest trace of weakness. Brute force radiated through his enormous biceps, his frame, his legs. He was a small but compact powerhouse. I knew I couldn't beat him. The best I could be was his punching bag. Till he decided to kill me.

He lifted me up into the air as if I were a rag doll, held

me aloft, then flung me across the lab into a wall. I fell down onto the floor, helpless. He'd knocked all the breath out of me. I wondered if I'd cracked a rib; I knew my wrist was sprained. There was no way I could stop this inhuman killing machine.

Upstairs I heard a pounding on the door. Help had arrived. But they couldn't get to me. Even if Darcy showed them the broken window, there was no chance they could get to me in time.

My head was swimming, I forced myself to my feet and tried to hobble away from him. He tackled me, knocking me against Amelia's tray table, the tools raining down around me, clattering to the floor. I tried to swing the chair at him, but I was so weak it didn't even count as an annoyance. He pushed it away, growling, as if angered that I had attempted to defend myself. I grabbed a pencil off her desk. I had read somewhere that you could kill someone with a pencil. If you knew how. Which I didn't. I pointed it toward him, but he snatched it away from me and snapped it between two fingers. Then he grabbed me by the collar and lifted me into the air, straight up into the air. And smiled at me.

I squirmed, trying to escape, but he had me totally under his control. He threw me again. It seemed as if I flew ten feet, like people do in the movies. In real life, no one is that strong, right? Except him. He was.

He kicked me in the stomach, then bashed me against the nearest wall. I hurt in every place that it was possible to hurt, and worse, I was ashamed. I had come to help my friend. I hadn't helped her at all. And now he would kill me. I'd seen his face, full and clear. He had no choice.

I tried to stand, but he hammered a fist into my jaw. This time I was certain I would lose it; consciousness was fading fast. Somehow I managed to crawl back toward Amelia's desk. I had to know if she was still alive. At least, if I had to die, please don't let it be in vain. Let me accomplish something before he destroys me.

He grabbed my feet and swung me around again. I smashed into Amelia's desk. Lightbulbs flashed before my eyes, a sure sign that I would not be awake for long. I was covered with blood, bleeding from so many different places I couldn't count them all. I reached out with my bloody hands, trying to find some purchase, anything . . .

I found Amelia's scissors. The big gardening shears.

He came at me again, reached for me with his left hand, but this time, just before he got me, I twisted around, pulled the scissors open, clamped them down on his fingers, and snapped them shut.

He cried out in pain, pulling his hand close to him, minus the two fingers I had just amputated. Blood spewed from the stumps. He was hurt, but I didn't fool myself into believing he was out of commission. At best, this was a temporary setback, an opportunity. I didn't let it go to waste. I crawled forward, glass crunching under my hands, lunged toward him, and plunged the scissors into his gut.

He screamed, howled like a wounded animal, which I suppose is more or less what he was. I pushed hard, jabbing the scissors farther into him, blood spurting everywhere, making sure he wouldn't be able to pull them out.

I rolled backward, crawling on hands and knees. I knew I didn't have long, and I wasn't going to waste it by trying anything as stupid as standing up. I crawled like a baby back to Amelia's desk, back to the blotch of white I'd first seen behind the desk.It was still there, on the floor, motionless. The white was her lab coat, of course. It was splayed open but still on her, even the parts that were no longer white because they were soaked with blood. I winced when I saw the *T* branded on her chest. But that wasn't the worst of it. Not by a long shot.

A huge cavity had been carved open in her chest.

He hadn't been content with a limb this time. Not an arm or a leg. Not even her face. He had ripped out her heart.

BOOK TWO

CALCULUS AND KABBALAH

"In spite of the gloomy dogmas of priests and superstition, the study of numbers is the true theology."

—Thomas Paine

32

JULY 28

GIVEN WHAT I'D SEEN, given what I'd let happen, I think I could be forgiven for wallowing in a multicolored array of multipurpose pills. None of it really worked, certainly not fast enough. At the least, I thought I might get a little sleep out of it. Even after they finally released me from the hospital, battered and bruised and stitched in about a dozen places, I needed sleep, especially after hours and hours of interrogation and questioning and all the blank stares that implied the same message, over and over again: How could you let this happen? To a fellow cop? To your friend? *How could you let it happen?*

When I was finally able to return to my apartment, I crawled into bed in my clothes, pulled a pillow between my legs, and curled up like an embryo, wanting to cry, not able to cry. I needed to talk to someone. I needed to know that someone was there.

I reached past the alarm clock and grabbed the four-leaf clover charm. I squeezed it tight in my fist.

Nothing happened. I tried again, this time clenching my eyes shut as well.

Still nothing happened.

David? *David?*

It wasn't working. I closed my eyes but all I saw was a

fog. Maybe he was out there somewhere—his smell, his taste, his strength—but I couldn't get to it. A hazy wall separated us.

A hazy, drug-induced wall.

Would I have done better if I hadn't been doped to the gills? Or worse? Would the pain I'd have felt slowed me down? Or would my brain, my empathic skills have been able to figure it all out sooner?

I didn't know and I didn't care. Right now, all I wanted was my David. And I couldn't get to him.

I threw the damn charm down and squeezed the pillow all the tighter, trying to make the world go away, David and Amelia and everyone else. Trying to make the pain disappear.

It didn't.

THE REPORT WAITING FOR ME on my desk when I returned to work told me everything I wanted to know—or more accurately, everything I didn't want but needed to know. Amelia had an unwanted baby when she was seventeen. She was poor, jobless. Didn't know what to do. But she was determined not to let it ruin her life. She ended up putting herself in the hands of one of those adoption brokers, who managed to sell the infant girl to a respectable childless family for enough money that Amelia could go to college and start a new life. She thought she did the right thing—but the acquiring parents turned out to be alcoholics. The mother was giving the daughter a bath while intoxicated and ended up drowning her. No one—at least no one sane—blamed Amelia, not even the DHS, but there was a record in the DHS database. And that was what killed her.

My God, poor Amelia. As well as I thought I knew her—I didn't know her at all. She had a secret she never told me, probably never told anyone. Not that I blamed her.

Now she was gone. I missed her. Not even thinking about my personal guilt, how badly I had failed her—I missed her. Seemed all my friends, everyone I cared for most in this world, evaporated like the morning mist.

Well, I could sit around feeling sorry for myself, or I could make damn sure the man in the interrogation room paid the price for what he had done. Which meant I had to understand what he had done and why he'd done it.

I made my way downstairs to the interrogation chamber. I hadn't been invited. But when had I ever let that stop me?

I don't go in for "turf wars." As far as I'm concerned, that's something that was invented by people who learned about police work from old episodes of *Baretta*. If someone else wants to do my work, fine, just don't screw it up. So there was nothing stereotypical about my major mad-on when I found out Granger was the lead interrogator working over the killer. I just knew he'd screw it up.

"Why would you turn him over to that nincompoop instead of me?" I asked the chief, trying not to sound strident. I really hate being strident. It's so predictable. "I'm the one who caught him."

"And about got yourself killed in the process," O'Bannon grunted. "Last I heard, you were in the hospital getting your ribs bandaged."

"Last I heard, the doctors were doing some serious work on him, too. So what? Let me in there."

O'Bannon shook his head. "You're too close."

"Why? Because he tried to turn me into a slab of ground round?"

"Because Amelia was your friend."

"Amelia was everybody here's friend."

"Not like that."

"Look, I'm a professional. I can separate—"

"And as far as I'm concerned," O'Bannon said, cutting me off, "you should be under suspension for disobeying my direct orders."

"What?"

"I told you to leave Darcy out of it. More than once."

"You said I could use him for the math stuff. That's all I was doing."

"Don't kid a kidder. The only reason he wasn't down in the crime lab getting the shit beat out of him is that his shoulders are too broad to fit through that damn little window."

"If it hadn't been for Darcy, I wouldn't have been able to figure out that Amelia was the next target." Amelia. My God, I almost choked when I said the word. Amelia had died, damn it. Died. Because I didn't get there in time. "And I wouldn't have caught the killer."

"Nonetheless, you disobeyed a direct order. I don't want Darcy to have anything to do with this mess."

"W-W-W-Wellll . . . m-maybe I do."

We both whirled around to find Darcy standing in the doorway. How long had he been listening?

O'Bannon's shoulders sagged wearily. "Darcy, this is a private conference. You should wait outside."

"Are you talking about me?"

"Well . . ."

"Th-Th-Then I will stay."

O'Bannon took a step forward. "Darcy . . . we're working on a case."

"Th-Th-Then I sh-should stay. I am also working on this case."

"You shouldn't be. Susan was out of line."

"Susan did not do anything. I worked on this case because I wanted to work on this case. I got into a crime scene using your badge."

I've seen O'Bannon go through a wide variety of emotions in my time, but this was the first time I'd ever seen him do "stunned." "*What?*"

"I-I-I-I want to do police work. I am good at it."

"Darcy, we all have things we want to do. Hell, I wanted to be a pro baseball player. What I didn't have was the ability."

"I can do police stuff."

"Darcy, you have to be realistic about your . . . disability."

"I-I-I do not have a d-d-d-disability! I can do this. I saw stuff that none of you saw!"

O'Bannon sighed. "Darcy . . . go home. We'll talk about this later."

"*No!*" I'd never heard Darcy raise his voice in my entire life—I wasn't sure he was capable of it. Until then. He turned on his heel and stomped away.

"You see what you've done?" O'Bannon bellowed at me. "This is your fault."

"Is it? I'm on his side. I think he'd make a hell of a cop."

"How could he be a cop when he can't even carry on a normal conversation, huh? Answer me that?"

"Who cares about conversation? Any idiot can do that. Granger can do that. But I don't know anyone who can do the things Darcy can do."

O'Bannon pressed his hand against his forehead. "Would you please just . . . drop this?"

"Fine. But I want in on the interrogation."

"It's Granger's."

"Uh-huh. And in three days, has he managed to get a damn thing out of the man?"

"Thanks to you, 'the man' is barely out of the hospital himself."

"But has Granger gotten anything?"

O'Bannon shook his head. I could tell he didn't want to give in, but he didn't have the strength to argue with me anymore. Somehow, the confrontation with Darcy had drained him in a way that I'd never managed to do. "Come on."

They had Tucker in the largest and most high-tech interrogation room; everything he did or said was being recorded on both audio- and videotape. We could stand behind the mirror and watch everything without Tucker knowing. Although after so many years of cop shows, you had to wonder if every suspect didn't assume there was someone watching behind what appeared to be a mirror.

The gods were with me. We arrived at just the right moment to catch Granger in full bellow. "That was how you got your jollies, wasn't it? Killing innocent people? You couldn't make it with a real girl. Maybe you don't even like girls!"

I felt it was safe to assume Granger was playing the bad cop. Despite his wild gesticulation, his endless ranting and raving, Tucker sat motionless, staring upward, not saying a word, not betraying the least emotion.

"That's why you had to kill all those people, isn't it? Kill them and cut them into pieces. Was that the only way you could get it up? I bet it was. Because you couldn't face up to the fact that you like boys more than you like girls. Because you're just a goddamned flaming faggot!"

Just watching this pathetic display made my stomach hurt. Fortunately, the sour expression on O'Bannon's face suggested that he wasn't enjoying it any more than I was. "Please," I said simply. "I beg you."

"Give him another minute."

"For what? That idiot couldn't get Edward the Confessor to confess."

"He won't talk to you, either."

"You don't know that."

"Susan—you cut off the man's fingers!"

"Well, the surgeons sewed them back on, didn't they?"

"They tried. We don't know if it's going to take or not."

"He slung me halfway across the room three times. He might be feeling remorse."

"Yeah. His history does indicate that he's a sensitive soul."

"C'mon. I can't do any worse than Granger."

"All right," he said, blowing air through his teeth. "But I'm not pulling Granger out."

"I can deal with that."

I turned the doorknob and stepped inside. Granger was still ranting. "Maybe your mommy liked to make you wear little dresses, is that what it was? And maybe you liked it. Maybe you still like it. Maybe I should go get a dress for you right now, huh?" He leaned into Tucker's face. "You'd like that, wouldn't you?"

I tapped Granger on the shoulder. "Take five, boss man."

He straightened. "What the hell are you doing in here?"

"O'Bannon sent me in. Thought you could use a break."

"Are you kidding?" Now he was ranting at me. "I was just starting to get somewhere."

"No, you weren't."

"You presumptuous— You think just because you're a shrink you're the only person on earth who can ask a question?"

"Obviously not. You've been asking questions for three days. You just aren't asking the right ones."

Tucker watched us as he might a tennis match, head moving left, then right, never changing expression, never saying a word.

"I know what I'm doing. Get the hell out of here."

"No."

"That's an order, Pulaski. Leave!"

"You don't get to give me orders anymore, remember?

And you don't know anything about the man you're interrogating."

"I know he hates sex." He turned back to Tucker. "That's why you hate porn and people who like porn, isn't it? Because those are all things you can't do. That's a world you'll never know because you're such a flaming faggot!"

"How old were you when he came to town?" I asked quietly.

Both men looked at me, neither sure to whom I was speaking.

"I'm guessing fourteen, maybe fifteen. Am I right, Granger?"

He stared at me with a total lack of comprehension. "I don't know what you're babbling about."

"The new boy. The one you liked."

"What?"

"You were young, confused. You didn't know the way the world worked. You just knew that you . . . liked this new boy. You thought he was pretty."

"What the hell? Who do you think you're interrogating?"

"You had strange feelings you didn't understand. You wanted so much to tell him about it. But you couldn't."

"You're . . . so nuts—"

That's when I glimpsed it. "No. You did tell him. You did tell him and it went badly. What happened? Did he laugh at you? Did he call you a flaming faggot? Is that why the phrase is so burned into your brain?"

"Spare me the pop psychology crap."

"He probably told the whole school. That's why you had to move to Vegas, isn't it? But moving wasn't enough. You never forgot that boy. Even after you signed up for the toughest, most manly profession you could imagine. You never forgot that boy."

"Pulaski, you are full of shit!"

"Until you met David."

He stopped and stared, gaping at me.

"My husband. Your partner. Small wonder you've never forgiven me for his death. You loved him."

"You don't know what you're talking about!"

"Just keep telling yourself that. We both know better."

He looked as if he were about to pounce. "You—This is—I'm reporting this to O'Bannon!"

"Cool. I'll interrogate the suspect."

Granger flew out of the room in a palpable rage, his face red and sweaty.

I smiled at Tucker. "I thought he'd never leave." I pulled out a chair and sat opposite him at the small table. We stared at each other for a good long time. I wasn't sure how to begin and didn't see any urgency to find out. He'd been sitting there for hours without speaking. I could take a minute to plan my approach.

As it turned out, it didn't take as long as I thought it might. Maybe five excruciating minutes passed before Tucker spoke. "You're a smart lady."

Far be it from me to disagree. "Is that good?"

He shrugged.

"Do you like smart ladies?"

He looked me straight in the eyes. "Yeah." He shifted his weight. I realized he was so short his feet didn't touch the ground when he sat back in his chair. "Sorry I hurt ya."

"Are you?"

Still looking at me. "Yeah."

I nodded. "I'm sorry about the fingers."

Another shrug. Another dead silence. I figured this time it was my turn.

"Why did you hate your father?"

"I never said I did."

"You didn't have to."

He looked down at his lap. "I don't wanna talk about him."

But, by implication, he did wanna talk about something. I just had to figure out what it was. "How many times have you wished you were dead?" I asked.

No response. Tiny twitch under his left eye. I was close, but not quite there.

I grabbed his left wrist and pulled it across the table. "How many times have you tried to kill yourself?"

He pulled his arm back before I could get a good look. "None. What about you? That's a pretty good scar on your left wrist."

Damn me and my monkey arms. They never make the sleeves long enough. "Skiing accident."

"Right."

"It's none of your business."

"Yeah? Why is it you get to ask me all these questions if I can't even ask you one?"

"Because I haven't murdered anybody."

Good answer—if I wanted him to clam up. Because that's what happened. And I was stuck trying to reboot the conversation one more time.

"Is it your body you despise? Or your brain?"

No answer. He wasn't biting.

"I know you're not gay."

"That's swell."

"But I don't understand why you killed all those people. I don't get the pattern. The mutilations. What's it all about?"

To my very great surprise, he answered. "The Kabbalah."

"The what?"

"It's a Jewish mystical . . . thing. Real old."

I squinted. He took his instructions from an ancient

religious text? He could barely explain to me what it was. "Are you good at math, Tucker?"

"Pitiful."

"Algebra?"

"Never saw the point."

If he was lying, he was the best damn liar I'd encountered in my entire life. Plus, I'd seen his school records, up to the tenth grade, when he dropped out. They didn't indicate any great proficiency at math. Or anything else. For reasons I couldn't even explain yet, I felt a cold chill grip the base of my spine. "Then why leave all those equations behind?"

"Because I was supposed to."

"The Kabbalah told you to do this?"

"No."

"You wanted me to catch you? So the killings would stop?"

"No." And then he laughed. It was short and unenthusiastic, but it was still the most harrowing thing I'd heard come out of his mouth yet. What was going on here? Five minutes with a creep and I should be able to zero in on him. But the magic wasn't working.

"As you might've heard, Granger thinks you enjoyed killing all those people. Did you?"

"No," he said succinctly—and I believed him.

"Then—why?"

"The Kabbalah."

That again. "This Jewish thingie said you had to kill people in the NDHS database?"

He didn't answer, but he didn't argue, either.

"Are you even Jewish? You don't look it."

"Hell, no."

"Then—" No, stop. Think of a better approach. "So you killed those people . . . because it gave you one more thing to despise about yourself."

"I told you—"

"Don't give me this Kabbalah crap. That's an excuse, not a reason. You did it because you hate yourself. You're counting on the state to put you out of your misery."

"No."

"I can help you, Tucker. I can even help you like yourself."

"I doubt that."

"Look, if I can make myself like myself, I can do the same for you." A supposition based on a false premise, but never mind that. "But only if you let me." I paused. "Tell me why you killed these people."

"I didn't want to do it."

"I know. But you did. Why?"

"I told you already."

"You told me nothing!"

Tucker smiled, and then, to my horror, he began to sing, softly, as if I weren't even in the room, as if it were his way of blocking me out. "Round and round the cobbler's bench, the monkey chased the weasel; The monkey thought twas all in fun—"

"Tucker—"

"*Pop!* Goes the weasel."

I almost jumped out of my chair when he shouted the "Pop!" He was really starting to creep me out. "Listen to me, Tucker. You killed five people. Five. You chose them in a weird way. You did sick things to their bodies. You hauled their corpses to distant locations. You only killed on prime number days and you chose your victims according to a formula I'm not sure you even understand. I don't believe you got all this out of some musty Hebrew text! So why the hell did you do it?"

He stared at me for the longest time. Finally, he must've decided it didn't matter. What could I do about it? "Because she told me to."

I felt as if he'd socked me in the gut, except somehow,

this hurt worse than the numerous times when he did just that. "*She*? Who's *she*?"

"I won't tell you. I'll never tell you."

"Why not?"

"Because it isn't finished yet."

My hands were shaking. I wished to God I could tell myself he was lying, that he was trying to absolve himself by inventing a co-conspirator. But in my heart, I knew better. It was all starting to make sense, all the contradictions, all the inconsistencies . . . "What isn't finished?"

"The plan. The deconstruction of the Sefirot."

"And what the hell is that?"

He wouldn't say.

"Does it involve more killing?"

"Yeah."

"But—But—how can she kill more people when her ace thug is in lockup?"

"I dunno. She'll find a way."

"I'd like to know what that way is."

"You won't have to wonder long."

I leaned across the table. "Why? Why do you say that?"

He smiled, as if perfectly at ease, content with himself and his role in the universe. "Twenty-nine is a prime number."

ESTHER FINISHED packing her bags, drove downtown, abandoned her car, then walked to the dingy motel room she had carefully reserved under an assumed name. She had no illusions about what was going to happen next.

It was only a matter of time before Tucker was caught. She'd known that from the first. If anything, he'd lasted longer than she'd expected. She'd known this time would come, so she'd prepared accordingly—made sure she could leave on a moment's notice. Not that he was likely to rat her out. The doofus was far too head over heels in love, or perhaps lust, for that. But you can never be too careful. So she'd arranged a false ID well in advance and bought another car under a fake name. From now on she would operate under enough of a disguise that no one could identify or recognize her.

Had she been wrong to drag Tucker into her personal quest? What had to be done had to be done. She was pregnant—very pregnant, now, and her strength was failing. She couldn't go on pretending she wasn't ill. Every day she felt a little weaker. She needed to conserve her energy. So it was only logical to . . . outsource as much of the ceremonial proceedings as possible. Tucker was important. But if she had to finish—so be it. She'd manage.

Poor sweet moronic Tucker. Statistically speaking, there was a perfect match somewhere in the world for everyone on earth. Except maybe Tucker. It was almost endearing—in a pathetic sort of way—how he had clamped on to her and held tight and forced himself to do anything she said, anything she wanted. Just to keep the sex coming? Not really. Just so she would stroke his hair and tell him he'd been a good boy. That was all he wanted. A lover, yes, but a parent most of all.

It was a shame that the DHS list had been discovered, but that too she had known was a contingent possibility. Didn't matter. There were other ways. Vegas would never run short of lousy parents. She had already made her remaining selections.

It was almost end game. One more individual for the 29th, the sixth member of the Sefirot—and then it would be time for the grand finale. The glorious conclusion to all she had done, everything she had calculated. The final expression so perfect even He would be forced to take notice. He would reveal Himself unto her.

And then? Then she'd give Him a piece of her mind.

33

JULY 29

"I DON'T BUY IT," Granger said. We were sitting in a conference room together, me and him and O'Bannon. Darcy had wanted to come in, but his father made him wait outside. "I think he's making up the accomplice. Trying to get himself off the hook."

"I don't want to believe it," I responded. "I thought this case was over. I wanted this case to be over." I hoped my voice didn't sound as desperate as I felt. "But he isn't lying."

"You don't know that."

"I do."

"Stop," O'Bannon interjected. "Bickering won't get us anywhere. Have either of you managed to get him to talk about this woman who supposedly told him what to do?"

"No," we both said simultaneously.

"But you think she'll carry on alone."

"Or enlist another Tucker, I don't know," I said. "But she doesn't have much time."

"So she skips a prime number. So what? She just waits for the next one."

"No. She'll do it on the appointed day. Everything has been so . . . meticulously planned. So orchestrated and orderly. She thinks she's figured out the universe, reduced it all to a common denominator. Who knows what might happen if she broke the pattern? The whole system might fall apart."

O'Bannon wrapped his hand around his jaw. "Puts us in a hell of a spot. We told the press we caught the guy."

"We did catch the guy," I said, not trying to be funny. "But now we have to catch the girl."

"And how are we going to do that? When he won't tell us who she is. We've checked all the forensic evidence. Fingerprints, footprints. It all points to him. There's no trace of a second person."

"She's out there, just the same."

"That's not good enough, Susan. You've got to find her. Fast."

"Got it. Fast. Reaching for the Bat-Phone."

"Don't give me—"

"But for starters," I interrupted, "I'm going to visit my friendly neighborhood rabbi."

I DIDN'T MIND meeting Rabbi Hoffman at the Friedman Jewish Community Center. If anything, I was relieved. Been a long time since I was in a church, frankly. Synagogue, whatever. Still, my mental image as I drove over was that I was going to see a man decked out in black, probably with a big bushy salt-and-pepper beard. Like in *Fiddler on the Roof*. A white scarf around his neck with a beaded Star of David sewn into it, hunched over a huge edition of the Torah, thinking studious thoughts.

I didn't expect to see him in gym shorts, at any rate.

"My apologies," he said, wiping his brow. "Racquetball game lasted longer than I expected." He was slim, clean-shaven, and young. Probably younger than me. More like a Calvin Klein model than a rabbi.

"No problem," I said, trying to rearrange my stereotyped anticipations and get a grip. "Did you win?"

"If I had, I'd have told you already."

He guided me into a small room—the reading room, according to the lettering on the door—just off the main lobby. "What can I do for you? I can't imagine how I could help with a police investigation."

"Well, this isn't exactly your average ordinary police investigation. We're looking for a serial killer—"

"Not the one I've been reading about in the paper. The deep fat fryer—"

"That's the one. All the murders have followed a strange mathematical pattern—"

"Really?" His eyes brightened. "My undergraduate degree was in math."

Which was why Colin had recommended this particular rabbi. "And now we have information indicating that there may be a religious connection. Something to do with the Kabbalah. You know anything about that?"

"About the killings? Or the Kabbalah?" He grinned. He was damned handsome, for a rabbi. I tried to remember—are rabbis allowed to marry? "I'm going to assume the latter. Yes, I've done quite a bit of research into Kabbalistic history. Against the advice of my colleagues."

"They don't care for the Kabbalah?"

"Not many do. It's become sort of the pop culture stepchild of Judaism. Madonna professes to be an adherent of the Kabbalah, and I think that pretty well says it all."

I stifled a laugh.

"When you talk about the Kabbalah, though, you're not talking about religion. It's mysticism. It may have evolved from Judaism, but please let me assure you it is not the same thing."

"Does it have anything to do with math?"

"A lot, actually. But then, so does Judaism. The Kabbalah didn't really come into its own until around the fifth century, but its mathematical origins can be traced back to Pythagoras. A great mathematician—but also a great mystic. You could argue that all the secret societies, the Masons, the Scottish Rites, whatever, date back to the secret society he formed way back when."

"Because they wanted to keep this big secret, right? The square root of two."

"You are well-informed."

"Well, I have good advisors."

"Not being able to reduce the square root of two to an integer may not seem like a big deal to you and me, but for the blue-star crowd—"

"The what?"

"The blue stars. Did you know that all the members of the Pythagorean secret society had tiny blue stars tattooed on the palm of their hand?"

"I didn't."

"That was how they identified themselves to one another. Predecessor to the secret handshake, I guess. Anyway, the secret motto of the Brethren of Purity was: God is number. And their definition of number was whole numbers, and the ratios between whole numbers. Problem is—whatever the square root of two is, it clearly is not a whole number. This was a devastating blow for the secret society. It challenged their understanding of the universe, of God. It suggested that God was not perfect."

"I'd think a simple look around town would prove that to them," I said, then immediately regretted it. "Sorry, Father. Brother. Whatever. What do rabbis call themselves?"

"Rabbis. But you can call me Mike. And don't worry about sending a little populist cynicism my way. Keeps me on my toes." He smiled again. Cute. "Anyway, they lived with this secret, but it is one reason they kept the society exclusive. It continued to thrive, even after Pythagoras's death—till a rival group of mystics called the Sybaris attacked and slaughtered them. A few got away and managed to record what they knew, but it was the end of the cult."

"Fascinating. But what has this got to do with the Kabbalah?"

"Are you familiar with the Jewish priesthood? How it started and all."

"Mmm . . . with Moses?"

"Darn close. His brother, Aaron. In this time, before written language, the priest was responsible for preserving wisdom orally. It wasn't until much later that the five books comprising the Torah were written down. And it wasn't until a thousand years later, during the Babylonian exile, that priests began to write the secret interpretations of the Torah. See, unlike the fundamentalists in a certain rival religion I won't name, we've never pretended that the stories in these books were literally true. We've always understood them to be allegorical. And we've never suggested that there can be only one correct interpretation of these texts, either. The Torah contains many interpretations. The Kabbalist reads the Torah on four different levels—the literal, the allegoric, the homiletic, and the secret. The point is to encourage debate. To make people think. Not to turn them into mindless puppets regurgitating nonsense they heard fifty years ago in Sunday school."

"So, uh, tell me, Mike—is this something you feel strongly about?"

I made him laugh. Hurrah! "Sorry. I get a little wound up sometimes."

"Is the Kabbalah part of the Torah?"

"Heavens, no. It's not even a written text, or wasn't originally. It came from another secret society, a Jewish one. Secret teachings, secret practices and prayers. The name literally means: the received tradition of the Jews. First in Spain in the eleventh century, then elsewhere, the Kabbalists organized to study the Torah and to look for hidden meanings and truths. Which soon led to thinking about numbers."

"It did?"

"Absolutely. Every letter in the Hebrew alphabet has a corresponding number."

The light dawned. "Like numerology."

"Exactly. This may be where that occult belief originated. The idea was that any words that had the same numerical value were linked in meaning. So the Kabbalists began to study the Torah focusing not on the meanings of words, but on these numeric connections. Sefirotic correspondences."

"And this caught on? Because frankly—it sounds kind of boring."

He held up a finger. "Not if you think you're unraveling the secrets of the universe."

"I don't know . . ."

"Not if you think you're forging a hotline to God. The Kabbalah has been very influential. Dante borrowed from it when he created his—extremely mathematically precise—*Divine Comedy.* Augustine, Aquinas, and many others you probably think of as Christian figures were influenced by the Kabbalah."

"Well . . . can you give me the Cliffs' Notes version?"

"The fundamental premise of Kabbalistic learning is the Sefirot, which is based upon the components of God's greatest creation."

I leaned forward eagerly. "The Sefirot? Our suspect mentioned that. What is it?"

"I won't bore you with the mathematical and translational methods by which this system was devised. Just think of it as a tree of life. It has been conceptualized different ways—with twelve parts, ten or seven. Seven is probably the favorite, because it's considered the most holy number in Judaism, the number that shows up the most often in important places in the Torah."

"Okay, let's go with seven."

"Fine. Now, envision a primordial human body. Each part of the Sefirot represents a limb of the body, each symbolizing man's closeness to God. Keter is the head. Binah is the face. Chesed is the arm. Netzach is the leg. Tiferet is the heart."

He must've read my reaction.

"What? Does this mean something?"

I could feel my pulse racing, but I managed to answer. "The mutilations. I mean—what the killer took each time. Face, head, arm, leg. Heart." Poor sweet Amelia. Because I wasn't there to help her, even after she'd helped me a hundred times. "The killer—or whoever is behind the killer—is hacking away each part of the Sefirot. And those names—that explains the letter branded on each victim." I paused to think. "What comes next? After the heart."

"Yesod, representing the genitals."

"Oh, God."

"And then Malchut, who is sometimes interpreted as representing the feet, but is also used to symbolize many people, or humanity itself. All mankind."

"I don't even want to think about how she accomplishes that part of her mission."

Rabbi Hoffman paused. "Your killer is not just dismembering the victims. She's dismembering Creation itself. She's severing our connection to God."

This was way too much for me, even with the tranquilizers. My head was spinning. "But—why?"

He turned his hands out helplessly. "I think that question falls more in your department than mine."

"Does this mean . . . the killer thinks he's the Antichrist?"

He shook his head. "Even in Christian theology, the Beast comes to tempt man, not to destroy him. In math, we have so-called apocalyptic numbers—Fibonacci numbers with precisely 666 digits. But that doesn't explain these murders."

"Maybe the killer wants to summon the Antichrist. Or maybe . . . to challenge the Church. Christianity."

"The person who destroys the Sefirot . . ." Hoffman looked at me helplessly. "It's a line in the Zohar, perhaps the most cherished of all Kabbalistic texts. 'He who destroys the Sefirot challenges the Aleph.' "

"The Aleph? What's that?"

"Remember when I told you that all the Hebrew letters had numeric correspondents? The Aleph is the first letter in the alphabet, or in numeric terms, one. Which is interpreted to mean oneness. Infinite nature." He took a deep breath. "In other words, God. He who destroys the Sefirot challenges God."

34

THOMAS STEVENS BROUGHT the close-up mirror practically next to his nose and scrutinized the cut of his beard. Left profile—perfect. Right profile—almost perfect. But not quite. He held the tiny scissors in his left hand—he was quite ambidextrous—and clipped the offending hairs until his beard lay as perfectly as if it had been sculpted by Michelangelo. Perfection!

He applied a little gel until he had his hair precisely the way he wanted it—chic, hip, youthful. None of that absurd comb-over Donald Trump stuff. Not that he had a bald spot, or ever would, but if he did, he wouldn't try to mask it in such an obvious fashion. It was beneath him. He dressed in one of his best suits, a black, always black, Armani number that had been specially tailored. A cane this evening? Yes, a cane, he thought. Added just the right panache. A tad eccentric, since he didn't need it to walk, but loaded with élan.

Stevens noticed that the latest in his long series of gentlemen's gentlemen had positioned himself just inside his dressing room door. He seemed to float soundlessly into the room; it was a bit eerie, actually. And his knowledge was equally impressive.

"There are representatives of the press positioned in the hotel lobby," the man announced. Stevens didn't know his name. He liked to call them all Jeeves; it was so literary. "Presumably awaiting your comments regarding the contemplated merger."

"That's fine. Just fine."

"Should I instruct the security officers to forcibly disperse them?"

"No, not necessary."

"Then should I instruct your press secretary to announce that you will give a brief statement?"

"No, not that, either," he answered, while knotting his tie.

The man stood granite-still, making only a small throat-clearing sound. Stevens knew this was his way of saying, Well, what the hell should I do, then?

"Leave them as they are. I have no objection to picking up a little publicity on my way to the deal. The more attention I can draw to the negotiations, the more likely this business will be completed in a satisfactory fashion."

"Then—"

"I won't say anything informative. Just a few cryptic comments on my way through the lobby. Then into the limousine and off I go."

"Perhaps I should have a security detail attend your automobile."

"Not necessary. Mercer can handle the crowd. No one can get into the garage unless they know the numeric password on the access lock pads." Mercer was his driver, had been for years. "Is my tie straight?"

"Your appearance is, as always, impeccable, sir."

"Good. Uh . . . tell me. Has there been . . . any activity from Mr. Wynn?"

"No, sir. Not to my knowledge. Were you expecting any?"

"You never know. Wynn loves attention." Steve Wynn was, of course, the other building mogul in Vegas, the big dog, the man with the global reputation, although as far as Stevens was concerned, it was based mostly on his talent for capturing media attention, not for his business acumen. Stevens could deal rings around him, though that didn't get him in the papers. These days, it was all about name recognition.

Stevens reached for his fur-lined jacket, even though it wasn't cold today and, in point of fact, was never cold in Vegas. Let PETA cry their hearts out; he looked good in it. "Will there be anything else?"

"Only if you wish it, sir."

"Then—how can I put it politely—why are you still here?"

His man cleared his throat again. "I know that you have been quite busy of late, sir, but may I assume that you are familiar with the series of unfortunate events that have occurred the last few weeks in our fair city?"

"You mean the murderer? The one who got Danielle?"

"The very same, sir. Quite a dangerous fellow."

"I thought they caught him."

"It seems, as is so often the case, the announcement of mission accomplished was premature. He is believed to have an accomplice who is still at liberty."

"So what's your point?"

"My point, sir, is that—" Here he cleared his throat again. "According to the morning *Courier,* the pattern that links all these killings together involves records at the Department of Human Services regarding parenting issues."

Stevens's neck stiffened ever so slightly. "And your point is?"

"I do not wish to give offense, sir—"

"Then don't."

"But I feel it is my duty—"

"I tell you what your duty is, understand me?"

His chin rose ever so slightly. "As you say, sir."

"Good. Glad we got that worked out." He smiled. "Don't mean to put you off, old boy, but I've got the best security system in town. No one can get to me." He grabbed his cane and started toward the door, but just before he reached it, he put the knob of his cane under his gentleman's gentleman's chin. "And tell the gang down in the servants' quarters to stop gossiping, would you? Something like that could cost a person their job. And jobs are hard to find these days. Especially for anyone who burns me."

THIS TIME, I didn't wait until Tucker was comfortable, didn't offer him a drink, didn't let the boss send out for sandwiches. I wanted him to be uncomfortable. If I didn't get the name of the woman who had been pushing his buttons today, it would be too late for someone.

With Darcy's help, we'd run our own homegrown version of the numerology program to come up with the next few likely victims in the DHS files. They were all under heavy surveillance. At the same time, I knew that Tucker's boss was anything but stupid. She knew we had him. That meant she probably knew we'd broken the code. That meant we couldn't count on her adhering to it. Tucker said he didn't know who the next victim would be, and sadly, I believed him. That meant my only chance of stopping the next murder was to find out who this woman was and to stop her.

I slid into the chair at the opposite end of the table in the interrogation room. Didn't even give him a chance to breathe. "Sexual slavery," I said. And waited for a response.

Tucker stared at me. He looked tired. I suppose I would be too if I'd had people grilling me for so long. He hadn't shaved, hadn't washed his hair. Dark bags under his eyes told me he hadn't slept well. All good. " 'Zat a question?"

"No, but this is. Are you familiar with the concept of sexual slavery?"

"No."

"I think you are."

"I don't go in for the kinky stuff."

"I think you do."

"You're wrong."

"Then was she the one who liked the kinky stuff?"

"No!"

I leaned forward, capitalizing as best I could on his defensiveness spike. "Are you sure?" I saw the look in his eye, and then I knew. "No, she acted as if she liked the kinky stuff, but it was all show. It was for you. And you knew it. That's how she kept you. How she controlled you."

"Don't know . . . what you're talkin' about."

"Sure you do. I already told you. Sexual slavery. You'd probably never been with a woman who gave you exactly what you craved most." I paused. God but his eyes were illuminating. "You'd never been with a woman at all, had you?"

"That's not true!"

"Sure it is. You were a thirty-something virgin till she came along. Reasonably pretty. Smart. Hell of a lot smarter than you. Did the stuff you secretly wanted her to do. Sure, she was a sadist. She hurt you. That explains those claw marks on your back." He stiffened, more than enough to tell me I was right. "A relationship based upon sexual servitude. And you were the compliant victim." I smiled. "That's why you don't have a record. You probably never committed a crime in your life till you met her. Tough childhood, sure, but I'm betting you never stole a gumball from a drugstore. She exploited your naivete and, it must be said, your stupidity.

What you didn't understand is that sexual sadists secretly despise members of the opposite sex. And in this case, I think your sexually confused master probably hates people of both sexes. That's why she was so hard on you. That's why she's so hard on everyone."

"You don't know what you're talkin' about."

"I do. And you know I do. She spotted you, broke you, used you. That simple. You've probably got DPD—dependent personality disorder. Your mistress has radar for finding men like you, and this city is full of them. Why else would they come here to self-destruct with gambling or booze or drugs? She seduced you, told you she loved you. And you're such a sap you actually believed her."

"That's not true!" he shouted. If he hadn't been chained down, he would've risen out of his seat. "She does love me. I know she does."

"Then why is she letting you take the rap for her crimes? Why is it you're the one in custody, the one suffering? The only one. Why did you always have to do all the dirty work?"

"I wanted to help her. It was my choice."

"Sure it was. If you wanted to keep the creepy sex coming. Once she seduced you, she reshaped your behavior, even your personality, with skillfully directed incentives, clever little behavior modification techniques. Guy like you—I'll bet a sulky pout was enough to get you crawling back to mommy. I'll bet she didn't want you to see your friends, your family, right? No, she wanted to keep you to herself, under her influence. And with every victim, your self-esteem dropped a little lower. Which made it all the easier for her to do her nasty work. To keep you under her finger."

"You're crazy!" he shouted. "We love each other!"

"Who does?"

"We do! Me and—and her."

He almost said it, damn it. He was that close. His mouth was forming the word. His mouth was open—her name probably begins with a vowel sound. He caught himself at the last moment—this time. But maybe if I kept pushing . . .

"Did she ever tie you up? Shove you in the closet?"

"Hell, no!"

"I'll bet she did. It would be consistent with everything I know about her. She tied you up—or maybe used those handcuffs you're so fond of—forced you down on your knees, locked you in the closet. Maybe . . . played with you. Sexually. Toyed with your body, your private parts. You hated it, but you never said anything, because you thought she liked it. What you didn't realize was that she was just wearing you down. Until you wouldn't care anymore. Until you'd be willing to do anything for her."

"We *love* each other!"

"Do you even know what love is? You want commitment and devotion, someone who cares about you. Not someone who's using you to do her dirty work. When you say 'I love you,' it's supposed to mean something. It's supposed to—" Damn it, my voice was choking. "—it's supposed to mean they're never going to leave you, that they understand you, that they care about you. Do you really think this woman loves you?"

Again he tried to rise out of his seat, rattling his chains. "I know she does!"

"Love is something someone gives you because they care about you, Tucker. You're not supposed to have to kill for it!" I paused, hoping my words were sinking in. "Is it really worth it, Tucker? All this killing for some damn math slut?"

"It wasn't like that!" He screamed and lunged, so hard that, despite the leg braces, he knocked the table forward into my chest.

While we both caught our breath, O'Bannon and

Granger rushed through the door. "Get out of here!" I shouted.

"But he—"

"I'm not done! Leave us alone!" To my happy surprise, they complied. Once the room had settled down, I reached out and did something none of them expected, least of all Tucker.

I took his hand and held it between both of mine. "Look into your heart, Tucker, and give me an honest answer. Do you really think she loves you? Truly? The way your mother loved you?"

His answer was bitter, but I noticed he did not remove his hand. "Leave my mother out of this."

"Why? Didn't she love you?"

"I said, leave her out of this!" This time, he took his hand back.

"Okay. We'll talk about your father." He looked up. "What did your father do?"

"Nothing! He never did anything to me, understand? Nothing! *Nothing!*"

My lips slowly parted. "I meant, what did he do for a living."

THOMAS STEVENS was a proud man, but the way he looked at it, he had a lot of reasons to be proud. He'd created himself from next to nothing, a classic self-made man. Sure, he inherited his first million the day he turned twenty-one, but the next 247 of them he'd earned, wheeling and dealing, mostly in real estate, with some periodic diversions into casinos, moving through a series of increasingly valuable projects, finally culminating in his first hotel on the Strip. The press liked to call him the New Steve Wynn, the Younger Steve Wynn, the Hipper Steve Wynn, the Sexier Steve Wynn.

Always some damned comparison to Steve Wynn. He was sick of it.

What had Steve Wynn ever done that was so great, anyway? Bought and sold a few hotels and casinos. The way people talked about him, you'd think he invented hotels and casinos. Not to mention restaurants, trams, shopping malls and, of course, his greatest achievement, Siegfried and Roy. Stevens was tired of being compared to that pretender.

After this new deal was consummated, they'd be calling Wynn the Old Thomas Stevens. The Has-Been Thomas Stevens. The Decrepit Thomas Stevens.

Now that had a nice ring to it.

Once this merger was complete, he would own more square footage on the Strip than Wynn or anybody else. And he would build and build until he controlled more rooms, more slot machines, more everything. No tacky architecture, no girlie shows, no pirate ships, no pretentious French restaurants, no bloody art gallery. He would give people what they really liked, not what they pretended they liked when they went home and told their friends about it. He would be huge.

After this merger, there would be no stopping him.

He stepped out of the elevator and passed through the media throng, waving, smiling, careful never to break his stride. If he stopped, even for a moment, he would be consumed. He had work to do.

"Mr. Stevens, is this a done deal?"

"Is it true you're borrowing more than a billion dollars?"

"When are you and Shalimar getting married?"

"Is it true Steve Wynn is secretly backing your acquisition?"

Okay, he had to stop for that one. "No, it is not. Mr. Wynn is playing no role in this operation." He paused before adding, with equal parts pleasure and elusiveness: "This is a respectable business deal."

He pushed his way through the mass of microphones

and paparazzi and entered his private elevator. The doors closed behind him and he descended to his private parking garage. He arrived, but the door didn't open. That required a ten-digit number to be punched into a keypad just above the floor buttons, a number only he and his driver knew. He punched it in—coincidentally the same as the number of one of his Swiss bank accounts—and stepped into the garage.

His car was waiting for him, chauffeur at the wheel.

He slid into the backseat and immediately poured himself a drink. "Damn reporters," he muttered, as if a profession of disgust would justify taking a drink this time of day. "Shatter your nerves like crystal."

The chauffeur didn't answer, but then, he usually didn't. He was the picture of decorum, eyes on the road—not the backseat, which was often very convenient—and none of the eye-rolling or presumptuous throat-clearing he got from the gentlemen's gentlemen. He'd drive all the way to the MGM silently, if Stevens allowed him. But he was in a chatty mood.

"Can you believe it, Mercer? We're finally going to make this dream a reality."

Still his chauffeur did not answer. Now this was just rude.

"Did you hear me? I mean, we're not that far apart. I said—"

He stopped. Something was wrong. His chauffeur—too narrow in the shoulders, and—there was blond hair tucked just inside the black coat, barely visible beneath the cap. "What's going on here?"

At last his driver spoke. It was a woman! "Mercer has the day off. He's . . . sleeping."

"I didn't authorize this."

In the rearview, he could see a small smile light the woman's face. "I did."

"You presumptuous little—Where's Mercer?"

"If you must know—he's tied up and gagged in a storage closet."

"What are you talking about?"

"How slow are you?" She took a hard left, and he suddenly realized they were not headed for the MGM. "You're being kidnapped."

"What?" All at once, Jeeves's words returned to him. "Who are you?"

"Haven't you read the papers?"

"Oh, my God. I'm getting out of here."

"I don't think so. The doors and windows are locked. I control them."

He removed his hard-soled Pierre Cardin shoe. "Then I'll break the window open."

"No, you won't."

"Why the hell not?"

"Because you took two quickies from the liquor bottle, as I knew you would, and it was laced with enough sedatives to put down a gorilla. You'll be unconscious in . . ." She checked her watch. "Oh, thirty seconds, at the most."

Damn! He *was* feeling . . . drowsy. As if he were . . . slipping away from himself. "But . . . the keypad . . . the security locks . . ." It was becoming more difficult to form words. His eyelids weighed on him like bricks. "You have to know the number . . ."

The chauffeur smiled as she turned off the main road. "I'm very good with numbers."

35

ESTHER WRUNG HER HANDS as she watched the heating element become a progressively lighter, more intense shade of red, almost blue. Soon it would be time to begin the ritual.

She had thought about this from the moment she knew Tucker had been captured. She didn't need him anymore, she told herself. She could do it alone.

But thinking about it and doing it are two different things altogether.

"Where the hell are my clothes?"

Showtime.

Esther returned to the center room where Thomas Stevens, the Vegas real estate mogul, was chained to an examining room table. "Your clothes were removed."

"Do you have any idea how much that jacket cost me, lady? Do you have any idea?"

"Do you know the square root of two?"

"Huh?"

"Then we're even." She checked her watch. The branding iron was almost ready. "Fear not. I've taken good care of your clothing."

"Why did you take them off?"

"I thought it would be easier while you were unconscious. I'm not a strong woman. And I'm in a delicate condition." She coughed. Her voice was becoming weaker, more gravelly, every day.

"Did you have to take my boxers?"

"Most especially," she said quietly.

"Look, can I cut to the chase? I mean, I don't want to interrupt your sick torture chamber thing or whatever it is you've got planned, but I'm a deal maker, okay? And I feel confident we can make a deal."

"I'm not interested."

"Yeah, that's what Merv Griffin said, too, but three weeks later, he was signing on the bottom line. Let's make this short and sweet. What is it you want?"

She hesitated a moment, then thought—why not? She replied: "God."

"Well, that's tougher. Still, I can help you. What is it you want to do? Build a church? A tabernacle or something?"

"Anything but."

"Oh, I get it. You're the Antichrist, aren't you? Fine, whatever. I'm a non-denominational deal maker. Will a million dollars take care of it?"

"A million dollars?"

"Why not? I figure you earned it. You caught me, fair and square. Don't know how you did it—"

"I programmed my laptop to run an algorithmic number generator that transmitted all conceivable ten-digit numbers in a little over three minutes."

"Whatever. Point is, you did it. So you've earned a little something. You let me go, I give you a million bucks. Then we both go home happy and you don't have to take my arm or leg or whatever it is this time."

"Something a bit more personal, I'm afraid."

"If you're not into cash, I can work with that. Diamonds, jewels."

"How about the family jewels?"

"The—hey, wait a minute, lady. What are you thinking?"

"I'm thinking . . ." She inhaled deeply. "I'm thinking it's time I started."

"Don't do this. I can tell you don't want to do this."

"What I *want* is . . . irrelevant." She coughed again. "Clearly the universe does not care what I want."

"Do you know what a million dollars can do for you? You could get anything. Anything!"

"Except," she said quietly, touching her hand lightly to her stomach, "the one thing I want most." She raised the branding iron.

"Wh-What are you planning to do with that?"

"You are Yesod, the sixth member of the Sefirot. Your holy attributes must be removed."

"But—why?" The branding iron was so close to his face he could feel the heat. He began to perspire. "Okay—make it two million!"

"You think your money can buy you anything. Just like it bought you all those little boys."

"Hey, those charges were totally unsubstantiated. Nothing was ever proven."

"I've talked to one of the boys. I know."

Sweat poured down his face. "Okay, fine, make it three, then. Three million bucks. But don't do this. Please."

"I have no choice. The numbers require it, and the numbers control the universe."

"Numbers? What—?"

"Thus sayeth the Kabbalah. Thus marks the pathway."

"The pathway to what?" He was screaming, twisting his head, trying to get away from the intense red-hot heat. "Enlightenment?"

The hand holding the branding iron trembled. "The path to becoming God."

"Becoming God? Why?"

She closed her eyes, tears slipping through the lids, and thrust the iron forward. "Because we deserve better."

"TELL ME about your father."

"No."

"Did he abuse you?"

"No."

"Would you tell me if he did?"

Silence.

"Tucker, I know he did. Tell me the truth. Was it physical? Or . . . sexual?"

"He never touched me!"

"But I—" Wait a minute. I wasn't listening. He just gave me the clue. The clue to the whole damn mess. "Do you have a little sister, Tucker?"

"No."

"Brother."

"No."

"You're lying. I know you do."

"No!"

"Tucker, it won't take the computer geeks five minutes to bring me the name and age of your little brother. So save us some time. How much younger is he?"

He glared at me, his eyes cold and filled with reproach. "Five years."

"And your father . . . slept with him?"

"No!"

"He beat him up. But only him. Never you. Even then, you were strong. Small but strong. You'd fight back. So he went after your helpless little brother. You couldn't stop it. And you've felt guilty ever since."

"You don't know what the hell you're talkin' about."

"I do. Your father would hit him, and he'd scream, maybe he'd even call out your name, but there was nothing you could do. You couldn't protect your best friend, the one boy who looked up to you and—"

"Why should I? It's not like Mother ever did!"

A remark so revealing it almost took my breath away. "That's it. It wasn't just you being helpless. It was your mother, too. She couldn't stop your father, he was big and mean, but afterward, afterward, he'd . . . what? Hit her, too?" I kept peering into his eyes. "No. She'd cradle your little brother. Stroke him, maybe? Caress him? Rock him to sleep? All the attention you wanted but never got. He got everything while you sat on the outside looking in, feeling like the ugliest, most unloved creature who ever lived."

"You're full of shit, you know that?"

"Tucker." I reached out to him again, but he snatched his hand away before I could get it. "Let it go."

"You don't understand anythin'!" He was shouting at me, spitting out his words.

"That's a song your father sang, isn't it?"

"I don't know what you're talking about!"

"Maybe when he was chasing your brother. 'Round and round the cobbler's bench, the monkey chased the weasel' . . ."

"Stop it!" he screamed, pressing his hands against his ears. "Stop it!"

"*Pop!* Goes the weasel!"

"I'm done with this. I'm outta here." He tried to get up, but the chains held him back. With his massive legs, he began dragging the table toward the window, staring into the musky reflection. "You hear me? I'm done. I want out of here. Now!"

"That's why you were so vulnerable," I said quietly. "That's why you felt so unloved. How you became convinced you were ugly, unlovable." I turned to him. "You're not, you know. I've known a lot worse. Hell, I've dated a lot worse."

"I want outta heeeeerrrrre!"

"I can see the attraction now. She's confident, sure, and smart, the one thing you'd convinced yourself you could never be. And she says she loves you. She's your substitute mother."

"No!" he screamed, whirling back at me. "She's nothing like my mother!"

"Ah. You hate your mother, too. Because she didn't protect your brother, but she loved him. More than she loved you. But you know what, Tucker?" I paused, waited until his eyes met mine. "At least your mother never asked you to kill anyone."

He grabbed the back of the third chair as if to raise it over his head. I slammed my boot down on it. "If you do that, Tucker, my friends will have to come in. And we're not done talking yet."

"Yes, we are!"

"I don't know why you're being so hostile, Tucker. I really don't. I understand. Truly. And who else has ever been able to say that to you? I'm even sympathetic. But Tucker." I reached out for the hand and this time I caught it. "How many people are going to have to die because you had crappy parents?"

I thought he'd lash out again, but he didn't. He just stared at me, as if utterly helpless. Despite his injuries, he squeezed my hand so tightly I could see it turning white. And then he crumpled. All at once. Tumbled into his chair and began to cry.

"I—I didn't—want to . . ." It took him half a minute to get it all out, amidst the sobs and stutters. "I—didn't—"

"I know you didn't, Tucker. But you did. Five people. And they had families, just like you did, better or worse. People who cared about each other. That kid in the Burger Bliss had four children, all of them under ten. Three girls and a baby boy who will never see their daddy again."

He buried his face in his arms. "I didn't—She told me—"

"Who, Tucker? *Who?* Who's your Kabbalah expert? Why is she taking the Sefirot apart piece by piece?"

"I can't tell you."

"You must tell me. I know you feel guilty about what you've done, Tucker. You're filled with remorse. You want to atone. Well, here's your chance. Tell me who she is. Help me stop her before she takes her next victim. Before she leaves another child without a parent."

"I—can't—"

"Let me share this horrible burden you've been carrying, Tucker. Please! Give me her name!"

He looked up at me, his face streaked with tears. "I—I didn't want to be bad. I never wanted to be b-bad."

"I know you didn't, Tucker. Give me her name."

"E-E-E—" He drew in his breath, mustered all his remaining strength, tried it again. "Esther."

"Esther?" It clicked immediately. "My God—not Esther Goldstein."

He nodded as if every little motion hurt his head. "She was laughing at you, when you came to visit her. She said you'd never catch her."

"But—" I closed my lips before I said it aloud. I met this woman. I talked with her. Me, the one with the keen psychological insight, the empathic gift. How could I have stood in the same room with her and not known she was the one?

My hand instinctively traveled to the pill bottle in my pocket. And then I knew the answer.

Granger broke into the room wanting all the details about Esther, how I knew her, where to find her. I gave him what he wanted and let him go after her. I didn't try to tag along. He wouldn't want me there, and it would be too damn embarrassing anyway. I'd have to admit I met the killer and didn't have the sense to know her for what she was. I'd have to admit to O'Bannon that I dragged Darcy out to see a cold-blooded killer.

I'd have to face that cold-blooded killer, knowing that she had laughed at me. Was probably still laughing at me.

No, I decided to just stay here at the office. And wish I had something stronger than Valium in my pocket.

36

DID THEY REALLY THINK I would be so stupid? Esther wondered, as she watched from a safe distance as the police converged on her house . Of course, she had moved the instant Tucker was captured. Now it was just her, and Stevens, and the ingredients she would use to make all those terribly dangerous very bad no good explosives. Amazing how easy those were to concoct, if you knew a little chemistry and math. She found the formula for homemade plastique on the Internet.

She was so close now, she could feel it. Was she the only one? Was it all one-sided? Or could God feel her breathing down His neck?

Never mind that. She had work to do. And she didn't like to rush. The baby didn't like it when she rushed.

WHEN THEY DIDN'T find Esther at any of the obvious places, everyone even remotely affiliated with the detectives' division was assigned to the investigation, including me. It was more than a little embarrassing. This was the second time we thought we had this case locked up—that I personally thought I'd cracked the case—only to have victory snatched away at the last moment. So I had to help, even if I wasn't happy about it. I felt as if I had let everyone down, as if I were personally responsible for every death that occurred after I interviewed Goldstein but failed to recognize that she was the killer—and I knew many of the others on the force felt the same way. Granger had been strangely silent. I expected him to use this gaffe to get me fired, but he hadn't. A rare moment of compassion? Or perhaps, after our contretemps in the interrogation room, he had finally realized it was best not to screw around with me.

I was up at the university, interviewing everyone in sight, every single member of the mathematics department, and you can imagine how exciting that would be. We heard the same things over and over again. She was quiet, kept to herself. Brilliant, but reclusive. A trifle strange, but what do you expect from someone specializing in cryptomathematics? From someone with the delusional idea that she was going to prove Reimann's hypothesis? Actually, what I sensed was a lot of jealousy; she was smarter than anyone else and they knew it and were secretly pleased she had turned out to be a psycho—not realizing, perhaps, what that said implicitly about the rest of the math geeks in residence. The only reason she wasn't running the place was that she didn't want to—didn't participate in office politics, didn't go to the Christmas party. No one had seen Tucker here or seen her with anyone else. She was strangely popular with her students, despite being a tough grader. I was beginning to despair of hearing anything of interest. Until I stood in the tiny, messy office that served as the nerve center for the graduate math school and picked up an interesting tidbit of information from the department president.

"She was *pregnant*?" I wasn't sure if this was a question or an exclamation.

"Yes," Lars Engle, the head of the department, replied.

"How pregnant?"

"I'm sure I don't know. It's an awkward thing to ask about, when a member of the faculty isn't, well, you know."

"Married?"

"Yes, that. She was wearing loose-fitting clothing to disguise the alteration to her figure." I thought back to the muumuu thing she had been wearing when I interviewed her. "But she was definitely pregnant. I took a message once from a doctor—de Alameida, was her name, I believe. An OB-GYN, I assume."

"And you don't know who the—"

"No idea." Engle lowered his eyebrows. "Can't even imagine."

"Student? Fellow faculty member?"

"I think both highly unlikely."

I pondered. I suppose it could have been Tucker, but I seriously doubted it. I couldn't imagine why she, the dominant member of the relationship, would even want a child, much less allow it to happen by accident, but in any case, she wouldn't have a child by her pet homunculus.

"Any knowledge of her outside activities? Habits? Places she haunted? Hobbies?"

He shrugged. "Esther was just as mysterious as her work."

"Second home? Vacation cabin?"

"Not to my knowledge." Or mine. If she had any such place, at least in her own name, it would've already shown up in our computer searches.

"Is there anything else I can do for you?" Engle asked.

I pressed my hand against my forehead. My head throbbed, my knees were wobbly, and the very worst of it all was—in a few more hours, it would no longer be the twenty-ninth. "Yeah. What's the next prime number after twenty-nine?"

"That would be . . . thirty-one."

Two days. Two lousy days. Then she went after mankind.

IT WAS ALMOST an hour before Stevens stopped crying, which threw Esther seriously off schedule. She was tempted to go right ahead with the operation anyway, but somehow, with the man squealing like a baby, she couldn't bring herself to do it. She didn't like listening to that incessant caterwauling, didn't like being in the same room with him. It was disturbing. And if it was upsetting to her, then it was almost certainly upsetting to the baby.

When at last he quieted, she returned to the room, wearing nothing but a black full-length robe. She liked it; it was comfortable, masked the bulge of her pregnancy, and lent a certain gravitas to the occasion.

"How pleads the defendant?" she asked, in appropriately somber tones.

Stevens peered at her through slitted eyes, his chest swollen and red and caked with blood. "I—I don't know—"

"You are charged with forsaking the trust of a child, the greatest sin it is possible to commit. You knowingly and willfully abused the foster home program to fulfill your own base needs, not once, but on repeated occasions."

"That's—that's all just gossip. It wasn't true—"

"You were eventually stricken from the list of suitable foster parents, but because of your power and money and influence you were never charged for your crimes, never tried. So you shall have that trial here, today." Her voice was weak and raspy; every day it became more difficult to speak.

"Nothing was ever proven because nothing ever happened."

"Count One: Duggan Phillips."

Stevens slowly recovered his voice. "He dropped his civil claims. The D.A. dropped the criminal charges."

"You paid him off!"

"I settled the claims."

"You gave him half a million dollars. That's not a settlement. That's a bribe."

"It would've cost me a lot more than that to defend, once you consider legal fees and the time taken away from my business. It was worth it."

"And the worst of it is, without a prosecuting witness, the District Attorney was forced to drop the charges."

Stevens struggled uselessly against his chains. He hadn't been able to escape when the branding iron had been pressed against his flesh and he couldn't escape now. "So you've appointed yourself judge and jury, is that it?"

Esther's eyes seemed to withdraw within herself. "I am the fallen one, cast out, unloved, but I will scratch and claw my way out of Purgatory, dismember the Sefirot one piece at a time, until creation itself is forced to come to me for its reckoning."

"Lady . . ." His voice had lost most of the self-confident abrasiveness. He was a desperate man now, one who knew his time was limited. "Don't take this the wrong way, but . . . you need help. You really do. And I can get you that help. I know the best docs in the city. Hell, the state."

"Silence."

"It's nothing to be ashamed of. Lots of good people have problems. I used to see a shrink."

"Count Two," Esther said, ignoring him. "Phillip Davis."

"He was trouble from the get-go. He heard about Duggan and figured if he made up a lot of stuff about me, I'd pay him some money."

"You violated his trust. You violated him."

"It wasn't like that."

"Don't lie to me!" Esther screamed. "Do you think I don't know what you're like? Do you think I don't remember? Coming into my bedroom, night after night. Raping a young girl, telling her it was fine, that was the way things were supposed to be!"

"A—A girl? I—I thought we were talking—"

"Never a thought to anyone else!" Esther continued ranting, tears streaming. "Never a thought to the damage you might be doing to—to . . . him." Her voice quieted. "Conrad Sweeney."

"Him? He wasn't even my—" He froze, pressed his lips and eyelids together.

"Wasn't even your *type?*" Esther screamed. "Is that what you were going to say? You inhuman monster." She reached inside her robe and withdrew a large knife with a sharp blade. "Do you know how fortunate you were to be entrusted with a child? It's a sacred trust, a holy privilege. Many people go their entire lives, wanting and praying for children, never getting them, or never getting them until it's too late, until—"

Esther stopped, trying to catch her breath. Her face was red from rage and lack of oxygen. She breathed deeply several times over, in and out, until she finally recovered herself. Stay calm. Think of the baby. Think of the child.

"I find you guilty. Sentence must therefore be rendered."

"Please don't hurt me. Please!"

"You are Yesod, part of the primordial Sefirot. You must sacrifice that which you represent in the greater scheme of creation."

"I beg you. Please!"

Her eyes slowly turned to black. "You will never hurt anyone again with your perverse fornicating lust. Never again."

"God, no. *God!*"

"God? If God has some objection to what I'm doing, then let Him tell me Himself. Just as I'm telling Him what I think of His work. Myself."

37

JULY 30

"FEDS?"

"Yup."

"Lots?"

"Yup."

"BSS?"

"Course."

"DMI?"

"Yup?"

"Us?"

"Lickspittle."

Darcy squinted his eyes as if he were having trouble seeing. "Are you two people speaking in a foreign language? Or is this maybe a code? Because I am usually good with codes but I cannot figure out what you are saying."

I smiled. Granger looked annoyed. In short, each did what we did best. "Sorry, Darcy. Cop talk. Shorthand for actual dialogue."

"Oh. Could I learn to talk cop talk? I would like to talk cop talk."

"I'm sure you'll pick it up in no time."

"What did you say?"

"Bottom line: We're about to be invaded by an infestation of FBI agents, specialists in serial killers, because they think we're doing such an incompetent job of handling this case. Once they arrive, we'll probably be delegated to paper-shuffling and answering the phone."

The three of us stood in the front lobby of downtown headquarters. The university interviews were over, and beyond the revelation that our sadistic killer was on the nest, it had proved pointless. Plainclothes officers were interrogating all of Esther Goldstein's neighbors, but I didn't expect it to be any more productive. This woman had obviously planned her escape carefully and arranged a hideaway, probably stocked with lots of cash. I had a call in to her doctor, but in the time-honored tradition of doctors everywhere, she was making me wait. Until she received a court order.

"It isn't fair," Granger grunted. He was as unpleasant as ever, but at least he was speaking to me again. Although I may have preferred it when he wasn't. "I've been busting my ass day and night on this case. We caught one of the perps."

"But the murders haven't stopped."

"But why feds? They're not any more likely to catch her than we are!"

Poor Granger, mourning over his lost turf. I could almost feel sorry for him, if I didn't despise him so intensely. "This die was cast the moment Joshua Brazee became one of the victims and Thomas Stevens went missing. In this celebrity culture of ours, media attention of that magnitude was bound to create a hue and cry for federal intervention. We'll just have to take it in stride." I didn't tell him my worst fear—that with the feds around, all nonessential personnel would be reassigned. Or that a consulting psychologist only hanging on to her job by a wing and a prayer would be dismissed.

Out the corner of my eye, I spotted O'Bannon lurching from his office, doing his best to make it appear that he didn't need the cane at all. He approached, didn't bother with pleasantries. "Pulaski, you're doing the press conference."

"Good morning to you, too," I replied. Had to make the smart remark before we got on with business. It was like my trademark. "What press conference? I thought the feds were invading."

"That's why we need a press conference. To, you know, explain the situation."

"To save face."

"Whatever. Wouldn't be bad if you gave the impression that we asked for federal assistance. Not that we needed it, but as a goodwill effort to becalm the tourists, yadda, yadda, yadda. The city is already on orange alert. Any more murders and the whole town will shut down."

"Chief . . ."

"Is it possible you could just do what you're told this once without arguing about it?"

"You've got it wrong. I think the press conference is a good idea. But—do you remember what happened the last time I did a press conference for you?"

"That won't happen again."

"You say that, but—"

"Back then, no one knew who or what you were. With the Edgar case, you earned their respect. No one's going to give you any crap."

"Chief," Granger cut in. Apparently he was incapable of allowing anyone else to talk to his boss for more than a minute without jamming himself into the conversation. "Nothing personal against Susan"—It isn't?—"but shouldn't the press conference be held by someone who is actually a member of the police force? Like maybe, the head of homicide?"

"Sorry, no. Gotta be Susan."

Even I was perplexed by this. "Why me?"

"The feds aren't idiots. They'll be watching CNN, too. They'll see this. So it has to be you."

"Because . . ."

"Because the feds are okay with you. In fact . . ." He glanced at Granger, then quickly looked away. "They want you to act as liaison between them and us."

"What?" The top of Granger's head almost flew off. "That's completely inappropriate. I'm the head of the department and—"

"It's not my call," O'Bannon grunted. "Seems the feds have a high opinion of you, Susan. Based on the work you did with them on the Edgar case. And some rather glowing reports written about you by their late colleague Patrick Chaffee."

Dear sweet Patrick. I might've known.

"So you're elected. Go home, put on something nice to wear, maybe even a little makeup for the cameras." He looked me straight in the eyes. "And make sure you're fit and ready for the conference at one P.M."

Message received and understood. "Will do, Chief."

He started to leave, then noticed Darcy hovering on the fringes. "Aren't you supposed to be at home?"

Darcy stared at the floor. "I—I have to be here in case . . . in case there is a math emergency."

"A math emergency?"

He didn't look up. "I am—I am—I—" He swallowed. "Susan made me her official math consultant."

O'Bannon said what I was thinking. "She did?"

He shook his head in a sideways direction. "I have been reviewing all of the evidence, looking for clues that we might have missed. Math clues."

O'Bannon scowled, gave me a glance, then lurched away. "Hope she pays you better than I'm paying her."

I was just about to inquire about the nature of our nascent consulting relationship when I heard Amanda David calling me across the office. "Susan! Telephone!"

I raced to the phone. "Please hold for Dr. de Alameida." As luck would have it, I got to talk to the doctor after only a two-hour wait. And I didn't even have to show her my health insurance card. "Dr. de Alameida here."

I explained who I was and why I was calling. She had read about Esther in the morning paper but assumed it must be someone else with the same name. "The woman I treated was quiet, thoughtful, introverted. Very maternal."

"So you're her OB-GYN?"

There was a pause. I never like pauses. "No, I'm an oncologist."

"A—" My turn to pause. "You weren't seeing her about her pregnancy?"

"No. I knew she was pregnant, of course, but that wasn't why I was seeing her. I'm a cancer specialist."

I tried not to let my eyes balloon. "Cancer? Esther Goldstein has cancer?"

"Of the throat, yes. Horrible thing, especially in a woman so young. Apparently she smoked in her younger days. Pity."

"And—what exactly is her condition?"

"Well . . . it's only a matter of time."

"You're telling me she's terminal?"

"I'm afraid so. The cancer is quite inoperable. And chemotherapy is out of the question, given that she's carrying a child. Not that it would be likely to succeed in any case."

I pressed my hands against the desktop, trying to get a grip on what I was hearing. "You're telling me that my sadistic killer is not only pregnant—but dying?"

"When last I saw her, there was a real question about whether she would be able to carry the child to term. I wanted to hospitalize her, but she refused. Said she had too much to do."

And so she did. Small wonder she didn't fear the death penalty. She knew the grim reaper would take her long before the criminal justice system.

"Doctor, do you know who the father of her child is?"

"I'm afraid not. She was quite silent on that question, and of course, it was really none of my business."

"Do you know anything about her friends, family? Places she might go?"

"No, sorry. I know this, though—she had been trying to become pregnant for a long time. Had visited fertility specialists—in fact, she was referred to me by one of them. A Dr. Landon Lorenz." A moment of silence, then a clicking of the tongue. "Rather ironic, really. And sad. All that time and money spent trying to become pregnant, and when she finally succeeds, she develops a fatal illness. Tragic, isn't it?"

Yes, tragic, I thought, as I hung up the phone. And just the thing that might push an already dangerously unstable personality over the brink.

I had some thinking to do.

38

"COME ON, ESTHER, I know you can learn this. You just need to apply yourself."

"Yes, Father."

"Now again, from the beginning."

"Thus said God: When I have gathered—"

"Thus said God the Lord."

"Thus said God the Lord: When I have gathered the house of Israel from the people among whom—"

"Peoples. Peoples!"

"From the peoples among whom they are scattered, and when—"

"No, no, no!" Esther's father threw his hands down in exasperation. "Esther, you're just not trying."

"It's hard, Father."

"It isn't hard. It's two little Bible verses. Your sister, Anna, can say it in Hebrew."

"It's *her* bat mitzvah."

"It's our bat mitzvah, Esther, the whole family's, hers and yours and mine. And I'll thank you not to give me any more of your negative attitude." He paused, sighing heavily, peering down at her with a stern expression. "Obviously, you will not be chosen tonight."

"I don't see why I have to know this at all. Anna is the one who has to say it at the party."

"So that you can help her, Esther." He was a lean, almost emaciated man, with a thin smile that sometimes seemed not to be a smile at all. "The bat mitzvah is an important day—far more than just a birthday. According to the Zohar, the joy the celebrant receives on this day should be as great as the day of her wedding. You want Anna to experience that joy, don't you?"

Esther didn't answer immediately.

"Esther," her father intoned, his brow creased. "Why are you here? Why were you born?"

"I am my sister's handmaiden."

"That's correct. And when your sister needs help . . . you must be ready to provide it. Do you understand that?"

She bowed her head. "Yes, Father."

"Everyone we know will be at the party. You want her to do well, don't you?"

"Will I get a present?"

The blow came so swiftly she was reeling before she knew what had hit her. She tumbled onto the floor, the red imprint of his hand still visible on her chubby eight-year-old cheek.

"That's the kind of selfish thinking that God doesn't like, Esther." He turned his back on her, then added, "We'll try this again in an hour. At that time you will know it perfectly. Or . . . there will be a punishment." He stretched his arm out to his other daughter, the taller, thinner, almost-twelve-year-old brunette. "Come along, Anna. I think you've earned some ice cream."

SHE STRUCK A MATCH, lit the candle at her bedside, then stared at the reflection in the window and the way it seemed to illuminate the stars, to light a pathway from herself to whoever was out there, whoever might be listening. She loved fire, loved to watch it flicker and dance, a modern dancer atop a candlewick. She could stare at it for hours.

Tefilah: "Heavenly Father, I'm sorry that I don't pray

enough, and I'm sorry that I can't pray to you in Hebrew because I know you like it better that way, but I hope that you'll listen to me anyway. I don't have the Kavanah and I haven't done the Berakhot one hundred times a day. I haven't even done it once and I'm not really sure how but my earthly father keeps talking about it so I know you like that. Even though I haven't done everything I should, could you please help me? I'm scared. I'm scared every day. I don't know what happened to my mother and my father doesn't like me. He almost never chooses me. He likes Anna much more and I think he only had me for her. Maybe it's because I still wet the bed, I don't know. Sometimes he gets so angry he can barely stand up and he shakes all over and I'm afraid he's going to seriously hurt me. I wish I had a mother but I don't so maybe you could bring me a mother. That would be the best thing in the whole world if I could just have a good mother. Everyone should have a good mother, isn't that what you said in the Torah? Even Cain had a good mother."

"DADDY! DADDY! Noah is dead!"

Esther raced downstairs as soon as she heard her sister screaming. Her father emerged from his study, wobbly. He knelt beside his oldest daughter and took her by the shoulders. "Calm down, darling. Tell your father what happened."

"Noah is dead. Barry Feldman killed him. He twisted Noah's neck till it broke!"

Esther's father's face seemed to awaken. "Barry? That little boy across the street? What is he, ten?"

"Eleven." Her narrow eyes turned slightly. "He goes to school with Esther."

"An eleven-year-old boy killed your cat? That's just—" He shook his head. "Are you sure about this, honey? Are you sure you saw him do it?"

"I didn't have to see him do it." She threw her hands back dramatically, flipping back her fake curls. "He told me he did it."

"But why?"

Esther watched as her sister slowly approached. "Because Esther made him."

"Oh, honey, don't be ridiculous."

"She did. Barry told me."

Esther took a step back. "You're being silly, Anna. How could I make him do anything?"

"He said you let him—do stuff to you. Let him touch you. Like—like daddy does."

Her father straightened. He braced himself against the landing. "What did you tell him about us, Anna? I've told you—"

"I didn't tell him anything. He said—"

"Esther, what have you been telling this boy?"

"Nothing, Father," she said quietly, staring at the floor.

"What have you been doing with this boy?"

"Nothing. But—didn't you say there was nothing wrong with it?"

"I—that's when—I mean, when I—Listen to me, Esther. This is a horrible thing, losing a pet. Do you understand that?"

"I've never had a pet."

"That doesn't matter. It's a horrible thing. You came into this world to give life, not to take it away. Did you put this boy up to this?"

She spread her hands and smiled beatifically. "How could I?"

Her father stared at her for a long moment, then returned his attention to Anna. "I'm so sorry this happened to you, dear. We'll get you a new kitty. And I'm going to have a talk with the parents of that Feldman boy." He drew in his breath. "But you shouldn't blame poor Esther. She would never do anything to harm you. She's here to save you."

Her father pulled Anna close and held her tight for a long time. But over his shoulder, one sister peered intently at the other.

SHE WAS THIRTEEN years old when her father woke her in the middle of the night. At first, she was elated. Did this mean that tonight she had been chosen? It had been so long since she had felt his warmth, his love. He almost always chose her sister. But tonight, there he was, in the blackness, hovering over her bed. In only a few short moments, though, she realized that he had not come for her. He had come for her kidney.

"It's time, Esther. We knew this day would come. We've talked about it. It's why you were brought into this world. Your sister needs you. Get dressed. Quickly. Anna is already at the hospital."

She fumbled in the darkness, trying to find her clothes, wondering why they couldn't turn on the light, wondering if it would hurt very much. She was scared. But she should not be scared, she told herself. She should feel lucky. After all, Cain slew Abel; all her big sister wanted was her kidney. They would be compatible so it would be all right. She wanted to help Anna because maybe if she helped Anna then her father would like her better. Maybe then her mother would come back from the fairy kingdom and they would be reunited. There was a buzzing in her head and she wished it would go away because it was making her nervous and unhappy and scared. She remembered what her teacher had taught her—when she was feeling scared, she should try counting to herself, counting sheep to relax herself, just running through numbers until she wasn't scared anymore, and she could do that because you never ran out of numbers. But just counting was so boring. She would count in multiples of three, she thought, as she slid out of her pajamas, her father watching, urging her to hurry. 3, 6, 9, 12, 15, 18, 21, she thought, as she slid into her best dress. Or perhaps she would see how high she could count in prime numbers. That would be more challenging. 1, 2, 3, 5, 7, 11, 13, 17, 19 . . .

SHE HAD NEVER seen her father like this before. She had seen him mean, violent, bitter, but never like this. Now he was silent, heavy; it was almost as if she didn't exist. When they walked through the front door, just the two of them, he didn't say a word. She wished he would hit her or kick her or something. Instead, he stumbled into the living room and pulled out that bottle, the one that smelled like the wine at the temple that she hated so much, and he collapsed in his recliner and he began to drink. She didn't know what to do. She was hungry and sad and tired and she didn't know what to do.

Esther decided to go upstairs and try to sleep. Or maybe she wouldn't sleep. Maybe she couldn't sleep. Maybe she would just wait for him. Surely now, now that it was just the two of them, she would be the chosen one.

When he arrived, he was staggering, smelly, he talked weird and he wandered about as if he couldn't tell where she was. It wasn't that dark.

"Whererya," he slurred, weaving around the end of the bed. "Where?"

"Are we going to play the kissing game?" Esther asked, her eyes bright and hopeful. "Am I going to be the mother? I'll be a good mother for you, Father. I promise I will."

Apparently her voice helped him locate her face. He swerved, zeroed in, and his hand barreled down on the target. Her head slammed against the headboard.

"Ya kilter," he said. He tore off his shirt, then knotted it like a noose between his hands. "Jus' like your mother. She dint likea screamin'. Yer gonna liket."

Esther panicked. After all the nights she spent wishing that he would come, here he was, at long last—and it was horrifying. It had been different when Anna was alive. Then it was like a competition between them. Now she didn't want him, didn't want to be chosen. He was scaring her. She tried to scramble out of the bed, but he grabbed her by the leg. She fell face-first down onto the covers.

"Jus' lie still," he said, as he crawled up onto the bed. "Ya killt my Anna. Pay fer killin' my Anna."

From where she lay, Esther could just barely reach the drawer of the end table. While he climbed on top of her, she managed to open the drawer, get out her matches, light one. She threw it at his face. He screamed, then reared up. That was all the opening she needed to scramble out from under him. The flame fell onto the bedspread and began to burn. He beat at it, barely able to hit the spot, snuffing it out. That gave her the time she needed to get downstairs and out the door.

She ran across the street till she reached the Feldmans' house and rang the bell. They would be surprised to find her standing on the doorstep in her nightgown at this hour of the night. But they would take her in. They hated her father, had always distrusted him, and she knew it. They would take care of her, at least for a little while. It would be all right.

She would be living with Barry Feldman. And she could get Barry to do anything she wanted.

HER FATHER LEFT the next morning. He emptied out the bank account, stopped making the mortgage payments, and disappeared. The authorities had no choice but to believe everything Esther told them, horrible though it was. She stayed with the Feldmans for six months, and that was good. They took care of her, gave her the things she needed, encouraged her interest in mathematics. Mr. Feldman introduced her to the Kabbalah, a Hebrew text her father had never mentioned. He said it was very old and very difficult but that she might like it because it had so much math in it.

He was right. She loved it. She loved the way every letter had a number, so every word had a meaning beyond the one you could find in the dictionary. She found and understood the numerical correspondences in the Sefirot, could calculate the sacred numbers in the Torah and the apocalyptic number from the Revelation of St. John. Some of it was too difficult for her, but even when she didn't understand it entirely, she loved the sound of the words, their meanings. We must realize that this life is a prison. Yes, she could understand that. But what she liked was that this was not the end point of the philosophy, but the start. Life might be a prison, but we all had a chance to open a crack in the cell door. We are all destined to become like God, but the darkness tricks us into believing otherwise, believing that we are trapped and there is nothing we can do to help ourselves. She liked that part a lot.

Eventually Esther was placed in a foster home. She was fourteen. The man of the house was abusive, but she tolerated it, because she thought she had no choice. And then one night, when she was tired and far too sleepy to resist, he raped her. Even then she kept quiet, did nothing. After the third time, she fled.

She lived on the streets for a long time, until at last she was picked up by the police. When she refused to return to her foster home, they delivered her to the human services department. They didn't believe her, but they eventually agreed to relocate her to a new home. This one was even worse. The mother came into her room the very first night, touching her in ways she knew she should not be touched. She left the next day, even though it was the dead of winter. She lived on the streets—giving blow jobs for small change, drinking cheap wine, eating table scraps, smoking other people's cigarettes. Sleeping in the park, in the snow. One night, she got frostbite. Esther found a free clinic that would treat her, eventually, but she still lost the small toe on her left foot. She had nothing to support her, nothing she could depend upon. Except math. Late at night, she would count, work imaginary equations in her head. No matter how bad things got, no matter how cold or sore or disgusted she was, the numbers were always the same. They were always there for her.

She lived like this for more than a year.

"YOUNG LADY," the judge intoned, sitting high in the oaken security of his bench, "I have reviewed your record and I must say—I am revolted. Have you no sense of decency? Have you no sense of morality? Do you not know that God is watching everything you do?"

Esther peered up at him through cold, slitted eyes. He was just like all the others, the dozens of judges she had been dragged before. He cared nothing for her. Eventually, he would put her in a juvenile facility or send her off to another home where she would be raped or beaten or abused and he would consider it a job well done. This judge might go through twenty, thirty children a day, treating them with the same contempt, the same cruel indifference. In many ways, he was the worst parent of them all.

"If God is watching me, why doesn't He do something to help?"

"It's not our position to question the ways of our maker, young lady. Our job is to follow His commandments, and in that regard, I regret to say you have fallen woefully short." He shuffled through his papers. "I'm very tempted to have you incarcerated. A little time in juvenile hall might do you well. But the counselors tell me you are highly intelligent and I hate to see that kind of potential go to waste. Even if you haven't done much with it so far." He frowned disapprovingly, an expression in which Esther took decided pleasure. "I'm going to give you one more chance, little girl. One chance only. I'm going to place you in a foster home—"

"Please, don't. I'd rather go to prison."

The judge drew himself up angrily. "I'm going to put you in a foster home. I am personally acquainted with these people and know them to be good, honest, Christian folk. I'll let them see if they can turn you around, teach you to make the most of your talents. And if they can't—" He shook his head. "Well, then may God have mercy on your soul."

This home was not so bad, at least not in the physical way. Here she had to endure lectures, constant berating about how she was a sinner, how her body was a temple and she had defiled it. He called her awful names, but at least he left her alone at night. And she was able to finish high school. She made poor grades in many of her classes; she couldn't have cared less about literature or art. But she excelled in math. She finished two years of trigonometry in one semester, then completed calculus and advanced calculus almost as quickly. They said she was a prodigy. And despite the ugly lectures she had to endure, being a prodigy was better than sleeping in the snow.

Her foster father offered to send her to college, assuming she got a math scholarship, which she did, and assuming she agreed to go to a Christian college, which she did. She was a wild thing, he said, and she needed Jesus Christ to enter her life and tame her, to teach her how to be a good person. The fact that she was Jewish seemed to have altogether escaped him. Didn't matter to her—just so she got out of the house. That was all she wanted. Out of the house. On her own. Free to do math—the one thing she loved in life.

And free to become a mother. She desperately wanted to be a parent. Because she would be a good parent, not like all the others she had been forced to endure, one after the other, over and over again. She would be a good mother.

"YOU MAY BE ASKING yourself—what does God have to do with mathematics? Well, let me answer that question for you. God has everything to do with mathematics. The world, indeed, the universe, has everything to do with mathematics. We are surrounded by it. Math is in the air, in the plants, in us, in nature, throughout the cosmos. God is not silent; He never has been. To the contrary, mathematics is how we know that God exists."

Esther watched the salt-and-pepper-bearded professor cross the stage of the small seminar room, always staring at the floor, never at the students, as if lost in thought. She had only taken this intersession class, Mathematics and Theology, because it sounded like an easy "A." During the past three years of college life, she had learned to ignore the fundamentalist claptrap that infected all her classes, even math. Did they not understand that this was what made math special? Its purity, the fact that it could not be corrupted by politics or science or theology. Math was unchanging, no matter where you went or what people believed, math was always the same. But as the two-week course progressed, she found herself more and more intrigued by his lectures. Not the nonsense about how God gave the Greeks math just in time to pave the way for Christ, so the Romans could build roads and improve trade and other such activities that would aid the spread of the Good News—that was obvious nonsense. But she was impressed by the impact numbers had made on the world.

She was fascinated to learn about Pythagoras, his enormous contribution to mathematics, and the society he founded to keep secrets out of the hands and minds of the public. She was amazed to learn that St. Augustine, perhaps the greatest of the early Christian writers, believed that numbers were the pathway to God. "Everywhere you find measures, numbers, and order, look for the craftsman. You will find none other than the One in whom there is supreme measure, supreme numericity, and supreme order. That is God, of whom it is most truly said that He arranged everything according to measure, and number, and weight." She was intrigued by the numerous efforts to devise a mathematical formula to prove that God exists, not only comic exercises like Euler's but serious attempts like those of William Hatcher. She learned to play Rithomachia, the ancient math/chess hybrid favored by ancient European mathematicians. But something was missing.

"I admit," the professor continued, "the message is insubstantial and incomplete, and in the end, perhaps it answers nothing more than simply to say, 'Yes, I am here. You are not alone.' But that itself is a potent message. If math can do that for us, if it can give us the language of God, perhaps it is left to us to interpret the message."

Not good enough for Esther, but perhaps she had the solution. The Kabbalah. The ancient text Feldman had introduced to her. What did it say? Life doesn't have to be a prison. We are all in the process of becoming God. She raced back to her dorm room, trying to find her copy, pulling it from the shelves. The world is a war between the forces of darkness and the forces of light. Yes, that was true enough. The forces of light are what we call God. The forces of darkness are discomfort, pain, unhappiness. But this was the good thing: Concealed in every moment of pain is an opportunity to become God.

That was the path, the key, the missing element that these bigoted fundamentalists would never stumble across. We could know God, we could communicate with God.

We could challenge God.

ESTHER WAS A GOOD TEACHER and a gifted mathematician. Her dissertation on Isaac Newton broke new ground, exploring the alchemical and biblical work that consumed more of his time than science or mathematics. Her first published paper won a major prize, guaranteeing her a tenured position with an excellent university. Rumor had it she was working on Reimann's hypothesis, the Holy Grail of mathematical proofs. A long shot—but if anyone could do it, she could. In her leisure moments, she studied the Kabbalah, became almost as knowledgeable about it as she was about math, linking the two, following Newton in his blending of math and theology, his progress from casual study to obsession. And once her professional life was stable, she began trying to become pregnant.

Given her background, sex did not come easy. She found it impossible to establish any kind of long-term relationship; every time she looked at a man, she saw her father's face, his or one of the abusive surrogate fathers she had endured throughout her childhood. She found it much easier to get through one-night stands, no commitment, no long-term involvement—and she never had to look them in the face. She became adept at picking men up, determining what would attract them, what they wanted, then using that to get what she wanted.

Or tried. In fact, she never got what she wanted. For years and years she tried without success to become pregnant. She sought out fertility specialists, unapproved drug therapies, even so-called specialists who she knew in her scientific heart were little better than witch doctors. It was so unfair! There were so many bad parents around—but she would be a good mother! She would be the best mother who ever lived. But never any luck. Nothing ever changed. Until that fateful day in October of last year. When everything changed.

She knew something was wrong the moment she saw the expression on Dr. Lorenz's face. "What's wrong with me? You said it was possible. You said I was capable of conceiving a child. Why isn't it happening?"

"Esther . . . please sit down."

"I'm not going to sit down. I'm not a child anymore. Tell me what you have to say."

He sighed wearily. "It would be better if you weren't standing."

"Stop treating me this way! Just tell me why I'm not pregnant!"

Slowly, he closed his clipboard. "You are pregnant."

"I—I am. *I am!* Then—what's wrong? Why are you looking at me like that?" She clutched the doctor's arms. "Oh my God. Is there something wrong with the baby? Is there something wrong with my baby?"

"No, no. The baby appears to be fine."

"Then what?"

Dr. Lorenz looked at her with the saddest eyes she had ever seen. "Esther . . . you've got cancer. Cancer of the throat."

Her lips parted, but only a choking sound came out where there should have been words. "How—How long do I have?"

"It's impossible to say. Some people live for years with your condition . . ."

"But I won't."

The doctor lowered his head. "I don't think so, no."

"Will it affect the baby?"

"No."

"Will I live long enough to deliver the baby?"

"I can't say. But even if you do . . ."

The doctor didn't have to complete the sentence. Esther knew what he was trying to say. Even if she did deliver the baby—she wouldn't live long enough to raise her child. She would never have a chance to be her baby's mother.

Esther sped home and collapsed on her bed, consumed with rage and tears. What kind of a God would allow this? She would have been a good mother, the best mother who ever lived. But now she would never have a chance. And with no father, her child would end up in one of those dreadful foster homes, full of rape and incest and perversion and sick minds inflicting their warped damaged psyches on the next generation. It wasn't fair. It just wasn't *fair*! How could God permit this? Why would He give all those wretched people children but deny them to her? He obviously didn't love children—look what He let happen to his own so-called son, what He let happen to his chosen people for centuries, how He allows those supposedly created in his image to lead hellish lonely lives. What was He thinking?

She had no answers. She could not fathom the inscrutable mind of God. But somewhere, just as something in one part of her brain was snapping, another part was stitching something together, something new and . . . workable. A way to ask her questions, to force God to answer. To let Him know what she thought of Him and His strange and mysterious ways. Math and magic, that was the answer. Calculus and the Kabbalah.

She would need a plan, a way to get His divine attention, to turn His own Holy Word against Him. And she would need a pawn, but by now, turning the minds of little men was child's play to her. Esther would take His bloody image apart piece by piece, destroy the Sefirot limb by limb, find her way from darkness to light by exposing the darkness *in* the light, the pathetic fallibility of God Himself. She would begin her work at once—calculate her plans and set them in motion.

And then, when she did, may God have mercy on His own goddamn soul.

39

JULY 31

"IF YOU'RE GOING TO get inside her head," I explained to the more than twenty federal officers crammed into the briefing room, "and you have to, if you're going to have any chance of catching her, then you have to understand what motivates her."

"Rage?" suggested one of the younger men in the front row, an agent Gilpin.

"Rage, certainly, but rage fueled by what?" The background checks on Esther Goldstein had come in, and they confirmed most of what I had already hypothesized and woven into my revised psychological profile.

"Frustration. Loss of the child she worked so hard to conceive."

"Certainly the child is a factor. But she doesn't know she's going to lose the child. There's only one thing she knows for certain."

"She won't be around to raise her child," agent Gilpin said quietly.

"Exactly so. All her life she's been surrounded by bad parents, at least in her mind. She was determined to be better, to be better than any of them. And now she's being cheated out of the chance. By God."

"Is that why she's using all the religious motifs?" one

of the senior officers, agent Ringold, asked. "Is this her way of . . . filing an appeal? With God?"

"I can't say for certain," I acknowledged. "But I don't think so. I don't think she's interested in an appeal. I think she knows it's hopeless. But all this imagery and philosophy and mathematics she has absorbed from the Kabbalah, all of it relates to the relationship between God and man. That we are made in His image. That we are all potentially in the process of becoming God."

"So she wants to be God. A deity of equal status. So she could overrule His decision."

"That too seems impossible, even in her delusional narcissistic state. I think she knows she's doomed, that she'll never have a chance to raise her child, at least not on this earthly plane."

"Then what? What does she want from Him? A miracle?"

I shook my head slowly. "Not a miracle. An accounting. She's not buying into all that C.S. Lewis misery-helps-us-appreciate-God's-mercy crap. Don't mean to offend anyone, but in Esther's mind, God is not only a son of a bitch—He's a mean son of a bitch. He's the Old Testament God, raining down death and destruction on those who don't deserve it, torturing the innocent, justifying it all in terms of some incomprehensible plan. And that's not good enough for Esther. She wants to deconstruct God's image while simultaneously taking down as many bad parents as possible, and in so doing, to make God answer for what He has done."

"That's . . . insane."

I arched an eyebrow. "And this surprises you?"

There was another voice from the back of the room. "Ms. Pulaski, we appreciate the work you've done on this case—and other cases as well. But we've all read your preliminary profile on this case and, well, to be blunt, you were dead wrong. You didn't even have the killer's gender correct."

"I'll be the first to admit I've made some boneheaded moves on this one," I said. Best defense is a good offense, right? "We had eyewitness accounts identifying the killer as male and I allowed them to influence me, even though there were contradictory indications: male/female, organized/disorganized, narcissistic/sympathetic. What I didn't realize—but should've—was that there were two people involved, one being controlled by the other. But there's no point dwelling on past mistakes. I've logged over twenty hours in the interrogation room with Tucker, in addition to all the other research and detective work I've done, and I'm here to tell you—I've got it right this time. So if you really want to catch this killer, memorize my report and treat it like your own personal Kabbalah." I closed my folder. "If you'll excuse me, I've got a press conference."

DARCY MET ME just outside the conference room.

"They found the body!"

Well, that was good to know. It must've been a more pleasant discovery than the part Esther left behind in Stevens's conference room. "Where was it?"

"Barely a mile away! And did you know this? Did you know that it was behind an apartment building! People went back and forth all the time, but it still took a long time before someone found it."

I wondered how she managed to get the body there without being caught. Late at night, probably. Wrapped in a rug or some such. A smart woman like Esther wouldn't have any trouble figuring out a way. "Seems like every body comes a little closer to headquarters. Any chance she's . . . I don't know. Slowly bringing her dirty deeds into our face? Teasing us or something?"

Darcy tilted his head slightly to one side. "Do you think that maybe . . . that maybe . . . there is some . . . pattern to the way the Math Lady gets rid of the bodies?"

"I wouldn't be surprised. There's been a pattern to everything else. Do you see any connections?"

He didn't answer. I'd seen that look before. He was off in Cloud-Cuckoo-Land, and if I had any brains, I wouldn't disturb him.

"You keep thinking, Darce. I've got to do this miserable press conference."

He snapped out of it. "Can I go with you?"

"To the press conference? I don't know, Darcy—your father never wanted you involved in this case, much less at a press conference."

"But you have to take me!"

"I do? Why?"

"Because—Because—" He raised his hands up and ran them back and forth through his hair. "Because I am your math consultant."

"I don't think the press will be asking any math questions."

"Then—because I am your good luck charm!"

"You are?"

"Of course I am. Do you think that I am? Do you believe in luck?"

"I think this is not the best time to get off on philosophical tangents. I have to—"

"And then after the press thing, we can go for custard."

I gave him a long look. "Darcy . . . we have a very tight deadline. Assuming she keeps to her pattern—the Math Lady is going to strike again today."

Against all odds, Darcy's expression brightened. "Then I will just have to stay with you until then."

IT WAS THE MOST COMPLEX algorithm she had ever devised, the most demanding computer program she had ever invented. And for what purpose? No one could possibly decipher this, at least not until it was far too late. So why bother?

Because she had no choice. The Kabbalah was all about numbers, yes, but also about fairness, justice. It dictated that all persons should have their opportunity to crawl out of the darkness into the light, to find their own path to becoming God. To be challenged in their own environments. That's why the amputations were always performed in the chosen one's workplace. That's why an escape hatch—however remote—had to be included in her final act of destruction. That's why, even though they did not deserve it, she would give them a chance. However slight.

Esther was still a little shaky after all she had been forced to do—the branding, the killing, the transportation of the body. She was glad she hadn't had to do it the other times as well. Her final stroke would be much larger, of course, but in its own way, less personal. Her physical presence was not required—just as well, given how weak she felt. The branding, the dismemberment, all that had become unnecessary. She was making a larger statement now, one that would symbolize a strike against all mankind.

When she was finished, she put the electronic detonator beside the blue folder containing her mathematical work, both representative of a lifetime of effort in her two chosen fields of endeavor. If all went well, these two objects would represent her legacy to her daughter, the culmination of a lifetime's work, a hard lifetime, but one to which she had never succumbed, never given in.

Esther poured herself a drink—nonalcoholic, because of the baby—and turned on the television. She had heard there was going to be a conference on what the press were now calling the "Math Slayings." Rumor had it they were expecting another murder soon. But why?

Was it possible they had discovered the prime number pattern? Much of their mathematical work had surprised and impressed her, including the discovery of the mathematical algorithmic scheme that allowed the Kabbalistic forces to determine who the victims for each aspect of the Sefirot would be. This was math of the highest order, but they had cracked it, and it had allowed them to capture Tucker, if not to save their own colleague. How was it done?

She was surprised to see Susan Pulaski leading the press conference. Given how severely—and repeatedly—Pulaski had blundered in this case, Esther was surprised to find her still employed at all, much less used in such a public capacity. Just as well, though. There was no chance of her cracking the codes Esther had devised.

She turned up the volume so she could hear what the pathetic woman had to say.

". . . but the most important thing is that we not start a panic. Yes, we have a killer in our midst, but if we're all careful, we can remain safe. She has never attacked anyone who is not a native of this city and there is no reason to believe that she will start now. On the other hand, if you have ever had any dealings with the Department of Human Services, or for any other reason might fall under this woman's twisted notion of what constitutes a bad parent, you need to take precautions. Stay home. Don't talk to strangers. Don't be alone, especially in your place of work. We'll be broadcasting the most recent pictures of her that we've been able to find, but this woman is smart enough to alter her appearance."

Wait a minute—did that Pulaski woman use the word "twisted"? Was it twisted to hold parents accountable for their wrongdoing? To punish those who committed atrocities on their young, who took advantage of them, abused them? Why would they even want to stop her? Why not let her take out the whole sorry lot of them?

Pulaski was fielding questions now, as best she was able when she knew basically nothing. A handsome reporter named Jonathan Wooley with a brown and gray goatee was grilling her. "Why hasn't the LVPD captured her? Why did the federal government have to send in assistance? What are the taxpayers getting for their money?"

"I assure you the LVPD has been giving this case its top priority, sir." An edge crept into Pulaski's voice, discernible and probably calculated. "If I may remind you, one of our own became the killer's fifth victim. A personal friend of mine." Pulaski was silent for a moment. "We are doing everything within our power. And we have captured the man who committed most of the murders."

"But not the mastermind of the whole operation."

Another significant pause. "No. But we will. Please bear in mind that, despite her delusional state, Dr. Esther Goldstein is intelligent and she has planned her crimes well in advance, very carefully. Nonetheless, we will catch her. And as for the involvement of the federal government, that's standard procedure in cases involving multiple murders. In no sense does it constitute an indictment of the LVPD. We've worked together before and we will no doubt—"

Esther stopped listening. Delusional state? Did that cheap harlot third-rate psychologist—a woman who didn't even have her *doctorate*!—actually have the audacity to say Esther was in a delusional state? What was wrong with these people? They should be applauding her efforts. She was stamping out the parents that destroyed children's lives. Was that delusional? Would Susan Pulaski find it so delusional if she had been raped by her father, her foster parents, if the courts had never listened to her, just sent her back again and again and again? Would she still—

Something on the television screen caught her eye. A

young man was standing behind Susan, staring at the floor.

It was the same kid she had brought with her when she came to the university—what was his name? David? Dwayne? No—Darcy. Darcy O'Bannon. The chief of police's son. He was the numbers whiz, the one who whipped through the continuing fractions most of her graduate students couldn't handle correctly, even though he'd never had any experience or training in the field. That was the answer! That must be how they were able to follow her clues, to solve the equations, to understand the secrets of the Kabbalah that guided her actions. That idiot savant was guiding their pathetic efforts to catch her.

If the final piece of the Sefirot were to be destroyed as planned, if the final piece of this majestic plan were to work, Darcy O'Bannon would have to be eliminated.

She turned off the television and logged onto the Internet. She hated to add a new factor to the plan this late in the game, with as little time left. But given all that was at stake, it would be worth the effort.

40

"WHERE'S DARCY?" I asked, when I didn't see him outside the conference room.

"Who cares?" Granger replied, with his usual touching concern. "Can't you do anything without that kid?"

"I don't want to consult with him. I want to know where he is." This was odd. Just before the press conference, he'd been threatening to stick with me until we caught Esther. I knew he'd come into the press conference room. So where was he now?

"Last I saw him," Granger said, "you were about halfway through the conference." He was tight-lipped, downright sullen. Probably still sulking because O'Bannon chose me to do the press conference instead of him.

"And he left? While I was talking?"

Granger shrugged. "Looked like he thought of something he'd forgotten. Or maybe saw something, someone. I don't know. Anyway, he started flapping his hands and then he ran out the back door."

"That doesn't make any sense. Why would he—"

"Have either of you seen Darcy?"

Granger and I both slowly pivoted to the left. Chief O'Bannon was asking the question.

"No," I answered.

"You got him on some . . . math quest or something?"

"No, nothing. I expected him to be here. Why?"

"Got a call from one of my neighbors. She's known Darcy since the day he was born. Says she heard some kind of commotion next door."

I felt an icy grip at the base of my spine.

"It's nothing," I said, sounding just as unconvincing as I felt. "You know how unpredictable Darcy is. Probably saw a rare species of butterfly or something."

The crease in O'Bannon's forehead deepened. "Is there any chance . . . any at all . . ."

I didn't need super-empathy to know where he was going. "Darcy doesn't fit the profile. Esther only kills bad parents."

"Tucker did his damnedest to take you out. Darcy was with you when you interviewed Goldstein."

My throat went dry. I felt shaky, anxious, barely able to breathe. *Darcy!*

"But why now?" Granger asked. "That interview was—" He snapped his fingers. "The press conference. She must've seen him at the press conference!"

"And then she realized how we've managed to decode all her little mathematical puzzles," I added somberly.

O'Bannon didn't waste a second. "Amanda! I want an APB out on my son. Now! Granger, mobilize every man you have available and—"

There was more, but I didn't hear it. I was already halfway to my car. I wanted to dig into my purse, wanted to pull out the pill bottle that would make the acidic aching eating away at my stomach lining go away. But I didn't. That was how I missed Esther the first time. I couldn't let it happen again. Darcy needed me. All of me, everything I had to give.

I just prayed to God I wasn't too late.

"HELLO, DARCY," Esther said. "Remember me?"

He was standing in the kitchen holding a book and a

folded piece of paper. He picked up a package of Pizza Hut chicken wings from the counter, tossed them into the microwave oven, then started it.

"What are you doing?" she demanded.

He looked at her strangely. "I thought you might be hungry."

She laughed at him. "Idiot savant. Mostly idiot. Do you remember who I am?"

"Of course. I remember the way you smell. The sound of your shoes. You are the Math Lady."

"Yes, I am," she said, smiling slightly. "What else do you know about me?"

"You made all those nice people die."

"They weren't nice people, Darcy."

"I do not think anyone is so bad they should get killed." His hands flapped wildly in the air. "I do not think people should kill each other. Killing is bad." Darcy didn't make eye contact with her. Instead, he sat down on the hardwood floor and crouched in a fetal position, arms around his legs, and rocked back and forth.

"I brought you some more math puzzles. You like puzzles, don't you?"

"Stay away from me. Please stay away from me."

She moved closer. "You don't have to hold yourself, Darcy. Here, let me hold you."

"No!" He scooted away from her. "I do not like for people to hold me. I do not like for people to touch me!"

"Oh, nonsense. You'll change your mind when you see what I have for you."

"I will not. Stay away from me!"

"I can't, Darcy. A smart boy like you, so gifted with numbers. You deserve a reward."

"A reward? Do you mean a treat? I like treats."

"All right, then. We'll call it a treat." She reached

inside her windbreaker and removed a large serrated knife. "I can't let you spoil my plans, Darcy, but I can let you become an important part of them." She smiled. "Come closer, dear. I have something very special for you."

41

HURRY! I SHOUTED without moving my lips as I barreled down the highway. I'd heard of backseat drivers before, but this was the first time I'd ever experienced being a backseat driver to myself. I careened through the neighborhood gateposts and tore down the road at a speed that sent trash, leaves, and a few small animals flying out of my path.

Even before I arrived at the O'Bannon residence, I could hear the alarm.

Some of the neighbors were gathered outside, huddled on the front lawn. "We tried to get in there," one of them shouted at me. "But we didn't have a key."

I didn't have a key, either, but thanks to Chief O'Bannon, I did have a gun. Three shots were enough to get the door open. I raced inside, throwing caution to the wind. I didn't have time to stealthily creep into each room, gun poised. I had to find Darcy.

"Darcy!" I shouted. "*Darcy?* Where are you?"

No answer.

Okay, *think,* I told myself. Calm down and think. Someone or something set off the alarm. So logically, he must have been here.

Or someone else was here. Or both.

I like to think of myself as an optimist, but even I couldn't kid myself that much. I knew what would happen if Esther, the cold-blooded mastermind behind half a dozen murders, were alone with Darcy, the boy who couldn't step on a spider. Darcy wouldn't stand a chance.

"Darcy!" I screeched, so loud it made my throat hurt. "Are you here?"

I knew from the time when I'd stayed here with him where all his favorite hiding spots were, nooks and crannies where he huddled when he was experiencing sensory overload. He wasn't in any of them.

I checked in the library, upstairs, downstairs, his room, the backyard. I was running at the speed of light, sending my heart into palpitations. I was certain he wasn't here. And that meant she hadn't killed him, right? Because if she had, I would have found the—

No. Not with this killer. She never left the corpses behind. Just pieces.

I found blood smeared on the wall about a foot off the floor in the entryway just beyond the front door. Enough to tell me someone was hurt.

Tears flooded my eyes. That goddamned—

The worst of it was, it was my fault. Again. Why had I brought him with me? Why had I let him come to the press conference? Why had I involved him in the case at all? Why had I been so doped up I couldn't spot a serial killer when I stared her in the face?

It was my fault, all the way. My fault.

Darcy!

ESTHER GRIPPED the steering wheel of her car and made her way downtown. That had been . . . unpleasant. But it didn't matter now. Her opportunity was at hand. She knew when she would be able to get in and out, to do what needed to be done . . . and then retreat and wait for the excitement to begin. The screaming of the sinners. The wailing of the worthless.

Till God came begging, crawling on His hands and knees. Begging her for forgiveness.

She parked her car just outside the courthouse. Nothing could stop her now. Nothing at all.

"ARE YOU SURE he isn't there?" Granger barked over his cell phone.

"Positive. Send your men somewhere else. Interview the neighbors. Go to the day-care center where he works. Someone must know something."

"I'm concerned about the clock, Susan. If your theory is correct, that killer is going to strike—"

"Never mind that, dammit." I talked while I raced to my car. "I'm going to get back to the office and see if I can find any trace of him. Or Esther. It's possible she took him captive." I said it, even though I didn't believe it. She had no reason to do anything other than kill him. "You work the other end of the equation. Find Darcy."

"I've pulled every man available onto this, but I can't justify anything more when we think the killer is about to strike."

"Granger, goddamn it, listen to me. Darcy comes first!"

"Susan, you're not being rational. According to your own report, her next attack could be a large-scale assault. I can't justify chasing one kid—"

"If you don't, Granger, so help me, I'll rip your fucking balls off!"

"You're a psycho, Pulaski."

"Granger—" I clamped my jaw shut. How many times would I have to try this approach with Granger before I realized it didn't work? I lowered my voice. "Granger . . . please. This is important. To the chief and to me. Find Darcy."

"I can't—"

"Do it for me," I blurted out, even though I felt like a fool. "Please. Do it for me."

"Why the hell should I?"

"Because . . . I think there was a time when you liked me. At least a little. And I know you liked David."

"Don't start—"

"Please, Granger," I whispered. "Find my Darcy." I snapped the cell phone closed and slid behind the wheel of my car.

He jumped out of the backseat so suddenly that I practically had a stroke. "Am I really *your* Darcy?"

"Darcy! Darcy! My God, Darcy!" I couldn't help myself, and I didn't care if he liked it or not. I threw my arms around him and hugged him tight. "Darcy! Oh, thank God you're safe."

He didn't hug back, but he wasn't resisting, either. "So when you called me your Darcy, does that mean you are ready to adopt me?"

I could barely speak. "Damn it, Darcy . . . I'll do anything you want me to do. Just . . . don't ever do that again."

"Do what? Did I do something bad? Can we go back to the part where I was your Darcy?"

I laughed and cried and choked and in the end just contented myself with hugging him so tightly it might not have been possible for him to breathe. "What have you been doing? Did you see Esther?"

"Oh, yes. She tried to kill me," he said, with the same inflection I might use to say, "She tried to sell me a new life insurance policy." "But she did not kill me."

"I can see that," I said, still laughing and crying hysterically. "So where the hell have you been?"

"I went home. Then I hid in my neighbor's yard. Then, when I saw your car, I came back. And," he added, "I saw the Math Lady. But I got away."

"You—" I was fighting mightily to stay in control,

keep my blood pressure down, and try to figure out what the hell happened. "But there was blood!"

"That was hers, not mine. I went home to get a book on Fibonacci numbers. Did you know that Fibonacci numbers are the most fascinating—"

"Stick to your story, Darcy."

"I knew the book by heart. But I wanted to prove it to you."

"Yes, yes. What happened when you saw the—I mean, Esther?"

"It was not a big deal," he said, shrugging. His modesty might be irritating, if I didn't know how unaware he was that he was doing anything. "When I saw her, I put some chicken wings in the microwave, but I left the aluminum foil in the box and started the oven. I knew that would start a fire." He looked down sheepishly. "Because I did it before."

"I know. I put it out, remember? What happened next?"

"I sat down on the floor and acted like I was scared and waited. A big fire came out of the oven, and the alarm went off, and I ran from the Math Lady with the knife. She shut off the microwave and put out the fire, and while she was doing it, I ran outside and hid. I did not mean to hurt her. I do not like to hurt anyone. But when I ran past her she tried to stab me so I dodged away from her and she fell and banged her forehead."

"The blood," I murmured. "Foreheads bleed profusely, even from a minor cut. But—are you telling me you went home just to get some book?"

"Yes. On Fibonacci numbers."

"And what have you been doing ever since?"

"Working out the math," he said, beaming from ear to ear. "I know where she's going to go next. I thought that we could stop her maybe, you and me. If we are not too late."

42

"HOW CAN YOU KNOW where she's going to strike?"

"From the math. When I got away from her, she shouted that it didn't matter, because she would make it all be over at four o'clock."

Four o'clock? I glanced at my watch. Less than thirty minutes.

"I got a map, too."

"Map? I thought you said 'math'? I don't get it."

"That is because you do not understand Fibonacci numbers."

I thumbed through the book Darcy thrust into my hands. "Rabbi Hoffman mentioned these. What on earth are they?"

"Did you know that the numbers followed a pattern? Do you see the pattern?"

"What numbers?"

"The numbers where she made all the bodies be placed." He pointed to a string of numbers typed on the first page: 1, 1, 2, 3, 5, 8, 13, 21, 34, 55, 89, 144, 233, 377 . . . "See? The third number is the sum of the first two, the fourth is the sum of the second and third, the fifth is the sum of—"

"Okay, I get the idea." I stared at the chain of numbers, as if there was any chance they might speak to me. "Do these numbers have some . . . religious significance?"

Darcy's head tilted slightly. I could almost see the gears turning. "I do not know about that. But this sequence occurs throughout nature, and God created nature, right?"

"That's what they tell me."

He thumbed through the book till he found the passage he wanted. It was illustrated with pictures of pinecones, sunflowers, plant life. He pointed and read: "This numerical sequence occurs with such regularity throughout nature that entire journals have been dedicated to documenting these occurrences." It seemed that the numerical sequence occurred in the petal arrangement of flowers, the spiral arrangement of pinecones and pineapples, the turning of leaves about the stem of various plants. Even genealogical charts followed a Fibonacci pattern. The book referred to it as the Divine Progression.

"I can see how this would appeal to Esther," I said, "but what has it got to do with the placement of the bodies?"

Darcy crouched down on the backseat of my car, butt up in the air, hovering over a map of the city. He had placed pins at all the locations where the bodies were found. "Did you know that all these locations follow a Fibonacci pattern?"

"But—how? There are no numbers."

"There are numbers!" he said, his eyes dancing with excitement. "There are always numbers! The Fibonacci numbers move backward. The numbers are miles."

"Darcy . . . I know the FBI experts have been over a map just like this one, looking for a pattern. They didn't find one."

"That is because they did not know where to start. Also it is hard, because she never got to put your friend Amelia's body where she wanted to, so that left a big hole in the equation. I bet the Math Lady must have hated that. I know I would. The FBI men measure the distances from one location to another. But that is wrong. They needed to measure distances in miles from each drop-off place to the center point."

"The center point? What's that?"

"The center of the spiral. The place all the drop-off locations are dancing around. If you measure the distance between the body locations and the center point in miles, look what you get." He pointed at the place where the first body was found. "Twenty-one miles." He moved his finger to the next one. "Eighteen miles." Then thirteen, then eight, then five, each location describing a circle around the center point and coming increasingly closer, the distance in miles always perpetuating the Fibonacci relationship.

"All of this has been building toward the final stroke against the Sefirot," I said, the light slowly dawning. "All the mutilations have been moving toward her final cataclysmic act of destruction. And all the drop-off locations have been pointing toward her final target." Hearing it aloud made it seem more convincing, almost logical, in a perverse sort of way. "This time, she won't have to move the body. Or bodies. They'll already be there." I looked up at him. "This is more than just the center point, Darcy. This is Ground Zero." I yanked the center pin out of the map, then gasped. "The county courthouse?"

"I know. I thought that was very strange. Do you think that is strange? Why would she want to hurt a whole courthouse?"

I turned the ignition and peeled toward downtown. "She doesn't want to take out the whole courthouse. She has a more specific target in mind."

ESTHER BROKE the window and crawled into the room, careful not to cut herself on the broken glass.

She'd already hurt herself once today; she didn't want to repeat the experience. Her illness made her weaker every day and she had to remain healthy—for her little girl's sake. She kicked the ladder away behind her, as soon as she didn't need it anymore. Sure, it would be found in time, if it wasn't destroyed in the explosion. But she would be long gone by then.

Esther preferred a more direct approach, but the metal detectors in the front lobby made that impossible. Still, security here at the county courthouse wasn't remotely comparable to that at the federal courthouse; it had only taken her a few visits, and some abstract mathematics, to figure out how she could get in undetected.

She smoothed her clothes and dusted off her all-important briefcase. Deciding how to dress had been a challenge. She had to look professional, so the baggy muumuus she had favored of late were out of the question. At the same time, her photograph had been in the newspaper; she was forced to dye her hair, wear glasses she didn't need and shoes that made her taller. There was one detail that she couldn't disguise, of course, but she didn't think it would be a problem. No one was ever suspicious of pregnant women.

Esther stepped out of the storeroom into the main corridor. Eyes straight ahead, slightly intense, focused, as if she belonged here (which she did) and as if there was nothing unusual about her presence. She knew exactly where she wanted to go. All she had to do was get there without any interference.

"Excuse me, ma'am. May I see your badge?"

The security guard was strictly going through the motions and she knew it. She smiled and remained calm. "I don't have one yet. I've been appointed to act as guardian ad litem in the Merriwether juvenile case, but I haven't seen the judge yet." It was useful to have a little experience in these matters.

The guard nodded with understanding, or perhaps it was just intense ennui. "You'd better wait inside. I'll tell the judge's clerk."

Who would just assume the judge forgot to tell him about something and do nothing whatsoever. Esther compliantly entered the room as the guard directed—since it was exactly where she had wanted to go in the first place. The architectural plans she'd pulled off the Internet indicated this was the dead center of the entire family court division. The court system she knew all too well. The system that had shuffled her from one horror home to the next, never once caring about her, never honoring their supposed duty to act as parens patriae—to protect a friendless child.

They were the worse parents of all.

She left her briefcase under the table, then fixed the lock so that if anyone stumbled upon her little package too early . . . they would be sorry. And then, as unobtrusively as she had arrived, she left, smiling.

I'D DRIVEN AS FAST as possible, but it was still less than twenty minutes till four. While I broke every traffic regulation imaginable, Darcy called Dispatch to call off the manhunt for him, then tried to call Granger, then his father, but he couldn't reach either. Presumably because they were all still out looking for him. I called for backup to comb the courthouse, then parked illegally just outside the front steps.

"Darcy, I'm going in."

"I do not think that is a good idea."

Of course it wasn't a good idea, but I was going to do it anyway, and fast. I hadn't been here since the last custody hearing over Rachel; I'd forgotten how damn long it took to climb all these stairs. I was almost at the top before I realized that Darcy was dogging my steps.

"Darcy! Go back to the car!"

He rotated his hands in circles around themselves. "I think that maybe it would be best if I stayed with you."

"No! It's too dangerous."

"You might need me."

"I will not—" I grabbed him by the shoulders. "Darcy, you have been a great help to me in this case. But this is police work."

"I want to be a policeman."

"I know. But you're not! And you never will be if I let you get killed."

"No one ever wants to let me do anything, even though I help them over and over again. You are just like my dad."

"Darcy—" I glanced at my watch. Barely ten minutes till four. I had to hurry. "Darcy, I can't sit here and argue with you. I'll explain it all later. But for now—go!"

I turned my back on him and ran as fast as I could. We had only ten more minutes. But I knew where she would strike.

At least I thought I did.

I raced past security, flashing my badge and telling them not to let anyone leave the building. I knew the elevators would be too slow. I jumped into the stairwell and bounded up to the third floor, taking the steps three at a time. Long legs were occasionally an advantage, assuming you didn't kill yourself. I broke through the door and into the corridor leading to the family court division.

If it hadn't been for the dinging bell of the elevator doors as they began to close I wouldn't have noticed. My head turned—

And there she was. No clumsy dye job or fake glasses were going to fool me, especially when the woman was nine months pregnant and looked ten. She recognized me, too. She slunk to the back of the elevator. I lurched, jutting my hand forward. It hurt like hell, but I managed to get my palm in sideways, fast enough to prevent the doors from closing. They reopened, and just as I prepared to step into her domain, she caught me off guard with a very heavy shoe to the gut.

I doubled over and she tried to run past me. I grabbed her leg. My head was flooded with conflicting emotions and motivations. I wanted to twist the ankle around and fling her to the ground, but I reminded myself that she was pregnant. The baby was an innocent. On the other hand, the mother was a psychopathic mass murderer. I couldn't let her escape.

I wrapped myself around her waist; she tried to drag me down the corridor, beating on me and clawing me with her nails. Where the hell were all those officers who were supposed to be combing the building? I grabbed her hand and gave her the Vulcan Death Grip—three fingers pressed into the soft spot between her thumb and forefinger. Her knees buckled, but she somehow managed to bring her other arm around and slam it into the side of my face. Maybe it was the protective maternal instinct at work. For a woman who was supposedly dying and about to give birth, she fought like hell.

"You are the Math Lady again!"

God in heaven, it was Darcy. Why didn't he listen to anything I ever said? He was grinning at her like she was some long-lost friend. "That was pretty funny when we played chase at my house. Did you know that I would be faster than you? I bet you thought you could sneak up on me and catch me. But you could not sneak up and catch me. I smelled you and heard you before you got into the kitchen."

Esther made a sort of growling noise and took a swing at him, well off the mark. It was just the distraction I needed. I grabbed her other arm and twisted it hard behind her back. The sudden pain forced her to her knees.

"I guess you could not catch Susan, either, could

you?" He grinned, then sniffed the air. "She smells like Aqua Velva."

What? Aftershave lotion? Why would she—

No. It had to be something else. Something that smelled like Aqua Velva.

Plastique.

I dug my knee into the small of her back. She cried out. I could tell Darcy didn't like it; he didn't like to see anyone hurt. But he didn't interfere. "Where's the bomb, Esther?"

"You'll know soon enough."

"I want to know now."

"There's nothing you can do to me that would make me tell you."

I checked my watch. "The bomb goes off at four, right?" I grabbed her by the shoulders and shook her as hard as I thought I could without inducing premature labor. "Where is it?"

Her only response was a placid smile.

"It isn't going to work, you know," I said. "God—if He even exists, which I have serious reason to doubt—isn't going to come down and have a chat with you just because you killed a lot of innocent people."

Now I had her attention. She was desperate to know how I knew what she wanted, how much more I might know. But she wouldn't allow herself to ask.

"You think Timothy McVeigh got a private audience with God? In this world or the next? I don't."

"He didn't do it right."

"No, and neither did you. This is a delusion, Esther, and somewhere deep inside, you know it. You are not accomplishing anything good here, not for you or your daughter. You're not Jesus Christ. You're Jack the Ripper."

Her eyes narrowed. Her breathing quickened. "You're wrong. Because you're still trapped in the prison. In the darkness. But I've found the pathway out. I'm on my way to becoming—"

"I have seen that briefcase before!" Darcy was screaming at me from the opposite end of the corridor, pointing at a window. "It is hers."

"Darcy! Come back!" I pushed Esther down the hallway, toward the conference room Darcy had just entered. Through the window, I watched him pull a briefcase out from under the table. Before I could yell at him not to do it, he had popped the latches.

Even from my distance, I could see the LED readout.

Barely more than four minutes left on the clock.

I ran around to the door, dragging Esther with me. It was locked.

She smiled at me. "I jammed the lock. You can't get in, and he can't get out." She closed her eyes. "I'm afraid your gifted friend is going to die."

43

"DARCY! GET OUT of there!" I screamed, but he wasn't listening, wasn't even looking at me. He was staring at the digital readout. I didn't know why. All I could see was a bunch of numbers. I called the bomb squad, then checked on the backup that was supposed to be coming. Neither one would arrive in time.

"Darcy! Get out!"

Esther shook her head. "I told you. He can't."

"We'll see about that." I pulled my gun out of its holster. I could probably shoot the lock off the door, but that would take longer. "Darcy! Get down!" Careful to aim away from the bomb, I fired two shots into the window.

Glass flew everywhere. Darcy crawled under the table, trying to get away from the noise and the flying shards. I grabbed Esther by the throat.

"Is there any way to shut that bomb down?" I shouted at her.

"Of course. But he won't figure it out. Not in time. The math is much too complex. The fractions just continue."

I whipped out my cuffs and locked Esther to the doorknob. "If that bomb goes off, you'll die." I paused, looking her square in the eye. "You and your baby girl."

Her face twitched, ever so slightly. "You won't go through with it."

"Watch me!"

"Fine. Then we both die. Better to die in flames than be subjected to the torment of being born unloved. Shuttled from one cruel home to another. Tortured and abused and—"

I didn't have time to relive her tragic life story. I shoved her down onto the floor. "Darcy! Crawl through the window."

He didn't answer. He was doing something, punching the numbers on a keypad beneath the readout. I would've been afraid that would trigger a premature explosion, but it didn't, thank God.

"Darcy! What are you doing?"

"I think—I, maybe if—" He was concentrating; obviously, I was a distraction. "I think it is a puzzle."

"A puzzle? Like what?"

"Like if I can solve this equation she wrote on the metal part, maybe it will stop the timer."

I turned back to Esther. "Is that true?"

She looked up at me but didn't answer. I was certain that meant the answer was yes.

"But there are so many different ways to solve it," Darcy continued, more to himself than to me. "I do not know which way is right."

"Darcy, there's no time. If you don't crawl out of there, I'm coming in after you."

"I want to solve the puzzle."

"Darcy, if you don't get out in time, you'll die."

For the first time, he looked up. "But there has not been time to evacuate the building, has there?"

Of course there hadn't. I wasn't going to lie to him.

"So if I do not solve the puzzle, everyone in this section of the building will die, right?"

Goddamn that stupid big heart of his! "Darcy, I'm ordering you—"

"Shhh! I am thinking. Maybe I can get this. Maybe."

"You can't. I mean, if anyone ever could, it would be you, Darcy. But no one can. Esther told me. Certainly not in"—I glanced at my watch—"less than three minutes. She said that no matter what you do, it just keeps continuing."

He tilted his head to one side, then his eyes brightened. "Continuing fractions? Like what the Math Lady had in her classroom?" He hunched over the keypad and punched the keys, rapid-fire.

Esther laughed. "When he was in my classroom, it took him an hour to solve three equations. Has he studied them since?"

I answered, even though my lips were dry and tremulous. "I don't think so."

"Then he doesn't have a chance."

I checked my watch. Barely more than two minutes till four. Assuming my watch was accurate. "Darcy! Give it up! We have to get out of here!"

He was still punching madly at the keypad. "I think that maybe I can get it." Long pause. "But there are so many equations. Each one leads to another."

"Darcy! There just isn't time!" I didn't know what to do. I could go in there and try to drag him out, but he would resist. I couldn't carry him out and get far enough away in time. "Darcy! It's going to detonate!"

"Did you know that thirty-seven percent of all detonators fail?"

I felt a hollow aching in my chest. "Hers won't." I climbed through the window. While he worked, I examined the bomb over his shoulder. I saw the clock that worked as the timer—less than a minute away from four o'clock. Two wires were attached to the minute hand—one leading to the power source and the other to the detonator—and there was a pin soldered in precisely at the four. I imagined there was a relay that cut off the triggering signal by stopping the clock, if the puzzle was solved in time, something that separated the power source from the detonator. I could see that the plugs and wires could not be pulled out—they'd been soldered into place, too. I didn't think my odds of snipping the right wire to defuse the bomb were high; it might not even be possible. Either Darcy solved this puzzle or a lot of people were going to die. Including Darcy.

And me. Because I wasn't leaving him here alone.

"Darcy," I murmured quietly. Beads of sweat were dripping down the sides of my face. My heart was pounding against the walls of my chest. "If there's anything I can do for you, please let me know."

He didn't. And what the hell could I do, anyway? Check his math? I just waited and watched the human calculator in motion. The Mozart of Math. Each time he solved an equation, a little beeping noise told him that he'd gotten it correct, but then another one appeared. I saw the target number—*seven*—scribbled just above the LED readout. This problem wouldn't be solved until that number turned up as a solution—a final solution. And there was no telling how long that might take.

Thirty seconds to go. Twenty.

"Darcy," I said quietly, "I don't want to distract you. I don't even want you to listen to me. But I have to say—I have to tell you—" I drew in my breath. "You're a good boy, Darcy. A very good boy." Pause. Ten seconds to go. "I'd be lucky to adopt a kid as great as you. And you'd make a hell of a good policeman."

Darcy's eyes widened. He let out a scream—

He stopped the clock with four seconds left to go. I don't really know what happened after that—Granger showed up with some of his men and they took control of the situation. Which was okay with me, because my legs had totally turned to Jell-O and I was lying on the carpet laughing and crying my eyes out.

44

AUGUST 5

"YOU HAVE GOT to be kidding," I said.

"I wouldn't kid about something this important."

I had my feet propped up on the desk. My first day back in the office after an enforced and unwanted medical leave, and I felt better than I had in months. And this time, it wasn't a case of Better Living Through Chemistry. "How many people have you shown this to, Colin?"

"Oh, about a hundred and five. Kiddo, I've been showing it to everyone I know since you found it in the woman's hotel room. I'm telling you, that little blue notebook is solid gold. In an intellectual sort of way."

"She wasn't delusional?"

"No! Well, maybe in the killing-people way, but her math is solid. I don't think I can explain how tremendous this accomplishment really is. People have been trying to solve Reimann's hypothesis for hundreds of years."

"That's what Esther told me. The first time I met her."

"And she's done it! At least, as far as anyone can tell so far. It has to go through peer review. These mathematical proofs are scrutinized for years before they're fully and finally accepted. But speaking for myself—I think it's the real deal. Can you imagine anything weirder than that?"

Yes, sadly enough, I could. I thought back to that first meeting with Esther, when she explained the theory of extreme intellectual capacity, the thin line between genius and madness. It seemed Esther had both, big time. What might she have become in a different world, with a different childhood? Different parents. Different everything.

"It's a shame, really," Colin mused. "Wasting a mind with that kind of ability. You think they'll let her do math in prison?"

I sighed. "I don't think it matters, Colin. She won't be there long."

I WAS GLAD the bomb did not explode while I was holding it. I was not worried well maybe just a little and maybe I should have been more worried but I did not have time to be more worried because I was busy solving the puzzle and I like it when I have puzzles to solve. Puzzles are fun. Everyone kept acting like I had done some wonderful thing but all I did was solve a puzzle and I like doing puzzles so what is so wonderful about that? It would be nice if everyone could get so much praise just for doing the things they like to do anyway.

I am glad we caught the Math Lady, but I feel sort of sorry for her, even though she did hurt people. I bet she liked to do puzzles too and now she probably will not get to do puzzles anymore. I would not like that.

I wish I understood why Susan started crying when the bomb did not explode. I would understand if she cried because the bomb did explode, but this does not make any sense to me. I guess I am just too stupid to understand things like that. But I still think I could be smarter. Especially if Susan would help me.

My dad kept saying that the best part of this case was when I outsmarted the Math Lady. But he was wrong.

The best part of this case was when Susan called me her Darcy.

"IT WOULD NEVER have worked, you know," I said, as I peered at the figure at the opposite end of the interrogation table. She seemed much smaller now, and it wasn't just because she had delivered the baby—a perfectly healthy seven-pound, nine-ounce girl. Esther named her Anna. "Never in a million years. No matter how many times you destroyed the Sefirot."

"That's your opinion," Esther said, through dark, hooded eyes. She looked feeble; I knew she wouldn't live much longer. She was being surprisingly cooperative, telling us everything we wanted to know. It wasn't so much the usual serial killer's narcissist pride in their brilliant master plan, at least I didn't think so. She was smart enough to know it was over. Everything. "Because you don't believe in God in the first place." Her tired eyes looked downward. "I believe in Him. I just hate the bastard."

"Whether God exists or not, I know this. He can't be accountable for everything that goes wrong." *Take good care of our son for us, okay?* "If He could, someone would've given Him the boot a long time ago."

I expected an argument, maybe something mathematical, maybe a long-winded Kabbalistic theological discursion, but I didn't get it. "She's beautiful, isn't she?"

I didn't have to ask who she was talking about. "Yes, she is." I smiled a little. "Favors her mother."

"No. She favors my sister. That's why I gave her that name. They weren't going to let me see her, you know. Not at first."

I did know. The DHS people argued that when a child is going up for adoption, it's standard procedure not to let the birth mother see her. But I came down on them in my inimitable fashion, explained that there was no chance of Esther ever interfering in the girl's life, so they relented. "I will monitor the adoption process," I told her. "Just like I promised. I have some experience with those people." Most of it bad, but I didn't tell her that. "I'll make sure your daughter ends up in a good home. A very good home. A safe home."

She smiled a little, not much, and her head fell lightly on her arms resting on the table. Her eyes seemed to go into soft focus, as if concentrating on something far far away.

"I would've been a good mother," she said quietly, tears suddenly filling her eyes.

I took her hand and squeezed it as tightly as I could. "I know."

DARCY HATED CROWDS, but I made sure every available body in the whole damn police force was there, just the same. And I made sure Chief O'Bannon was the one who made the presentation.

"Darcy O'Bannon," the chief said, clearing his throat. He hated giving speeches in front of crowds, which was another reason I made sure as many people as possible were present. "In commendation for your public service, and in recognition of your outstanding acts of courage and personal bravery, I am pleased to award you the LVPD's Citation of Honor, which is"—his voice choked—"which is the highest civilian award we have." He wrapped the medal around Darcy's neck (Darcy only writhed slightly) and shook his hand. "Congratulations, son."

The crowd burst into applause. Tony, Jodie, even Granger. They cheered and gave him a round of "For He's a Jolly Good Fellow." Darcy looked as if he didn't really know what was happening, and I suppose in a way, he didn't. But I also think that in a way, he did.

"And about that civilian business." The chief shuffled

his feet, stared at the floor, then continued. "I am pleased to inform you that your—your application to the Las Vegas Police Academy has been accepted. You start next month."

Darcy's eyes widened. This part he understood. "But—B-B-But—" He took a deep breath and started again. "But I did not make an application to the police academy."

His father placed his hand gently under Darcy's chin, forcing him, just this once, to make eye contact. "I did it for you."

Well, this called for a celebration. I joined Darcy and about a thousand other cops at Grady's after the ceremony, but he was devoting too much time to me. This was his chance to learn that he had other friends on the police force, friends who might be useful to him in the days ahead. And I knew I was going to see him tomorrow.

And I had a ceremony of my own to perform. Not quite as fancy as cracking a bottle of champagne over the masthead of a ship, but still nice in its own way.

I poured several bottles of pills into the toilet.

I hadn't used any of them in more than a week. The exercise was mostly symbolic. But it meant something to me.

I would never know for certain. Esther was smart, clever, the exact antithesis of what you expect a serial killer to be. Maybe I wouldn't have made her anyway. But with my natural gifts suppressed, with my brain doped to the gills, I had no chance of recognizing her for what she was.

And then she killed four more people. Including Amelia.

I would never make that mistake again.

In Amelia's memory, I pulled the coffee table she bought me out of the bathroom and brought it downstairs. I looked at my old table, with its preposterous chewed-up leg, scratched and clawed surface, one last time.

"So let me see if I have this straight. The dog died. But you kept the table he ruined?"

David gave me that smile, the big one, the one I could never resist. "I loved that dog."

"He chewed up your table!" We were newlyweds. I was more concerned about material possessions back then.

"But he was still a great dog. Helped me through the toughest years of a tough adolescence. Didn't matter what I did. Gabby was always there for me. And what did he ask in return? Nothing. A little food and water every now and again, that's all. His love was unconditional." He paused, then gazed at me with those endless baby blues of his. "Love like that is hard to find."

"Don't I know it."

"When Gabby died, I was so . . . depressed. I can't describe it to you. I couldn't get out of bed in the morning. Even when I started functioning again—I wasn't really functioning. The hurt was always with me. I couldn't get over the loss. Thought I'd never stop being sad." He raised my hand to his lips and kissed it. "But I did, in time. Eventually—you have to move on. You know what I mean?"

Yes, David, I thought, as I carried the old table out to the Dumpster. I know what you mean.

Later that night, after I crawled into my jammies and turned out the lights, I reached toward my alarm clock—

And found the four-leaf clover. I squeezed it tightly.

There he was.

He wasn't really there, of course. But I could smell him. I could taste him. I could even . . . feel him, in a way. He was real to me. Back where he belonged.

Tonight, one last time, we were going to spend the night together. And then it would be time to move on.

"MY GOD, these are heavy," I said, as I tossed the U-Haul box onto the sofa. "I'm a strong girl, but I'm going to need some serious rehabilitative therapy after this move is over. Maybe an all-day massage."

"I think that maybe you should rest for a minute," Darcy said. "You sit on the sofa and I will get the rest of them."

"There are hundreds of them!"

He thought a moment. "It might be more than a minute. Would you like to watch television?"

I couldn't help but laugh. "What's in all these boxes, anyway?"

"Books!"

"Of course. Stupid me."

"Do you mean that you do not like books?"

"No. But there's nothing on earth heavier to move."

"I think a home without books would not really be a home. And I have never had a home. I mean, a home away from home, I mean—"

"I know what you mean." Moving into an apartment, away from his father, for the first time in his twenty-six-year-old life was hard enough on him. I wasn't going to traumatize him any further by making him do anything so demanding as speaking coherently. "Sit down with me for a minute, buddy." He sat at the end of the sofa, near my feet. "Have I mentioned how proud of you I am?"

"No. Does this mean you are going to adopt me?"

"Darcy." I gave him my straight talk look. "You don't need anyone to adopt you. You can take care of yourself." He looked so stricken, I felt compelled to add, "Of course, it's always good to have friends. And I will always be your friend."

"Friends?"

"Friends. And believe me—there's nothing in the world more important."

He was trying hard not to appear disappointed, but he wasn't exactly the master of deception, much less of his emotions. "I think that you would like me more if I were not so weird."

"Darcy, you're not weird."

"I am. You know I am and I know I am. I am not . . . normal."

I wouldn't patronize him by arguing. "Darcy . . . if God made you different—"

"I thought you didn't believe in God."

I took a deep breath and started again. "If God made you different, it was for a reason. I mean—hell, He makes us all different. And for a reason. With all our great obstacles come great gifts. The trick is to learn how to overcome the obstacles. So you can take advantage of the gifts. That's what you're learning to do. Better than me. Better than anyone I've known in my entire life."

He rubbed his hands together and stared at his feet. "I still wish that I were normal. I think you would like me better if I were normal."

"Darcy, if you were normal—whatever the hell that is—we would never have caught Esther. And I'd be dead."

That seemed to get through to him. His head rose. His eyes brightened. I could see the wheels turning once again. "I am glad that you are not dead." He turned toward me and gave me something perilously close to direct eye contact. "Maybe it is okay to not be normal."

"It's more than okay, Darcy." I leaned over and gave him a big bear hug, whether he liked it or not. "I wouldn't have you any other way."

Read on for a sneak preview
of William Bernhardt's

NEMESIS

THE FINAL CASE OF ELIOT NESS

PROLOGUE

SEPTEMBER 16, 1957

THE DAYS WERE all the same now.

The best part of Eliot Ness's day was breakfast with Bobby. His marriage with Betty had its ups and downs, as had his previous two marriages. She was an artist, a sculptor. He had no idea whether she was talented but she certainly had an artist's temperament. Her suggestion that they adopt a child, however, had been a brilliant stroke that had transformed their lives, only for the better. All his life he had been a little awkward around children. Now he was a doting father who never missed an opportunity to spend time with his only son.

Most people expected a corporate president to be a busy man. Instead, Ness found himself getting idler by the day. The North Ridge Alliance Corporation had been in trouble for a long time now, almost from the start. It had seemed like such a brilliant idea. They would produce checks that could not be forged using a special watermarking technique. He would be providing a useful service—and still stopping crime, in a new way.

But the truth was, he had no head for business. One of his partners had run off with the corporate secrets and started his own corporation. Then they were denied a patent because there were other pre-existing watermarking firms. They had moved their offices from Cleveland to

Coudersport, Pennsylvania, a small town near the New York border, to reduce expenses. But it wasn't enough. They were holding on by their fingertips now and the money coming in wasn't nearly enough to pay the bills.

And that was how the great hero of the Prohibition era ended up in a backwater burg in Pennsylvania without a penny in savings and exceedingly poor prospects. Who would blame him if he took lunch at the same bar and grill every day, a pastrami sandwich with a whiskey chaser? Maybe two. A quick stop at the store and he was home with far too little to do until Betty and Bobby got home. He would pour a drink, sit in his favorite easy chair, and remember the days when every day had been packed with more excitement and activity than most people could handle . . .

The doorbell rang.

"Hey, Oscar. You're early."

"That okay?"

"Sure. I'm not doing anything."

"I just wanted to get some work done before you were . . . you know. Before you got too tired. It's hard, trying to remember stuff that happened so long ago."

"Yeah."

Ness let Oscar Fraley into his home. He liked Fraley. He was a good listener. He was a friend of his partner, Joe Phelps. A sportswriter, by trade. They'd met in a bar where Ness was telling his stories, as usual. But unlike most, Fraley seemed genuinely interested. He believed what Ness told him, or at least acted as if he did. And unlike most of the young punks at the Bar and Grill these days, Fraley remembered who Al Capone was.

"Like a drink?" Ness asked, hiccupping.

"No thanks," Fraley said. "Not while I'm working. But you go on ahead."

"Don't mind if I do," Ness replied, refilling his glass. "Helps me remember."

"Can we pick up where we left off last time? You and your people had finally put away Al Capone. For tax evasion."

"Yeah. People made fun of us for putting away a killer on such lame grounds. But it worked. Me and my boys kept him busy, pre-occupied, a constant thorn in his side, while Frank Wilson slowly put together a case proving Capone wasn't paying his taxes. We got him off the street, out of Chicago. He wasted away in prison—he had syphilis, you know. He got out, but my people tell me he was a broken man, barely able to dress himself or go to the toilet without help. Finally died about ten years ago. The tax charge did what we wanted. It put an end to the bloody reign of Al Capone."

"I gather you feel no shame about the way you did it."

"None at all. On the contrary, we were proud of ourselves for using our brains for once. Being creative. That's what the times were like back then. Learning something different every day. New scientific discoveries. Forensic labs solving crimes detectives couldn't. How long could criminals survive in this brave new scientific world? We thought we'd found the cure for crime. We thought we could end it for all time."

His eyes darkened. "But it turns out, crime is more resilient than we realized. It's—what's that term scientists are using now? It's a mutating organism. It adapts to new environments. Builds up resistance to the vaccine. We may have figured out how to deal with people like Capone, but something new, something different came along to take their place. Something we had no idea how to handle."

"Are you talking about Cleveland? The Torso Murderer?"

Ness took a long draw from his drink. "I don't want to talk about that."

"Why not? It's a great story. Scary, suspenseful, and filled with—"

"I don't want to talk about it. I don't want anything about it in this book you're writing. You understand me? Nothing!"

Oscar held up his hands. "All right, Eliot, stay calm. Don't work yourself up. We'll stick with the Capone saga."

"Good." There was no reason to get into the rest of it. No reason at all. So few knew anything about it these days, outside of Cleveland, anyway. Better to keep it that way.

If only there was some way he could make himself forget . . .